# Short Stories

# 1886

# Anton Chekhov

Copyright © this edition Will Jonson

First Edition, 2013

ISBN: 978-1484956762

The author has asserted their moral right under the Copyright, Designs and Patents Act, 1988, to be identified as the author of this work.

All Rights reserved. No part of this publication may be reproduced, copied, stored in a retrieval system, or transmitted, in any form or by any means, without the prior written consent of the copyright holder, nor be otherwise circulated in any form of binding or cover other than that in which it is published and without a similar condition being imposed on the subsequent purchaser. This is a work of fiction: any resemblance to persons living or dead is purely coincidental.

# CONTENTS

| | |
|---|---|
| Art | 7 |
| A Blunder | 13 |
| Children | 16 |
| Misery | 22 |
| An Upheaval | 29 |
| An Actor's End | 37 |
| The Requiem | 44 |
| Anyuta | 50 |
| Ivan Matveyitch | 55 |
| The Witch | 62 |
| A Story without an End | 76 |
| A Joke | 86 |
| Agafya | 91 |
| A Nightmare | 103 |
| Grisha | 118 |
| Love | 122 |
| Easter Eve | 129 |
| Ladies | 141 |
| Strong Impressions | 146 |
| A Gentleman Friend | 151 |
| A Happy Man | 155 |
| The Privy Councillor | 161 |

| | |
|---|---|
| A Day in the Country | 179 |
| At a Summer Villa | 186 |
| Panic Fears | 192 |
| The Chemist's Wife | 199 |
| Not Wanted | 206 |
| The Chorus Girl | 213 |
| The Schoolmaster | 220 |
| A Troublesome Visitor | 228 |
| The Husband | 236 |
| A Misfortune | 242 |
| A Pink Stocking | 256 |
| Martyrs | 260 |
| The First Class Passenger | 267 |
| Talent | 275 |
| The Dependents | 280 |
| The Jeune Premier | 287 |
| In the Dark | 293 |
| A Trivial Incident | 299 |
| A Tripping Tongue | 310 |
| A Trifle from Life | 314 |
| Difficult People | 321 |
| In the Court | 330 |
| A Peculiar Man | 338 |

| | |
|---|---|
| Mire | 343 |
| Dreams | 363 |
| Hush! | 372 |
| Excellent People | 376 |
| An Incident | 387 |
| The Orator | 393 |
| A Work of Art | 397 |
| Who Was To Blame? | 402 |
| Vanka | 406 |
| On the Road | 410 |

# ART

A gloomy winter morning.

On the smooth and glittering surface of the river Bystryanka, sprinkled here and there with snow, stand two peasants, scrubby little Seryozhka and the church beadle, Matvey. Seryozhka, a short-legged, ragged, mangy-looking fellow of thirty, stares angrily at the ice. Tufts of wool hang from his shaggy sheepskin like a mangy dog. In his hands he holds a compass made of two pointed sticks. Matvey, a fine-looking old man in a new sheepskin and high felt boots, looks with mild blue eyes upwards where on the high sloping bank a village nestles picturesquely. In his hands there is a heavy crowbar.

"Well, are we going to stand like this till evening with our arms folded?" says Seryozhka, breaking the silence and turning his angry eyes on Matvey. "Have you come here to stand about, old fool, or to work?"

"Well, you . . . er . . . show me . . ." Matvey mutters, blinking mildly.

"Show you. . . . It's always me: me to show you, and me to do it. They have no sense of their own! Mark it out with the compasses, that's what's wanted! You can't break the ice without marking it out. Mark it! Take the compass."

Matvey takes the compasses from Seryozhka's hands, and, shuffling heavily on the same spot and jerking with his elbows in all directions, he begins awkwardly trying to describe a circle on the ice. Seryozhka screws up his eyes contemptuously and obviously enjoys his awkwardness and incompetence.

"Eh-eh-eh!" he mutters angrily. "Even that you can't do! The fact is you are a stupid peasant, a wooden-head! You ought to be grazing geese and not making a Jordan! Give the compasses here! Give them here, I say!"

Seryozhka snatches the compasses out of the hands of the perspiring Matvey, and in an instant, jauntily twirling round on one heel, he describes a circle on the ice. The outline of the new Jordan is ready now, all that is left to do is to break the ice. . .

But before proceeding to the work Seryozhka spends a long time in airs and graces, whims and reproaches. . .

"I am not obliged to work for you! You are employed in the church, you do it!

He obviously enjoys the peculiar position in which he has been placed by the fate that has bestowed on him the rare talent of surprising the whole parish once a year by his art. Poor mild Matvey has to listen to many venomous and contemptuous words from him. Seryozhka sets to work with vexation, with anger. He is lazy. He has hardly described the circle when he is already itching to go up to the village to drink tea, lounge about, and babble. . .

"I'll be back directly," he says, lighting his cigarette, "and meanwhile you had better bring something to sit on and sweep up, instead of standing there counting the crows."

Matvey is left alone. The air is grey and harsh but still. The white church peeps out genially from behind the huts scattered on the river bank. Jackdaws are incessantly circling round its golden crosses. On one side of the village where the river bank breaks off and is steep a hobbled horse is standing at the very edge, motionless as a stone, probably asleep or deep in thought.

Matvey, too, stands motionless as a statue, waiting patiently. The dreamily brooding look of the river, the circling of the jackdaws, and the sight of the horse make him drowsy. One hour passes, a second, and still Seryozhka does not come. The river has long been swept and a box brought to sit on, but the drunken fellow does not appear. Matvey waits and merely yawns. The feeling of boredom is one of which he knows nothing. If he were told to stand on the river for a day, a month, or a year he would stand there.

At last Seryozhka comes into sight from behind the huts. He walks with a lurching gait, scarcely moving. He is too lazy to go the long way round, and he comes not by the road, but prefers a short cut in a straight line down the bank, and sticks in the snow, hangs on to the bushes, slides on his back as he comes  -  and all this slowly, with pauses.

"What are you about?" he cries, falling on Matvey at once. "Why are you standing there doing nothing! When are you going to break the ice?"

Matvey crosses himself, takes the crowbar in both hands, and begins breaking the ice, carefully keeping to the circle that has been drawn. Seryozhka sits down on the box and watches the heavy clumsy movements of his assistant.

"Easy at the edges! Easy there!" he commands. "If you can't do it properly, you shouldn't undertake it, once you have undertaken it you should do it. You!"

A crowd collects on the top of the bank. At the sight of the spectators Seryozhka becomes even more excited.

"I declare I am not going to do it . . ." he says, lighting a stinking cigarette and spitting on the ground. "I should like to see how you get on without me. Last year at Kostyukovo, Styopka Gulkov undertook to make a Jordan as I do. And what did it amount to - it was a laughing-stock. The Kostyukovo folks came to ours - crowds and crowds of them! The people flocked from all the villages."

"Because except for ours there is nowhere a proper Jordan . . ."

"Work, there is no time for talking. . . . Yes, old man . . . you won't find another Jordan like it in the whole province. The soldiers say you would look in vain, they are not so good even in the towns. Easy, easy!"

Matvey puffs and groans. The work is not easy. The ice is firm and thick; and he has to break it and at once take the pieces away that the open space may not be blocked up.

But, hard as the work is and senseless as Seryozhka's commands are, by three o'clock there is a large circle of dark water in the Bystryanka.

"It was better last year," says Seryozhka angrily. "You can't do even that! Ah, dummy! To keep such fools in the temple of God! Go and bring a board to make the pegs! Bring the ring, you crow! And er . . . get some bread somewhere. . . and some cucumbers, or something."

Matvey goes off and soon afterwards comes back, carrying on his shoulders an immense wooden ring which had been painted in previous years in patterns of various colours. In the centre of the ring is a red cross, at the circumference holes for the pegs. Seryozhka takes the ring and covers the hole in the ice with it.

"Just right . . . it fits. . . . We have only to renew the paint and it will be first-rate. . . . Come, why are you standing still? Make the lectern. Or - er - go and get logs to make the cross . . ."

Matvey, who has not tasted food or drink all day, trudges up the hill again. Lazy as Seryozhka is, he makes the pegs with his own hands. He knows that those pegs have a miraculous power: whoever gets hold of a peg after the blessing of the water will be lucky for the whole year. Such work is really worth doing.

But the real work begins the following day. Then Seryozhka displays himself before the ignorant Matvey in all the greatness of his talent. There is no end to his babble, his fault-finding, his whims and fancies. If Matvey nails two big pieces of wood to make a cross, he is dissatisfied and tells him to do it again. If Matvey stands still, Seryozhka asks him angrily why he does not go; if he moves, Seryozhka shouts to him not to go away but to do his work. He is not satisfied with his tools, with the weather, or with his own talent; nothing pleases him.

Matvey saws out a great piece of ice for a lectern.

"Why have you broken off the corner?" cries Seryozhka, and glares at him furiously. "Why have you broken off the corner? I ask you."

"Forgive me, for Christ's sake."

"Do it over again!"

Matvey saws again . . . and there is no end to his sufferings. A lectern is to stand by the hole in the ice that is covered by the painted ring; on the lectern is to be carved the cross and the open gospel. But that is not all. Behind the lectern there is to be a high cross to be seen by all the crowd and to glitter in the sun as though sprinkled with diamonds and rubies. On the cross is to be a dove carved out of ice. The path from the church to the Jordan is to be strewn with branches of fir and juniper. All this is their task.

First of all Seryozhka sets to work on the lectern. He works with a file, a chisel, and an awl. He is perfectly successful in the cross on the lectern, the gospel, and the drapery that hangs down from the lectern. Then he begins on the dove. While he is trying to carve an expression of meekness and humility on the face of the dove, Matvey, lumbering about like a bear, is coating with ice the cross he has made of wood. He takes the cross and dips it in the hole. Waiting till the water has frozen on the cross he dips it in a second time, and so on till the cross is covered with a thick layer of ice. It is a difficult job, calling for a great deal of strength and patience.

But now the delicate work is finished. Seryozhka races about the village like one possessed. He swears and vows he will go at once to the river and smash all his work. He is looking for suitable paints.

His pockets are full of ochre, dark blue, red lead, and verdigris; without paying a farthing he rushes headlong from one shop to another. The shop is next door to the tavern. Here he has a drink; with a wave of his hand he darts off without paying. At one hut he gets beetroot leaves, at another an onion skin, out of which he makes a yellow colour. He swears, shoves, threatens, and not a soul murmurs! They all smile at him, they sympathise with him, call him Sergey Nikititch; they all feel that his art is not his personal affair but something that concerns them all, the whole people. One creates, the others help him. Seryozhka in himself is a nonentity, a sluggard, a drunkard, and a wastrel, but when he has his red lead or compasses in his hand he is at once something higher, a servant of God.

Epiphany morning comes. The precincts of the church and both banks of the river for a long distance are swarming with people. Everything that makes up the Jordan is scrupulously concealed under new mats. Seryozhka is meekly moving about near the mats, trying to control his emotion. He sees thousands of people. There are many here from other parishes; these people have come many a mile on foot through the frost and the snow merely to see his celebrated Jordan. Matvey, who had finished his coarse, rough work, is by now back in the church, there is no sight, no sound of him; he is already forgotten. . . . The weather is lovely. . . . There is not a cloud in the sky. The sunshine is dazzling.

The church bells ring out on the hill . . . Thousands of heads are bared, thousands of hands are moving, there are thousands of signs of the cross!

And Seryozhka does not know what to do with himself for impatience. But now they are ringing the bells for the Sacrament; then half an hour later a certain agitation is perceptible in the belfry and among the people. Banners are borne out of the church one after the other, while the bells peal in joyous haste. Seryozhka, trembling, pulls away the mat . . . and the people behold something extraordinary. The lectern, the wooden ring, the pegs, and the cross in the ice are iridescent with thousands of colors. The cross and the dove glitter so dazzlingly that it hurts the eyes to look at them. Merciful God, how fine it is! A murmur of wonder and delight runs through the crowd; the bells peal more loudly still, the day grows brighter; the banners oscillate and move over the crowd as over the waves. The procession, glittering with the settings of the ikons and the vestments of the clergy, comes slowly down the road and turns towards the Jordan. Hands are waved to the belfry for the ringing to cease, and the blessing of the water begins. The priests conduct the service slowly, deliberately, evidently trying to prolong the ceremony and the joy of praying all gathered together. There is perfect stillness.

But now they plunge the cross in, and the air echoes with an extraordinary din. Guns are fired, the bells peal furiously, loud exclamations of delight, shouts, and a rush to get the pegs. Seryozhka listens to this uproar, sees thousands of eyes fixed upon him, and the lazy fellow's soul is filled with a sense of glory and triumph.

# A BLUNDER

Ilya Sergeitch Peplov and his wife Kleopatra Petrovna were standing at the door, listening greedily. On the other side in the little drawing-room a love scene was apparently taking place between two persons: their daughter Natashenka and a teacher of the district school, called Shchupkin.

"He's rising!" whispered Peplov, quivering with impatience and rubbing his hands. "Now, Kleopatra, mind; as soon as they begin talking of their feelings, take down the ikon from the wall and we'll go in and bless them.... We'll catch him.... A blessing with an ikon is sacred and binding... He couldn't get out of it, if he brought it into court."

On the other side of the door this was the conversation:

"Don't go on like that!" said Shchupkin, striking a match against his checked trousers. "I never wrote you any letters!"

"I like that! As though I didn't know your writing!" giggled the girl with an affected shriek, continually peeping at herself in the glass. "I knew it at once! And what a queer man you are! You are a writing master, and you write like a spider! How can you teach writing if you write so badly yourself?"

"H'm!... That means nothing. The great thing in writing lessons is not the hand one writes, but keeping the boys in order. You hit one on the head with a ruler, make another kneel down.... Besides, there's nothing in handwriting! Nekrassov was an author, but his handwriting's a disgrace, there's a specimen of it in his collected works."

"You are not Nekrassov...." (A sigh). "I should love to marry an author. He'd always be writing poems to me."

"I can write you a poem, too, if you like."

"What can you write about?"

"Love - passion - your eyes. You'll be crazy when you read it. It would draw a tear from a stone! And if I write you a real poem, will you let me kiss your hand?"

"That's nothing much! You can kiss it now if you like."

Shchupkin jumped up, and making sheepish eyes, bent over the fat little hand that smelt of egg soap.

"Take down the ikon," Peplov whispered in a fluster, pale with excitement, and buttoning his coat as he prodded his wife with his elbow. "Come along, now!"

And without a second's delay Peplov flung open the door.

"Children," he muttered, lifting up his arms and blinking tearfully, "the Lord bless you, my children. May you live - be fruitful - and multiply."

"And - and I bless you, too," the mamma brought out, crying with happiness. "May you be happy, my dear ones! Oh, you are taking from me my only treasure!" she said to Shchupkin. "Love my girl, be good to her. . . ."

Shchupkin's mouth fell open with amazement and alarm. The parents' attack was so bold and unexpected that he could not utter a single word.

"I'm in for it! I'm spliced!" he thought, going limp with horror. "It's all over with you now, my boy! There's no escape!"

And he bowed his head submissively, as though to say, "Take me, I'm vanquished."

"Ble-blessings on you," the papa went on, and he, too, shed tears. "Natashenka, my daughter, stand by his side. Kleopatra, give me the ikon."

But at this point the father suddenly left off weeping, and his face was contorted with anger.

"You ninny!" he said angrily to his wife. "You are an idiot! Is that the ikon?"

"Ach, saints alive!"

What had happened? The writing master raised himself and saw that he was saved; in her flutter the mamma had snatched from the wall the portrait of Lazhetchnikov, the author, in mistake for the ikon. Old Peplov and his wife stood disconcerted in the middle of the room, holding the portrait aloft, not knowing what to do or what to say. The writing master took advantage of the general confusion and slipped away.

# CHILDREN

Papa and mamma and Aunt Nadya are not at home. They have gone to a christening party at the house of that old officer who rides on a little grey horse. While waiting for them to come home, Grisha, Anya, Alyosha, Sonya, and the cook's son, Andrey, are sitting at the table in the dining-room, playing at loto. To tell the truth, it is bedtime, but how can one go to sleep without hearing from mamma what the baby was like at the christening, and what they had for supper? The table, lighted by a hanging lamp, is dotted with numbers, nutshells, scraps of paper, and little bits of glass. Two cards lie in front of each player, and a heap of bits of glass for covering the numbers. In the middle of the table is a white saucer with five kopecks in it. Beside the saucer, a half-eaten apple, a pair of scissors, and a plate on which they have been told to put their nutshells. The children are playing for money. The stake is a kopeck. The rule is: if anyone cheats, he is turned out at once. There is no one in the dining-room but the players, and nurse, Agafya Ivanovna, is in the kitchen, showing the cook how to cut a pattern, while their elder brother, Vasya, a schoolboy in the fifth class, is lying on the sofa in the drawing-room, feeling bored.

They are playing with zest. The greatest excitement is expressed on the face of Grisha. He is a small boy of nine, with a head cropped so that the bare skin shows through, chubby cheeks, and thick lips like a negro's. He is already in the preparatory class, and so is regarded as grown up, and the cleverest. He is playing entirely for the sake of the money. If there had been no kopecks in the saucer, he would have been asleep long ago. His brown eyes stray uneasily and jealously over the other players' cards. The fear that he may not win, envy, and the financial combinations of which his cropped head is full, will not let him sit still and concentrate his mind. He fidgets as though he were sitting on thorns. When he wins, he snatches up the money greedily, and instantly puts it in his pocket. His sister, Anya, a girl of eight, with a sharp chin and clever shining eyes, is also afraid that someone else may win. She flushes and turns pale, and watches the players keenly. The kopecks do not interest her. Success in the game is for her a question of vanity. The other sister, Sonya, a child of six with a curly head, and a complexion such as is seen only in very healthy children, expensive dolls, and the faces on bonbon boxes, is playing loto for the process of the game itself. There is bliss all over her face. Whoever wins, she laughs and claps her hands. Alyosha, a chubby, spherical little figure, gasps, breathes hard through his nose, and stares open-eyed at the cards. He is moved neither by covetousness nor vanity. So long as he is not driven out of the room, or sent to bed, he is thankful. He looks phlegmatic, but at heart he is rather a little beast. He is not there so much for the sake of the loto, as for the sake of the misunderstandings which are inevitable in the game. He is greatly delighted if one hits another, or calls him names. He ought to have run off somewhere long ago, but he won't leave the table for a minute, for fear they should steal his counters or his kopecks. As he can only count the units and numbers which end in nought, Anya covers his numbers for him. The fifth player, the cook's son, Andrey, a dark-skinned and sickly looking boy in a cotton shirt, with a copper cross on his breast, stands motionless, looking dreamily at the numbers. He takes no interest in winning, or in the success of the others, because he is entirely engrossed by the arithmetic of the game, and its far from complex theory; "How many numbers there are in the world," he is thinking, "and how is it they don't get mixed up?"

They all shout out the numbers in turn, except Sonya and Alyosha. To vary the monotony, they have invented in the course of time a number of synonyms and comic nicknames. Seven, for instance, is called the "ovenrake," eleven the "sticks," seventy-seven "Semyon Semyonitch," ninety "grandfather," and so on. The game is going merrily.

"Thirty-two," cries Grisha, drawing the little yellow cylinders out of his father's cap. "Seventeen! Ovenrake! Twenty-eight! Lay them straight. . . ."

Anya sees that Andrey has let twenty-eight slip. At any other time she would have pointed it out to him, but now when her vanity lies in the saucer with the kopecks, she is triumphant.

"Twenty-three!" Grisha goes on, "Semyon Semyonitch! Nine!"

"A beetle, a beetle," cries Sonya, pointing to a beetle running across the table. "Aie!"

"Don't kill it," says Alyosha, in his deep bass, "perhaps it's got children . . . ."

Sonya follows the black beetle with her eyes and wonders about its children: what tiny little beetles they must be!

"Forty-three! One!" Grisha goes on, unhappy at the thought that Anya has already made two fours. "Six!"

"Game! I have got the game!" cries Sonya, rolling her eyes coquettishly and giggling.

The players' countenances lengthen.

"Must make sure!" says Grisha, looking with hatred at Sonya.

Exercising his rights as a big boy, and the cleverest, Grisha takes upon himself to decide. What he wants, that they do. Sonya's reckoning is slowly and carefully verified, and to the great regret of her fellow players, it appears that she has not cheated. Another game is begun.

"I did see something yesterday!" says Anya, as though to herself. "Filipp Filippitch turned his eyelids inside out somehow and his eyes looked red and dreadful, like an evil spirit's."

"I saw it too," says Grisha. "Eight! And a boy at our school can move his ears. Twenty-seven!"

Andrey looks up at Grisha, meditates, and says:

"I can move my ears too. . . ."

"Well then, move them."

Andrey moves his eyes, his lips, and his fingers, and fancies that his ears are moving too. Everyone laughs.

"He is a horrid man, that Filipp Filippitch," sighs Sonya. "He came into our nursery yesterday, and I had nothing on but my chemise . . . And I felt so improper!"

"Game!" Grisha cries suddenly, snatching the money from the saucer. "I've got the game! You can look and see if you like."

The cook's son looks up and turns pale.

"Then I can't go on playing any more," he whispers.

"Why not?"

"Because . . . because I have got no more money."

"You can't play without money," says Grisha.

Andrey ransacks his pockets once more to make sure. Finding nothing in them but crumbs and a bitten pencil, he drops the corners of his mouth and begins blinking miserably. He is on the point of crying. . . .

"I'll put it down for you!" says Sonya, unable to endure his look of agony. "Only mind you must pay me back afterwards."

The money is brought and the game goes on.

"I believe they are ringing somewhere," says Anya, opening her eyes wide.

They all leave off playing and gaze open-mouthed at the dark window. The reflection of the lamp glimmers in the darkness.

"It was your fancy."

"At night they only ring in the cemetery," says Andrey.

"And what do they ring there for?"

"To prevent robbers from breaking into the church. They are afraid of the bells."

"And what do robbers break into the church for?" asks Sonya.

"Everyone knows what for: to kill the watchmen."

A minute passes in silence. They all look at one another, shudder, and go on playing. This time Andrey wins.

"He has cheated," Alyosha booms out, apropos of nothing.

"What a lie, I haven't cheated."

Andrey turns pale, his mouth works, and he gives Alyosha a slap on the head! Alyosha glares angrily, jumps up, and with one knee on the table, slaps Andrey on the cheek! Each gives the other a second blow, and both howl. Sonya, feeling such horrors too much for her, begins crying too, and the dining-room resounds with lamentations on various notes. But do not imagine that that is the end of the game. Before five minutes are over, the children are laughing and talking peaceably again. Their faces are tear-stained, but that does not prevent them from smiling; Alyosha is positively blissful, there has been a squabble!

Vasya, the fifth form schoolboy, walks into the dining-room. He looks sleepy and disillusioned.

"This is revolting!" he thinks, seeing Grisha feel in his pockets in which the kopecks are jingling. "How can they give children money? And how can they let them play games of chance? A nice way to bring them up, I must say! It's revolting!"

But the children's play is so tempting that he feels an inclination to join them and to try his luck.

"Wait a minute and I'll sit down to a game," he says.

"Put down a kopeck!"

"In a minute," he says, fumbling in his pockets. "I haven't a kopeck, but here is a rouble. I'll stake a rouble."

"No, no, no. . . . You must put down a kopeck."

"You stupids. A rouble is worth more than a kopeck anyway," the schoolboy explains. "Whoever wins can give me change."

"No, please! Go away!"

The fifth form schoolboy shrugs his shoulders, and goes into the kitchen to get change from the servants. It appears there is not a single kopeck in the kitchen.

"In that case, you give me change," he urges Grisha, coming back from the kitchen. "I'll pay you for the change. Won't you? Come, give me ten kopecks for a rouble."

Grisha looks suspiciously at Vasya, wondering whether it isn't some trick, a swindle.

"I won't," he says, holding his pockets.

Vasya begins to get cross, and abuses them, calling them idiots and blockheads.

"I'll put down a stake for you, Vasya!" says Sonya. "Sit down." He sits down and lays two cards before him. Anya begins counting the numbers.

"I've dropped a kopeck!" Grisha announces suddenly, in an agitated voice. "Wait!"

He takes the lamp, and creeps under the table to look for the kopeck. They clutch at nutshells and all sorts of nastiness, knock their heads together, but do not find the kopeck. They begin looking again, and look till Vasya takes the lamp out of Grisha's hands and puts it in its place. Grisha goes on looking in the dark. But at last the kopeck is found. The players sit down at the table and mean to go on playing.

"Sonya is asleep!" Alyosha announces.

Sonya, with her curly head lying on her arms, is in a sweet, sound, tranquil sleep, as though she had been asleep for an hour. She has fallen asleep by accident, while the others were looking for the kopeck.

"Come along, lie on mamma's bed!" says Anya, leading her away from the table. "Come along!"

They all troop out with her, and five minutes later mamma's bed presents a curious spectacle. Sonya is asleep. Alyosha is snoring beside her. With their heads to the others' feet, sleep Grisha and Anya. The cook's son, Andrey too, has managed to snuggle in beside them. Near them lie the kopecks, that have lost their power till the next game. Good-night!

# MISERY

*"To whom shall I tell my grief?"*

The twilight of evening. Big flakes of wet snow are whirling lazily about the street lamps, which have just been lighted, and lying in a thin soft layer on roofs, horses' backs, shoulders, caps. Iona Potapov, the sledge-driver, is all white like a ghost. He sits on the box without stirring, bent as double as the living body can be bent. If a regular snowdrift fell on him it seems as though even then he would not think it necessary to shake it off. . . . His little mare is white and motionless too. Her stillness, the angularity of her lines, and the stick-like straightness of her legs make her look like a halfpenny gingerbread horse. She is probably lost in thought. Anyone who has been torn away from the plough, from the familiar gray landscapes, and cast into this slough, full of monstrous lights, of unceasing uproar and hurrying people, is bound to think.

It is a long time since Iona and his nag have budged. They came out of the yard before dinnertime and not a single fare yet. But now the shades of evening are falling on the town. The pale light of the street lamps changes to a vivid color, and the bustle of the street grows noisier.

"Sledge to Vyborgskaya!" Iona hears. "Sledge!"

Iona starts, and through his snow-plastered eyelashes sees an officer in a military overcoat with a hood over his head.

"To Vyborgskaya," repeats the officer. "Are you asleep? To Vyborgskaya!"

In token of assent Iona gives a tug at the reins which sends cakes of snow flying from the horse's back and shoulders. The officer gets into the sledge. The sledge-driver clicks to the horse, cranes his neck like a swan, rises in his seat, and more from habit than necessity brandishes his whip. The mare cranes her neck, too, crooks her stick-like legs, and hesitatingly sets of. . . .

"Where are you shoving, you devil?" Iona immediately hears shouts from the dark mass shifting to and fro before him. "Where the devil are you going? Keep to the r-right!"

"You don't know how to drive! Keep to the right," says the officer angrily.

A coachman driving a carriage swears at him; a pedestrian crossing the road and brushing the horse's nose with his shoulder looks at him angrily and shakes the snow off his sleeve. Iona fidgets on the box as though he were sitting on thorns, jerks his elbows, and turns his eyes about like one possessed as though he did not know where he was or why he was there.

"What rascals they all are!" says the officer jocosely. "They are simply doing their best to run up against you or fall under the horse's feet. They must be doing it on purpose."

Iona looks as his fare and moves his lips. . . . Apparently he means to say something, but nothing comes but a sniff.

"What?" inquires the officer.

Iona gives a wry smile, and straining his throat, brings out huskily: "My son . . . er . . . my son died this week, sir."

"H'm! What did he die of?"

Iona turns his whole body round to his fare, and says:

"Who can tell! It must have been from fever. . . . He lay three days in the hospital and then he died. . . . God's will."

"Turn round, you devil!" comes out of the darkness. "Have you gone cracked, you old dog? Look where you are going!"

"Drive on! drive on! . . ." says the officer. "We shan't get there till to-morrow going on like this. Hurry up!"

The sledge-driver cranes his neck again, rises in his seat, and with heavy grace swings his whip. Several times he looks round at the officer, but the latter keeps his eyes shut and is apparently disinclined to listen.

Putting his fare down at Vyborgskaya, Iona stops by a restaurant, and again sits huddled up on the box. . . . Again the wet snow paints him and his horse white. One hour passes, and then another. . . .

Three young men, two tall and thin, one short and hunchbacked, come up, railing at each other and loudly stamping on the pavement with their goloshes.

"Cabby, to the Police Bridge!" the hunchback cries in a cracked voice. "The three of us, . . . twenty kopecks!"

Iona tugs at the reins and clicks to his horse. Twenty kopecks is not a fair price, but he has no thoughts for that. Whether it is a rouble or whether it is five kopecks does not matter to him now so long as he has a fare. . . . The three young men, shoving each other and using bad language, go up to the sledge, and all three try to sit down at once. The question remains to be settled: Which are to sit down and which one is to stand? After a long altercation, ill-temper, and abuse, they come to the conclusion that the hunchback must stand because he is the shortest.

"Well, drive on," says the hunchback in his cracked voice, settling himself and breathing down Iona's neck. "Cut along! What a cap you've got, my friend! You wouldn't find a worse one in all Petersburg. . . ."

"He-he! . . . he-he! . . ." laughs Iona. "It's nothing to boast of!"

"Well, then, nothing to boast of, drive on! Are you going to drive like this all the way? Eh? Shall I give you one in the neck?"

"My head aches," says one of the tall ones. "At the Dukmasovs' yesterday Vaska and I drank four bottles of brandy between us."

"I can't make out why you talk such stuff," says the other tall one angrily. "You lie like a brute."

"Strike me dead, it's the truth! . . ."

"It's about as true as that a louse coughs."

"He-he!" grins Iona. "Me-er-ry gentlemen!"

"Tfoo! the devil take you!" cries the hunchback indignantly. "Will you get on, you old plague, or won't you? Is that the way to drive? Give her one with the whip. Hang it all, give it her well."

Iona feels behind his back the jolting person and quivering voice of the hunchback. He hears abuse addressed to him, he sees people, and the feeling of loneliness begins little by little to be less heavy on his heart. The hunchback swears at him, till he chokes over some elaborately whimsical string of epithets and is overpowered by his cough. His tall companions begin talking of a certain Nadyezhda Petrovna. Iona looks round at them. Waiting till there is a brief pause, he looks round once more and says:

"This week . . . er. . . my. . . er. . . son died!"

"We shall all die, . . ." says the hunchback with a sigh, wiping his lips after coughing. "Come, drive on! drive on! My friends, I simply cannot stand crawling like this! When will he get us there?"

"Well, you give him a little encouragement . . . one in the neck!"

"Do you hear, you old plague? I'll make you smart. If one stands on ceremony with fellows like you one may as well walk. Do you hear, you old dragon? Or don't you care a hang what we say? "

And Iona hears rather than feels a slap on the back of his neck.

"He-he! . . . " he laughs. "Merry gentlemen . . . . God give you health!"

"Cabman, are you married?" asks one of the tall ones.

"I? He he! Me-er-ry gentlemen. The only wife for me now is the damp earth. . . . He-ho-ho!. . . .The grave that is! . . . Here my son's dead and I am alive. . . . It's a strange thing, death has come in at the wrong door. . . . Instead of coming for me it went for my son. . . ."

And Iona turns round to tell them how his son died, but at that point the hunchback gives a faint sigh and announces that, thank God! they have arrived at last. After taking his twenty kopecks, Iona gazes for a long while after the revelers, who disappear into a dark entry. Again he is alone and again there is silence for him. . . . The misery which has been for a brief space eased comes back again and tears his heart more cruelly than ever. With a look of anxiety and suffering Iona's eyes stray restlessly among the crowds moving to and fro on both sides of the street: can he not find among those thousands someone who will listen to him? But the crowds flit by heedless of him and his misery.... His misery is immense, beyond all bounds. If Iona's heart were to burst and his misery to flow out, it would flood the whole world, it seems, but yet it is not seen. It has found a hiding-place in such an insignificant shell that one would not have found it with a candle by daylight....

Iona sees a house-porter with a parcel and makes up his mind to address him.

"What time will it be, friend?" he asks.

"Going on for ten.... Why have you stopped here? Drive on!"

Iona drives a few paces away, bends himself double, and gives himself up to his misery. He feels it is no good to appeal to people. But before five minutes have passed he draws himself up, shakes his head as though he feels a sharp pain, and tugs at the reins.... He can bear it no longer.

"Back to the yard!" he thinks. "To the yard!"

And his little mare, as though she knew his thoughts, falls to trotting. An hour and a half later Iona is sitting by a big dirty stove. On the stove, on the floor, and on thebenches are people snoring. The air is full of smells and stuffiness. Iona looks at the sleeping figures, scratches himself, and regrets that he has come home so early....

"I have not earned enough to pay for the oats, even," he thinks. "That's why I am so miserable. A man who knows how to do his work, ... who has had enough to eat, and whose horse has had enough to eat, is always at ease...."

In one of the corners a young cabman gets up, clears his throat sleepily, and makes for the water-bucket.

"Want a drink?" Iona asks him.

"Seems so."

"May it do you good. . . . But my son is dead, mate. . . . Do you hear? This week in the hospital. . . . It's a queer business. . . ."

Iona looks to see the effect produced by his words, but he sees nothing. The young man has covered his head over and is already asleep. The old man sighs and scratches himself. . . . Just as the young man had been thirsty for water, he thirsts for speech. His son will soon have been dead a week, and he has not really talked to anybody yet . . . . He wants to talk of it properly, with deliberation. . . . He wants to tell how his son was taken ill, how he suffered, what he said before he died, how he died. . . . He wants to describe the funeral, and how he went to the hospital to get his son's clothes. He still has his daughter Anisya in the country. . . . And he wants to talk about her too. . . . Yes, he has plenty to talk about now. His listener ought to sigh and exclaim and lament. . . . It would be even better to talk to women. Though they are silly creatures, they blubber at the first word.

"Let's go out and have a look at the mare," Iona thinks. "There is always time for sleep. . . . You'll have sleep enough, no fear. . . ."

He puts on his coat and goes into the stables where his mare is standing. He thinks about oats, about hay, about the weather. . . . He cannot think about his son when he is alone. . . . To talk about him with someone is possible, but to think of him and picture him is insufferable anguish. . . .

"Are you munching?" Iona asks his mare, seeing her shining eyes. "There, munch away, munch away. . . . Since we have not earned enough for oats, we will eat hay. . . . Yes, . . . I have grown too old to drive. . . . My son ought to be driving, not I. . . . He was a real cabman. . . . He ought to have lived. . . ."

Iona is silent for a while, and then he goes on:

"That's how it is, old girl. . . . Kuzma Ionitch is gone. . . . He said good-by to me. . . . He went and died for no reason. . . . Now, suppose you had a little colt, and you were own mother to that little colt. . . . And all at once that same little colt went and died. . . . You'd be sorry, wouldn't you? . . ."

The little mare munches, listens, and breathes on her master's hands. Iona is carried away and tells her all about it.

# AN UPHEAVAL

Mashenka Pavletsky, a young girl who had only just finished her studies at a boarding school, returning from a walk to the house of the Kushkins, with whom she was living as a governess, found the household in a terrible turmoil. Mihailo, the porter who opened the door to her, was excited and red as a crab.

Loud voices were heard from upstairs.

"Madame Kushkin is in a fit, most likely, or else she has quarrelled with her husband," thought Mashenka.

In the hall and in the corridor she met maid-servants. One of them was crying. Then Mashenka saw, running out of her room, the master of the house himself, Nikolay Sergeitch, a little man with a flabby face and a bald head, though he was not old. He was red in the face and twitching all over. He passed the governess without noticing her, and throwing up his arms, exclaimed:

"Oh, how horrible it is! How tactless! How stupid! How barbarous! Abominable!"

Mashenka went into her room, and then, for the first time in her life, it was her lot to experience in all its acuteness the feeling that is so familiar to persons in dependent positions, who eat the bread of the rich and powerful, and cannot speak their minds. There was a search going on in her room. The lady of the house, Fedosya Vassilyevna, a stout, broad shouldered, uncouth woman with thick black eyebrows, a faintly perceptible moustache, and red hands, who was exactly like a plain, illiterate cook in face and manners, was standing, without her cap on, at the table, putting back into Mashenka's workbag balls of wool, scraps of materials, and bits of paper. . . . Evidently the governess's arrival took her by surprise, since, on looking round and seeing the girl's pale and astonished face, she was a little taken aback, and muttered:

"*Pardon.* I . . . I upset it accidentally. . . . My sleeve caught in it. . ."

And saying something more, Madame Kushkin rustled her long skirts and went out. Mashenka looked round her room with wondering eyes, and, unable to understand it, not knowing what to think, shrugged her shoulders, and turned cold with dismay. What had Fedosya Vassilyevna been looking for in her work-bag? If she really had, as she said, caught her sleeve in it and upset everything, why had Nikolay Sergeitch dashed out of her room so excited and red in the face? Why was one drawer of the table pulled out a little way? The money-box, in which the governess put away ten kopeck pieces and old stamps, was open. They had opened it, but did not know how to shut it, though they had scratched the lock all over. The whatnot with her books on it, the things on the table, the bed - all bore fresh traces of a search. Her linen-basket, too. The linen had been carefully folded, but it was not in the same order as Mashenka had left it when she went out. So the search had been thorough, most thorough. But what was it for? Why? What had happened? Mashenka remembered the excited porter, the general turmoil which was still going on, the weeping servant-girl; had it not all some connection with the search that had just been made in her room? Was not she mixed up in something dreadful? Mashenka turned pale, and feeling cold all over, sank on to her linen-basket.

A maid-servant came into the room.

"Liza, you don't know why they have been rummaging in my room?" the governess asked her.

"Mistress has lost a brooch worth two thousand," said Liza.

"Yes, but why have they been rummaging in my room?"

"They've been searching every one, miss. They've searched all my things, too. They stripped us all naked and searched us. . . . God knows, miss, I never went near her toilet-table, let alone touching the brooch. I shall say the same at the police-station."

"But . . . why have they been rummaging here?" the governess still wondered.

"A brooch has been stolen, I tell you. The mistress has been rummaging in everything with her own hands. She even searched Mihailo, the porter, herself. It's a perfect disgrace! Nikolay Sergeitch simply looks on and cackles like a hen. But you've no need to tremble like that, miss. They found nothing here. You've nothing to be afraid of if you didn't take the brooch."

"But, Liza, it's vile . . . it's insulting," said Mashenka, breathless with indignation. "It's so mean, so low! What right had she to suspect me and to rummage in my things?"

"You are living with strangers, miss," sighed Liza. "Though you are a young lady, still you are . . . as it were . . . a servant. . . . It's not like living with your papa and mamma."

Mashenka threw herself on the bed and sobbed bitterly. Never in her life had she been subjected to such an outrage, never had she been so deeply insulted. . . . She, well-educated, refined, the daughter of a teacher, was suspected of theft; she had been searched like a street-walker! She could not imagine a greater insult. And to this feeling of resentment was added an oppressive dread of what would come next. All sorts of absurd ideas came into her mind. If they could suspect her of theft, then they might arrest her, strip her naked, and search her, then lead her through the street with an escort of soldiers, cast her into a cold, dark cell with mice and woodlice, exactly like the dungeon in which Princess Tarakanov was imprisoned. Who would stand up for her? Her parents lived far away in the provinces; they had not the money to come to her. In the capital she was as solitary as in a desert, without friends or kindred. They could do what they liked with her.

"I will go to all the courts and all the lawyers," Mashenka thought, trembling. "I will explain to them, I will take an oath. . . . They will believe that I could not be a thief!"

Mashenka remembered that under the sheets in her basket she had some sweetmeats, which, following the habits of her schooldays, she had put in her pocket at dinner and carried off to her room. She felt hot all over, and was ashamed at the thought that her little secret was known to the lady of the house; and all this terror, shame, resentment, brought on an attack of palpitation of the heart, which set up a throbbing in her temples, in her heart, and deep down in her stomach.

"Dinner is ready," the servant summoned Mashenka.

"Shall I go, or not?"

Mashenka brushed her hair, wiped her face with a wet towel, and went into the dining-room. There they had already begun dinner. At one end of the table sat Fedosya Vassilyevna with a stupid, solemn, serious face; at the other end Nikolay Sergeitch. At the sides there were the visitors and the children. The dishes were handed by two footmen in swallowtails and white gloves. Every one knew that there was an upset in the house, that Madame Kushkin was in trouble, and every one was silent. Nothing was heard but the sound of munching and the rattle of spoons on the plates.

The lady of the house, herself, was the first to speak.

"What is the third course?" she asked the footman in a weary, injured voice.

"*Esturgeon à la russe*," answered the footman.

"I ordered that, Fenya," Nikolay Sergeitch hastened to observe. "I wanted some fish. If you don't like it, *ma chère*, don't let them serve it. I just ordered it. . . ."

Fedosya Vassilyevna did not like dishes that she had not ordered herself, and now her eyes filled with tears.

Come, don't let us agitate ourselves," Mamikov, her household doctor, observed in a honeyed voice, just touching her arm, with a smile as honeyed. "We are nervous enough as it is. Let us forget the brooch! Health is worth more than two thousand roubles!"

"It's not the two thousand I regret," answered the lady, and a big tear rolled down her cheek. "It's the fact itself that revolts me! I cannot put up with thieves in my house. I don't regret it - I regret nothing; but to steal from me is such ingratitude! That's how they repay me for my kindness. . . ."

They all looked into their plates, but Mashenka fancied after the lady's words that every one was looking at her. A lump rose in her throat; she began crying and put her handkerchief to her lips.

"*Pardon*," she muttered. "I can't help it. My head aches. I'll go away."

And she got up from the table, scraping her chair awkwardly, and went out quickly, still more overcome with confusion.

"It's beyond everything!" said Nikolay Sergeitch, frowning. "What need was there to search her room? How out of place it was!"

"I don't say she took the brooch," said Fedosya Vassilyevna, "but can you answer for her? To tell the truth, I haven't much confidence in these learned paupers."

"It really was unsuitable, Fenya. . . . Excuse me, Fenya, but you've no kind of legal right to make a search."

"I know nothing about your laws. All I know is that I've lost my brooch. And I will find the brooch!" She brought her fork down on the plate with a clatter, and her eyes flashed angrily. "And you eat your dinner, and don't interfere in what doesn't concern you!"

Nikolay Sergeitch dropped his eyes mildly and sighed. Meanwhile Mashenka, reaching her room, flung herself on her bed. She felt now neither alarm nor shame, but she felt an intense longing to go and slap the cheeks of this hard, arrogant, dull-witted, prosperous woman.

Lying on her bed she breathed into her pillow and dreamed of how nice it would be to go and buy the most expensive brooch and fling it into the face of this bullying woman. If only it were God's will that Fedosya Vassilyevna should come to ruin and wander about begging, and should taste all the horrors of poverty and dependence, and that Mashenka, whom she had insulted, might give her alms! Oh, if only she could come in for a big fortune, could buy a carriage, and could drive noisily past the windows so as to be envied by that woman!

But all these were only dreams, in reality there was only one thing left to do - to get away as quickly as possible, not to stay another hour in this place. It was true it was terrible to lose her place, to go back to her parents, who had nothing; but what could she do? Mashenka could not bear the sight of the lady of the house nor of her little room; she felt stifled and wretched here. She was so disgusted with Fedosya Vassilyevna, who was so obsessed by her illnesses and her supposed aristocratic rank, that everything in the world seemed to have become coarse and unattractive because this woman was living in it. Mashenka jumped up from the bed and began packing.

"May I come in?" asked Nikolay Sergeitch at the door; he had come up noiselessly to the door, and spoke in a soft, subdued voice. "May I?"

"Come in."

He came in and stood still near the door. His eyes looked dim and his red little nose was shiny. After dinner he used to drink beer, and the fact was perceptible in his walk, in his feeble, flabby hands.

"What's this?" he asked, pointing to the basket.

"I am packing. Forgive me, Nikolay Sergeitch, but I cannot remain in your house. I feel deeply insulted by this search!"

"I understand. . . . Only you are wrong to go. Why should you? They've searched your things, but you . . . what does it matter to you? You will be none the worse for it."

Mashenka was silent and went on packing. Nikolay Sergeitch pinched his moustache, as though wondering what he should say next, and went on in an ingratiating voice:

"I understand, of course, but you must make allowances. You know my wife is nervous, headstrong; you mustn't judge her too harshly."

Mashenka did not speak.

"If you are so offended," Nikolay Sergeitch went on, "well, if you like, I'm ready to apologise. I ask your pardon."

Mashenka made no answer, but only bent lower over her box. This exhausted, irresolute man was of absolutely no significance in the household. He stood in the pitiful position of a dependent and hanger-on, even with the servants, and his apology meant nothing either.

"H'm! . . . You say nothing! That's not enough for you. In that case, I will apologise for my wife. In my wife's name. . . . She behaved tactlessly, I admit it as a gentleman. . . ."

Nikolay Sergeitch walked about the room, heaved a sigh, and went on:

"Then you want me to have it rankling here, under my heart. . . . You want my conscience to torment me. . . ."

"I know it's not your fault, Nikolay Sergeitch," said Mashenka, looking him full in the face with her big tear-stained eyes. "Why should you worry yourself?"

"Of course, no. . . . But still, don't you. . . go away. I entreat you."

Mashenka shook her head. Nikolay Sergeitch stopped at the window and drummed on the pane with his finger-tips.

"Such misunderstandings are simply torture to me," he said. "Why, do you want me to go down on my knees to you, or what? Your pride is wounded, and here you've been crying and packing up to go; but I have pride, too, and you do not spare it! Or do you want me to tell you what I would not tell as Confession? Do you? Listen; you want me to tell you what I won't tell the priest on my deathbed?"

Mashenka made no answer.

"I took my wife's brooch," Nikolay Sergeitch said quickly. "Is that enough now? Are you satisfied? Yes, I . . . took it. . . . But, of course, I count on your discretion. . . . For God's sake, not a word, not half a hint to any one!"

Mashenka, amazed and frightened, went on packing; she snatched her things, crumpled them up, and thrust them anyhow into the box and the basket. Now, after this candid avowal on the part of Nikolay Sergeitch, she could not remain another minute, and could not understand how she could have gone on living in the house before.

"And it's nothing to wonder at," Nikolay Sergeitch went on after a pause. "It's an everyday story! I need money, and she . . . won't give it to me. It was my father's money that bought this house and everything, you know! It's all mine, and the brooch belonged to my mother, and . . . it's all mine! And she took it, took possession of everything. . . . I can't go to law with her, you'll admit. . . . I beg you most earnestly, overlook it . . . stay on. *Tout comprendre, tout pardonner.* Will you stay?"

"No!" said Mashenka resolutely, beginning to tremble. "Let me alone, I entreat you!"

"Well, God bless you!" sighed Nikolay Sergeitch, sitting down on the stool near the box. "I must own I like people who still can feel resentment, contempt, and so on. I could sit here forever and look at your indignant face.... So you won't stay, then? I understand.... It's bound to be so... Yes, of course.... It's all right for you, but for me - wo-o-o-o!... I can't stir a step out of this cellar. I'd go off to one of our estates, but in every one of them there are some of my wife's rascals... stewards, experts, damn them all! They mortgage and remortgage.... You mustn't catch fish, must keep off the grass, mustn't break the trees."

"Nikolay Sergeitch!" his wife's voice called from the drawing-room. "Agnia, call your master!"

"Then you won't stay?" asked Nikolay Sergeitch, getting up quickly and going towards the door. "You might as well stay, really. In the evenings I could come and have a talk with you. Eh? Stay! If you go, there won't be a human face left in the house. It's awful!"

Nikolay Sergeitch's pale, exhausted face besought her, but Mashenka shook her head, and with a wave of his hand he went out.

Half an hour later she was on her way.

# AN ACTOR'S END

Shtchiptsov, the "heavy father" and "good-hearted simpleton," a tall and thick-set old man, not so much distinguished by his talents as an actor as by his exceptional physical strength, had a desperate quarrel with the manager during the performance, and just when the storm of words was at its height felt as though something had snapped in his chest. Zhukov, the manager, as a rule began at the end of every heated discussion to laugh hysterically and to fall into a swoon; on this occasion, however, Shtchiptsov did not remain for this climax, but hurried home. The high words and the sensation of something ruptured in his chest so agitated him as he left the theatre that he forgot to wash off his paint, and did nothing but take off his beard.

When he reached his hotel room, Shtchiptsov spent a long time pacing up and down, then sat down on the bed, propped his head on his fists, and sank into thought. He sat like that without stirring or uttering a sound till two o'clock the next afternoon, when Sigaev, the comic man, walked into his room.

"Why is it you did not come to the rehearsal, Booby Ivanitch?" the comic man began, panting and filling the room with fumes of vodka. "Where have you been?"

Shtchiptsov made no answer, but simply stared at the comic man with lustreless eyes, under which there were smudges of paint.

"You might at least have washed your phiz!" Sigaev went on. "You are a disgraceful sight! Have you been boozing, or . . . are you ill, or what? But why don't you speak? I am asking you: are you ill?"

Shtchiptsov did not speak. In spite of the paint on his face, the comic man could not help noticing his striking pallor, the drops of sweat on his forehead, and the twitching of his lips. His hands and feet were trembling too, and the whole huge figure of the "good-natured simpleton" looked somehow crushed and flattened. The comic man took a rapid glance round the room, but saw neither bottle nor flask nor any other suspicious vessel.

"I say, Mishutka, you know you are ill!" he said in a flutter. "Strike me dead, you are ill! You don't look yourself!"

Shtchiptsov remained silent and stared disconsolately at the floor.

"You must have caught cold," said Sigaev, taking him by the hand. "Oh, dear, how hot your hands are! What's the trouble?"

"I wa-ant to go home," muttered Shtchiptsov.

"But you are at home now, aren't you?"

"No. . . . To Vyazma. . . ."

"Oh, my, anywhere else! It would take you three years to get to your Vyazma. . . . What? do you want to go and see your daddy and mummy? I'll be bound, they've kicked the bucket years ago, and you won't find their graves. . . ."

"My ho-ome's there."

"Come, it's no good giving way to the dismal dumps. These neurotic feelings are the limit, old man. You must get well, for you have to play Mitka in 'The Terrible Tsar' to-morrow. There is nobody else to do it. Drink something hot and take some castor-oil? Have you got the money for some castor-oil? Or, stay, I'll run and buy some."

The comic man fumbled in his pockets, found a fifteen-kopeck piece, and ran to the chemist's. A quarter of an hour later he came back.

"Come, drink it," he said, holding the bottle to the "heavy father's" mouth. "Drink it straight out of the bottle. . . . All at a go! That's the way. . . . Now nibble at a clove that your very soul mayn't stink of the filthy stuff."

The comic man sat a little longer with his sick friend, then kissed him tenderly, and went away. Towards evening the *jeune premier,* Brama-Glinsky, ran in to see Shtchiptsov. The gifted actor was wearing a pair of prunella boots, had a glove on his left hand, was smoking a cigar, and even smelt of heliotrope, yet nevertheless he strongly suggested a traveller cast away in some land in which there were neither baths nor laundresses nor tailors. . . .

"I hear you are ill?" he said to Shtchiptsov, twirling round on his heel. "What's wrong with you? What's wrong with you, really? . . ."

Shtchiptsov did not speak nor stir.

"Why don't you speak? Do you feel giddy? Oh well, don't talk, I won't pester you . . . don't talk. . . ."

Brama-Glinsky (that was his stage name, in his passport he was called Guskov) walked away to the window, put his hands in his pockets, and fell to gazing into the street. Before his eyes stretched an immense waste, bounded by a grey fence beside which ran a perfect forest of last year's burdocks. Beyond the waste ground was a dark, deserted factory, with windows boarded up. A belated jackdaw was flying round the chimney. This dreary, lifeless scene was beginning to be veiled in the dusk of evening.

"I must go home!" the *jeune premier* heard.

"Where is home?"

"To Vyazma . . . to my home. . . ."

"It is a thousand miles to Vyazma . . . my boy," sighed Brama-Glinsky, drumming on the window-pane. "And what do you want to go to Vyazma for?"

"I want to die there."

"What next! Now he's dying! He has fallen ill for the first time in his life, and already he fancies that his last hour is come. . . . No, my boy, no cholera will carry off a buffalo like you. You'll live to be a hundred. . . . Where's the pain?"

"There's no pain, but I . . . feel . . ."

"You don't feel anything, it all comes from being too healthy. Your surplus energy upsets you. You ought to get jolly tight — drink, you know, till your whole inside is topsy-turvy. Getting drunk is wonderfully restoring. . . . Do you remember how screwed you were at Rostov on the Don? Good Lord, the very thought of it is alarming! Sashka and I together could only just carry in the barrel, and you emptied it alone, and even sent for rum afterwards. . . . You got so drunk you were catching devils in a sack and pulled a lamp-post up by the roots. Do you remember? Then you went off to beat the Greeks. . . ."

Under the influence of these agreeable reminiscences Shtchiptsov's face brightened a little and his eyes began to shine.

"And do you remember how I beat Savoikin the manager?" he muttered, raising his head. "But there! I've beaten thirty-three managers in my time, and I can't remember how many smaller fry. And what managers they were! Men who would not permit the very winds to touch them! I've beaten two celebrated authors and one painter!"

"What are you crying for?"

"At Kherson I killed a horse with my fists. And at Taganrog some roughs fell upon me at night, fifteen of them. I took off their caps and they followed me, begging: 'Uncle, give us back our caps.' That's how I used to go on."

"What are you crying for, then, you silly?"

"But now it's all over . . . I feel it. If only I could go to Vyazma!"

A pause followed. After a silence Shtchiptsov suddenly jumped up and seized his cap. He looked distraught.

"Good-bye! I am going to Vyazma!" he articulated, staggering.

"And the money for the journey?"

"H'm! . . . I shall go on foot!"

"You are crazy. . . ."

The two men looked at each other, probably because the same thought - of the boundless plains, the unending forests and swamps - struck both of them at once.

"Well, I see you have gone off your head," the *jeune premier* commented. "I'll tell you what, old man. . . . First thing, go to bed, then drink some brandy and tea to put you into a sweat. And some castor-oil, of course. Stay, where am I to get some brandy?"

Brama-Glinsky thought a minute, then made up his mind to go to a shopkeeper called Madame Tsitrinnikov to try and get it from her on tick: who knows? perhaps the woman would feel for them and let them have it. The *jeune premier* went off, and half an hour later returned with a bottle of brandy and some castor-oil. Shtchiptsov was sitting motionless, as before, on the bed, gazing dumbly at the floor. He drank the castor-oil offered him by his friend like an automaton, with no consciousness of what he was doing. Like an automaton he sat afterwards at the table, and drank tea and brandy; mechanically he emptied the whole bottle and let the *jeune premier* put him to bed. The latter covered him up with a quilt and an overcoat, advised him to get into a perspiration, and went away.

The night came on; Shtchiptsov had drunk a great deal of brandy, but he did not sleep. He lay motionless under the quilt and stared at the dark ceiling; then, seeing the moon looking in at the window, he turned his eyes from the ceiling towards the companion of the earth, and lay so with open eyes till the morning. At nine o'clock in the morning Zhukov, the manager, ran in.

"What has put it into your head to be ill, my angel?" he cackled, wrinkling up his nose. "Aie, aie! A man with your physique has no business to be ill! For shame, for shame! Do you know, I was quite frightened. 'Can our conversation have had such an effect on him?' I wondered. My dear soul, I hope it's not through me you've fallen ill! You know you gave me as good . . . er . . . And, besides, comrades can never get on without words. You called me all sorts of names . . . and have gone at me with your fists too, and yet I am fond of you! Upon my soul, I am. I respect you and am fond of you! Explain, my angel, why I am so fond of you. You are neither kith nor kin nor wife, but as soon as I heard you had fallen ill it cut me to the heart."

Zhukov spent a long time declaring his affection, then fell to kissing the invalid, and finally was so overcome by his feelings that he began laughing hysterically, and was even meaning to fall into a swoon, but, probably remembering that he was not at home nor at the theatre, put off the swoon to a more convenient opportunity and went away.

Soon after him Adabashev, the tragic actor, a dingy, short-sighted individual who talked through his nose, made his appearance. . . . For a long while he looked at Shtchiptsov, for a long while he pondered, and at last he made a discovery.

"Do you know what, Mifa?" he said, pronouncing through his nose "f" instead of "sh," and assuming a mysterious expression. "Do you know what? You ought to have a dose of castor-oil!"

Shtchiptsov was silent. He remained silent, too, a little later as the tragic actor poured the loathsome oil into his mouth. Two hours later Yevlampy, or, as the actors for some reason called him, Rigoletto, the hairdresser of the company, came into the room. He too, like the tragic man, stared at Shtchiptsov for a long time, then sighed like a steam-engine, and slowly and deliberately began untying a parcel he had brought with him. In it there were twenty cups and several little flasks.

"You should have sent for me and I would have cupped you long ago," he said, tenderly baring Shtchiptsov's chest. "It is easy to neglect illness."

Thereupon Rigoletto stroked the broad chest of the "heavy father" and covered it all over with suction cups.

"Yes . . ." he said, as after this operation he packed up his paraphernalia, crimson with Shtchiptsov's blood. "You should have sent for me, and I would have come. . . . You needn't trouble about payment. . . . I do it from sympathy. Where are you to get the money if that idol won't pay you? Now, please take these drops. They are nice drops! And now you must have a dose of this castor-oil. It's the real thing. That's right! I hope it will do you good. Well, now, good-bye. . . ."

Rigoletto took his parcel and withdrew, pleased that he had been of assistance to a fellow-creature.

The next morning Sigaev, the comic man, going in to see Shtchiptsov, found him in a terrible condition. He was lying under his coat, breathing in gasps, while his eyes strayed over the ceiling. In his hands he was crushing convulsively the crumpled quilt.

"To Vyazma!" he whispered, when he saw the comic man. "To Vyazma."

"Come, I don't like that, old man!" said the comic man, flinging up his hands. "You see . . . you see . . . you see, old man, that's not the thing! Excuse me, but . . . it's positively stupid. . . ."

"To go to Vyazma! My God, to Vyazma!"

"I . . . I did not expect it of you," the comic man muttered, utterly distracted. "What the deuce do you want to collapse like this for? Aie . . . aie . . . aie! . . . that's not the thing. A giant as tall as a watch-tower, and crying. Is it the thing for actors to cry?"

"No wife nor children," muttered Shtchiptsov. "I ought not to have gone for an actor, but have stayed at Vyazma. My life has been wasted, Semyon! Oh, to be in Vyazma!"

"Aie . . . aie . . . aie! . . . that's not the thing! You see, it's stupid . . . contemptible indeed!"

Recovering his composure and setting his feelings in order, Sigaev began comforting Shtchiptsov, telling him untruly that his comrades had decided to send him to the Crimea at their expense, and so on, but the sick man did not listen and kept muttering about Vyazma. . . . At last, with a wave of his hand, the comic man began talking about Vyazma himself to comfort the invalid.

"It's a fine town," he said soothingly, "a capital town, old man! It's famous for its cakes. The cakes are classical, but - between ourselves - h'm! - they are a bit groggy. For a whole week after eating them I was . . . h'm! . . . But what is fine there is the merchants! They are something like merchants. When they treat you they do treat you!"

The comic man talked while Shtchiptsov listened in silence and nodded his head approvingly.

Towards evening he died.

# THE REQUIEM

In the village church of Verhny Zaprudy mass was just over. The people had begun moving and were trooping out of church. The only one who did not move was Andrey Andreyitch, a shopkeeper and old inhabitant of Verhny Zaprudy. He stood waiting, with his elbows on the railing of the right choir. His fat and shaven face, covered with indentations left by pimples, expressed on this occasion two contradictory feelings: resignation in the face of inevitable destiny, and stupid, unbounded disdain for the smocks and striped kerchiefs passing by him. As it was Sunday, he was dressed like a dandy. He wore a long cloth overcoat with yellow bone buttons, blue trousers not thrust into his boots, and sturdy goloshes - the huge clumsy goloshes only seen on the feet of practical and prudent persons of firm religious convictions.

His torpid eyes, sunk in fat, were fixed upon the ikon stand. He saw the long familiar figures of the saints, the verger Matvey puffing out his cheeks and blowing out the candles, the darkened candle stands, the threadbare carpet, the sacristan Lopuhov running impulsively from the altar and carrying the holy bread to the churchwarden. . . . All these things he had seen for years, and seen over and over again like the five fingers of his hand. . . . There was only one thing, however, that was somewhat strange and unusual. Father Grigory, still in his vestments, was standing at the north door, twitching his thick eyebrows angrily.

"Who is it he is winking at? God bless him!" thought the shopkeeper. "And he is beckoning with his finger! And he stamped his foot! What next! What's the matter, Holy Queen and Mother! Whom does he mean it for?"

Andrey Andreyitch looked round and saw the church completely deserted. There were some ten people standing at the door, but they had their backs to the altar.

"Do come when you are called! Why do you stand like a graven image?" he heard Father Grigory's angry voice. "I am calling you."

The shopkeeper looked at Father Grigory's red and wrathful face, and only then realized that the twitching eyebrows and beckoning finger might refer to him. He started, left the railing, and hesitatingly walked towards the altar, tramping with his heavy goloshes.

"Andrey Andreyitch, was it you asked for prayers for the rest of Mariya's soul?" asked the priest, his eyes angrily transfixing the shopkeeper's fat, perspiring face.

"Yes, Father."

"Then it was you wrote this? You?" And Father Grigory angrily thrust before his eyes the little note.

And on this little note, handed in by Andrey Andreyitch before mass, was written in big, as it were staggering, letters:

"For the rest of the soul of the servant of God, the harlot Mariya."

"Yes, certainly I wrote it, . . ." answered the shopkeeper.

"How dared you write it?" whispered the priest, and in his husky whisper there was a note of wrath and alarm.

The shopkeeper looked at him in blank amazement; he was perplexed, and he, too, was alarmed. Father Grigory had never in his life spoken in such a tone to a leading resident of Verhny Zaprudy. Both were silent for a minute, staring into each other's face. The shopkeeper's amazement was so great that his fat face spread in all directions like spilt dough.

"How dared you?" repeated the priest.

"Wha . . . what?" asked Andrey Andreyitch in bewilderment.

"You don't understand?" whispered Father Grigory, stepping back in astonishment and clasping his hands. "What have you got on your shoulders, a head or some other object? You send a note up to the altar, and write a word in it which it would be unseemly even to utter in the street! Why are you rolling your eyes? Surely you know the meaning of the word?"

"Are you referring to the word harlot?" muttered the shopkeeper, flushing crimson and blinking. "But you know, the Lord in His mercy .

. . forgave this very thing, . . . forgave a harlot. . . . He has prepared a place for her, and indeed from the life of the holy saint, Mariya of Egypt, one may see in what sense the word is used  -  excuse me . . ."

The shopkeeper wanted to bring forward some other argument in his justification, but took fright and wiped his lips with his sleeve

"So that's what you make of it!" cried Father Grigory, clasping his hands. "But you see God has forgiven her  -  do you understand? He has forgiven, but you judge her, you slander her, call her by an unseemly name, and whom! Your own deceased daughter! Not only in Holy Scripture, but even in worldly literature you won't read of such a sin! I tell you again, Andrey, you mustn't be over-subtle! No, no, you mustn't be over-subtle, brother! If God has given you an inquiring mind, and if you cannot direct it, better not go into things. . . . Don't go into things, and hold your peace!"

"But you know, she, . . . excuse my mentioning it, was an actress!" articulated Andrey Andreyitch, overwhelmed.

"An actress! But whatever she was, you ought to forget it all now she is dead, instead of writing it on the note."

"Just so, . . ." the shopkeeper assented.

"You ought to do penance," boomed the deacon from the depths of the altar, looking contemptuously at Andrey Andreyitch's embarrassed face, "that would teach you to leave off being so clever! Your daughter was a well-known actress. There were even notices of her death in the newspapers. . . . Philosopher!"

"To be sure, . . . certainly," muttered the shopkeeper, "the word is not a seemly one; but I did not say it to judge her, Father Grigory, I only meant to speak spiritually, . . . that it might be clearer to you for whom you were praying. They write in the memorial notes the various callings, such as the infant John, the drowned woman Pelagea, the warrior Yegor, the murdered Pavel, and so on. . . . I meant to do the same."

"It was foolish, Andrey! God will forgive you, but beware another time. Above all, don't be subtle, but think like other people. Make ten bows and go your way."

"I obey," said the shopkeeper, relieved that the lecture was over, and allowing his face to resume its expression of importance and dignity. "Ten bows? Very good, I understand. But now, Father, allow me to ask you a favor. . . . Seeing that I am, anyway, her father, . . . you know yourself, whatever she was, she was still my daughter, so I was, . . . excuse me, meaning to ask you to sing the requiem today. And allow me to ask you, Father Deacon!"

"Well, that's good," said Father Grigory, taking off his vestments. "That I commend. I can approve of that! Well, go your way. We will come out immediately."

Andrey Andreyitch walked with dignity from the altar, and with a solemn, requiem-like expression on his red face took his stand in the middle of the church. The verger Matvey set before him a little table with the memorial food upon it, and a little later the requiem service began.

There was perfect stillness in the church. Nothing could be heard but the metallic click of the censer and slow singing. . . . Near Andrey Andreyitch stood the verger Matvey, the midwife Makaryevna, and her one-armed son Mitka. There was no one else. The sacristan sang badly in an unpleasant, hollow bass, but the tune and the words were so mournful that the shopkeeper little by little lost the expression of dignity and was plunged in sadness. He thought of his Mashutka, . . . he remembered she had been born when he was still a lackey in the service of the owner of Verhny Zaprudy. In his busy life as a lackey he had not noticed how his girl had grown up. That long period during which she was being shaped into a graceful creature, with a little flaxen head and dreamy eyes as big as kopeck-pieces passed unnoticed by him. She had been brought up like all the children of favorite lackeys, in ease and comfort in the company of the young ladies. The gentry, to fill up their idle time, had taught her to read, to write, to dance; he had had no hand in her bringing up. Only from time to time casually meeting her at the gate or on the landing of the stairs, he would remember that she was his daughter, and would, so far as he had leisure for it, begin teaching her the prayers and the scripture. Oh, even then he had the reputation of an authority on the church rules and the holy scriptures! Forbidding and stolid as her father's face was, yet the girl listened readily. She repeated the prayers after him yawning, but on the other hand, when he, hesitating and trying to express himself elaborately, began telling her stories, she was all attention. Esau's pottage, the punishment of Sodom, and the troubles of the boy Joseph made her turn pale and open her blue eyes wide.

Afterwards when he gave up being a lackey, and with the money he had saved opened a shop in the village, Mashutka had gone away to Moscow with his master's family. . . .

Three years before her death she had come to see her father. He had scarcely recognized her. She was a graceful young woman with the manners of a young lady, and dressed like one. She talked cleverly, as though from a book, smoked, and slept till midday. When Andrey Andreyitch asked her what she was doing, she had announced, looking him boldly straight in the face: "I am an actress." Such frankness struck the former flunkey as the acme of cynicism. Mashutka had begun boasting of her successes and her stage life; but seeing that her father only turned crimson and threw up his hands, she ceased. And they spent a fortnight together without speaking or looking at one another till the day she went away. Before she went away she asked her father to come for a walk on the bank of the river. Painful as it was for him to walk in the light of day, in the sight of all honest people, with a daughter who was an actress, he yielded to her request.

"What a lovely place you live in!" she said enthusiastically. "What ravines and marshes! Good heavens, how lovely my native place is!"

And she had burst into tears.

"The place is simply taking up room, . . ." Andrey Andreyitch had thought, looking blankly at the ravines, not understanding his daughter's enthusiasm. "There is no more profit from them than milk from a billy-goat."

And she had cried and cried, drawing her breath greedily with her whole chest, as though she felt she had not a long time left to breathe.

Andrey Andreyitch shook his head like a horse that has been bitten, and to stifle painful memories began rapidly crossing himself. . . .

"Be mindful, O Lord," he muttered, "of Thy departed servant, the harlot Mariya, and forgive her sins, voluntary or involuntary. . . ."

The unseemly word dropped from his lips again, but he did not notice it: what is firmly imbedded in the consciousness cannot be driven out by Father Grigory's exhortations or even knocked out by a nail. Makaryevna sighed and whispered something, drawing in a deep breath, while one-armed Mitka was brooding over something. . . .

"Where there is no sickness, nor grief, nor sighing," droned the sacristan, covering his right cheek with his hand.

Bluish smoke coiled up from the censer and bathed in the broad, slanting patch of sunshine which cut across the gloomy, lifeless emptiness of the church. And it seemed as though the soul of the dead woman were soaring into the sunlight together with the smoke. The coils of smoke like a child's curls eddied round and round, floating upwards to the window and, as it were, holding aloof from the woes and tribulations of which that poor soul was full.

# ANYUTA

In the cheapest room of a big block of furnished apartments Stepan Klotchkov, a medical student in his third year, was walking to and fro, zealously conning his anatomy. His mouth was dry and his forehead perspiring from the unceasing effort to learn it by heart.

In the window, covered by patterns of frost, sat on a stool the girl who shared his room - Anyuta, a thin little brunette of five-and-twenty, very pale with mild grey eyes. Sitting with bent back she was busy embroidering with red thread the collar of a man's shirt. She was working against time. . . . The clock in the passage struck two drowsily, yet the little room had not been put to rights for the morning. Crumpled bed-clothes, pillows thrown about, books, clothes, a big filthy slop-pail filled with soap-suds in which cigarette ends were swimming, and the litter on the floor - all seemed as though purposely jumbled together in one confusion. . . .

"The right lung consists of three parts . . ." Klotchkov repeated. "Boundaries! Upper part on anterior wall of thorax reaches the fourth or fifth rib, on the lateral surface, the fourth rib . . . behind to the *spina scapulæ*. . ."

Klotchkov raised his eyes to the ceiling, striving to visualise what he had just read. Unable to form a clear picture of it, he began feeling his upper ribs through his waistcoat.

"These ribs are like the keys of a piano," he said. "One must familiarise oneself with them somehow, if one is not to get muddled over them. One must study them in the skeleton and the living body. . . . I say, Anyuta, let me pick them out."

Anyuta put down her sewing, took off her blouse, and straightened herself up. Klotchkov sat down facing her, frowned, and began counting her ribs.

"H'm! . . . One can't feel the first rib; it's behind the shoulder-blade. . . . This must be the second rib. . . . Yes . . . this is the third . . . this is the fourth. . . . H'm! . . . yes. . . . Why are you wriggling?"

"Your fingers are cold!"

"Come, come . . . it won't kill you. Don't twist about. That must be the third rib, then . . . this is the fourth. . . . You look such a skinny thing, and yet one can hardly feel your ribs. That's the second . . . that's the third. . . . Oh, this is muddling, and one can't see it clearly. . . . I must draw it. . . . Where's my crayon?"

Klotchkov took his crayon and drew on Anyuta's chest several parallel lines corresponding with the ribs.

"First-rate. That's all straightforward. . . . Well, now I can sound you. Stand up!"

Anyuta stood up and raised her chin. Klotchkov began sounding her, and was so absorbed in this occupation that he did not notice how Anyuta's lips, nose, and fingers turned blue with cold. Anyuta shivered, and was afraid the student, noticing it, would leave off drawing and sounding her, and then, perhaps, might fail in his exam.

"Now it's all clear," said Klotchkov when he had finished. "You sit like that and don't rub off the crayon, and meanwhile I'll learn up a little more."

And the student again began walking to and fro, repeating to himself. Anyuta, with black stripes across her chest, looking as though she had been tattooed, sat thinking, huddled up and shivering with cold. She said very little as a rule; she was always silent, thinking and thinking. . . .

In the six or seven years of her wanderings from one furnished room to another, she had known five students like Klotchkov. Now they had all finished their studies, had gone out into the world, and, of course, like respectable people, had long ago forgotten her. One of them was living in Paris, two were doctors, the fourth was an artist, and the fifth was said to be already a professor. Klotchkov was the sixth. . . . Soon he, too, would finish his studies and go out into the world. There was a fine future before him, no doubt, and Klotchkov probably would become a great man, but the present was anything but bright; Klotchkov had no tobacco and no tea, and there were only four lumps of sugar left. She must make haste and finish her embroidery, take it to the woman who had ordered it, and with the quarter rouble she would get for it, buy tea and tobacco.

"Can I come in?" asked a voice at the door.

Anyuta quickly threw a woollen shawl over her shoulders. Fetisov, the artist, walked in.

"I have come to ask you a favour," he began, addressing Klotchkov, and glaring like a wild beast from under the long locks that hung over his brow. "Do me a favour; lend me your young lady just for a couple of hours! I'm painting a picture, you see, and I can't get on without a model."

"Oh, with pleasure," Klotchkov agreed. "Go along, Anyuta."

"The things I've had to put up with there," Anyuta murmured softly.

"Rubbish! The man's asking you for the sake of art, and not for any sort of nonsense. Why not help him if you can?"

Anyuta began dressing.

"And what are you painting?" asked Klotchkov.

"Psyche; it's a fine subject. But it won't go, somehow. I have to keep painting from different models. Yesterday I was painting one with blue legs. 'Why are your legs blue?' I asked her. 'It's my stockings stain them,' she said. And you're still grinding! Lucky fellow! You have patience."

"Medicine's a job one can't get on with without grinding."

"H'm! . . . Excuse me, Klotchkov, but you do live like a pig! It's awful the way you live!"

"How do you mean? I can't help it. . . . I only get twelve roubles a month from my father, and it's hard to live decently on that."

"Yes . . . yes . . ." said the artist, frowning with an air of disgust; "but, still, you might live better. . . . An educated man is in duty bound to have taste, isn't he? And goodness knows what it's like here! The bed not made, the slops, the dirt . . . yesterday's porridge in the plates. . . Tfoo!"

"That's true," said the student in confusion; "but Anyuta has had no time to-day to tidy up; she's been busy all the while."

When Anyuta and the artist had gone out Klotchkov lay down on the sofa and began learning, lying down; then he accidentally dropped asleep, and waking up an hour later, propped his head on his fists and sank into gloomy reflection. He recalled the artist's words that an educated man was in duty bound to have taste, and his surroundings actually struck him now as loathsome and revolting. He saw, as it were in his mind's eye, his own future, when he would see his patients in his consulting-room, drink tea in a large dining-room in the company of his wife, a real lady. And now that slop-pail in which the cigarette ends were swimming looked incredibly disgusting. Anyuta, too, rose before his imagination - a plain, slovenly, pitiful figure . . . and he made up his mind to part with her at once, at all costs.

When, on coming back from the artist's, she took off her coat, he got up and said to her seriously:

"Look here, my good girl . . . sit down and listen. We must part! The fact is, I don't want to live with you any longer."

Anyuta had come back from the artist's worn out and exhausted. Standing so long as a model had made her face look thin and sunken, and her chin sharper than ever. She said nothing in answer to the student's words, only her lips began to tremble.

"You know we should have to part sooner or later, anyway," said the student. "You're a nice, good girl, and not a fool; you'll understand ."

Anyuta put on her coat again, in silence wrapped up her embroidery in paper, gathered together her needles and thread: she found the screw of paper with the four lumps of sugar in the window, and laid it on the table by the books

"That's . . . your sugar . . . " she said softly, and turned away to conceal her tears.

"Why are you crying?" asked Klotchkov.

He walked about the room in confusion, and said:

"You are a strange girl, really. . . . Why, you know we shall have to part. We can't stay together forever."

She had gathered together all her belongings, and turned to say good-bye to him, and he felt sorry for her.

"Shall I let her stay on here another week?" he thought. "She really may as well stay, and I'll tell her to go in a week;" and vexed at his own weakness, he shouted to her roughly:

"Come, why are you standing there? If you are going, go; and if you don't want to, take off your coat and stay! You can stay!"

Anyuta took off her coat, silently, stealthily, then blew her nose also stealthily, sighed, and noiselessly returned to her invariable position on her stool by the window.

The student drew his textbook to him and began again pacing from corner to corner. "The right lung consists of three parts," he repeated; "the upper part, on anterior wall of thorax, reaches the fourth or fifth rib . . . ."

In the passage some one shouted at the top of his voice: "Grigory! The samovar!"

# IVAN MATVEYITCH

Between five and six in the evening. A fairly well-known man of learning - we will call him simply the man of learning - is sitting in his study nervously biting his nails.

"It's positively revolting," he says, continually looking at his watch. "It shows the utmost disrespect for another man's time and work. In England such a person would not earn a farthing, he would die of hunger. You wait a minute, when you do come . . . ."

And feeling a craving to vent his wrath and impatience upon someone, the man of learning goes to the door leading to his wife's room and knocks.

"Listen, Katya," he says in an indignant voice. "If you see Pyotr Danilitch, tell him that decent people don't do such things. It's abominable! He recommends a secretary, and does not know the sort of man he is recommending! The wretched boy is two or three hours late with unfailing regularity every day. Do you call that a secretary? Those two or three hours are more precious to me than two or three years to other people. When he does come I will swear at him like a dog, and won't pay him and will kick him out. It's no use standing on ceremony with people like that!"

"You say that every day, and yet he goes on coming and coming."

"But to-day I have made up my mind. I have lost enough through him. You must excuse me, but I shall swear at him like a cabman."

At last a ring is heard. The man of learning makes a grave face; drawing himself up, and, throwing back his head, he goes into the entry. There his amanuensis Ivan Matveyitch, a young man of eighteen, with a face oval as an egg and no moustache, wearing a shabby, mangy overcoat and no goloshes, is already standing by the hatstand. He is in breathless haste, and scrupulously wipes his huge clumsy boots on the doormat, trying as he does so to conceal from the maidservant a hole in his boot through which a white sock is peeping. Seeing the man of learning he smiles with that broad, prolonged, somewhat foolish smile which is seen only on the faces of children or very good-natured people.

"Ah, good evening!" he says, holding out a big wet hand. "Has your sore throat gone?"

"Ivan Matveyitch," says the man of learning in a shaking voice, stepping back and clasping his hands together. "Ivan Matveyitch."

Then he dashes up to the amanuensis, clutches him by the shoulders, and begins feebly shaking him.

"What a way to treat me!" he says with despair in his voice. "You dreadful, horrid fellow, what a way to treat me! Are you laughing at me, are you jeering at me? Eh?"

Judging from the smile which still lingered on his face Ivan Matveyitch had expected a very different reception, and so, seeing the man of learning's countenance eloquent of indignation, his oval face grows longer than ever, and he opens his mouth in amazement.

"What is . . . what is it?" he asks.

"And you ask that?" the man of learning clasps his hands. "You know how precious time is to me, and you are so late. You are two hours late! . . . Have you no fear of God?"

"I haven't come straight from home," mutters Ivan Matveyitch, untying his scarf irresolutely. "I have been at my aunt's name-day party, and my aunt lives five miles away. . . . If I had come straight from home, then it would have been a different thing."

"Come, reflect, Ivan Matveyitch, is there any logic in your conduct? Here you have work to do, work at a fixed time, and you go flying off after name-day parties and aunts! But do make haste and undo your wretched scarf! It's beyond endurance, really!"

The man of learning dashes up to the amanuensis again and helps him to disentangle his scarf.

"You are done up like a peasant woman, . . . Come along, . . . Please make haste!"

Blowing his nose in a dirty, crumpled-up handkerchief and pulling down his grey reefer jacket, Ivan Matveyitch goes through the hall and the drawing-room to the study. There a place and paper and even cigarettes had been put ready for him long ago.

"Sit down, sit down," the man of learning urges him on, rubbing his hands impatiently. "You are an unsufferable person. . . . You know the work has to be finished by a certain time, and then you are so late. One is forced to scold you. Come, write, . . . Where did we stop?"

Ivan Matveyitch smooths his bristling cropped hair and takes up his pen. The man of learning walks up and down the room, concentrates himself, and begins to dictate:

"The fact is . . . comma . . . that so to speak fundamental forms . . . have you written it? . . . forms are conditioned entirely by the essential nature of those principles . . . comma . . . which find in them their expression and can only be embodied in them. . . . New line, . . . There's a stop there, of course. . . . More independence is found . . . is found . . . by the forms which have not so much a political . . . comma . . . as a social character . . ."

"The high-school boys have a different uniform now . . . a grey one," said Ivan Matveyitch, "when I was at school it was better: they used to wear regular uniforms."

"Oh dear, write please!" says the man of learning wrathfully. "Character . . . have you written it? Speaking of the forms relating to the organization . . . of administrative functions, and not to the regulation of the life of the people . . . comma . . . it cannot be said that they are marked by the nationalism of their forms . . . the last three words in inverted commas. . . . Aie, aie . . . tut, tut . so what did you want to say about the high school?"

"That they used to wear a different uniform in my time."

"Aha! . . . indeed, . . . Is it long since you left the high school?"

"But I told you that yesterday. It is three years since I left school. . . . I left in the fourth class."

"And why did you give up high school?" asks the man of learning, looking at Ivan Matveyitch's writing.

"Oh, through family circumstances."

"Must I speak to you again, Ivan Matveyitch? When will you get over your habit of dragging out the lines? There ought not to be less than forty letters in a line."

"What, do you suppose I do it on purpose?" says Ivan Matveyitch, offended. "There are more than forty letters in some of the other lines. . . . You count them. And if you think I don't put enough in the line, you can take something off my pay."

"Oh dear, that's not the point. You have no delicacy, really. . . . At the least thing you drag in money. The great thing is to be exact, Ivan Matveyitch, to be exact is the great thing. You ought to train yourself to be exact."

The maidservant brings in a tray with two glasses of tea on it, and a basket of rusks. . . . Ivan Matveyitch takes his glass awkwardly with both hands, and at once begins drinking it. The tea is too hot. To avoid burning his mouth Ivan Matveyitch tries to take a tiny sip. He eats one rusk, then a second, then a third, and, looking sideways, with embarrassment, at the man of learning, timidly stretches after a fourth. . . . The noise he makes in swallowing, the relish with which he smacks his lips, and the expression of hungry greed in his raised eyebrows irritate the man of learning.

"Make haste and finish, time is precious."

"You dictate, I can drink and write at the same time. . . . I must confess I was hungry."

"I should think so after your walk!"

"Yes, and what wretched weather! In our parts there is a scent of spring by now. . . . There are puddles everywhere; the snow is melting."

"You are a southerner, I suppose?"

"From the Don region. . . . It's quite spring with us by March. Here it is frosty, everyone's in a fur coat, . . . but there you can see the grass . . . it's dry everywhere, and one can even catch tarantulas."

"And what do you catch tarantulas for?"

"Oh! . . . to pass the time . . ." says Ivan Matveyitch, and he sighs. "It's fun catching them. You fix a bit of pitch on a thread, let it down into their hole and begin hitting the tarantula on the back with the pitch, and the brute gets cross, catches hold of the pitch with his claws, and gets stuck. . . . And what we used to do with them! We used to put a basinful of them together and drop a bihorka in with them."

"What is a bihorka?"

"That's another spider, very much the same as a tarantula. In a fight one of them can kill a hundred tarantulas."

"H'm! . . . But we must write, . . . Where did we stop?"

The man of learning dictates another twenty lines, then sits plunged in meditation.

Ivan Matveyitch, waiting while the other cogitates, sits and, craning his neck, puts the collar of his shirt to rights. His tie will not set properly, the stud has come out, and the collar keeps coming apart.

"H'm! . . ." says the man of learning. "Well, haven't you found a job yet, Ivan Matveyitch?"

"No. And how is one to find one? I am thinking, you know, of volunteering for the army. But my father advises my going into a chemist's."

"H'm! . . . But it would be better for you to go into the university. The examination is difficult, but with patience and hard work you could get through. Study, read more. . . . Do you read much?"

"Not much, I must own . . ." says Ivan Matveyitch, lighting a cigarette.

"Have you read Turgenev?"

"N-no. . . ."

"And Gogol?"

"Gogol. H'm! . . . Gogol. . . . No, I haven't read him!"

"Ivan Matveyitch! Aren't you ashamed? Aie! aie! You are such a nice fellow, so much that is original in you . . . you haven't even read Gogol! You must read him! I will give you his works! It's essential to read him! We shall quarrel if you don't!"

Again a silence follows. The man of learning meditates, half reclining on a soft lounge, and Ivan Matveyitch, leaving his collar in peace, concentrates his whole attention on his boots. He has not till then noticed that two big puddles have been made by the snow melting off his boots on the floor. He is ashamed.

"I can't get on to-day . . ." mutters the man of learning. "I suppose you are fond of catching birds, too, Ivan Matveyitch?"

"That's in autumn, . . . I don't catch them here, but there at home I always did."

"To be sure . . . very good. But we must write, though."

The man of learning gets up resolutely and begins dictating, but after ten lines sits down on the lounge again.

"No. . . . Perhaps we had better put it off till to-morrow morning," he says. "Come to-morrow morning, only come early, at nine o'clock. God preserve you from being late!"

Ivan Matveyitch lays down his pen, gets up from the table and sits in another chair. Five minutes pass in silence, and he begins to feel it is time for him to go, that he is in the way; but in the man of learning's study it is so snug and light and warm, and the impression of the nice rusks and sweet tea is still so fresh that there is a pang at his heart at the mere thought of home. At home there is poverty, hunger, cold, his grumbling father, scoldings, and here it is so quiet and unruffled, and interest even is taken in his tarantulas and birds.

The man of learning looks at his watch and takes up a book.

"So you will give me Gogol?' says Ivan Matveyitch, getting up.

"Yes, yes! But why are you in such a hurry, my dear boy? Sit down and tell me something . . ."

Ivan Matveyitch sits down and smiles broadly. Almost every evening he sits in this study and always feels something extraordinarily soft, attracting him, as it were akin, in the voice and the glance of the man of learning. There are moments when he even fancies that the man of learning is becoming attached to him, used to him, and that if he scolds him for being late, it's simply because he misses his chatter about tarantulas and how they catch goldfinches on the Don.

# THE WITCH

It was approaching nightfall. The sexton, Savély Gykin, was lying in his huge bed in the hut adjoining the church. He was not asleep, though it was his habit to go to sleep at the same time as the hens. His coarse red hair peeped from under one end of the greasy patchwork quilt, made up of coloured rags, while his big unwashed feet stuck out from the other. He was listening. His hut adjoined the wall that encircled the church and the solitary window in it looked out upon the open country. And out there a regular battle was going on. It was hard to say who was being wiped off the face of the earth, and for the sake of whose destruction nature was being churned up into such a ferment; but, judging from the unceasing malignant roar, someone was getting it very hot. A victorious force was in full chase over the fields, storming in the forest and on the church roof, battering spitefully with its fists upon the windows, raging and tearing, while something vanquished was howling and wailing. . . . A plaintive lament sobbed at the window, on the roof, or in the stove. It sounded not like a call for help, but like a cry of misery, a consciousness that it was too late, that there was no salvation. The snowdrifts were covered with a thin coating of ice; tears quivered on them and on the trees; a dark slush of mud and melting snow flowed along the roads and paths. In short, it was thawing, but through the dark night the heavens failed to see it, and flung flakes of fresh snow upon the melting earth at a terrific rate. And the wind staggered like a drunkard. It would not let the snow settle on the ground, and whirled it round in the darkness at random.

Savély listened to all this din and frowned. The fact was that he knew, or at any rate suspected, what all this racket outside the window was tending to and whose handiwork it was.

"I know!" he muttered, shaking his finger menacingly under the bedclothes; "I know all about it."

On a stool by the window sat the sexton's wife, Raïssa Nilovna. A tin lamp standing on another stool, as though timid and distrustful of its powers, shed a dim and flickering light on her broad shoulders, on the handsome, tempting-looking contours of her person, and on her thick plait, which reached to the floor. She was making sacks out of coarse hempen stuff. Her hands moved nimbly, while her whole body, her eyes, her eyebrows, her full lips, her white neck were as still as though they were asleep, absorbed in the monotonous, mechanical toil. Only from time to time she raised her head to rest her weary neck, glanced for a moment towards the window, beyond which the snowstorm was raging, and bent again over her sacking. No desire, no joy, no grief, nothing was expressed by her handsome face with its turned-up nose and its dimples. So a beautiful fountain expresses nothing when it is not playing.

But at last she had finished a sack. She flung it aside, and, stretching luxuriously, rested her motionless, lack-lustre eyes on the window. The panes were swimming with drops like tears, and white with short-lived snowflakes which fell on the window, glanced at Raïssa, and melted. . . .

"Come to bed!" growled the sexton. Raïssa remained mute. But suddenly her eyelashes flickered and there was a gleam of attention in her eye. Savély, all the time watching her expression from under the quilt, put out his head and asked:

"What is it?"

"Nothing. . . . I fancy someone's coming," she answered quietly.

The sexton flung the quilt off with his arms and legs, knelt up in bed, and looked blankly at his wife. The timid light of the lamp illuminated his hirsute, pock-marked countenance and glided over his rough matted hair.

"Do you hear?" asked his wife.

Through the monotonous roar of the storm he caught a scarcely audible thin and jingling monotone like the shrill note of a gnat when it wants to settle on one's cheek and is angry at being prevented.

"It's the post," muttered Savély, squatting on his heels.

Two miles from the church ran the posting road. In windy weather, when the wind was blowing from the road to the church, the inmates of the hut caught the sound of bells.

"Lord! fancy people wanting to drive about in such weather," sighed Raïssa.

"It's government work. You've to go whether you like or not."

The murmur hung in the air and died away.

"It has driven by," said Savély, getting into bed.

But before he had time to cover himself up with the bedclothes he heard a distinct sound of the bell. The sexton looked anxiously at his wife, leapt out of bed and walked, waddling, to and fro by the stove. The bell went on ringing for a little, then died away again as though it had ceased.

"I don't hear it," said the sexton, stopping and looking at his wife with his eyes screwed up.

But at that moment the wind rapped on the window and with it floated a shrill jingling note. Savély turned pale, cleared his throat, and flopped about the floor with his bare feet again.

"The postman is lost in the storm," he wheezed out glancing malignantly at his wife. "Do you hear? The postman has lost his way! . . I . . . I know! Do you suppose I . . don't understand? " he muttered. "I know all about it, curse you!"

"What do you know?" Raïssa asked quietly, keeping her eyes fixed on the window.

"I know that it's all your doing, you she-devil! Your doing, damn you! This snowstorm and the post going wrong, you've done it all - you!"

"You're mad, you silly," his wife answered calmly.

"I've been watching you for a long time past and I've seen it. From the first day I married you I noticed that you'd bitch's blood in you!"

"Tfoo!" said Raïssa, surprised, shrugging her shoulders and crossing herself. "Cross yourself, you fool!"

"A witch is a witch," Savély pronounced in a hollow, tearful voice, hurriedly blowing his nose on the hem of his shirt; "though you are my wife, though you are of a clerical family, I'd say what you are even at confession. . . . Why, God have mercy upon us! Last year on the Eve of the Prophet Daniel and the Three Young Men there was a snowstorm, and what happened then? The mechanic came in to warm himself. Then on St. Alexey's Day the ice broke on the river and the district policeman turned up, and he was chatting with you all night . . . the damned brute! And when he came out in the morning and I looked at him, he had rings under his eyes and his cheeks were hollow! Eh? During the August fast there were two storms and each time the huntsman turned up. I saw it all, damn him! Oh, she is redder than a crab now, aha!"

"You didn't see anything."

"Didn't I! And this winter before Christmas on the Day of the Ten Martyrs of Crete, when the storm lasted for a whole day and night - do you remember? - the marshal's clerk was lost, and turned up here, the hound. . . . Tfoo! To be tempted by the clerk! It was worth upsetting God's weather for him! A drivelling scribbler, not a foot from the ground, pimples all over his mug and his neck awry! If he were good-looking, anyway - but he, tfoo! he is as ugly as Satan!"

The sexton took breath, wiped his lips and listened. The bell was not to be heard, but the wind banged on the roof, and again there came a tinkle in the darkness.

"And it's the same thing now!" Savély went on. "It's not for nothing the postman is lost! Blast my eyes if the postman isn't looking for you! Oh, the devil is a good hand at his work; he is a fine one to help! He will turn him round and round and bring him here. I know, I see! You can't conceal it, you devil's bauble, you heathen wanton! As soon as the storm began I knew what you were up to."

"Here's a fool!" smiled his wife. "Why, do you suppose, you thick-head, that I make the storm?"

"H'm! . . . Grin away! Whether it's your doing or not, I only know that when your blood's on fire there's sure to be bad weather, and when there's bad weather there's bound to be some crazy fellow turning up here. It happens so every time! So it must be you!"

To be more impressive the sexton put his finger to his forehead, closed his left eye, and said in a singsong voice:

"Oh, the madness! oh, the unclean Judas! If you really are a human being and not a witch, you ought to think what if he is not the mechanic, or the clerk, or the huntsman, but the devil in their form! Ah! You'd better think of that!"

"Why, you are stupid, Savély," said his wife, looking at him compassionately. "When father was alive and living here, all sorts of people used to come to him to be cured of the ague: from the village, and the hamlets, and the Armenian settlement. They came almost every day, and no one called them devils. But if anyone once a year comes in bad weather to warm himself, you wonder at it, you silly, and take all sorts of notions into your head at once."

His wife's logic touched Savély. He stood with his bare feet wide apart, bent his head, and pondered. He was not firmly convinced yet of the truth of his suspicions, and his wife's genuine and unconcerned tone quite disconcerted him. Yet after a moment's thought he wagged his head and said:

"It's not as though they were old men or bandy-legged cripples; it's always young men who want to come for the night. . . . Why is that? And if they only wanted to warm themselves - - But they are up to mischief. No, woman; there's no creature in this world as cunning as your female sort! Of real brains you've not an ounce, less than a starling, but for devilish slyness - oo-oo-oo! The Queen of Heaven protect us! There is the postman's bell! When the storm was only beginning I knew all that was in your mind. That's your witchery, you spider!"

"Why do you keep on at me, you heathen?" His wife lost her patience at last. "Why do you keep sticking to it like pitch?"

"I stick to it because if anything - God forbid - happens to-night . . . do you hear? . . . if anything happens to-night, I'll go straight off to-morrow morning to Father Nikodim and tell him all about it. 'Father Nikodim,' I shall say, 'graciously excuse me, but she is a witch.' 'Why so?' 'H'm! do you want to know why?' 'Certainly. . . .' And I shall tell him. And woe to you, woman! Not only at the dread Seat of Judgment, but in your earthly life you'll be punished, too! It's not for nothing there are prayers in the breviary against your kind!"

Suddenly there was a knock at the window, so loud and unusual that Savély turned pale and almost dropped backwards with fright. His wife jumped up, and she, too, turned pale.

"For God's sake, let us come in and get warm!" they heard in a trembling deep bass. "Who lives here? For mercy's sake! We've lost our way."

"Who are you?" asked Raïssa, afraid to look at the window.

"The post," answered a second voice.

"You've succeeded with your devil's tricks," said Savély with a wave of his hand. "No mistake; I am right! Well, you'd better look out!"

The sexton jumped on to the bed in two skips, stretched himself on the feather mattress, and sniffing angrily, turned with his face to the wall. Soon he felt a draught of cold air on his back. The door creaked and the tall figure of a man, plastered over with snow from head to foot, appeared in the doorway. Behind him could be seen a second figure as white.

"Am I to bring in the bags?" asked the second in a hoarse bass voice.

"You can't leave them there." Saying this, the first figure began untying his hood, but gave it up, and pulling it off impatiently with his cap, angrily flung it near the stove. Then taking off his greatcoat, he threw that down beside it, and, without saying good-evening, began pacing up and down the hut.

He was a fair-haired, young postman wearing a shabby uniform and black rusty-looking high boots. After warming himself by walking to and fro, he sat down at the table, stretched out his muddy feet towards the sacks and leaned his chin on his fist. His pale face, reddened in places by the cold, still bore vivid traces of the pain and terror he had just been through. Though distorted by anger and bearing traces of recent suffering, physical and moral, it was handsome in spite of the melting snow on the eyebrows, moustaches, and short beard.

"It's a dog's life!" muttered the postman, looking round the walls and seeming hardly able to believe that he was in the warmth. "We were nearly lost! If it had not been for your light, I don't know what would have happened. Goodness only knows when it will all be over! There's no end to this dog's life! Where have we come?" he asked, dropping his voice and raising his eyes to the sexton's wife.

"To the Gulyaevsky Hill on General Kalinovsky's estate," she answered, startled and blushing.

"Do you hear, Stepan?" The postman turned to the driver, who was wedged in the doorway with a huge mail-bag on his shoulders. "We've got to Gulyaevsky Hill."

"Yes . . . we're a long way out." Jerking out these words like a hoarse sigh, the driver went out and soon after returned with another bag, then went out once more and this time brought the postman's sword on a big belt, of the pattern of that long flat blade with which Judith is portrayed by the bedside of Holofernes in cheap woodcuts. Laying the bags along the wall, he went out into the outer room, sat down there and lighted his pipe.

"Perhaps you'd like some tea after your journey?" Raïssa inquired.

"How can we sit drinking tea?" said the postman, frowning. "We must make haste and get warm, and then set off, or we shall be late for the mail train. We'll stay ten minutes and then get on our way. Only be so good as to show us the way."

"What an infliction it is, this weather!" sighed Raïssa.

"H'm, yes. . . . Who may you be?"

"We? We live here, by the church. . . . We belong to the clergy. . . . There lies my husband. Savély, get up and say good-evening! This used to be a separate parish till eighteen months ago. Of course, when the gentry lived here there were more people, and it was worth while to have the services. But now the gentry have gone, and I need not tell you there's nothing for the clergy to live on. The nearest village is Markovka, and that's over three miles away. Savély is on the retired list now, and has got the watchman's job; he has to look after the church. . . ."

And the postman was immediately informed that if Savély were to go to the General's lady and ask her for a letter to the bishop, he would be given a good berth. "But he doesn't go to the General's lady because he is lazy and afraid of people. We belong to the clergy all the same . . ." added Raïssa.

"What do you live on?" asked the postman.

"There's a kitchen garden and a meadow belonging to the church. Only we don't get much from that," sighed Raïssa. "The old skinflint, Father Nikodim, from the next village celebrates here on St. Nicolas' Day in the winter and on St. Nicolas' Day in the summer, and for that he takes almost all the crops for himself. There's no one to stick up for us!"

"You are lying," Savély growled hoarsely. "Father Nikodim is a saintly soul, a luminary of the Church; and if he does take it, it's the regulation!"

"You've a cross one!" said the postman, with a grin. "Have you been married long?"

"It was three years ago the last Sunday before Lent. My father was sexton here in the old days, and when the time came for him to die, he went to the Consistory and asked them to send some unmarried man to marry me that I might keep the place. So I married him."

"Aha, so you killed two birds with one stone!" said the postman, looking at Savély's back. "Got wife and job together."

Savély wriggled his leg impatiently and moved closer to the wall. The postman moved away from the table, stretched, and sat down on the mail-bag. After a moment's thought he squeezed the bags with his hands, shifted his sword to the other side, and lay down with one foot touching the floor.

"It's a dog's life," he muttered, putting his hands behind his head and closing his eyes. "I wouldn't wish a wild Tatar such a life."

69

Soon everything was still. Nothing was audible except the sniffing of Savély and the slow, even breathing of the sleeping postman, who uttered a deep prolonged "h-h-h" at every breath. From time to time there was a sound like a creaking wheel in his throat, and his twitching foot rustled against the bag.

Savély fidgeted under the quilt and looked round slowly. His wife was sitting on the stool, and with her hands pressed against her cheeks was gazing at the postman's face. Her face was immovable, like the face of some one frightened and astonished.

"Well, what are you gaping at?" Savély whispered angrily.

"What is it to you? Lie down!" answered his wife without taking her eyes off the flaxen head.

Savély angrily puffed all the air out of his chest and turned abruptly to the wall. Three minutes later he turned over restlessly again, knelt up on the bed, and with his hands on the pillow looked askance at his wife. She was still sitting motionless, staring at the visitor. Her cheeks were pale and her eyes were glowing with a strange fire. The sexton cleared his throat, crawled on his stomach off the bed, and going up to the postman, put a handkerchief over his face.

"What's that for?" asked his wife.

"To keep the light out of his eyes."

"Then put out the light!"

Savély looked distrustfully at his wife, put out his lips towards the lamp, but at once thought better of it and clasped his hands.

"Isn't that devilish cunning?" he exclaimed. "Ah! Is there any creature slyer than womenkind?"

"Ah, you long-skirted devil!" hissed his wife, frowning with vexation. "You wait a bit!"

And settling herself more comfortably, she stared at the postman again.

It did not matter to her that his face was covered. She was not so much interested in his face as in his whole appearance, in the novelty of this man. His chest was broad and powerful, his hands were slender and well formed, and his graceful, muscular legs were much comelier than Savély's stumps. There could be no comparison, in fact.

"Though I am a long-skirted devil," Savély said after a brief interval, "they've no business to sleep here. . . . It's government work; we shall have to answer for keeping them. If you carry the letters, carry them, you can't go to sleep. . . . Hey! you!" Savély shouted into the outer room. "You, driver. What's your name? Shall I show you the way? Get up; postmen mustn't sleep!"

And Savély, thoroughly roused, ran up to the postman and tugged him by the sleeve.

"Hey, your honour, if you must go, go; and if you don't, it's not the thing. . . . Sleeping won't do."

The postman jumped up, sat down, looked with blank eyes round the hut, and lay down again.

"But when are you going?" Savély pattered away. "That's what the post is for - to get there in good time, do you hear? I'll take you."

The postman opened his eyes. Warmed and relaxed by his first sweet sleep, and not yet quite awake, he saw as through a mist the white neck and the immovable, alluring eyes of the sexton's wife. He closed his eyes and smiled as though he had been dreaming it all.

"Come, how can you go in such weather!" he heard a soft feminine voice; "you ought to have a sound sleep and it would do you good!"

"And what about the post?" said Savély anxiously. "Who's going to take the post? Are you going to take it, pray, you?"

The postman opened his eyes again, looked at the play of the dimples on Raïssa's face, remembered where he was, and understood Savély. The thought that he had to go out into the cold darkness sent a chill shudder all down him, and he winced.

"I might sleep another five minutes," he said, yawning. "I shall be late, anyway. . . ."

"We might be just in time," came a voice from the outer room. "All days are not alike; the train may be late for a bit of luck."

The postman got up, and stretching lazily began putting on his coat.

Savély positively neighed with delight when he saw his visitors were getting ready to go.

"Give us a hand," the driver shouted to him as he lifted up a mail-bag.

The sexton ran out and helped him drag the post-bags into the yard. The postman began undoing the knot in his hood. The sexton's wife gazed into his eyes, and seemed trying to look right into his soul.

"You ought to have a cup of tea . . ." she said.

"I wouldn't say no . . . but, you see, they're getting ready," he assented. "We are late, anyway."

"Do stay," she whispered, dropping her eyes and touching him by the sleeve.

The postman got the knot undone at last and flung the hood over his elbow, hesitating. He felt it comfortable standing by Raïssa.

"What a . . . neck you've got! . . ." And he touched her neck with two fingers. Seeing that she did not resist, he stroked her neck and shoulders.

"I say, you are . . ."

"You'd better stay . . . have some tea."

"Where are you putting it?" The driver's voice could be heard outside. "Lay it crossways."

"You'd better stay. . . . Hark how the wind howls."

And the postman, not yet quite awake, not yet quite able to shake off the intoxicating sleep of youth and fatigue, was suddenly overwhelmed by a desire for the sake of which mail-bags, postal trains . . . and all things in the world, are forgotten. He glanced at the door in a frightened way, as though he wanted to escape or hide himself, seized Raïssa round the waist, and was just bending over the lamp to put out the light, when he heard the tramp of boots in the outer room, and the driver appeared in the doorway. Savély peeped in over his shoulder. The postman dropped his hands quickly and stood still as though irresolute.

"It's all ready," said the driver. The postman stood still for a moment, resolutely threw up his head as though waking up completely, and followed the driver out. Raïssa was left alone.

"Come, get in and show us the way!" she heard.

One bell sounded languidly, then another, and the jingling notes in a long delicate chain floated away from the hut.

When little by little they had died away, Raïssa got up and nervously paced to and fro. At first she was pale, then she flushed all over. Her face was contorted with hate, her breathing was tremulous, her eyes gleamed with wild, savage anger, and, pacing up and down as in a cage, she looked like a tigress menaced with red-hot iron. For a moment she stood still and looked at her abode. Almost half of the room was filled up by the bed, which stretched the length of the whole wall and consisted of a dirty feather-bed, coarse grey pillows, a quilt, and nameless rags of various sorts. The bed was a shapeless ugly mass which suggested the shock of hair that always stood up on Savély's head whenever it occurred to him to oil it. From the bed to the door that led into the cold outer room stretched the dark stove surrounded by pots and hanging clouts. Everything, including the absent Savély himself, was dirty, greasy, and smutty to the last degree, so that it was strange to see a woman's white neck and delicate skin in such surroundings.

Raïssa ran up to the bed, stretched out her hands as though she wanted to fling it all about, stamp it underfoot, and tear it to shreds. But then, as though frightened by contact with the dirt, she leapt back and began pacing up and down again.

When Savély returned two hours later, worn out and covered with snow, she was undressed and in bed. Her eyes were closed, but from the slight tremor that ran over her face he guessed that she was not asleep. On his way home he had vowed inwardly to wait till next day and not to touch her, but he could not resist a biting taunt at her.

"Your witchery was all in vain: he's gone off," he said, grinning with malignant joy.

His wife remained mute, but her chin quivered. Savély undressed slowly, clambered over his wife, and lay down next to the wall.

"To-morrow I'll let Father Nikodim know what sort of wife you are!" he muttered, curling himself up.

Raïssa turned her face to him and her eyes gleamed.

"The job's enough for you, and you can look for a wife in the forest, blast you!" she said. "I am no wife for you, a clumsy lout, a slug-a-bed, God forgive me!"

"Come, come . . . go to sleep!"

"How miserable I am!" sobbed his wife. "If it weren't for you, I might have married a merchant or some gentleman! If it weren't for you, I should love my husband now! And you haven't been buried in the snow, you haven't been frozen on the highroad, you Herod!"

Raïssa cried for a long time. At last she drew a deep sigh and was still. The storm still raged without. Something wailed in the stove, in the chimney, outside the walls, and it seemed to Savély that the wailing was within him, in his ears. This evening had completely confirmed him in his suspicions about his wife. He no longer doubted that his wife, with the aid of the Evil One, controlled the winds and the post sledges. But to add to his grief, this mysteriousness, this supernatural, weird power gave the woman beside him a peculiar, incomprehensible charm of which he had not been conscious before. The fact that in his stupidity he unconsciously threw a poetic glamour over her made her seem, as it were, whiter, sleeker, more unapproachable.

"Witch!" he muttered indignantly. "Tfoo, horrid creature!"

Yet, waiting till she was quiet and began breathing evenly, he touched her head with his finger . . . held her thick plait in his hand for a minute. She did not feel it. Then he grew bolder and stroked her neck.

"Leave off!" she shouted, and prodded him on the nose with her elbow with such violence that he saw stars before his eyes.

The pain in his nose was soon over, but the torture in his heart remained.

## A STORY WITHOUT AN END

Soon after two o'clock one night, long ago, the cook, pale and agitated, rushed unexpectedly into my study and informed me that Madame Mimotih, the old woman who owned the house next door, was sitting in her kitchen.

"She begs you to go in to her, sir . . ." said the cook, panting. "Something bad has happened about her lodger. . . . He has shot himself or hanged himself. . . ."

"What can I do?" said I. "Let her go for the doctor or for the police!"

"How is she to look for a doctor! She can hardly breathe, and she has huddled under the stove, she is so frightened. . . . You had better go round, sir."

I put on my coat and hat and went to Madame Mimotih's house. The gate towards which I directed my steps was open. After pausing beside it, uncertain what to do, I went into the yard without feeling for the porter's bell. In the dark and dilapidated porch the door was not locked. I opened it and walked into the entry. Here there was not a glimmer of light, it was pitch dark, and, moreover, there was a marked smell of incense. Groping my way out of the entry I knocked my elbow against something made of iron, and in the darkness stumbled against a board of some sort which almost fell to the floor. At last the door covered with torn baize was found, and I went into a little hall.

I am not at the moment writing a fairy tale, and am far from intending to alarm the reader, but the picture I saw from the passage was fantastic and could only have been drawn by death. Straight before me was a door leading to a little drawing-room. Three five-kopeck wax candles, standing in a row, threw a scanty light on the faded slate-coloured wallpaper. A coffin was standing on two tables in the middle of the little room. The two candles served only to light up a swarthy yellow face with a half-open mouth and sharp nose. Billows of muslin were mingled in disorder from the face to the tips of the two shoes, and from among the billows peeped out two pale motionless hands, holding a wax cross. The dark gloomy corners of the little drawing-room, the ikons behind the coffin, the coffin itself, everything except the softly glimmering lights, were still as death, as the tomb itself.

"How strange!" I thought, dumbfounded by the unexpected panorama of death. "Why this haste? The lodger has hardly had time to hang himself, or shoot himself, and here is the coffin already!"

I looked round. On the left there was a door with a glass panel; on the right a lame hat-stand with a shabby fur coat on it. . . .

"Water. . . ." I heard a moan.

The moan came from the left, beyond the door with the glass panel. I opened the door and walked into a little dark room with a solitary window, through which there came a faint light from a street lamp outside.

"Is anyone here?" I asked.

And without waiting for an answer I struck a match. This is what I saw while it was burning. A man was sitting on the blood-stained floor at my very feet. If my step had been a longer one I should have trodden on him. With his legs thrust forward and his hands pressed on the floor, he was making an effort to raise his handsome face, which was deathly pale against his pitch-black beard. In the big eyes which he lifted upon me, I read unutterable terror, pain, and entreaty. A cold sweat trickled in big drops down his face. That sweat, the expression of his face, the trembling of the hands he leaned upon, his hard breathing and his clenched teeth, showed that he was suffering beyond endurance. Near his right hand in a pool of blood lay a revolver.

"Don't go away," I heard a faint voice when the match had gone out. "There's a candle on the table."

I lighted the candle and stood still in the middle of the room not knowing what to do next. I stood and looked at the man on the floor, and it seemed to me that I had seen him before.

"The pain is insufferable," he whispered, "and I haven't the strength to shoot myself again. Incomprehensible lack of will."

I flung off my overcoat and attended to the sick man. Lifting him from the floor like a baby, I laid him on the American leather covered sofa and carefully undressed him. He was shivering and cold when I took off his clothes; the wound which I saw was not in keeping either with his shivering nor the expression on his face. It was a trifling one. The bullet had passed between the fifth and sixth ribs on the left side, only piercing the skin and the flesh. I found the bullet itself in the folds of the coat-lining near the back pocket. Stopping the bleeding as best I could and making a temporary bandage of a pillow-case, a towel, and two handkerchiefs, I gave the wounded man some water and covered him with a fur coat that was hanging in the passage. We neither of us said a word while the bandaging was being done. I did my work while he lay motionless looking at me with his eyes screwed up as though he were ashamed of his unsuccessful shot and the trouble he was giving me.

"Now I must trouble you to lie still," I said, when I had finished the bandaging, "while I run to the chemist and get something."

"No need!" he muttered, clutching me by the sleeve and opening his eyes wide.

I read terror in his eyes. He was afraid of my going away.

"No need! Stay another five minutes . . . ten. If it doesn't disgust you, do stay, I entreat you."

As he begged me he was trembling and his teeth were chattering. I obeyed, and sat down on the edge of the sofa. Ten minutes passed in silence. I sat silent, looking about the room into which fate had brought me so unexpectedly. What poverty! This man who was the possessor of a handsome, effeminate face and a luxuriant well-tended beard, had surroundings which a humble working man would not have envied. A sofa with its American-leather torn and peeling, a humble greasy-looking chair, a table covered with a little of paper, and a wretched oleograph on the wall, that was all I saw. Damp, gloomy, and grey.

"What a wind!" said the sick man, without opening his eyes, "How it whistles!"

"Yes," I said. "I say, I fancy I know you. Didn't you take part in some private theatricals in General Luhatchev's villa last year?"

"What of it?" he asked, quickly opening his eyes.

A cloud seemed to pass over his face.

"I certainly saw you there. Isn't your name Vassilyev?"

"If it is, what of it? It makes it no better that you should know me."

"No, but I just asked you."

Vassilyev closed his eyes and, as though offended, turned his face to the back of the sofa.

"I don't understand your curiosity," he muttered. "You'll be asking me next what it was drove me to commit suicide!"

Before a minute had passed, he turned round towards me again, opened his eyes and said in a tearful voice:

"Excuse me for taking such a tone, but you'll admit I'm right! To ask a convict how he got into prison, or a suicide why he shot himself is not generous . . . and indelicate. To think of gratifying idle curiosity at the expense of another man's nerves!"

"There is no need to excite yourself. . . . It never occurred to me to question you about your motives."

"You would have asked. . . . It's what people always do. Though it would be no use to ask. If I told you, you would not believe or understand. . . . I must own I don't understand it myself. . . . There are phrases used in the police reports and newspapers such as: 'unrequited love,' and 'hopeless poverty,' but the reasons are not known. . . . They are not known to me, nor to you, nor to your newspaper offices, where they have the impudence to write 'The diary of a suicide.' God alone understands the state of a man's soul when he takes his own life; but men know nothing about it."

"That is all very nice," I said, "but you oughtn't to talk. . . ."

But my suicide could not be stopped, he leaned his head on his fist, and went on in the tone of some great professor:

"Man will never understand the psychological subtleties of suicide! How can one speak of reasons? To-day the reason makes one snatch up a revolver, while to-morrow the same reason seems not worth a rotten egg. It all depends most likely on the particular condition of the individual at the given moment. . . . Take me for instance. Half an hour ago, I had a passionate desire for death, now when the candle is lighted, and you are sitting by me, I don't even think of the hour of death. Explain that change if you can! Am I better off, or has my wife risen from the dead? Is it the influence of the light on me, or the presence of an outsider?"

"The light certainly has an influence . . . " I muttered for the sake of saying something. "The influence of light on the organism. . . ."

"The influence of light. . . . We admit it! But you know men do shoot themselves by candle-light! And it would be ignominious indeed for the heroes of your novels if such a trifling thing as a candle were to change the course of the drama so abruptly. All this nonsense can be explained perhaps, but not by us. It's useless to ask questions or give explanations of what one does not understand. . . ."

"Forgive me," I said, "but . . . judging by the expression of your face, it seems to me that at this moment you . . . are posing."

"Yes," Vassilyev said, startled. "It's very possible! I am naturally vain and fatuous. Well, explain it, if you believe in your power of reading faces! Half an hour ago I shot myself, and just now I am posing. . . . Explain that if you can."

These last words Vassilyev pronounced in a faint, failing voice. He was exhausted, and sank into silence. A pause followed. I began scrutinising his face. It was as pale as a dead man's. It seemed as though life were almost extinct in him, and only the signs of the suffering that the "vain and fatuous" man was feeling betrayed that it was still alive. It was painful to look at that face, but what must it have been for Vassilyev himself who yet had the strength to argue and, if I were not mistaken, to pose?

"You here - are you here ?" he asked suddenly, raising himself on his elbow. "My God, just listen!"

I began listening. The rain was pattering angrily on the dark window, never ceasing for a minute. The wind howled plaintively and lugubriously.

" 'And I shall be whiter than snow, and my ears will hear gladness and rejoicing.' " Madame Mimotih, who had returned, was reading in the drawing-room in a languid, weary voice, neither raising nor dropping the monotonous dreary key.

"It is cheerful, isn't it?" whispered Vassilyev, turning his frightened eyes towards me. "My God, the things a man has to see and hear! If only one could set this chaos to music! As Hamlet says, 'it would -

"Confound the ignorant, and amaze indeed,
The very faculties of eyes and ears."

How well I should have understood that music then! How I should have felt it! What time is it?"

"Five minutes to three."

"Morning is still far off. And in the morning there's the funeral. A lovely prospect! One follows the coffin through the mud and rain. One walks along, seeing nothing but the cloudy sky and the wretched scenery. The muddy mutes, taverns, woodstacks. . . . One's trousers drenched to the knees. The never-ending streets. The time dragging out like eternity, the coarse people. And on the heart a stone, a stone!"

After a brief pause he suddenly asked: "Is it long since you saw General Luhatchev?"

"I haven't seen him since last summer."

"He likes to be cock of the walk, but he is a nice little old chap. And are you still writing?"

"Yes, a little."

"Ah. . . . Do you remember how I pranced about like a needle, like an enthusiastic ass at those private theatricals when I was courting Zina? It was stupid, but it was good, it was fun. The very memory of it brings back a whiff of spring. . . . And now! What a cruel change of scene! There is a subject for you! Only don't you go in for writing 'the diary of a suicide.' That's vulgar and conventional. You make something humorous of it."

"Again you are . . . posing," I said. "There's nothing humorous in your position."

"Nothing laughable? You say nothing laughable?" Vassilyev sat up, and tears glistened in his eyes. An expression of bitter distress came into his pale face. His chin quivered.

"You laugh at the deceit of cheating clerks and faithless wives," he said, "but no clerk, no faithless wife has cheated as my fate has cheated me! I have been deceived as no bank depositor, no duped husband has ever been deceived! Only realise what an absurd fool I have been made! Last year before your eyes I did not know what to do with myself for happiness. And now before your eyes. . . ."

Vassilyev's head sank on the pillow and he laughed.

"Nothing more absurd and stupid than such a change could possibly be imagined. Chapter one: spring, love, honeymoon . . . honey, in fact; chapter two: looking for a job, the pawnshop, pallor, the chemist's shop, and . . . to-morrow's splashing through the mud to the graveyard."

He laughed again. I felt acutely uncomfortable and made up my mind to go.

"I tell you what," I said, "you lie down, and I will go to the chemist's."

He made no answer. I put on my great-coat and went out of his room. As I crossed the passage I glanced at the coffin and Madame Mimotih reading over it. I strained my eyes in vain, I could not recognise in the swarthy, yellow face Zina, the lively, pretty *ingénue* of Luhatchev's company.

"*Sic transit*," I thought.

With that I went out, not forgetting to take the revolver, and made my way to the chemist's. But I ought not to have gone away. When I came back from the chemist's, Vassilyev lay on the sofa fainting. The bandages had been roughly torn off, and blood was flowing from the reopened wound. It was daylight before I succeeded in restoring him to consciousness. He was raving in delirium, shivering, and looking with unseeing eyes about the room till morning had come, and we heard the booming voice of the priest as he read the service over the dead.

When Vassilyev's rooms were crowded with old women and mutes, when the coffin had been moved and carried out of the yard, I advised him to remain at home. But he would not obey me, in spite of the pain and the grey, rainy morning. He walked bareheaded and in silence behind the coffin all the way to the cemetery, hardly able to move one leg after the other, and from time to time clutching convulsively at his wounded side. His face expressed complete apathy. Only once when I roused him from his lethargy by some insignificant question he shifted his eyes over the pavement and the grey fence, and for a moment there was a gleam of gloomy anger in them.

" 'Weelright,' " he read on a signboard. "Ignorant, illiterate people, devil take them!"

I led him home from the cemetery.

\*\*\*\*

Only one year has passed since that night, and Vassilyev has hardly had time to wear out the boots in which he tramped through the mud behind his wife's coffin.

At the present time as I finish this story, he is sitting in my drawing-room and, playing on the piano, is showing the ladies how provincial misses sing sentimental songs. The ladies are laughing, and he is laughing too. He is enjoying himself.

I call him into my study. Evidently not pleased at my taking him from agreeable company, he comes to me and stands before me in the attitude of a man who has no time to spare. I give him this story, and ask him to read it. Always condescending about my authorship, he stifles a sigh, the sigh of a lazy reader, sits down in an armchair and begins upon it.

"Hang it all, what horrors," he mutters with a smile.

But the further he gets into the reading, the graver his face becomes. At last, under the stress of painful memories, he turns terribly pale, he gets up and goes on reading as he stands. When he has finished he begins pacing from corner to corner.

"How does it end?" I ask him.

"How does it end? H'm. . . ."

He looks at the room, at me, at himself. . . . He sees his new fashionable suit, hears the ladies laughing and . . . sinking on a chair, begins laughing as he laughed on that night.

"Wasn't I right when I told you it was all absurd? My God! I have had burdens to bear that would have broken an elephant's back; the devil knows what I have suffered - no one could have suffered more, I think, and where are the traces? It's astonishing. One would have thought the imprint made on a man by his agonies would have been everlasting, never to be effaced or eradicated. And yet that imprint wears out as easily as a pair of cheap boots. There is nothing left, not a scrap. It's as though I hadn't been suffering then, but had been dancing a mazurka. Everything in the world is transitory, and that transitoriness is absurd! A wide field for humorists! Tack on a humorous end, my friend!"

"Pyotr Nikolaevitch, are you coming soon?" The impatient ladies call my hero.

"This minute," answers the "vain and fatuous" man, setting his tie straight. "It's absurd and pitiful, my friend, pitiful and absurd, but what's to be done? *Homo sum*. . . . And I praise Mother Nature all the same for her transmutation of substances. If we retained an agonising memory of toothache and of all the terrors which every one of us has had to experience, if all that were everlasting, we poor mortals would have a bad time of it in this life."

I look at his smiling face and I remember the despair and the horror with which his eyes were filled a year ago when he looked at the dark window. I see him, entering into his habitual rôle of intellectual chatterer, prepare to show off his idle theories, such as the transmutation of substances before me, and at the same time I recall him sitting on the floor in a pool of blood with his sick imploring eyes.

"How will it end?" I ask myself aloud.

Vassilyev, whistling and straightening his tie, walks off into the drawing-room, and I look after him, and feel vexed. For some reason I regret his past sufferings, I regret all that I felt myself on that man's account on that terrible night. It is as though I had lost something. . . .

# A JOKE

It was a bright winter midday. . . . There was a sharp snapping frost and the curls on Nadenka's temples and the down on her upper lip were covered with silvery frost. She was holding my arm and we were standing on a high hill. From where we stood to the ground below there stretched a smooth sloping descent in which the sun was reflected as in a looking-glass. Beside us was a little sledge lined with bright red cloth.

"Let us go down, Nadyezhda Petrovna!" I besought her. "Only once! I assure you we shall be all right and not hurt."

But Nadenka was afraid. The slope from her little goloshes to the bottom of the ice hill seemed to her a terrible, immensely deep abyss. Her spirit failed her, and she held her breath as she looked down, when I merely suggested her getting into the sledge, but what would it be if she were to risk flying into the abyss! She would die, she would go out of her mind.

"I entreat you!" I said. "You mustn't be afraid! You know it's poor-spirited, it's cowardly!"

Nadenka gave way at last, and from her face I saw that she gave way in mortal dread. I sat her in the sledge, pale and trembling, put my arm round her and with her cast myself down the precipice.

The sledge flew like a bullet. The air cleft by our flight beat in our faces, roared, whistled in our ears, tore at us, nipped us cruelly in its anger, tried to tear our heads off our shoulders. We had hardly strength to breathe from the pressure of the wind. It seemed as though the devil himself had caught us in his claws and was dragging us with a roar to hell. Surrounding objects melted into one long furiously racing streak . . . another moment and it seemed we should perish.

"I love you, Nadya!" I said in a low voice.

The sledge began moving more and more slowly, the roar of the wind and the whirr of the runners was no longer so terrible, it was easier to breathe, and at last we were at the bottom. Nadenka was more dead than alive. She was pale and scarcely breathing. . . . I helped her to get up.

"Nothing would induce me to go again," she said, looking at me with wide eyes full of horror. "Nothing in the world! I almost died!"

A little later she recovered herself and looked enquiringly into my eyes, wondering had I really uttered those four words or had she fancied them in the roar of the hurricane. And I stood beside her smoking and looking attentively at my glove.

She took my arm and we spent a long while walking near the ice-hill. The riddle evidently would not let her rest. . . . Had those words been uttered or not? . . . Yes or no? Yes or no? It was the question of pride, or honour, of life - a very important question, the most important question in the world. Nadenka kept impatiently, sorrowfully looking into my face with a penetrating glance; she answered at random, waiting to see whether I would not speak. Oh, the play of feeling on that sweet face! I saw that she was struggling with herself, that she wanted to say something, to ask some question, but she could not find the words; she felt awkward and frightened and troubled by her joy. . . .

"Do you know what," she said without looking at me.

"Well?" I asked.

"Let us . . . slide down again."

We clambered up the ice-hill by the steps again. I sat Nadenka, pale and trembling, in the sledge; again we flew into the terrible abyss, again the wind roared and the runners whirred, and again when the flight of our sledge was at its swiftest and noisiest, I said in a low voice:

"I love you, Nadenka!"

When the sledge stopped, Nadenka flung a glance at the hill down which we had both slid, then bent a long look upon my face, listened to my voice which was unconcerned and passionless, and the whole of her little figure, every bit of it, even her muff and her hood expressed the utmost bewilderment, and on her face was written: "What does it mean? Who uttered *those* words? Did he, or did I only fancy it?"

The uncertainty worried her and drove her out of all patience. The poor girl did not answer my questions, frowned, and was on the point of tears.

"Hadn't we better go home?" I asked.

"Well, I . . . I like this tobogganning," she said, flushing. "Shall we go down once more?"

She "liked" the tobogganning, and yet as she got into the sledge she was, as both times before, pale, trembling, hardly able to breathe for terror.

We went down for the third time, and I saw she was looking at my face and watching my lips. But I put my handkerchief to my lips, coughed, and when we reached the middle of the hill I succeeded in bringing out:

"I love you, Nadya!"

And the mystery remained a mystery! Nadenka was silent, pondering on something. . . . I saw her home, she tried to walk slowly, slackened her pace and kept waiting to see whether I would not say those words to her, and I saw how her soul was suffering, what effort she was making not to say to herself:

"It cannot be that the wind said them! And I don't want it to be the wind that said them!"

Next morning I got a little note:

"If you are tobogganning to-day, come for me. - N."

And from that time I began going every day tobogganning with Nadenka, and as we flew down in the sledge, every time I pronounced in a low voice the same words: "I love you, Nadya!"

Soon Nadenka grew used to that phrase as to alcohol or morphia. She could not live without it. It is true that flying down the ice-hill terrified her as before, but now the terror and danger gave a peculiar fascination to words of love - words which as before were a mystery and tantalized the soul. The same two - the wind and I were still suspected. . . . Which of the two was making love to her she did not know, but apparently by now she did not care; from which goblet one drinks matters little if only the beverage is intoxicating.

It happened I went to the skating-ground alone at midday; mingling with the crowd I saw Nadenka go up to the ice-hill and look about for me. . . then she timidly mounted the steps. . . . She was frightened of going alone - oh, how frightened! She was white as the snow, she was trembling, she went as though to the scaffold, but she went, she went without looking back, resolutely. She had evidently determined to put it to the test at last: would those sweet amazing words be heard when I was not there? I saw her, pale, her lips parted with horror, get into the sledge, shut her eyes and saying good-bye forever to the earth, set off. . . . "Whrrr!" whirred the runners. Whether Nadenka heard those words I do not know. I only saw her getting up from the sledge looking faint and exhausted. And one could tell from her face that she could not tell herself whether she had heard anything or not. Her terror while she had been flying down had deprived of her all power of hearing, of discriminating sounds, of understanding.

But then the month of March arrived . . . the spring sunshine was more kindly. . . . Our ice-hill turned dark, lost its brilliance and finally melted. We gave up tobogganning. There was nowhere now where poor Nadenka could hear those words, and indeed no one to utter them, since there was no wind and I was going to Petersburg - for long, perhaps forever.

It happened two days before my departure I was sitting in the dusk in the little garden which was separated from the yard of Nadenka's house by a high fence with nails in it. . . . It was still pretty cold, there was still snow by the manure heap, the trees looked dead but there was already the scent of spring and the rooks were cawing loudly as they settled for their night's rest. I went up to the fence and stood for a long while peeping through a chink. I saw Nadenka come out into the porch and fix a mournful yearning gaze on the sky. The spring wind was blowing straight into her pale dejected face. . . . It reminded her of the wind which roared at us on the ice-hill when she heard those four words, and her face became very, very sorrowful, a tear trickled down her cheek, and the poor child held out both arms as though begging the wind to bring her those words once more. And waiting for the wind I said in a low voice:

"I love you, Nadya!"

Mercy! The change that came over Nadenka! She uttered a cry, smiled all over her face and looking joyful, happy and beautiful, held out her arms to meet the wind.

And I went off to pack up. . . .

That was long ago. Now Nadenka is married; she married - whether of her own choice or not does not matter - a secretary of the Nobility Wardenship and now she has three children. That we once went tobogganning together, and that the wind brought her the words "I love you, Nadenka," is not forgotten; it is for her now the happiest, most touching, and beautiful memory in her life. . . .

But now that I am older I cannot understand why I uttered those words, what was my motive in that joke. . . .

# AGAFYA

During my stay in the district of S. I often used to go to see the watchman Savva Stukatch, or simply Savka, in the kitchen gardens of Dubovo. These kitchen gardens were my favorite resort for so-called "mixed" fishing, when one goes out without knowing what day or hour one may return, taking with one every sort of fishing tackle as well as a store of provisions. To tell the truth, it was not so much the fishing that attracted me as the peaceful stroll, the meals at no set time, the talk with Savka, and being for so long face to face with the calm summer nights. Savka was a young man of five-and-twenty, well grown and handsome, and as strong as a flint. He had the reputation of being a sensible and reasonable fellow. He could read and write, and very rarely drank, but as a workman this strong and healthy young man was not worth a farthing. A sluggish, overpowering sloth was mingled with the strength in his muscles, which were strong as cords. Like everyone else in his village, he lived in his own hut, and had his share of land, but neither tilled it nor sowed it, and did not work at any sort of trade. His old mother begged alms at people's windows and he himself lived like a bird of the air; he did not know in the morning what he would eat at midday. It was not that he was lacking in will, or energy, or feeling for his mother; it was simply that he felt no inclination for work and did not recognize the advantage of it. His whole figure suggested unruffled serenity, an innate, almost artistic passion for living carelessly, never with his sleeves tucked up. When Savka's young, healthy body had a physical craving for muscular work, the young man abandoned himself completely for a brief interval to some free but nonsensical pursuit, such as sharpening skates not wanted for any special purpose, or racing about after the peasant women. His favorite attitude was one of concentrated immobility. He was capable of standing for hours at a stretch in the same place with his eyes fixed on the same spot without stirring. He never moved except on impulse, and then only when an occasion presented itself for some rapid and abrupt action: catching a running dog by the tail, pulling off a woman's kerchief, or jumping over a big hole. It need hardly be said that with such parsimony of movement Savka was as poor as a mouse and lived worse than any homeless outcast. As time went on, I suppose he accumulated arrears of taxes and, young and sturdy as he was, he was sent by the commune to do an old man's job - to be watchman and scarecrow in the kitchen gardens. However much they laughed at him for his premature senility he did not object to it. This position, quiet and convenient for motionless contemplation, exactly fitted his temperament.

It happened I was with this Savka one fine May evening. I remember I was lying on a torn and dirty sackcloth cover close to the shanty from which came a heavy, fragrant scent of hay. Clasping my hands under my head I looked before me. At my feet was lying a wooden fork. Behind it Savka's dog Kutka stood out like a black patch, and not a dozen feet from Kutka the ground ended abruptly in the steep bank of the little river. Lying down I could not see the river; I could only see the tops of the young willows growing thickly on the nearer bank, and the twisting, as it were gnawed away, edges of the opposite bank. At a distance beyond the bank on the dark hillside the huts of the village in which Savka lived lay huddling together like frightened young partridges. Beyond the hill the afterglow of sunset still lingered in the sky. One pale crimson streak was all that was left, and even that began to be covered by little clouds as a fire with ash.

A copse with alder-trees, softly whispering, and from time to time shuddering in the fitful breeze, lay, a dark blur, on the right of the kitchen gardens; on the left stretched the immense plain. In the distance, where the eye could not distinguish between the sky and the plain, there was a bright gleam of light. A little way off from me sat Savka. With his legs tucked under him like a Turk and his head hanging, he looked pensively at Kutka. Our hooks with live bait on them had long been in the river, and we had nothing left to do but to abandon ourselves to repose, which Savka, who was never exhausted and always rested, loved so much. The glow had not yet quite died away, but the summer night was already enfolding nature in its caressing, soothing embrace.

Everything was sinking into its first deep sleep except some night bird unfamiliar to me, which indolently uttered a long, protracted cry in several distinct notes like the phrase, "Have you seen Ni-ki-ta?" and immediately answered itself, "Seen him, seen him, seen him!"

"Why is it the nightingales aren't singing tonight?" I asked Savka.

He turned slowly towards me. His features were large, but his face was open, soft, and expressive as a woman's. Then he gazed with his mild, dreamy eyes at the copse, at the willows, slowly pulled a whistle out of his pocket, put it in his mouth and whistled the note of a hen-nightingale. And at once, as though in answer to his call, a landrail called on the opposite bank.

"There's a nightingale for you . . ." laughed Savka. "Drag-drag! drag-drag! just like pulling at a hook, and yet I bet he thinks he is singing, too."

"I like that bird," I said. "Do you know, when the birds are migrating the landrail does not fly, but runs along the ground? It only flies over the rivers and the sea, but all the rest it does on foot."

"Upon my word, the dog . . ." muttered Savka, looking with respect in the direction of the calling landrail.

Knowing how fond Savka was of listening, I told him all I had learned about the landrail from sportsman's books. From the landrail I passed imperceptibly to the migration of the birds. Savka listened attentively, looking at me without blinking, and smiling all the while with pleasure.

"And which country is most the bird's home? Ours or those foreign parts?" he asked.

"Ours, of course. The bird itself is hatched here, and it hatches out its little ones here in its native country, and they only fly off there to escape being frozen."

"It's interesting," said Savka. "Whatever one talks about it is always interesting. Take a bird now, or a man . . . or take this little stone; there's something to learn about all of them. . . . Ah, sir, if I had known you were coming I wouldn't have told a woman to come here this evening. . . . She asked to come to-day."

"Oh, please don't let me be in your way," I said. "I can lie down in the wood. . . ."

"What next! She wouldn't have died if she hadn't come till to-morrow. . . . If only she would sit quiet and listen, but she always wants to be slobbering. . . . You can't have a good talk when she's here."

"Are you expecting Darya?" I asked, after a pause.

"No . . . a new one has asked to come this evening . . . Agafya, the signalman's wife."

Savka said this in his usual passionless, somewhat hollow voice, as though he were talking of tobacco or porridge, while I started with surprise. I knew Agafya. . . . She was quite a young peasant woman of nineteen or twenty, who had been married not more than a year before to a railway signalman, a fine young fellow. She lived in the village, and her husband came home there from the line every night.

"Your goings on with the women will lead to trouble, my boy," said I.

"Well, may be . . . ."

And after a moment's thought Savka added:

"I've said so to the women; they won't heed me. . . .They don't trouble about it, the silly things!"

Silence followed. . . . Meanwhile the darkness was growing thicker and thicker, and objects began to lose their contours. The streak behind the hill had completely died away, and the stars were growing brighter and more luminous. . . . The mournfully monotonous chirping of the grasshoppers, the call of the landrail, and the cry of the quail did not destroy the stillness of the night, but, on the contrary, gave it an added monotony. It seemed as though the soft sounds that enchanted the ear came, not from birds or insects, but from the stars looking down upon us from the sky. . . .

Savka was the first to break the silence. He slowly turned his eyes from black Kutka and said:

"I see you are dull, sir. Let's have supper."

And without waiting for my consent he crept on his stomach into the shanty, rummaged about there, making the whole edifice tremble like a leaf; then he crawled back and set before me my vodka and an earthenware bowl; in the bowl there were baked eggs, lard scones made of rye, pieces of black bread, and something else.... We had a drink from a little crooked glass that wouldn't stand, and then we fell upon the food.... Coarse grey salt, dirty, greasy cakes, eggs tough as india-rubber, but how nice it all was!

"You live all alone, but what lots of good things you have," I said, pointing to the bowl. "Where do you get them from?"

"The women bring them," mumbled Savka.

"What do they bring them to you for?"

"Oh . . . from pity."

Not only Savka's menu, but his clothing, too, bore traces of feminine "pity." Thus I noticed that he had on, that evening, a new woven belt and a crimson ribbon on which a copper cross hung round his dirty neck. I knew of the weakness of the fair sex for Savka, and I knew that he did not like talking about it, and so I did not carry my inquiries any further. Besides there was not time to talk.... Kutka, who had been fidgeting about near us and patiently waiting for scraps, suddenly pricked up his ears and growled. We heard in the distance repeated splashing of water.

"Someone is coming by the ford," said Savka.

Three minutes later Kutka growled again and made a sound like a cough.

"Shsh!" his master shouted at him.

In the darkness there was a muffled thud of timid footsteps, and the silhouette of a woman appeared out of the copse. I recognized her, although it was dark - it was Agafya. She came up to us diffidently and stopped, breathing hard. She was breathless, probably not so much from walking as from fear and the unpleasant sensation everyone experiences in wading across a river at night. Seeing near the shanty not one but two persons, she uttered a faint cry and fell back a step.

"Ah . . . that is you!" said Savka, stuffing a scone into his mouth.

"Ye-es . . . I," she muttered, dropping on the ground a bundle of some sort and looking sideways at me. "Yakov sent his greetings to you and told me to give you . . . something here. . . ."

"Come, why tell stories? Yakov!" laughed Savka. "There is no need for lying; the gentleman knows why you have come! Sit down; you shall have supper with us."

Agafya looked sideways at me and sat down irresolutely.

"I thought you weren't coming this evening," Savka said, after a prolonged silence. "Why sit like that? Eat! Or shall I give you a drop of vodka?"

"What an idea!" laughed Agafya; "do you think you have got hold of a drunkard? . . ."

"Oh, drink it up. . . . Your heart will feel warmer. . . . There!"

Savka gave Agafya the crooked glass. She slowly drank the vodka, ate nothing with it, but drew a deep breath when she had finished.

"You've brought something," said Savka, untying the bundle and throwing a condescending, jesting shade into his voice. "Women can never come without bringing something. Ah, pie and potatoes. . . . They live well," he sighed, turning to me. "They are the only ones in the whole village who have got potatoes left from the winter!"

In the darkness I did not see Agafya's face, but from the movement of her shoulders and head it seemed to me that she could not take her eyes off Savka's face. To avoid being the third person at this tryst, I decided to go for a walk and got up. But at that moment a nightingale in the wood suddenly uttered two low contralto notes. Half a minute later it gave a tiny high trill and then, having thus tried its voice, began singing. Savka jumped up and listened.

"It's the same one as yesterday," he said. "Wait a minute."

And, getting up, he went noiselessly to the wood.

"Why, what do you want with it?" I shouted out after him, "Stop!"

Savka shook his hand as much as to say, "Don't shout," and vanished into the darkness. Savka was an excellent sportsman and fisherman when he liked, but his talents in this direction were as completely thrown away as his strength. He was too slothful to do things in the routine way, and vented his passion for sport in useless tricks. For instance, he would catch nightingales only with his hands, would shoot pike with a fowling piece, he would spend whole hours by the river trying to catch little fish with a big hook.

Left alone with me, Agafya coughed and passed her hand several times over her forehead. . . . She began to feel a little drunk from the vodka.

"How are you getting on, Agasha?" I asked her, after a long silence, when it began to be awkward to remain mute any longer.

"Very well, thank God. . . . Don't tell anyone, sir, will you?" she added suddenly in a whisper.

"That's all right," I reassured her. "But how reckless you are, Agasha! . . . What if Yakov finds out?"

"He won't find out."

But what if he does?"

"No . . . I shall be at home before he is. He is on the line now, and he will come back when the mail train brings him, and from here I can hear when the train's coming. . . ."

Agafya once more passed her hand over her forehead and looked away in the direction in which Savka had vanished. The nightingale was singing. Some night bird flew low down close to the ground and, noticing us, was startled, fluttered its wings and flew across to the other side of the river.

Soon the nightingale was silent, but Savka did not come back. Agafya got up, took a few steps uneasily, and sat down again.

"What is he doing?" she could not refrain from saying. "The train's not coming in to-morrow! I shall have to go away directly."

"Savka," I shouted. "Savka."

I was not answered even by an echo. Agafya moved uneasily and sat down again.

"It's time I was going," she said in an agitated voice. "The train will be here directly! I know when the trains come in."

The poor woman was not mistaken. Before a quarter of an hour had passed a sound was heard in the distance.

Agafya kept her eyes fixed on the copse for a long time and moved her hands impatiently.

"Why, where can he be?" she said, laughing nervously. "Where has the devil carried him? I am going! I really must be going."

Meanwhile the noise was growing more and more distinct. By now one could distinguish the rumble of the wheels from the heavy gasps of the engine. Then we heard the whistle, the train crossed the bridge with a hollow rumble . . . another minute and all was still.

"I'll wait one minute more," said Agafya, sitting down resolutely. "So be it, I'll wait.

At last Savka appeared in the darkness. He walked noiselessly on the crumbling earth of the kitchen gardens and hummed something softly to himself.

"Here's a bit of luck; what do you say to that now?" he said gaily. "As soon as I got up to the bush and began taking aim with my hand it left off singing! Ah, the bald dog! I waited and waited to see when it would begin again, but I had to give it up."

Savka flopped clumsily down to the ground beside Agafya and, to keep his balance, clutched at her waist with both hands.

"Why do you look cross, as though your aunt were your mother?" he asked.

With all his soft-heartedness and good-nature, Savka despised women. He behaved carelessly, condescendingly with them, and even stooped to scornful laughter of their feelings for himself. God knows, perhaps this careless, contemptuous manner was one of the causes of his irresistible attraction for the village Dulcineas. He was handsome and well-built; in his eyes there was always a soft friendliness, even when he was looking at the women he so despised, but the fascination was not to be explained by merely external qualities. Apart from his happy exterior and original manner, one must suppose that the touching position of Savka as an acknowledged failure and an unhappy exile from his own hut to the kitchen gardens also had an influence upon the women.

"Tell the gentleman what you have come here for!" Savka went on, still holding Agafya by the waist. "Come, tell him, you good married woman! Ho-ho! Shall we have another drop of vodka, friend Agasha?"

I got up and, threading my way between the plots, I walked the length of the kitchen garden. The dark beds looked like flattened-out graves. They smelt of dug earth and the tender dampness of plants beginning to be covered with dew. . . . A red light was still gleaming on the left. It winked genially and seemed to smile.

I heard a happy laugh. It was Agafya laughing.

"And the train?" I thought. "The train has come in long ago."

Waiting a little longer, I went back to the shanty. Savka was sitting motionless, his legs crossed like a Turk, and was softly, scarcely audibly humming a song consisting of words of one syllable something like: "Out on you, fie on you . . . I and you." Agafya, intoxicated by the vodka, by Savka's scornful caresses, and by the stifling warmth of the night, was lying on the earth beside him, pressing her face convulsively to his knees. She was so carried away by her feelings that she did not even notice my arrival.

"Agasha, the train has been in a long time," I said.

"It's time - it's time you were gone," Savka, tossing his head, took up my thought. "What are you sprawling here for? You shameless hussy!"

Agafya started, took her head from his knees, glanced at me, and sank down beside him again.

"You ought to have gone long ago," I said.

Agafya turned round and got up on one knee. . . . She was unhappy. . . . For half a minute her whole figure, as far as I could distinguish it through the darkness, expressed conflict and hesitation. There was an instant when, seeming to come to herself, she drew herself up to get upon her feet, but then some invincible and implacable force seemed to push her whole body, and she sank down beside Savka again.

"Bother him!" she said, with a wild, guttural laugh, and reckless determination, impotence, and pain could be heard in that laugh.

I strolled quietly away to the copse, and from there down to the river, where our fishing lines were set. The river slept. Some soft, fluffy-petalled flower on a tall stalk touched my cheek tenderly like a child who wants to let one know it's awake. To pass the time I felt for one of the lines and pulled at it. It yielded easily and hung limply - nothing had been caught. . . . The further bank and the village could not be seen. A light gleamed in one hut, but soon went out. I felt my way along the bank, found a hollow place which I had noticed in the daylight, and sat down in it as in an arm-chair. I sat there a long time. . . . I saw the stars begin to grow misty and lose their brightness; a cool breath passed over the earth like a faint sigh and touched the leaves of the slumbering osiers. . . .

"A-ga-fya!" a hollow voice called from the village. "Agafya!"

It was the husband, who had returned home, and in alarm was looking for his wife in the village. At that moment there came the sound of unrestrained laughter: the wife, forgetful of everything, sought in her intoxication to make up by a few hours of happiness for the misery awaiting her next day.

I dropped asleep.

When I woke up Savka was sitting beside me and lightly shaking my shoulder. The river, the copse, both banks, green and washed, trees and fields - all were bathed in bright morning light. Through the slim trunks of the trees the rays of the newly risen sun beat upon my back.

"So that's how you catch fish?" laughed Savka. "Get up!"

I got up, gave a luxurious stretch, and began greedily drinking in the damp and fragrant air.

"Has Agasha gone?" I asked.

"There she is," said Savka, pointing in the direction of the ford.

I glanced and saw Agafya. Dishevelled, with her kerchief dropping off her head, she was crossing the river, holding up her skirt. Her legs were scarcely moving. . . .

"The cat knows whose meat it has eaten," muttered Savka, screwing up his eyes as he looked at her. "She goes with her tail hanging down. . . . They are sly as cats, these women, and timid as hares. . . . She didn't go, silly thing, in the evening when we told her to! Now she will catch it, and they'll flog me again at the peasant court . . . all on account of the women. . . ."

Agafya stepped upon the bank and went across the fields to the village. At first she walked fairly boldly, but soon terror and excitement got the upper hand; she turned round fearfully, stopped and took breath.

"Yes, you are frightened!" Savka laughed mournfully, looking at the bright green streak left by Agafya in the dewy grass. "She doesn't want to go! Her husband's been standing waiting for her for a good hour. . . . Did you see him?"

Savka said the last words with a smile, but they sent a chill to my heart. In the village, near the furthest hut, Yakov was standing in the road, gazing fixedly at his returning wife. He stood without stirring, and was as motionless as a post. What was he thinking as he looked at her? What words was he preparing to greet her with? Agafya stood still a little while, looked round once more as though expecting help from us, and went on. I have never seen anyone, drunk or sober, move as she did. Agafya seemed to be shrivelled up by her husband's eyes. At one time she moved in zigzags, then she moved her feet up and down without going forward, bending her knees and stretching out her hands, then she staggered back. When she had gone another hundred paces she looked round once more and sat down.

"You ought at least to hide behind a bush . . ." I said to Savka. "If the husband sees you . . ."

"He knows, anyway, who it is Agafya has come from. . . . The women don't go to the kitchen garden at night for cabbages - we all know that."

I glanced at Savka's face. It was pale and puckered up with a look of fastidious pity such as one sees in the faces of people watching tortured animals.

"What's fun for the cat is tears for the mouse. . ." he muttered.

Agafya suddenly jumped up, shook her head, and with a bold step went towards her husband. She had evidently plucked up her courage and made up her mind.

# A NIGHTMARE

Kunin, a young man of thirty, who was a permanent member of the Rural Board, on returning from Petersburg to his district, Borisovo, immediately sent a mounted messenger to Sinkino, for the priest there, Father Yakov Smirnov.

Five hours later Father Yakov appeared.

"Very glad to make your acquaintance," said Kunin, meeting him in the entry. "I've been living and serving here for a year; it seems as though we ought to have been acquainted before. You are very welcome! But . . . how young you are!" Kunin added in surprise. "What is your age?"

"Twenty-eight,. . ." said Father Yakov, faintly pressing Kunin's outstretched hand, and for some reason turning crimson.

Kunin led his visitor into his study and began looking at him more attentively.

"What an uncouth womanish face!" he thought.

There certainly was a good deal that was womanish in Father Yakov's face: the turned-up nose, the bright red cheeks, and the large grey-blue eyes with scanty, scarcely perceptible eyebrows. His long reddish hair, smooth and dry, hung down in straight tails on to his shoulders. The hair on his upper lip was only just beginning to form into a real masculine moustache, while his little beard belonged to that class of good-for-nothing beards which among divinity students are for some reason called "ticklers." It was scanty and extremely transparent; it could not have been stroked or combed, it could only have been pinched. . . . All these scanty decorations were put on unevenly in tufts, as though Father Yakov, thinking to dress up as a priest and beginning to gum on the beard, had been interrupted halfway through. He had on a cassock, the colour of weak coffee with chicory in it, with big patches on both elbows.

"A queer type," thought Kunin, looking at his muddy skirts. "Comes to the house for the first time and can't dress decently.

"Sit down, Father," he began more carelessly than cordially, as he moved an easy-chair to the table. "Sit down, I beg you."

Father Yakov coughed into his fist, sank awkwardly on to the edge of the chair, and laid his open hands on his knees. With his short figure, his narrow chest, his red and perspiring face, he made from the first moment a most unpleasant impression on Kunin. The latter could never have imagined that there were such undignified and pitiful-looking priests in Russia; and in Father Yakov's attitude, in the way he held his hands on his knees and sat on the very edge of his chair, he saw a lack of dignity and even a shade of servility.

"I have invited you on business, Father. . . ." Kunin began, sinking back in his low chair. "It has fallen to my lot to perform the agreeable duty of helping you in one of your useful undertakings. . . . On coming back from Petersburg, I found on my table a letter from the Marshal of Nobility. Yegor Dmitrevitch suggests that I should take under my supervision the church parish school which is being opened in Sinkino. I shall be very glad to, Father, with all my heart. . . . More than that, I accept the proposition with enthusiasm."

Kunin got up and walked about the study.

"Of course, both Yegor Dmitrevitch and probably you, too, are aware that I have not great funds at my disposal. My estate is mortgaged, and I live exclusively on my salary as the permanent member. So that you cannot reckon on very much assistance, but I will do all that is in my power. . . . And when are you thinking of opening the school Father?"

"When we have the money, . . ." answered Father Yakov.

"You have some funds at your disposal already?"

"Scarcely any. . . . The peasants settled at their meeting that they would pay, every man of them, thirty kopecks a year; but that's only a promise, you know! And for the first beginning we should need at least two hundred roubles. . . ."

"M'yes. . . . Unhappily, I have not that sum now," said Kunin with a sigh. "I spent all I had on my tour and got into debt, too. Let us try and think of some plan together."

Kunin began planning aloud. He explained his views and watched Father Yakov's face, seeking signs of agreement or approval in it. But the face was apathetic and immobile, and expressed nothing but constrained shyness and uneasiness. Looking at it, one might have supposed that Kunin was talking of matters so abstruse that Father Yakov did not understand and only listened from good manners, and was at the same time afraid of being detected in his failure to understand.

"The fellow is not one of the brightest, that's evident . . ." thought Kunin. "He's rather shy and much too stupid."

Father Yakov revived somewhat and even smiled only when the footman came into the study bringing in two glasses of tea on a tray and a cake-basket full of biscuits. He took his glass and began drinking at once.

"Shouldn't we write at once to the bishop?" Kunin went on, meditating aloud. "To be precise, you know, it is not we, not the Zemstvo, but the higher ecclesiastical authorities, who have raised the question of the church parish schools. They ought really to apportion the funds. I remember I read that a sum of money had been set aside for the purpose. Do you know nothing about it?"

Father Yakov was so absorbed in drinking tea that he did not answer this question at once. He lifted his grey-blue eyes to Kunin, thought a moment, and as though recalling his question, he shook his head in the negative. An expression of pleasure and of the most ordinary prosaic appetite overspread his face from ear to ear. He drank and smacked his lips over every gulp. When he had drunk it to the very last drop, he put his glass on the table, then took his glass back again, looked at the bottom of it, then put it back again. The expression of pleasure faded from his face. . . . Then Kunin saw his visitor take a biscuit from the cake-basket, nibble a little bit off it, then turn it over in his hand and hurriedly stick it in his pocket.

"Well, that's not at all clerical!" thought Kunin, shrugging his shoulders contemptuously. "What is it, priestly greed or childishness?"

After giving his visitor another glass of tea and seeing him to the entry, Kunin lay down on the sofa and abandoned himself to the unpleasant feeling induced in him by the visit of Father Yakov.

"What a strange wild creature!" he thought. "Dirty, untidy, coarse, stupid, and probably he drinks. . . . My God, and that's a priest, a spiritual father! That's a teacher of the people! I can fancy the irony there must be in the deacon's face when before every mass he booms out: 'Thy blessing, Reverend Father!' A fine reverend Father! A reverend Father without a grain of dignity or breeding, hiding biscuits in his pocket like a schoolboy. . . . Fie! Good Lord, where were the bishop's eyes when he ordained a man like that? What can he think of the people if he gives them a teacher like that? One wants people here who . . ."

And Kunin thought what Russian priests ought to be like.

"If I were a priest, for instance. . . . An educated priest fond of his work might do a great deal. . . . I should have had the school opened long ago. And the sermons? If the priest is sincere and is inspired by love for his work, what wonderful rousing sermons he might give!"

Kunin s hut his eyes and began mentally composing a sermon. A little later he sat down to the table and rapidly began writing.

"I'll give it to that red-haired fellow, let him read it in church, . . ." he thought.

The following Sunday Kunin drove over to Sinkino in the morning to settle the question of the school, and while he was there to make acquaintance with the church of which he was a parishioner. In spite of the awful state of the roads, it was a glorious morning. The sun was shining brightly and cleaving with its rays the layers of white snow still lingering here and there. The snow as it took leave of the earth glittered with such diamonds that it hurt the eyes to look, while the young winter corn was hastily thrusting up its green beside it. The rooks floated with dignity over the fields. A rook would fly, drop to earth, and give several hops before standing firmly on its feet. . . .

The wooden church up to which Kunin drove was old and grey; the columns of the porch had once been painted white, but the colour had now completely peeled off, and they looked like two ungainly shafts. The ikon over the door looked like a dark smudged blur. But its poverty touched and softened Kunin. Modestly dropping his eyes, he went into the church and stood by the door. The service had only just begun. An old sacristan, bent into a bow, was reading the "Hours" in a hollow indistinct tenor. Father Yakov, who conducted the service without a deacon, was walking about the church, burning incense. Had it not been for the softened mood in which Kunin found himself on entering the poverty-stricken church, he certainly would have smiled at the sight of Father Yakov. The short priest was wearing a crumpled and extremely long robe of some shabby yellow material; the hem of the robe trailed on the ground.

The church was not full. Looking at the parishioners, Kunin was struck at the first glance by one strange circumstance: he saw nothing but old people and children. . . . Where were the men of working age? Where was the youth and manhood? But after he had stood there a little and looked more attentively at the aged-looking faces, Kunin saw that he had mistaken young people for old. He did not, however, attach any significance to this little optical illusion.

The church was as cold and grey inside as outside. There was not one spot on the ikons nor on the dark brown walls which was not begrimed and defaced by time. There were many windows, but the general effect of colour was grey, and so it was twilight in the church.

"Anyone pure in soul can pray here very well," thought Kunin. "Just as in St. Peter's in Rome one is impressed by grandeur, here one is touched by the lowliness and simplicity."

But his devout mood vanished like smoke as soon as Father Yakov went up to the altar and began mass. Being still young and having come straight from the seminary bench to the priesthood, Father Yakov had not yet formed a set manner of celebrating the service. As he read he seemed to be vacillating between a high tenor and a thin bass; he bowed clumsily, walked quickly, and opened and shut the gates abruptly. . . . The old sacristan, evidently deaf and ailing, did not hear the prayers very distinctly, and this very often led to slight misunderstandings. Before Father Yakov had time to finish what he had to say, the sacristan began chanting his response, or else long after

Father Yakov had finished the old man would be straining his ears, listening in the direction of the altar and saying nothing till his skirt was pulled. The old man had a sickly hollow voice and an asthmatic quavering lisp. . . . The complete lack of dignity and decorum was emphasized by a very small boy who seconded the sacristan and whose head was hardly visible over the railing of the choir. The boy sang in a shrill falsetto and seemed to be trying to avoid singing in tune. Kunin stayed a little while, listened and went out for a smoke. He was disappointed, and looked at the grey church almost with dislike.

"They complain of the decline of religious feeling among the people. . ." he sighed. "I should rather think so! They'd better foist a few more priests like this one on them!"

Kunin went back into the church three times, and each time he felt a great temptation to get out into the open air again. Waiting till the end of the mass, he went to Father Yakov's. The priest's house did not differ outwardly from the peasants' huts, but the thatch lay more smoothly on the roof and there were little white curtains in the windows. Father Yakov led Kunin into a light little room with a clay floor and walls covered with cheap paper; in spite of some painful efforts towards luxury in the way of photographs in frames and a clock with a pair of scissors hanging on the weight the furnishing of the room impressed him by its scantiness. Looking at the furniture, one might have supposed that Father Yakov had gone from house to house and collected it in bits; in one place they had given him a round three-legged table, in another a stool, in a third a chair with a back bent violently backwards; in a fourth a chair with an upright back, but the seat smashed in; while in a fifth they had been liberal and given him a semblance of a sofa with a flat back and a lattice-work seat. This semblance had been painted dark red and smelt strongly of paint. Kunin meant at first to sit down on one of the chairs, but on second thoughts he sat down on the stool.

"This is the first time you have been to our church?" asked Father Yakov, hanging his hat on a huge misshapen nail.

"Yes it is. I tell you what, Father, before we begin on business, will you give me some tea? My soul is parched."

Father Yakov blinked, gasped, and went behind the partition wall. There was a sound of whispering.

"With his wife, I suppose," thought Kunin; "it would be interesting to see what the red-headed fellow's wife is like."

A little later Father Yakov came back, red and perspiring and with an effort to smile, sat down on the edge of the sofa.

"They will heat the samovar directly," he said, without looking at his visitor.

"My goodness, they have not heated the samovar yet!" Kunin thought with horror. "A nice time we shall have to wait."

"I have brought you," he said, "the rough draft of the letter I have written to the bishop. I'll read it after tea; perhaps you may find something to add. . . ."

"Very well."

A silence followed. Father Yakov threw furtive glances at the partition wall, smoothed his hair, and blew his nose.

"It's wonderful weather, . . ." he said.

"Yes. I read an interesting thing yesterday. . . . the Volsky Zemstvo have decided to give their schools to the clergy, that's typical."

Kunin got up, and pacing up and down the clay floor, began to give expression to his reflections.

"That would be all right," he said, "if only the clergy were equal to their high calling and recognized their tasks. I am so unfortunate as to know priests whose standard of culture and whose moral qualities make them hardly fit to be army secretaries, much less priests. You will agree that a bad teacher does far less harm than a bad priest."

Kunin glanced at Father Yakov; he was sitting bent up, thinking intently about something and apparently not listening to his visitor.

"Yasha, come here!" a woman's voice called from behind the partition. Father Yakov started and went out. Again a whispering began.

Kunin felt a pang of longing for tea.

"No; it's no use my waiting for tea here," he thought, looking at his watch. "Besides I fancy I am not altogether a welcome visitor. My host has not deigned to say one word to me; he simply sits and blinks."

Kunin took up his hat, waited for Father Yakov to return, and said good-bye to him.

"I have simply wasted the morning," he thought wrathfully on the way home. "The blockhead! The dummy! He cares no more about the school than I about last year's snow. . . . No, I shall never get anything done with him! We are bound to fail! If the Marshal knew what the priest here was like, he wouldn't be in such a hurry to talk about a school. We ought first to try and get a decent priest, and then think about the school."

By now Kunin almost hated Father Yakov. The man, his pitiful, grotesque figure in the long crumpled robe, his womanish face, his manner of officiating, his way of life and his formal restrained respectfulness, wounded the tiny relic of religious feeling which was stored away in a warm corner of Kunin's heart together with his nurse's other fairy tales. The coldness and lack of attention with which Father Yakov had met Kunin's warm and sincere interest in what was the priest's own work was hard for the former's vanity to endure. . . .

On the evening of the same day Kunin spent a long time walking about his rooms and thinking. Then he sat down to the table resolutely and wrote a letter to the bishop. After asking for money and a blessing for the school, he set forth genuinely, like a son, his opinion of the priest at Sinkino.

"He is young," he wrote, "insufficiently educated, leads, I fancy, an intemperate life, and altogether fails to satisfy the ideals which the Russian people have in the course of centuries formed of what a pastor should be."

After writing this letter Kunin heaved a deep sigh, and went to bed with the consciousness that he had done a good deed.

On Monday morning, while he was still in bed, he was informed that Father Yakov had arrived. He did not want to get up, and instructed the servant to say he was not at home. On Tuesday he went away to a sitting of the Board, and when he returned on Saturday he was told by the servants that Father Yakov had called every day in his absence.

"He liked my biscuits, it seems," he thought.

Towards evening on Sunday Father Yakov arrived. This time not only his skirts, but even his hat, was bespattered with mud. Just as on his first visit, he was hot and perspiring, and sat down on the edge of his chair as he had done then. Kunin determined not to talk about the school - not to cast pearls.

"I have brought you a list of books for the school, Pavel Mihailovitch, . . ." Father Yakov began.

"Thank you."

But everything showed that Father Yakov had come for something else besides the list. His whole figure was expressive of extreme embarrassment, and at the same time there was a look of determination upon his face, as on the face of a man suddenly inspired by an idea. He struggled to say something important, absolutely necessary, and strove to overcome his timidity.

"Why is he dumb?" Kunin thought wrathfully. "He's settled himself comfortably! I haven't time to be bothered with him."

To smoothe over the awkwardness of his silence and to conceal the struggle going on within him, the priest began to smile constrainedly, and this slow smile, wrung out on his red perspiring face, and out of keeping with the fixed look in his grey-blue eyes, made Kunin turn away. He felt moved to repulsion.

"Excuse me, Father, I have to go out," he said.

Father Yakov started like a man asleep who has been struck a blow, and, still smiling, began in his confusion wrapping round him the skirts of his cassock. In spite of his repulsion for the man, Kunin felt suddenly sorry for him, and he wanted to soften his cruelty.

"Please come another time, Father," he said, "and before we part I want to ask you a favour. I was somehow inspired to write two sermons the other day. . . . I will give them to you to look at. If they are suitable, use them."

"Very good," said Father Yakov, laying his open hand on Kunin's sermons which were lying on the table. "I will take them."

After standing a little, hesitating and still wrapping his cassock round him, he suddenly gave up the effort to smile and lifted his head resolutely.

"Pavel Mihailovitch, " he said, evidently trying to speak loudly and distinctly.

"What can I do for you?"

"I have heard that you . . . er . . . have dismissed your secretary, and . . . and are looking for a new one. . . ."

"Yes, I am. . . . Why, have you someone to recommend?"

"I. . . er . . . you see . . . I . . . Could you not give the post to me?"

"Why, are you giving up the Church?" said Kunin in amazement.

"No, no," Father Yakov brought out quickly, for some reason turning pale and trembling all over. "God forbid! If you feel doubtful, then never mind, never mind. You see, I could do the work between whiles,. . so as to increase my income. . . . Never mind, don't disturb yourself!"

"H'm! . . . your income. . . . But you know, I only pay my secretary twenty roubles a month."

"Good heavens! I would take ten," whispered Father Yakov, looking about him. "Ten would be enough! You . . . you are astonished, and everyone is astonished. The greedy priest, the grasping priest, what does he do with his money? I feel myself I am greedy, . . . and I blame myself, I condemn myself. . . . I am ashamed to look people in the face. . . . I tell you on my conscience, Pavel Mihailovitch. . . . I call the God of truth to witness. . . . "

Father Yakov took breath and went on:

"On the way here I prepared a regular confession to make you, but . . . I've forgotten it all; I cannot find a word now. I get a hundred and fifty roubles a year from my parish, and everyone wonders what I do with the money. . . . But I'll explain it all truly. . . . I pay forty roubles a year to the clerical school for my brother Pyotr. He has everything found there, except that I have to provide pens and paper."

"Oh, I believe you; I believe you! But what's the object of all this?" said Kunin, with a wave of the hand, feeling terribly oppressed by this outburst of confidence on the part of his visitor, and not knowing how to get away from the tearful gleam in his eyes.

"Then I have not yet paid up all that I owe to the consistory for my place here. They charged me two hundred roubles for the living, and I was to pay ten roubles a month. . . . You can judge what is left! And, besides, I must allow Father Avraamy at least three roubles a month."

"What Father Avraamy?"

"Father Avraamy who was priest at Sinkino before I came. He was deprived of the living on account of . . . his failing, but you know, he is still living at Sinkino! He has nowhere to go. There is no one to keep him. Though he is old, he must have a corner, and food and clothing - I can't let him go begging on the roads in his position! It would be on my conscience if anything happened! It would be my fault! He is. . . in debt all round; but, you see, I am to blame for not paying for him."

Father Yakov started up from his seat and, looking frantically at the floor, strode up and down the room.

"My God, my God!" he muttered, raising his hands and dropping them again. "Lord, save us and have mercy upon us! Why did you take such a calling on yourself if you have so little faith and no strength? There is no end to my despair! Save me, Queen of Heaven!"

"Calm yourself, Father," said Kunin.

"I am worn out with hunger, Pavel Mihailovitch," Father Yakov went on. "Generously forgive me, but I am at the end of my strength. . . . I know if I were to beg and to bow down, everyone would help, but . . . I cannot! I am ashamed. How can I beg of the peasants? You are on the Board here, so you know. . . . How can one beg of a beggar? And to beg of richer people, of landowners, I cannot! I have pride! I am ashamed!"

Father Yakov waved his hand, and nervously scratched his head with both hands.

"I am ashamed! My God, I am ashamed! I am proud and can't bear people to see my poverty! When you visited me, Pavel Mihailovitch, I had no tea in the house! There wasn't a pinch of it, and you know it was pride prevented me from telling you! I am ashamed of my clothes, of these patches here. . . . I am ashamed of my vestments, of being hungry. . . . And is it seemly for a priest to be proud?"

Father Yakov stood still in the middle of the study, and, as though he did not notice Kunin's presence, began reasoning with himself.

"Well, supposing I endure hunger and disgrace - but, my God, I have a wife! I took her from a good home! She is not used to hard work; she is soft; she is used to tea and white bread and sheets on her bed. . . . At home she used to play the piano. . . . She is young, not twenty yet. . . . She would like, to be sure, to be smart, to have fun, go out to see people. . . . And she is worse off with me than any cook; she is ashamed to show herself in the street. My God, my God! Her only treat is when I bring an apple or some biscuit from a visit. . . ."

Father Yakov scratched his head again with both hands.

"And it makes us feel not love but pity for each other. . . . I cannot look at her without compassion! And the things that happen in this life, O Lord! Such things that people would not believe them if they saw them in the newspaper. . . . And when will there be an end to it all!"

"Hush, Father!" Kunin almost shouted, frightened at his tone. "Why take such a gloomy view of life?"

"Generously forgive me, Pavel Mihailovitch . . ." muttered Father Yakov as though he were drunk, "Forgive me, all this . . . doesn't matter, and don't take any notice of it. . . . Only I do blame myself, and always shall blame myself . . . always."

Father Yakov looked about him and began whispering:

"One morning early I was going from Sinkino to Lutchkovo; I saw a woman standing on the river bank, doing something. . . . I went up close and could not believe my eyes. . . . It was horrible! The wife of the doctor, Ivan Sergeitch, was sitting there washing her linen. . . . A doctor's wife, brought up at a select boarding-school! She had got up you see, early and gone half a mile from the village that people should not see her. . . . She couldn't get over her pride! When she saw that I was near her and noticed her poverty, she turned red all over. . . . I was flustered - I was frightened, and ran up to help her, but she hid her linen from me; she was afraid I should see her ragged chemises. . . ."

"All this is positively incredible," said Kunin, sitting down and looking almost with horror at Father Yakov's pale face.

"Incredible it is! It's a thing that has never been! Pavel Mihailovitch, that a doctor's wife should be rinsing the linen in the river! Such a thing does not happen in any country! As her pastor and spiritual father, I ought not to allow it, but what can I do? What? Why, I am always trying to get treated by her husband for nothing myself! It is true that, as you say, it is all incredible! One can hardly believe one's eyes. During Mass, you know, when I look out from the altar and see my congregation, Avraamy starving, and my wife, and think of the doctor's wife - how blue her hands were from the cold water - would you believe it, I forget myself and stand senseless like a fool, until the sacristan calls to me. . . . It's awful!"

Father Yakov began walking about again.

"Lord Jesus!" he said, waving his hands, "holy Saints! I can't officiate properly. . . . Here you talk to me about the school, and I sit like a dummy and don't understand a word, and think of nothing but food. . . . Even before the altar. . . . But . . . what am I doing?" Father Yakov pulled himself up suddenly. "You want to go out. Forgive me, I meant nothing. . . . Excuse . . ."

Kunin shook hands with Father Yakov without speaking, saw him into the hall, and going back into his study, stood at the window. He saw Father Yakov go out of the house, pull his wide-brimmed rusty-looking hat over his eyes, and slowly, bowing his head, as though ashamed of his outburst, walk along the road.

"I don't see his horse," thought Kunin.

Kunin did not dare to think that the priest had come on foot every day to see him; it was five or six miles to Sinkino, and the mud on the road was impassable. Further on he saw the coachman Andrey and the boy Paramon, jumping over the puddles and splashing Father Yakov with mud, run up to him for his blessing. Father Yakov took off his hat and slowly blessed Andrey, then blessed the boy and stroked his head.

Kunin passed his hand over his eyes, and it seemed to him that his hand was moist. He walked away from the window and with dim eyes looked round the room in which he still seemed to hear the timid droning voice. He glanced at the table. Luckily, Father Yakov, in his haste, had forgotten to take the sermons. Kunin rushed up to them, tore them into pieces, and with loathing thrust them under the table.

"And I did not know!" he moaned, sinking on to the sofa. "After being here over a year as member of the Rural Board, Honorary Justice of the Peace, member of the School Committee! Blind puppet, egregious idiot! I must make haste and help them, I must make haste!"

He turned from side to side uneasily, pressed his temples and racked his brains.

"On the twentieth I shall get my salary, two hundred roubles. . . . On some good pretext I will give him some, and some to the doctor's wife. . . . I will ask them to perform a special service here, and will get up an illness for the doctor. . . . In that way I shan't wound their pride. And I'll help Father Avraamy too. . . ."

He reckoned his money on his fingers, and was afraid to own to himself that those two hundred roubles would hardly be enough for him to pay his steward, his servants, the peasant who brought the meat. . . . He could not help remembering the recent past when he was senselessly squandering his father's fortune, when as a puppy of twenty he had given expensive fans to prostitutes, had paid ten roubles a day to Kuzma, his cab-driver, and in his vanity had made presents to actresses. Oh, how useful those wasted rouble, three-rouble, ten-rouble notes would have been now!

"Father Avraamy lives on three roubles a month!" thought Kunin. "For a rouble the priest's wife could get herself a chemise, and the doctor's wife could hire a washerwoman. But I'll help them, anyway! I must help them."

Here Kunin suddenly recalled the private information he had sent to the bishop, and he writhed as from a sudden draught of cold air. This remembrance filled him with overwhelming shame before his inner self and before the unseen truth.

So had begun and had ended a sincere effort to be of public service on the part of a well-intentioned but unreflecting and over-comfortable person.

# GRISHA

Grisha, a chubby little boy, born two years and eight months ago, is walking on the boulevard with his nurse. He is wearing a long, wadded pelisse, a scarf, a big cap with a fluffy pom-pom, and warm over-boots. He feels hot and stifled, and now, too, the rollicking April sunshine is beating straight in his face, and making his eyelids tingle.

The whole of his clumsy, timidly and uncertainly stepping little figure expresses the utmost bewilderment.

Hitherto Grisha has known only a rectangular world, where in one corner stands his bed, in the other nurse's trunk, in the third a chair, while in the fourth there is a little lamp burning. If one looks under the bed, one sees a doll with a broken arm and a drum; and behind nurse's trunk, there are a great many things of all sorts: cotton reels, boxes without lids, and a broken Jack-a-dandy. In that world, besides nurse and Grisha, there are often mamma and the cat. Mamma is like a doll, and puss is like papa's fur-coat, only the coat hasn't got eyes and a tail. From the world which is called the nursery a door leads to a great expanse where they have dinner and tea. There stands Grisha's chair on high legs, and on the wall hangs a clock which exists to swing its pendulum and chime. From the dining-room, one can go into a room where there are red arm-chairs. Here, there is a dark patch on the carpet, concerning which fingers are still shaken at Grisha. Beyond that room is still another, to which one is not admitted, and where one sees glimpses of papa - an extremely enigmatical person! Nurse and mamma are comprehensible: they dress Grisha, feed him, and put him to bed, but what papa exists for is unknown. There is another enigmatical person, auntie, who presented Grisha with a drum. She appears and disappears. Where does she disappear to? Grisha has more than once looked under the bed, behind the trunk, and under the sofa, but she was not there.

In this new world, where the sun hurts one's eyes, there are so many papas and mammas and aunties, that there is no knowing to whom to run. But what is stranger and more absurd than anything is the horses. Grisha gazes at their moving legs, and can make nothing of it. He looks at his nurse for her to solve the mystery, but she does not speak.

All at once he hears a fearful tramping. . . . A crowd of soldiers, with red faces and bath brooms under their arms, move in step along the boulevard straight upon him. Grisha turns cold all over with terror, and looks inquiringly at nurse to know whether it is dangerous. But nurse neither weeps nor runs away, so there is no danger. Grisha looks after the soldiers, and begins to move his feet in step with them himself.

Two big cats with long faces run after each other across the boulevard, with their tongues out, and their tails in the air. Grisha thinks that he must run too, and runs after the cats.

"Stop!" cries nurse, seizing him roughly by the shoulder. "Where are you off to? Haven't you been told not to be naughty?"

Here there is a nurse sitting holding a tray of oranges. Grisha passes by her, and, without saying anything, takes an orange.

"What are you doing that for?" cries the companion of his travels, slapping his hand and snatching away the orange. "Silly!"

Now Grisha would have liked to pick up a bit of glass that was lying at his feet and gleaming like a lamp, but he is afraid that his hand will be slapped again.

"My respects to you!" Grisha hears suddenly, almost above his ear, a loud thick voice, and he sees a tall man with bright buttons.

To his great delight, this man gives nurse his hand, stops, and begins talking to her. The brightness of the sun, the noise of the carriages, the horses, the bright buttons are all so impressively new and not dreadful, that Grisha's soul is filled with a feeling of enjoyment and he begins to laugh.

"Come along! Come along!" he cries to the man with the bright buttons, tugging at his coattails.

"Come along where?" asks the man.

"Come along!" Grisha insists.

He wants to say that it would be just as well to take with them papa, mamma, and the cat, but his tongue does not say what he wants to.

A little later, nurse turns out of the boulevard, and leads Grisha into a big courtyard where there is still snow; and the man with the bright buttons comes with them too. They carefully avoid the lumps of snow and the puddles, then, by a dark and dirty staircase, they go into a room. Here there is a great deal of smoke, there is a smell of roast meat, and a woman is standing by the stove frying cutlets. The cook and the nurse kiss each other, and sit down on the bench together with the man, and begin talking in a low voice. Grisha, wrapped up as he is, feels insufferably hot and stifled.

"Why is this?" he wonders, looking about him.

He sees the dark ceiling, the oven fork with two horns, the stove which looks like a great black hole.

"Mam-ma," he drawls.

"Come, come, come!" cries the nurse. "Wait a bit!"

The cook puts a bottle on the table, two wine-glasses, and a pie. The two women and the man with the bright buttons clink glasses and empty them several times, and, the man puts his arm round first the cook and then the nurse. And then all three begin singing in an undertone.

Grisha stretches out his hand towards the pie, and they give him a piece of it. He eats it and watches nurse drinking. . . . He wants to drink too.

"Give me some, nurse!" he begs.

The cook gives him a sip out of her glass. He rolls his eyes, blinks, coughs, and waves his hands for a long time afterwards, while the cook looks at him and laughs.

When he gets home Grisha begins to tell mamma, the walls, and the bed where he has been, and what he has seen. He talks not so much with his tongue, as with his face and his hands. He shows how the sun shines, how the horses run, how the terrible stove looks, and how the cook drinks. . . .

In the evening he cannot get to sleep. The soldiers with the brooms, the big cats, the horses, the bit of glass, the tray of oranges, the bright buttons, all gathered together, weigh on his brain. He tosses from side to side, babbles, and, at last, unable to endure his excitement, begins crying.

"You are feverish," says mamma, putting her open hand on his forehead. "What can have caused it?

"Stove!" wails Grisha. "Go away, stove!"

"He must have eaten too much . . ." mamma decides.

And Grisha, shattered by the impressions of the new life he has just experienced, receives a spoonful of castor-oil from mamma.

# LOVE

"Three o'clock in the morning. The soft April night is looking in at my windows and caressingly winking at me with its stars. I can't sleep, I am so happy!

"My whole being from head to heels is bursting with a strange, incomprehensible feeling. I can't analyse it just now - I haven't the time, I'm too lazy, and there - hang analysis! Why, is a man likely to interpret his sensations when he is flying head foremost from a belfry, or has just learned that he has won two hundred thousand? Is he in a state to do it?"

This was more or less how I began my love-letter to Sasha, a girl of nineteen with whom I had fallen in love. I began it five times, and as often tore up the sheets, scratched out whole pages, and copied it all over again. I spent as long over the letter as if it had been a novel I had to write to order. And it was not because I tried to make it longer, more elaborate, and more fervent, but because I wanted endlessly to prolong the process of this writing, when one sits in the stillness of one's study and communes with one's own day-dreams while the spring night looks in at one's window. Between the lines I saw a beloved image, and it seemed to me that there were, sitting at the same table writing with me, spirits as naïvely happy, as foolish, and as blissfully smiling as I. I wrote continually, looking at my hand, which still ached deliciously where hers had lately pressed it, and if I turned my eyes away I had a vision of the green trellis of the little gate. Through that trellis Sasha gazed at me after I had said goodbye to her. When I was saying good-bye to Sasha I was thinking of nothing and was simply admiring her figure as every decent man admires a pretty woman; when I saw through the trellis two big eyes, I suddenly, as though by inspiration, knew that I was in love, that it was all settled between us, and fully decided already, that I had nothing left to do but to carry out certain formalities.

It is a great delight also to seal up a love-letter, and, slowly putting on one's hat and coat, to go softly out of the house and to carry the treasure to the post. There are no stars in the sky now: in their place there is a long whitish streak in the east, broken here and there by clouds above the roofs of the dingy houses; from that streak the whole sky is flooded with pale light. The town is asleep, but already the water-carts have come out, and somewhere in a far-away factory a whistle sounds to wake up the workpeople. Beside the postbox, slightly moist with dew, you are sure to see the clumsy figure of a house porter, wearing a bell-shaped sheepskin and carrying a stick. He is in a condition akin to catalepsy: he is not asleep or awake, but something between.

If the boxes knew how often people resort to them for the decision of their fate, they would not have such a humble air. I, anyway, almost kissed my postbox, and as I gazed at it I reflected that the post is the greatest of blessings.

I beg anyone who has ever been in love to remember how one usually hurries home after dropping the letter in the box, rapidly gets into bed and pulls up the quilt in the full conviction that as soon as one wakes up in the morning one will be overwhelmed with memories of the previous day and look with rapture at the window, where the daylight will be eagerly making its way through the folds of the curtain.

Well, to facts. . . . Next morning at midday, Sasha's maid brought me the following answer: "I am delited be sure to come to us to day please I shall expect you. Your S."

Not a single comma. This lack of punctuation, and the misspelling of the word "delighted," the whole letter, and even the long, narrow envelope in which it was put filled my heart with tenderness. In the sprawling but diffident handwriting I recognised Sasha's walk, her way of raising her eyebrows when she laughed, the movement of her lips. . . . But the contents of the letter did not satisfy me. In the first place, poetical letters are not answered in that way, and in the second, why should I go to Sasha's house to wait till it should occur to her stout mamma, her brothers, and poor relations to leave us alone together? It would never enter their heads, and nothing is more hateful than to have to restrain one's raptures simply because of the intrusion of some animate trumpery in the shape of a half-deaf old woman or little girl pestering one with questions. I sent an answer by the maid asking Sasha to select some park or boulevard for a rendezvous. My suggestion was readily accepted. I had struck the right chord, as the saying is.

Between four and five o'clock in the afternoon I made my way to the furthest and most overgrown part of the park. There was not a soul in the park, and the tryst might have taken place somewhere nearer in one of the avenues or arbours, but women don't like doing it by halves in romantic affairs; in for a penny, in for a pound - if you are in for a tryst, let it be in the furthest and most impenetrable thicket, where one runs the risk of stumbling upon some rough or drunken man. When I went up to Sasha she was standing with her back to me, and in that back I could read a devilish lot of mystery. It seemed as though that back and the nape of her neck, and the black spots on her dress were saying: Hush! . . . The girl was wearing a simple cotton dress over which she had thrown a light cape. To add to the air of mysterious secrecy, her face was covered with a white veil. Not to spoil the effect, I had to approach on tiptoe and speak in a half whisper.

From what I remember now, I was not so much the essential point of the rendezvous as a detail of it. Sasha was not so much absorbed in the interview itself as in its romantic mysteriousness, my kisses, the silence of the gloomy trees, my vows. . . . There was not a minute in which she forgot herself, was overcome, or let the mysterious expression drop from her face, and really if there had been any Ivan Sidoritch or Sidor Ivanitch in my place she would have felt just as happy. How is one to make out in such circumstances whether one is loved or not? Whether the love is "the real thing" or not?

From the park I took Sasha home with me. The presence of the beloved woman in one's bachelor quarters affects one like wine and music. Usually one begins to speak of the future, and the confidence and self-reliance with which one does so is beyond bounds. You make plans and projects, talk fervently of the rank of general though you have not yet reached the rank of a lieutenant, and altogether you fire off such high-flown nonsense that your listener must have a great deal of love and ignorance of life to assent to it. Fortunately for men, women in love are always blinded by their feelings and never know anything of life. Far from not assenting, they actually turn pale with holy awe, are full of reverence and hang greedily on the maniac's words. Sasha listened to me with attention, but I soon detected an absent-minded expression on her face, she did not understand me. The future of which I talked interested her only in its external aspect and I was wasting time in displaying my plans and projects before her. She was keenly interested in knowing which would be her room, what paper she would have in the room, why I had an upright piano instead of a grand piano, and so on. She examined carefully all the little things on my table, looked at the photographs, sniffed at the bottles, peeled the old stamps off the envelopes, saying she wanted them for something.

"Please collect old stamps for me!" she said, making a grave face. "Please do."

Then she found a nut in the window, noisily cracked it and ate it.

"Why don't you stick little labels on the backs of your books?" she asked, taking a look at the bookcase.

"What for?"

"Oh, so that each book should have its number. And where am I to put my books? I've got books too, you know."

"What books have you got?" I asked.

Sasha raised her eyebrows, thought a moment and said:

"All sorts."

And if it had entered my head to ask her what thoughts, what convictions, what aims she had, she would no doubt have raised her eyebrows, thought a minute, and have said in the same way: "All sorts."

Later I saw Sasha home and left her house regularly, officially engaged, and was so reckoned till our wedding. If the reader will allow me to judge merely from my personal experience, I maintain that to be engaged is very dreary, far more so than to be a husband or nothing at all. An engaged man is neither one thing nor the other, he has left one side of the river and not reached the other, he is not married and yet he can't be said to be a bachelor, but is in something not unlike the condition of the porter whom I have mentioned above.

Every day as soon as I had a free moment I hastened to my fiancée. As I went I usually bore within me a multitude of hopes, desires, intentions, suggestions, phrases. I always fancied that as soon as the maid opened the door I should, from feeling oppressed and stifled, plunge at once up to my neck into a sea of refreshing happiness. But it always turned out otherwise in fact. Every time I went to see my fiancée I found all her family and other members of the household busy over the silly trousseau. (And by the way, they were hard at work sewing for two months and then they had less than a hundred roubles' worth of things). There was a smell of irons, candle grease and fumes. Bugles scrunched under one's feet. The two most important rooms were piled up with billows of linen, calico, and muslin and from among the billows peeped out Sasha's little head with a thread between her teeth. All the sewing party welcomed me with cries of delight but at once led me off into the dining-room where I could not hinder them nor see what only husbands are permitted to behold. In spite of my feelings, I had to sit in the dining-room and converse with Pimenovna, one of the poor relations. Sasha, looking worried and excited, kept running by me with a thimble, a skein of wool or some other boring object.

"Wait, wait, I shan't be a minute," she would say when I raised imploring eyes to her. "Only fancy that wretch Stepanida has spoilt the bodice of the barège dress!"

And after waiting in vain for this grace, I lost my temper, went out of the house and walked about the streets in the company of the new cane I had bought. Or I would want to go for a walk or a drive with my fiancée, would go round and find her already standing in the hall with her mother, dressed to go out and playing with her parasol.

"Oh, we are going to the Arcade," she would say. "We have got to buy some more cashmere and change the hat."

My outing is knocked on the head. I join the ladies and go with them to the Arcade. It is revoltingly dull to listen to women shopping, haggling and trying to outdo the sharp shopman. I felt ashamed when Sasha, after turning over masses of material and knocking down the prices to a minimum, walked out of the shop without buying anything, or else told the shopman to cut her some half rouble's worth.

When they came out of the shop, Sasha and her mamma with scared and worried faces would discuss at length having made a mistake, having bought the wrong thing, the flowers in the chintz being too dark, and so on.

Yes, it is a bore to be engaged! I'm glad it's over.

Now I am married. It is evening. I am sitting in my study reading. Behind me on the sofa Sasha is sitting munching something noisily. I want a glass of beer.

"Sasha, look for the corkscrew. . . ." I say. "It's lying about somewhere."

Sasha leaps up, rummages in a disorderly way among two or three heaps of papers, drops the matches, and without finding the corkscrew, sits down in silence. . . . Five minutes pass - ten. . . I begin to be fretted both by thirst and vexation.

"Sasha, do look for the corkscrew," I say.

Sasha leaps up again and rummages among the papers near me. Her munching and rustling of the papers affects me like the sound of sharpening knives against each other. . . . I get up and begin looking for the corkscrew myself. At last it is found and the beer is uncorked. Sasha remains by the table and begins telling me something at great length.

"You'd better read something, Sasha," I say.

She takes up a book, sits down facing me and begins moving her lips. . . . I look at her little forehead, moving lips, and sink into thought.

"She is getting on for twenty. . . ." I reflect. "If one takes a boy of the educated class and of that age and compares them, what a difference! The boy would have knowledge and convictions and some intelligence."

But I forgive that difference just as the low forehead and moving lips are forgiven. I remember in my old Lovelace days I have cast off women for a stain on their stockings, or for one foolish word, or for not cleaning their teeth, and now I forgive everything: the munching, the muddling about after the corkscrew, the slovenliness, the long talking about nothing that matters; I forgive it all almost unconsciously, with no effort of will, as though Sasha's mistakes were my mistakes, and many things which would have made me wince in old days move me to tenderness and even rapture. The explanation of this forgiveness of everything lies in my love for Sasha, but what is the explanation of the love itself, I really don't know.

## EASTER EVE

I was standing on the bank of the River Goltva, waiting for the ferry-boat from the other side. At ordinary times the Goltva is a humble stream of moderate size, silent and pensive, gently glimmering from behind thick reeds; but now a regular lake lay stretched out before me. The waters of spring, running riot, had overflowed both banks and flooded both sides of the river for a long distance, submerging vegetable gardens, hayfields and marshes, so that it was no unusual thing to meet poplars and bushes sticking out above the surface of the water and looking in the darkness like grim solitary crags.

The weather seemed to me magnificent. It was dark, yet I could see the trees, the water and the people. . . . The world was lighted by the stars, which were scattered thickly all over the sky. I don't remember ever seeing so many stars. Literally one could not have put a finger in between them. There were some as big as a goose's egg, others tiny as hempseed. . . . They had come out for the festival procession, every one of them, little and big, washed, renewed and joyful, and everyone of them was softly twinkling its beams. The sky was reflected in the water; the stars were bathing in its dark depths and trembling with the quivering eddies. The air was warm and still. . . . Here and there, far away on the further bank in the impenetrable darkness, several bright red lights were gleaming. . . .

A couple of paces from me I saw the dark silhouette of a peasant in a high hat, with a thick knotted stick in his hand.

"How long the ferry-boat is in coming!" I said.

"It is time it was here," the silhouette answered.

"You are waiting for the ferry-boat, too?"

"No I am not," yawned the peasant - "I am waiting for the illumination. I should have gone, but to tell you the truth, I haven't the five kopecks for the ferry."

"I'll give you the five kopecks."

"No; I humbly thank you. . . . With that five kopecks put up a candle for me over there in the monastery. . . . That will be more interesting, and I will stand here. What can it mean, no ferry-boat, as though it had sunk in the water!"

The peasant went up to the water's edge, took the rope in his hands, and shouted; "Ieronim! Ieron - im!"

As though in answer to his shout, the slow peal of a great bell floated across from the further bank. The note was deep and low, as from the thickest string of a double bass; it seemed as though the darkness itself had hoarsely uttered it. At once there was the sound of a cannon shot. It rolled away in the darkness and ended somewhere in the far distance behind me. The peasant took off his hat and crossed himself.

"'Christ is risen," he said.

Before the vibrations of the first peal of the bell had time to die away in the air a second sounded, after it at once a third, and the darkness was filled with an unbroken quivering clamour. Near the red lights fresh lights flashed, and all began moving together and twinkling restlessly.

"Ieron - im!" we heard a hollow prolonged shout.

"They are shouting from the other bank," said the peasant, "so there is no ferry there either. Our Ieronim has gone to sleep."

The lights and the velvety chimes of the bell drew one towards them. . . . I was already beginning to lose patience and grow anxious, but behold at last, staring into the dark distance, I saw the outline of something very much like a gibbet. It was the long-expected ferry. It moved towards us with such deliberation that if it had not been that its lines grew gradually more definite, one might have supposed that it was standing still or moving to the other bank.

"Make haste! Ieronim!" shouted my peasant. "The gentleman's tired of waiting!"

The ferry crawled to the bank, gave a lurch and stopped with a creak. A tall man in a monk's cassock and a conical cap stood on it, holding the rope.

"Why have you been so long?" I asked jumping upon the ferry.

"Forgive me, for Christ's sake," Ieronim answered gently. "Is there no one else?"

"No one. . . ."

Ieronim took hold of the rope in both hands, bent himself to the figure of a mark of interrogation, and gasped. The ferry-boat creaked and gave a lurch. The outline of the peasant in the high hat began slowly retreating from me - so the ferry was moving off. Ieronim soon drew himself up and began working with one hand only. We were silent, gazing towards the bank to which we were floating. There the illumination for which the peasant was waiting had begun. At the water's edge barrels of tar were flaring like huge camp fires. Their reflections, crimson as the rising moon, crept to meet us in long broad streaks. The burning barrels lighted up their own smoke and the long shadows of men flitting about the fire; but further to one side and behind them from where the velvety chime floated there was still the same unbroken black gloom. All at once, cleaving the darkness, a rocket zigzagged in a golden ribbon up the sky; it described an arc and, as though broken to pieces against the sky, was scattered crackling into sparks. There was a roar from the bank like a far-away hurrah.

"How beautiful!" I said.

"Beautiful beyond words!" sighed Ieronim. "Such a night, sir! Another time one would pay no attention to the fireworks, but to-day one rejoices in every vanity. Where do you come from?"

I told him where I came from.

"To be sure . . . a joyful day to-day. . . ." Ieronim went on in a weak sighing tenor like the voice of a convalescent. "The sky is rejoicing and the earth and what is under the earth. All the creatures are keeping holiday. Only tell me kind sir, why, even in the time of great rejoicing, a man cannot forget his sorrows?"

I fancied that this unexpected question was to draw me into one of those endless religious conversations which bored and idle monks are so fond of. I was not disposed to talk much, and so I only asked:

"What sorrows have you, father?"

"As a rule only the same as all men, kind sir, but to-day a special sorrow has happened in the monastery: at mass, during the reading of the Bible, the monk and deacon Nikolay died."

"Well, it's God's will!" I said, falling into the monastic tone. "We must all die. To my mind, you ought to rejoice indeed. . . . They say if anyone dies at Easter he goes straight to the kingdom of heaven."

"That's true."

We sank into silence. The figure of the peasant in the high hat melted into the lines of the bank. The tar barrels were flaring up more and more.

"The Holy Scripture points clearly to the vanity of sorrow and so does reflection," said Ieronim, breaking the silence, "but why does the heart grieve and refuse to listen to reason? Why does one want to weep bitterly?"

Ieronim shrugged his shoulders, turned to me and said quickly:

"If I died, or anyone else, it would not be worth notice perhaps; but, you see, Nikolay is dead! No one else but Nikolay! Indeed, it's hard to believe that he is no more! I stand here on my ferry-boat and every minute I keep fancying that he will lift up his voice from the bank. He always used to come to the bank and call to me that I might not be afraid on the ferry. He used to get up from his bed at night on purpose for that. He was a kind soul. My God! how kindly and gracious! Many a mother is not so good to her child as Nikolay was to me! Lord, save his soul!"

Ieronim took hold of the rope, but turned to me again at once.

"And such a lofty intelligence, your honour," he said in a vibrating voice. "Such a sweet and harmonious tongue! Just as they will sing immediately at early matins: 'Oh lovely! oh sweet is Thy Voice!' Besides all other human qualities, he had, too, an extraordinary gift!"

"What gift?" I asked.

The monk scrutinized me, and as though he had convinced himself that he could trust me with a secret, he laughed good-humouredly.

"He had a gift for writing hymns of praise," he said. "It was a marvel, sir; you couldn't call it anything else! You would be amazed if I tell you about it. Our Father Archimandrite comes from Moscow, the Father Sub-Prior studied at the Kazan academy, we have wise monks and elders, but, would you believe it, no one could write them; while Nikolay, a simple monk, a deacon, had not studied anywhere, and had not even any outer appearance of it, but he wrote them! A marvel! A real marvel!" Ieronim clasped his hands and, completely forgetting the rope, went on eagerly:

"The Father Sub-Prior has great difficulty in composing sermons; when he wrote the history of the monastery he worried all the brotherhood and drove a dozen times to town, while Nikolay wrote canticles! Hymns of praise! That's a very different thing from a sermon or a history!"

"Is it difficult to write them?" I asked.

"There's great difficulty!" Ieronim wagged his head. "You can do nothing by wisdom and holiness if God has not given you the gift. The monks who don't understand argue that you only need to know the life of the saint for whom you are writing the hymn, and to make it harmonize with the other hymns of praise. But that's a mistake, sir. Of course, anyone who writes canticles must know the life of the saint to perfection, to the least trivial detail. To be sure, one must make them harmonize with the other canticles and know where to begin and what to write about. To give you an instance, the first response begins everywhere with 'the chosen' or 'the elect.' The first line must always begin with the 'angel.' In the canticle of praise to Jesus the Most Sweet, if you are interested in the subject, it begins like this: 'Of angels Creator and Lord of all powers!' In the canticle to the Holy Mother of God: 'Of angels the foremost sent down from on high,' to Nikolay, the Wonder-worker - 'An angel in semblance, though in substance a man,' and so on. Everywhere you begin with the angel. Of course, it would be impossible without making them harmonize, but the lives of the saints and conformity with the others is not what matters; what matters is the beauty and sweetness of it. Everything must be harmonious, brief and complete. There must be in every line softness, graciousness and tenderness; not one word should be harsh or rough or unsuitable. It must be written so that the worshipper may rejoice at heart and weep, while his mind is stirred and he is thrown into a tremor. In the canticle to the Holy Mother are the words: 'Rejoice, O Thou too high for human thought to reach! Rejoice, O Thou too deep for angels' eyes to fathom!' In another place in the same canticle: 'Rejoice, O tree that bearest the fair fruit of light that is the food of the faithful! Rejoice, O tree of gracious spreading shade, under which there is shelter for multitudes!' "

Ieronim hid his face in his hands, as though frightened at something or overcome with shame, and shook his head.

"Tree that bearest the fair fruit of light . . . tree of gracious spreading shade. . . ." he muttered. "To think that a man should find words like those! Such a power is a gift from God! For brevity he packs many thoughts into one phrase, and how smooth and complete it all is! 'Light-radiating torch to all that be . . .' comes in the canticle to Jesus the Most Sweet. 'Light-radiating!' There is no such word in conversation or in books, but you see he invented it, he found it in his mind! Apart from the smoothness and grandeur of language, sir, every line must be beautified in every way, there must be flowers and lightning and wind and sun and all the objects of the visible world. And every exclamation ought to be put so as to be smooth and easy for the ear. 'Rejoice, thou flower of heavenly growth!' comes in the hymn to Nikolay the Wonder-worker. It's not simply 'heavenly flower,' but 'flower of heavenly growth.' It's smoother so and sweet to the ear. That was just as Nikolay wrote it! Exactly like that! I can't tell you how he used to write!"

"Well, in that case it is a pity he is dead," I said; "but let us get on, father. or we shall be late."

Ieronim started and ran to the rope; they were beginning to peal all the bells. Probably the procession was already going on near the monastery, for all the dark space behind the tar barrels was now dotted with moving lights.

"Did Nikolay print his hymns?" I asked Ieronim.

"How could he print them?" he sighed. "And indeed, it would be strange to print them. What would be the object? No one in the monastery takes any interest in them. They don't like them. They knew Nikolay wrote them, but they let it pass unnoticed. No one esteems new writings nowadays, sir!"

"Were they prejudiced against him?"

"Yes, indeed. If Nikolay had been an elder perhaps the brethren would have been interested, but he wasn't forty, you know. There were some who laughed and even thought his writing a sin."

"What did he write them for?"

"Chiefly for his own comfort. Of all the brotherhood, I was the only one who read his hymns. I used to go to him in secret, that no one else might know of it, and he was glad that I took an interest in them. He would embrace me, stroke my head, speak to me in caressing words as to a little child. He would shut his cell, make me sit down beside him, and begin to read. . . ."

Ieronim left the rope and came up to me.

"We were dear friends in a way," he whispered, looking at me with shining eyes. 'Where he went I would go. If I were not there he would miss me. And he cared more for me than for anyone, and all because I used to weep over his hymns. It makes me sad to remember. Now I feel just like an orphan or a widow. You know, in our monastery they are all good people, kind and pious, but . . . there is no one with softness and refinement, they are just like peasants. They all speak loudly, and tramp heavily when they walk; they are noisy, they clear their throats, but Nikolay always talked softly, caressingly, and if he noticed that anyone was asleep or praying he would slip by like a fly or a gnat. His face was tender, compassionate. . . ."

Ieronim heaved a deep sigh and took hold of the rope again. We were by now approaching the bank. We floated straight out of the darkness and stillness of the river into an enchanted realm, full of stifling smoke, crackling lights and uproar. By now one could distinctly see people moving near the tar barrels. The flickering of the lights gave a strange, almost fantastic, expression to their figures and red faces. From time to time one caught among the heads and faces a glimpse of a horse's head motionless as though cast in copper.

"They'll begin singing the Easter hymn directly, . . ." said Ieronim, "and Nikolay is gone; there is no one to appreciate it. . . . There was nothing written dearer to him than that hymn. He used to take in every word! You'll be there, sir, so notice what is sung; it takes your breath away!"

"Won't you be in church, then?"

"I can't; . . . I have to work the ferry. . . ."

"But won't they relieve you?"

"I don't know. . . . I ought to have been relieved at eight; but, as you see, they don't come!. . . And I must own I should have liked to be in the church. . . ."

"Are you a monk?"

"Yes . . . that is, I am a lay-brother."

The ferry ran into the bank and stopped. I thrust a five-kopeck piece into Ieronim's hand for taking me across and jumped on land. Immediately a cart with a boy and a sleeping woman in it drove creaking onto the ferry. Ieronim, with a faint glow from the lights on his figure, pressed on the rope, bent down to it, and started the ferry back. . . .

I took a few steps through mud, but a little farther walked on a soft freshly trodden path. This path led to the dark monastery gates, that looked like a cavern through a cloud of smoke, through a disorderly crowd of people, unharnessed horses, carts and chaises. All this crowd was rattling, snorting, laughing, and the crimson light and wavering shadows from the smoke flickered over it all. . . . A perfect chaos! And in this hubbub the people yet found room to load a little cannon and to sell cakes. There was no less commotion on the other side of the wall in the monastery precincts, but there was more regard for decorum and order. Here there was a smell of juniper and incense. They talked loudly, but there was no sound of laughter or snorting. Near the tombstones and crosses people pressed close to one another with Easter cakes and bundles in their arms. Apparently many had come from a long distance for their cakes to be blessed and now were exhausted. Young lay brothers, making a metallic sound with their boots, ran busily along the iron slabs that paved the way from the monastery gates to the church door. They were busy and shouting on the belfry, too.

"What a restless night!" I thought. "How nice!"

One was tempted to see the same unrest and sleeplessness in all nature, from the night darkness to the iron slabs, the crosses on the tombs and the trees under which the people were moving to and fro. But nowhere was the excitement and restlessness so marked as in the church. An unceasing struggle was going on in the entrance between the inflowing stream and the outflowing stream. Some were going in, others going out and soon coming back again to stand still for a little and begin moving again. People were scurrying from place to place, lounging about as though they were looking for something. The stream flowed from the entrance all round the church, disturbing even the front rows, where persons of weight and dignity were standing. There could be no thought of concentrated prayer. There were no prayers at all, but a sort of continuous, childishly irresponsible joy, seeking a pretext to break out and vent itself in some movement, even in senseless jostling and shoving.

The same unaccustomed movement is striking in the Easter service itself. The altar gates are flung wide open, thick clouds of incense float in the air near the candelabra; wherever one looks there are lights, the gleam and splutter of candles. . . . There is no reading; restless and lighthearted singing goes on to the end without ceasing. After each hymn the clergy change their vestments and come out to burn the incense, which is repeated every ten minutes.

I had no sooner taken a place, when a wave rushed from in front and forced me back. A tall thick-set deacon walked before me with a long red candle; the grey-headed archimandrite in his golden mitre hurried after him with the censer. When they had vanished from sight the crowd squeezed me back to my former position. But ten minutes had not passed before a new wave burst on me, and again the deacon appeared. This time he was followed by the Father Sub-Prior, the man who, as Ieronim had told me, was writing the history of the monastery.

As I mingled with the crowd and caught the infection of the universal joyful excitement, I felt unbearably sore on Ieronim's account. Why did they not send someone to relieve him? Why could not someone of less feeling and less susceptibility go on the ferry? 'Lift up thine eyes, O Sion, and look around,' they sang in the choir, 'for thy children have come to thee as to a beacon of divine light from north and south, and from east and from the sea. . . .'

I looked at the faces; they all had a lively expression of triumph, but not one was listening to what was being sung and taking it in, and not one was 'holding his breath.' Why was not Ieronim released? I could fancy Ieronim standing meekly somewhere by the wall, bending forward and hungrily drinking in the beauty of the holy phrase. All this that glided by the ears of the people standing by me he would have eagerly drunk in with his delicately sensitive soul, and would have been spell-bound to ecstasy, to holding his breath, and there would not have been a man happier than he in all the church. Now he was plying to and fro over the dark river and grieving for his dead friend and brother.

The wave surged back. A stout smiling monk, playing with his rosary and looking round behind him, squeezed sideways by me, making way for a lady in a hat and velvet cloak. A monastery servant hurried after the lady, holding a chair over our heads.

I came out of the church. I wanted to have a look at the dead Nikolay, the unknown canticle writer. I walked about the monastery wall, where there was a row of cells, peeped into several windows, and, seeing nothing, came back again. I do not regret now that I did not see Nikolay; God knows, perhaps if I had seen him I should have lost the picture my imagination paints for me now. I imagine the lovable poetical figure solitary and not understood, who went out at nights to call to Ieronim over the water, and filled his hymns with flowers, stars and sunbeams, as a pale timid man with soft mild melancholy features. His eyes must have shone, not only with intelligence, but with kindly tenderness and that hardly restrained childlike enthusiasm which I could hear in Ieronim's voice when he quoted to me passages from the hymns.

When we came out of church after mass it was no longer night. The morning was beginning. The stars had gone out and the sky was a morose greyish blue. The iron slabs, the tombstones and the buds on the trees were covered with dew There was a sharp freshness in the air. Outside the precincts I did not find the same animated scene as I had beheld in the night. Horses and men looked exhausted, drowsy, scarcely moved, while nothing was left of the tar barrels but heaps of black ash. When anyone is exhausted and sleepy he fancies that nature, too, is in the same condition. It seemed to me that the trees and the young grass were asleep. It seemed as though even the bells were not pealing so loudly and gaily as at night. The restlessness was over, and of the excitement nothing was left but a pleasant weariness, a longing for sleep and warmth.

Now I could see both banks of the river; a faint mist hovered over it in shifting masses. There was a harsh cold breath from the water. When I jumped on to the ferry, a chaise and some two dozen men and women were standing on it already. The rope, wet and as I fancied drowsy, stretched far away across the broad river and in places disappeared in the white mist.

"Christ is risen! Is there no one else?" asked a soft voice.

I recognized the voice of Ieronim. There was no darkness now to hinder me from seeing the monk. He was a tall narrow-shouldered man of five-and-thirty, with large rounded features, with half-closed listless-looking eyes and an unkempt wedge shaped beard. He had an extraordinarily sad and exhausted look.

"They have not relieved you yet?" I asked in surprise.

"Me?" he answered, turning to me his chilled and dewy face with a smile. "There is no one to take my place now till morning. They'll all be going to the Father Archimandrite's to break the fast directly."

With the help of a little peasant in a hat of reddish fur that looked like the little wooden tubs in which honey is sold, he threw his weight on the rope; they gasped simultaneously, and the ferry started.

We floated across, disturbing on the way the lazily rising mist. Everyone was silent. Ieronim worked mechanically with one hand. He slowly passed his mild lustreless eyes over us; then his glance rested on the rosy face of a young merchant's wife with black eyebrows, who was standing on the ferry beside me silently shrinking from the mist that wrapped her about. He did not take his eyes off her face all the way.

There was little that was masculine in that prolonged gaze. It seemed to me that Ieronim was looking in the woman's face for the soft and tender features of his dead friend.

# LADIES

Fyodor Petrovitch the Director of Elementary Schools in the N. District, who considered himself a just and generous man, was one day interviewing in his office a schoolmaster called Vremensky.

"No, Mr. Vremensky," he was saying, "your retirement is inevitable. You cannot continue your work as a schoolmaster with a voice like that! How did you come to lose it?"

"I drank cold beer when I was in a perspiration. . ." hissed the schoolmaster.

"What a pity! After a man has served fourteen years, such a calamity all at once! The idea of a career being ruined by such a trivial thing. What are you intending to do now?"

The schoolmaster made no answer.

"Are you a family man?" asked the director.

"A wife and two children, your Excellency . . ." hissed the schoolmaster.

A silence followed. The director got up from the table and walked to and fro in perturbation.

"I cannot think what I am going to do with you!" he said. "A teacher you cannot be, and you are not yet entitled to a pension. . . . To abandon you to your fate, and leave you to do the best you can, is rather awkward. We look on you as one of our men, you have served fourteen years, so it is our business to help you. . . . But how are we to help you? What can I do for you? Put yourself in my place: what can I do for you?"

A silence followed; the director walked up and down, still thinking, and Vremensky, overwhelmed by his trouble, sat on the edge of his chair, and he, too, thought. All at once the director began beaming, and even snapped his fingers.

"I wonder I did not think of it before!" he began rapidly. "Listen, this is what I can offer you. Next week our secretary at the Home is retiring. If you like, you can have his place! There you are!"

Vremensky, not expecting such good fortune, beamed too.

"That's capital," said the director. "Write the application to-day."

Dismissing Vremensky, Fyodor Petrovitch felt relieved and even gratified: the bent figure of the hissing schoolmaster was no longer confronting him, and it was agreeable to recognize that in offering a vacant post to Vremensky he had acted fairly and conscientiously, like a good-hearted and thoroughly decent person. But this agreeable state of mind did not last long. When he went home and sat down to dinner his wife, Nastasya Ivanovna, said suddenly:

"Oh yes, I was almost forgetting! Nina Sergeyevna came to see me yesterday and begged for your interest on behalf of a young man. I am told there is a vacancy in our Home...."

Yes, but the post has already been promised to someone else," said the director, and he frowned. "And you know my rule: I never give posts through patronage."

"I know, but for Nina Sergeyevna, I imagine, you might make an exception. She loves us as though we were relations, and we have never done anything for her. And don't think of refusing, Fedya! You will wound both her and me with your whims."

"Who is it that she is recommending?"

"Polzuhin!"

"What Polzuhin? Is it that fellow who played Tchatsky at the party on New Year's Day? Is it that gentleman? Not on any account!"

The director left off eating.

"Not on any account!" he repeated. "Heaven preserve us!"

"But why not?"

"Understand, my dear, that if a young man does not set to work directly, but through women, he must be good for nothing! Why doesn't he come to me himself?"

After dinner the director lay on the sofa in his study and began reading the letters and newspapers he had received.

"Dear Fyodor Petrovitch," wrote the wife of the Mayor of the town. "You once said that I knew the human heart and understood people. Now you have an opportunity of verifying this in practice. K. N. Polzuhin, whom I know to be an excellent young man, will call upon you in a day or two to ask you for the post of secretary at our Home. He is a very nice youth. If you take an interest in him you will be convinced of it." And so on.

"On no account!" was the director's comment. "Heaven preserve me!"

After that, not a day passed without the director's receiving letters recommending Polzuhin. One fine morning Polzuhin himself, a stout young man with a close-shaven face like a jockey's, in a new black suit, made his appearance. . . .

"I see people on business not here but at the office," said the director drily, on hearing his request.

"Forgive me, your Excellency, but our common acquaintances advised me to come here."

"H'm!" growled the director, looking with hatred at the pointed toes of the young man's shoes. "To the best of my belief your father is a man of property and you are not in want," he said. "What induces you to ask for this post? The salary is very trifling!"

"It's not for the sake of the salary. . . . It's a government post, any way . . ."

"H'm. . . . It strikes me that within a month you will be sick of the job and you will give it up, and meanwhile there are candidates for whom it would be a career for life. There are poor men for whom . . ."

"I shan't get sick of it, your Excellency," Polzuhin interposed. "Honour bright, I will do my best!"

It was too much for the director.

"Tell me," he said, smiling contemptuously, "why was it you didn't apply to me direct but thought fitting instead to trouble ladies as a preliminary?"

"I didn't know that it would be disagreeable to you," Polzuhin answered, and he was embarrassed. "But, your Excellency, if you attach no significance to letters of recommendation, I can give you a testimonial. . . ."

He drew from his pocket a letter and handed it to the director. At the bottom of the testimonial, which was written in official language and handwriting, stood the signature of the Governor. Everything pointed to the Governor's having signed it unread, simply to get rid of some importunate lady.

"There's nothing for it, I bow to his authority. . . I obey . . ." said the director, reading the testimonial, and he heaved a sigh.

"Send in your application to-morrow. . . . There's nothing to be done. . . ."

And when Polzuhin had gone out, the director abandoned himself to a feeling of repulsion.

"Sneak!" he hissed, pacing from one corner to the other. "He has got what he wanted, one way or the other, the good-for-nothing toady! Making up to the ladies! Reptile! Creature!"

The director spat loudly in the direction of the door by which Polzuhin had departed, and was immediately overcome with embarrassment, for at that moment a lady, the wife of the Superintendent of the Provincial Treasury, walked in at the door.

"I've come for a tiny minute . . . a tiny minute. . ." began the lady. "Sit down, friend, and listen to me attentively. . . . Well, I've been told you have a post vacant. . . . To-day or to-morrow you will receive a visit from a young man called Polzuhin. . . ."

The lady chattered on, while the director gazed at her with lustreless, stupefied eyes like a man on the point of fainting, gazed and smiled from politeness.

And the next day when Vremensky came to his office it was a long time before the director could bring himself to tell the truth. He hesitated, was incoherent, and could not think how to begin or what to say. He wanted to apologize to the schoolmaster, to tell him the whole truth, but his tongue halted like a drunkard's, his ears burned, and he was suddenly overwhelmed with vexation and resentment that he should have to play such an absurd part - in his own office, before his subordinate. He suddenly brought his fist down on the table, leaped up, and shouted angrily:

"I have no post for you! I have not, and that's all about it! Leave me in peace! Don't worry me! Be so good as to leave me alone!"

And he walked out of the office.

# STRONG IMPRESSIONS

It happened not so long ago in the Moscow circuit court. The jurymen, left in the court for the night, before lying down to sleep fell into conversation about strong impressions. They were led to this discussion by recalling a witness who, by his own account, had begun to stammer and had gone grey owing to a terrible moment. The jurymen decided that before going to sleep, each one of them should ransack among his memories and tell something that had happened to him. Man's life is brief, but yet there is no man who cannot boast that there have been terrible moments in his past.

One juryman told the story of how he was nearly drowned; another described how, in a place where there were neither doctors nor chemists, he had one night poisoned his own son through giving him zinc vitriol by mistake for soda. The child did not die, but the father nearly went out of his mind. A third, a man not old but in bad health, told how he had twice attempted to commit suicide: the first time by shooting himself and the second time by throwing himself before a train.

The fourth, a foppishly dressed, fat little man, told us the following story:

"I was not more than twenty-two or twenty-three when I fell head over ears in love with my present wife and made her an offer. Now I could with pleasure thrash myself for my early marriage, but at the time, I don't know what would have become of me if Natasha had refused me. My love was absolutely the real thing, just as it is described in novels - frantic, passionate, and so on. My happiness overwhelmed me and I did not know how to get away from it, and I bored my father and my friends and the servants, continually talking about the fervour of my passion. Happy people are the most sickening bores. I was a fearful bore; I feel ashamed of it even now. . . .

"Among my friends there was in those days a young man who was beginning his career as a lawyer. Now he is a lawyer known all over Russia; in those days he was only just beginning to gain recognition and was not rich and famous enough to be entitled to cut an old friend when he met him. I used to go and see him once or twice a week. We used to loll on sofas and begin discussing philosophy.

"One day I was lying on his sofa, arguing that there was no more ungrateful profession than that of a lawyer. I tried to prove that as soon as the examination of witnesses is over the court can easily dispense with both the counsels for the prosecution and for the defence, because they are neither of them necessary and are only in the way. If a grown-up juryman, morally and mentally sane, is convinced that the ceiling is white, or that Ivanov is guilty, to struggle with that conviction and to vanquish it is beyond the power of any Demosthenes. Who can convince me that I have a red moustache when I know that it is black? As I listen to an orator I may perhaps grow sentimental and weep, but my fundamental conviction, based for the most part on unmistakable evidence and fact, is not changed in the least. My lawyer maintained that I was young and foolish and that I was talking childish nonsense. In his opinion, for one thing, an obvious fact becomes still more obvious through light being thrown upon it by conscientious, well-informed people; for another, talent is an elemental force, a hurricane capable of turning even stones to dust, let alone such trifles as the convictions of artisÊans and merchants of the second guild. It is as hard for human weakness to struggle against talent as to look at the sun without winking, or to stop the wind. One simple mortal by the power of the word turns thousands of convinced savages to Christianity; Odysseus was a man of the firmest convictions, but he succumbed to theSyrens, and so on. All history consists of similar examples, and in life they are met with at every turn; and so it is bound to be, or the intelligent and talented man would have no superiority over the stupid and incompetent.

"I stuck to my point, and went on maintaining that convictions are stronger than any talent, though, frankly speaking, I could not have defined exactly what I meant by conviction or what I meant by talent. Most likely I simply talked for the sake of talking.

" 'Take you, for example,' said the lawyer. 'You are convinced at this moment that your fiancée is an angel and that there is not a man in the whole town happier than you. But I tell you: ten or twenty minutes would be enough for me to make you sit down to this table and write to your fiancée, breaking off your engagement.

"I laughed.

" 'Don't laugh, I am speaking seriously,' said my friend. 'If I choose, in twenty minutes you will be happy at the thought that you need not get married. Goodness knows what talent I have, but you are not one of the strong sort.'

" 'Well, try it on!' said I.

" 'No, what for? I am only telling you this. You are a good boy and it would be cruel to subject you to such an experiment. And besides I am not in good form to-day.'

"We sat down to supper. The wine and the thought of Natasha, my beloved, flooded my whole being with youth and happiness. My happiness was so boundless that the lawyer sitting opposite to me with his green eyes seemed to me an unhappy man, so small, so grey. . . .

" 'Do try!' I persisted. 'Come, I entreat you!

"The lawyer shook his head and frowned. Evidently I was beginning to bore him.

" 'I know,' he said, 'after my experiment you will say, thank you, and will call me your saviour; but you see I must think of your fiancée too. She loves you; your jilting her would make her suffer. And what a charming creature she is! I envy you.'

"The lawyer sighed, sipped his wine, and began talking of how charming my Natasha was. He had an extraordinary gift of description. He could knock you off a regular string of words about a woman's eyelashes or her little finger. I listened to him with relish.

" 'I have seen a great many women in my day,' he said, 'but I give you my word of honour, I speak as a friend, your Natasha Andreyevna is a pearl, a rare girl. Of course she has her defects - many of them, in fact, if you like - but still she is fascinating.'

"And the lawyer began talking of my fiancée's defects. Now I understand very well that he was talking of women in general, of their weak points in general, but at the time it seemed to me that he was talking only of Natasha. He went into ecstasies over her turn-up nose, her shrieks, her shrill laugh, her airs and graces, precisely all the things I so disliked in her. All that was, to his thinking, infinitely sweet, graceful, and feminine.

"Without my noticing it, he quickly passed from his enthusiastic tone to one of fatherly admonition, and then to a light and derisive one. . . . There was no presiding judge and no one to check the diffusiveness of the lawyer. I had not time to open my mouth, besides, what could I say? What my friend said was not new, it was what everyone has known for ages, and the whole venom lay not in what he said, but in the damnable form he put it in. It really was beyond anything!

"As I listened to him then I learned that the same word has thousands of shades of meaning according to the tone in which it is pronounced, and the form which is given to the sentence. Of course I cannot reproduce the tone or the form; I can only say that as I listened to my friend and walked up and down the room, I was moved to resentment, indignation, and contempt together with him. I even believed him when with tears in his eyes he informed me that I was a great man, that I was worthy of a better fate, that I was destined to achieve something in the future which marriage would hinder!

" 'My friend!' he exclaimed, pressing my hand. 'I beseech you, I adjure you: stop before it is too late. Stop! May Heaven preserve you from this strange, cruel mistake! My friend, do not ruin your youth!'

"Believe me or not, as you choose, but the long and the short of it was that I sat down to the table and wrote to my fiancée, breaking off the engagement. As I wrote I felt relieved that it was not yet too late to rectify my mistake. Sealing the letter, I hastened out into the street to post it. The lawyer himself came with me.

" 'Excellent! Capital!' he applauded me as my letter to Natasha disappeared into the darkness of the box. 'I congratulate you with all my heart. I am glad for you.'

"After walking a dozen paces with me the lawyer went on:

" 'Of course, marriage has its good points. I, for instance, belong to the class of people to whom marriage and home life is everything.'

"And he proceeded to describe his life, and lay before me all the hideousness of a solitary bachelor existence.

"He spoke with enthusiasm of his future wife, of the sweets of ordinary family life, and was so eloquent, so sincere in his ecstasies that by the time we had reached his door, I was in despair.

" 'What are you doing to me, you horrible man?' I said, gasping. 'You have ruined me! Why did you make me write that cursed letter? I love her, I love her!'

"And I protested my love. I was horrified at my conduct which now seemed to me wild and senseless. It is impossible, gentlemen, to imagine a more violent emotion than I experienced at that moment. Oh, what I went through, what I suffered! If some kind person had thrust a revolver into my hand at that moment, I should have put a bullet through my brains with pleasure.

" 'Come, come . . .' said the lawyer, slapping me on the shoulder, and he laughed. 'Give over crying. The letter won't reach your fiancée. It was not you who wrote the address but I, and I muddled it so they won't be able to make it out at the post-office. It will be a lesson to you not to argue about what you don't understand.'

"Now, gentlemen, I leave it to the next to speak."

The fifth juryman settled himself more comfortably, and had just opened his mouth to begin his story when we heard the clock strike on Spassky Tower.

"Twelve . . ." one of the jurymen counted. "And into which class, gentlemen, would you put the emotions that are being experienced now by the man we are trying? He, that murderer, is spending the night in a convict cell here in the court, sitting or lying down and of course not sleeping, and throughout the whole sleepless night listening to that chime. What is he thinking of? What visions are haunting him?"

And the jurymen all suddenly forgot about strong impressions; what their companion who had once written a letter to his Natasha had suffered seemed unimportant, even not amusing; and no one said anything more; they began quietly and in silence lying down to sleep.

# A GENTLEMAN FRIEND

The charming Vanda, or, as she was described in her passport, the "Honourable Citizen Nastasya Kanavkin," found herself, on leaving the hospital, in a position she had never been in before: without a home to go to or a farthing in her pocket. What was she to do?

The first thing she did was to visit a pawn-broker's and pawn her turquoise ring, her one piece of jewellery. They gave her a rouble for the ring . . . but what can you get for a rouble? You can't buy for that sum a fashionable short jacket, nor a big hat, nor a pair of bronze shoes, and without those things she had a feeling of being, as it were, undressed. She felt as though the very horses and dogs were staring and laughing at the plainness of her dress. And clothes were all she thought about: the question what she should eat and where she should sleep did not trouble her in the least.

"If only I could meet a gentleman friend," she thought to herself, "I could get some money. . . . There isn't one who would refuse me, I know. . ."

But no gentleman she knew came her way. It would be easy enough to meet them in the evening at the "Renaissance," but they wouldn't let her in at the "Renaissance "in that shabby dress and with no hat. What was she to do?

After long hesitation, when she was sick of walking and sitting and thinking, Vanda made up her mind to fall back on her last resource: to go straight to the lodgings of some gentleman friend and ask for money.

She pondered which to go to. "Misha is out of the question; he's a married man. . . . The old chap with the red hair will be at his office at this time. . ."

Vanda remembered a dentist, called Finkel, a converted Jew, who six months ago had given her a bracelet, and on whose head she had once emptied a glass of beer at the supper at the German Club. She was awfully pleased at the thought of Finkel.

"He'll be sure to give it me, if only I find him at home," she thought, as she walked in his direction. "If he doesn't, I'll smash all the lamps in the house."

Before she reached the dentist's door she thought out her plan of action: she would run laughing up the stairs, dash into the dentist's room and demand twenty-five roubles. But as she touched the bell, this plan seemed to vanish from her mind of itself. Vanda began suddenly feeling frightened and nervous, which was not at all her way. She was bold and saucy enough at drinking parties, but now, dressed in everyday clothes, feeling herself in the position of an ordinary person asking a favour, who might be refused admittance, she felt suddenly timid and humiliated. She was ashamed and frightened.

"Perhaps he has forgotten me by now," she thought, hardly daring to pull the bell. "And how can I go up to him in such a dress, looking like a beggar or some working girl?"

And she rang the bell irresolutely.

She heard steps coming: it was the porter.

"Is the doctor at home?" she asked.

She would have been glad now if the porter had said "No," but the latter, instead of answering ushered her into the hall, and helped her off with her coat. The staircase impressed her as luxurious, and magnificent, but of all its splendours what caught her eye most was an immense looking-glass, in which she saw a ragged figure without a fashionable jacket, without a big hat, and without bronze shoes. And it seemed strange to Vanda that, now that she was humbly dressed and looked like a laundress or sewing girl, she felt ashamed, and no trace of her usual boldness and sauciness remained, and in her own mind she no longer thought of herself as Vanda, but as the Nastasya Kanavkin she used to be in the old days. . . .

"Walk in, please," said a maidservant, showing her into the consulting-room. "The doctor will be here in a minute. Sit down."

Vanda sank into a soft arm-chair.

"I'll ask him to lend it me," she thought; "that will be quite proper, for, after all, I do know him. If only that servant would go. I don't like to ask before her. What does she want to stand there for?"

Five minutes later the door opened and Finkel came in. He was a tall, dark Jew, with fat cheeks and bulging eyes. His cheeks, his eyes, his chest, his body, all of him was so well fed, so loathsome and repellent! At the "Renaissance" and the German Club he had usually been rather tipsy, and would spend his money freely on women, and be very long-suffering and patient with their pranks (when Vanda, for instance, poured the beer over his head, he simply smiled and shook his finger at her): now he had a cross, sleepy expression and looked solemn and frigid like a police captain, and he kept chewing something.

"What can I do for you?" he asked, without looking at Vanda.

Vanda looked at the serious countenance of the maid and the smug figure of Finkel, who apparently did not recognize her, and she turned red.

"What can I do for you?" repeated the dentist a little irritably.

"I've got toothache," murmured Vanda.

"Aha! . . . Which is the tooth? Where?"

Vanda remembered she had a hole in one of her teeth.

"At the bottom . . . on the right . . ." she said.

"Hm! . . . Open your mouth."

Finkel frowned and, holding his breath, began examining the tooth.

"Does it hurt?" he asked, digging into it with a steel instrument.

"Yes," Vanda replied, untruthfully.

"Shall I remind him?" she was wondering. "He would be sure to remember me. But that servant! Why will she stand there?"

Finkel suddenly snorted like a steam engine right into her mouth, and said:

"I don't advise you to have it stopped. That tooth will never be worth keeping anyhow."

After probing the tooth a little more and soiling Vanda's lips and gums with his tobacco-stained fingers, he held his breath again, and put something cold into her mouth. Vanda suddenly felt a sharp pain, cried out, and clutched at Finkel's hand.

"It's all right, it's all right," he muttered; "don't you be frightened! That tooth would have been no use to you, anyway . . . you must be brave. . ."

And his tobacco-stained fingers, smeared with blood, held up the tooth to her eyes, while the maid approached and put a basin to her mouth.

"You wash out your mouth with cold water when you get home, and that will stop the bleeding," said Finkel.

He stood before her with the air of a man expecting her to go, waiting to be left in peace.

"Good-day," she said, turning towards the door.

"Hm! . . . and how about my fee?" enquired Finkel, in a jesting tone.

"Oh, yes!" Vanda remembered, blushing, and she handed the Jew the rouble that had been given her for her ring.

When she got out into the street she felt more overwhelmed with shame than before, but now it was not her poverty she was ashamed of. She was unconscious now of not having a big hat and a fashionable jacket. She walked along the street, spitting blood, and brooding on her life, her ugly, wretched life, and the insults she had endured, and would have to endure to-morrow, and next week, and all her life, up to the very day of her death.

"Oh! how awful it is! My God, how fearful!"

Next day, however, she was back at the "Renaissance," and dancing there. She had on an enormous new red hat, a new fashionable jacket, and bronze shoes. And she was taken out to supper by a young merchant up from Kazan.

# A HAPPY MAN

The passenger train is just starting from Bologoe, the junction on the Petersburg-Moscow line. In a second-class smoking compartment five passengers sit dozing, shrouded in the twilight of the carriage. They had just had a meal, and now, snugly ensconced in their seats, they are trying to go to sleep. Stillness.

The door opens and in there walks a tall, lanky figure straight as a poker, with a ginger-coloured hat and a smart overcoat, wonderfully suggestive of a journalist in Jules Verne or on the comic stage.

The figure stands still in the middle of the compartment for a long while, breathing heavily, screwing up his eyes and peering at the seats.

"No, wrong again!" he mutters. "What the deuce! It's positively revolting! No, the wrong one again!"

One of the passengers stares at the figure and utters a shout of joy:

"Ivan Alexyevitch! what brings you here? Is it you?"

The poker-like gentleman starts, stares blankly at the passenger, and recognizing him claps his hands with delight.

"Ha! Pyotr Petrovitch," he says. "How many summers, how many winters! I didn't know you were in this train."

"How are you getting on?"

"I am all right; the only thing is, my dear fellow, I've lost my compartment and I simply can't find it. What an idiot I am! I ought to be thrashed!"

The poker-like gentleman sways a little unsteadily and sniggers.

"Queer things do happen!" he continues. "I stepped out just after the second bell to get a glass of brandy. I got it, of course. Well, I thought, since it's a long way to the next station, it would be as well to have a second glass. While I was thinking about it and drinking it the third bell rang. . . . I ran like mad and jumped into the first carriage. I am an idiot! I am the son of a hen!"

"But you seem in very good spirits," observes Pyotr Petrovitch. "Come and sit down! There's room and a welcome."

"No, no. . . . I'm off to look for my carriage. Good-bye!"

"You'll fall between the carriages in the dark if you don't look out! Sit down, and when we get to a station you'll find your own compartment. Sit down!"

Ivan Alexyevitch heaves a sigh and irresolutely sits down facing Pyotr Petrovitch. He is visibly excited, and fidgets as though he were sitting on thorns.

"Where are you travelling to?" Pyotr Petrovitch enquires.

"I? Into space. There is such a turmoil in my head that I couldn't tell where I am going myself. I go where fate takes me. Ha-ha! My dear fellow, have you ever seen a happy fool? No? Well, then, take a look at one. You behold the happiest of mortals! Yes! Don't you see something from my face?"

"Well, one can see you're a bit . . . a tiny bit so-so."

"I dare say I look awfully stupid just now. Ach! it's a pity I haven't a looking-glass, I should like to look at my counting-house. My dear fellow, I feel I am turning into an idiot, honour bright. Ha-ha! Would you believe it, I'm on my honeymoon. Am I not the son of a hen?"

"You? Do you mean to say you are married?"

"To-day, my dear boy. We came away straight after the wedding."

Congratulations and the usual questions follow. "Well, you are a fellow!" laughs Pyotr Petrovitch. "That's why you are rigged out such a dandy."

"Yes, indeed. . . . To complete the illusion, I've even sprinkled myself with scent. I am over my ears in vanity! No care, no thought, nothing but a sensation of something or other . . . deuce knows what to call it . . . beatitude or something? I've never felt so grand in my life!"

Ivan Alexyevitch shuts his eyes and waggles his head.

"I'm revoltingly happy," he says. "Just think; in a minute I shall go to my compartment. There on the seat near the window is sitting a being who is, so to say, devoted to you with her whole being. A little blonde with a little nose . . . little fingers. . . . My little darling! My angel! My little poppet! Phylloxera of my soul! And her little foot! Good God! A little foot not like our beetle-crushers, but something miniature, fairylike, allegorical. I could pick it up and eat it, that little foot! Oh, but you don't understand! You're a materialist, of course, you begin analyzing at once, and one thing and another. You are cold-hearted bachelors, that's what you are! When you get married you'll think of me. 'Where's Ivan Alexyevitch now?' you'll say. Yes; so in a minute I'm going to my compartment. There she is waiting for me with impatience . . . in joyful anticipation of my appearance. She'll have a smile to greet me. I sit down beside her and take her chin with my two fingers.

Ivan Alexyevitch waggles his head and goes off into a chuckle of delight.

"Then I lay my noddle on her shoulder and put my arm round her waist. Around all is silence, you know . . . poetic twilight. I could embrace the whole world at such a moment. Pyotr Petrovitch, allow me to embrace you!"

"Delighted, I'm sure." The two friends embrace while the passengers laugh in chorus. And the happy bridegroom continues:

"And to complete the idiocy, or, as the novelists say, to complete the illusion, one goes to the refreshment-room and tosses off two or three glasses. And then something happens in your head and your heart, finer than you can read of in a fairy tale. I am a man of no importance, but I feel as though I were limitless. I embrace the whole world!"

The passengers, looking at the tipsy and blissful bridegroom, are infected by his cheerfulness and no longer feel sleepy. Instead of one listener, Ivan Alexyevitch has now an audience of five. He wriggles and splutters, gesticulates, and prattles on without ceasing. He laughs and they all laugh.

"Gentlemen, gentlemen, don't think so much! Damn all this analysis! If you want a drink, drink, no need to philosophize as to whether it's bad for you or not. . . . Damn all this philosophy and psychology!"

The guard walks through the compartment.

"My dear fellow," the bridegroom addresses him, "when you pass through the carriage No. 209 look out for a lady in a grey hat with a white bird and tell her I'm here!"

"Yes, sir. Only there isn't a No. 209 in this train; there's 219!"

"Well, 219, then! It's all the same. Tell that lady, then, that her husband is all right!"

Ivan Alexyevitch suddenly clutches his head and groans:

"Husband. . . . Lady. . . . All in a minute! Husband. . . . Ha-ha! I am a puppy that needs thrashing, and here I am a husband! Ach, idiot! But think of her! . . . Yesterday she was a little girl, a midget . . . it s simply incredible!"

"Nowadays it really seems strange to see a happy man," observes one of the passengers; "one as soon expects to see a white elephant."

"Yes, and whose fault is it?" says Ivan Alexyevitch, stretching his long legs and thrusting out his feet with their very pointed toes. "If you are not happy it's your own fault! Yes, what else do you suppose it is? Man is the creator of his own happiness. If you want to be happy you will be, but you don't want to be! You obstinately turn away from happiness."

"Why, what next! How do you make that out?"

"Very simply. Nature has ordained that at a certain stage in his life man should love. When that time comes you should love like a house on fire, but you won't heed the dictates of nature, you keep waiting for something. What's more, it's laid down by law that the normal man should enter upon matrimony. There's no happiness without marriage. When the propitious moment has come, get married. There's no use in shilly-shallying. . . . But you don't get married, you keep waiting for something! Then the Scriptures tell us that 'wine maketh glad the heart of man.' . . . If you feel happy and you want to feel better still, then go to the refreshment bar and have a drink. The great thing is not to be too clever, but to follow the beaten track! The beaten track is a grand thing!"

"You say that man is the creator of his own happiness. How the devil is he the creator of it when a toothache or an ill-natured mother-in-law is enough to scatter his happiness to the winds? Everything depends on chance. If we had an accident at this moment you'd sing a different tune."

"Stuff and nonsense!" retorts the bridegroom. "Railway accidents only happen once a year. I'm not afraid of an accident, for there is no reason for one. Accidents are exceptional! Confound them! I don't want to talk of them! Oh, I believe we're stopping at a station."

"Where are you going now?" asks Pyotr Petrovitch. "To Moscow or somewhere further south?

"Why, bless you! How could I go somewhere further south, when I'm on my way to the north?"

"But Moscow isn't in the north."

"I know that, but we're on our way to Petersburg," says Ivan Alexyevitch.

"We are going to Moscow, mercy on us!"

"To Moscow? What do you mean?" says the bridegroom in amazement.

"It's queer. . . . For what station did you take your ticket?"

"For Petersburg."

"In that case I congratulate you. You've got into the wrong train."

There follows a minute of silence. The bridegroom gets up and looks blankly round the company.

"Yes, yes," Pyotr Petrovitch explains. "You must have jumped into the wrong train at Bologoe. . . . After your glass of brandy you succeeded in getting into the down-train "

Ivan Alexyevitch turns pale, clutches his head, and begins pacing rapidly about the carriage.

"Ach, idiot that I am!" he says in indignation. "Scoundrel! The devil devour me! Whatever am I to do now? Why, my wife is in that train! She's there all alone, expecting me, consumed by anxiety. Ach, I'm a motley fool!"

The bridegroom falls on the seat and writhes as though someone had trodden on his corns.

"I am un-unhappy man!" he moans. "What am I to do, what am I to do?"

"There, there!" the passengers try to console him. "It's all right. . . . You must telegraph to your wife and try to change into the Petersburg express. In that way you'll overtake her."

"The Petersburg express!" weeps the bridegroom, the creator of his own happiness. "And how am I to get a ticket for the Petersburg express? All my money is with my wife."

The passengers, laughing and whispering together, make a collection and furnish the happy man with funds.

# THE PRIVY COUNCILLOR

At the beginning of April in 1870 my mother, Klavdia Arhipovna, the widow of a lieutenant, received from her brother Ivan, a privy councillor in Petersburg, a letter in which, among other things, this passage occurred: "My liver trouble forces me to spend every summer abroad, and as I have not at the moment the money in hand for a trip to Marienbad, it is very possible, dear sister, that I may spend this summer with you at Kotchuevko...."

On reading the letter my mother turned pale and began trembling all over; then an expression of mingled tears and laughter came into her face. She began crying and laughing. This conflict of tears and laughter always reminds me of the flickering and spluttering of a brightly burning candle when one sprinkles it with water. Reading the letter once more, mother called together all the household, and in a voice broken with emotion began explaining to us that there had been four Gundasov brothers: one Gundasov had died as a baby; another had gone to the war, and he, too, was dead; the third, without offence to him be it said, was an actor; the fourth...

"The fourth has risen far above us," my mother brought out tearfully. "My own brother, we grew up together; and I am all of a tremble, all of a tremble!... A privy councillor with the rank of a general! How shall I meet him, my angel brother? What can I, a foolish, uneducated woman, talk to him about? It's fifteen years since I've seen him! Andryushenka," my mother turned to me, "you must rejoice, little stupid! It's a piece of luck for you that God is sending him to us!"

After we had heard a detailed history of the Gundasovs, there followed a fuss and bustle in the place such as I had been accustomed to see only before Christmas and Easter. The sky above and the water in the river were all that escaped; everything else was subjected to a merciless cleansing, scrubbing, painting. If the sky had been lower and smaller and the river had not flowed so swiftly, they would have scoured them, too, with bath brick and rubbed them, too, with tow. Our walls were as white as snow, but they were whitewashed; the floors were bright and shining, but they were washed every day. The cat Bobtail (as a small child I had cut off a good quarter of his tail with the knife used for chopping the sugar, and that was why he was called Bobtail) was carried off to the kitchen and put in charge of Anisya; Fedka was told that if any of the dogs came near the front-door "God would punish him." But no one was so badly treated as the poor sofas, easy-chairs, and rugs! They had never, before been so violently beaten as on this occasion in preparation for our visitor. My pigeons took fright at the loud thud of the sticks, and were continually flying up into the sky.

The tailor Spiridon, the only tailor in the whole district who ventured to make for the gentry, came over from Novostroevka. He was a hard-working capable man who did not drink and was not without a certain fancy and feeling for form, but yet he was an atrocious tailor. His work was ruined by hesitation. . . . The idea that his cut was not fashionable enough made him alter everything half a dozen times, walk all the way to the town simply to study the dandies, and in the end dress us in suits that even a caricaturist would have called *outre* and grotesque. We cut a dash in impossibly narrow trousers and in such short jackets that we always felt quite abashed in the presence of young ladies.

This Spiridon spent a long time taking my measure. He measured me all over lengthways and crossways, as though he meant to put hoops round me like a barrel; then he spent a long time noting down my measurements with a thick pencil on a bit of paper, and ticked off all the measurements with triangular signs. When he had finished with me he set to work on my tutor, Yegor Alexyevitch Pobyedimsky. My beloved tutor was then at the stage when young men watch the growth of their moustache and are critical of their clothes, and so you can imagine the devout awe with which Spiridon approached him. Yegor Alexyevitch had to throw back his head, to straddle his legs like an inverted V, first lift up his arms, then let them fall. Spiridon measured him several times, walking round him during the process like a love-sick pigeon round its mate, going down on one knee, bending double. . . . My mother, weary, exhausted by her exertions and heated by ironing, watched these lengthy proceedings, and said:

"Mind now, Spiridon, you will have to answer for it to God if you spoil the cloth! And it will be the worse for you if you don't make them fit!"

Mother's words threw Spiridon first into a fever, then into a perspiration, for he was convinced that he would not make them fit. He received one rouble twenty kopecks for making my suit, and for

Pobyedimsky's two roubles, but we provided the cloth, the lining, and the buttons. The price cannot be considered excessive, as Novostroevka was about seven miles from us, and the tailor came to fit us four times. When he came to try the things on and we squeezed ourselves into the tight trousers and jackets adorned with basting threads, mother always frowned contemptuously and expressed her surprise:

"Goodness knows what the fashions are coming to nowadays! I am positively ashamed to look at them. If brother were not used to Petersburg I would not get you fashionable clothes!"

Spiridon, relieved that the blame was thrown on the fashion and not on him, shrugged his shoulders and sighed, as though to say:

"There's no help for it; it's the spirit of the age!"

The excitement with which we awaited the arrival of our guest can only be compared with the strained suspense with which spiritualists wait from minute to minute the appearance of a ghost. Mother went about with a sick headache, and was continually melting into tears. I lost my appetite, slept badly, and did not learn my lessons. Even in my dreams I was haunted by an impatient longing to see a general - that is, a man with epaulettes and an embroidered collar sticking up to his ears, and with a naked sword in his hands, exactly like the one who hung over the sofa in the drawing-room and glared with terrible black eyes at everybody who dared to look at him. Pobyedimsky was the only one who felt himself in his element. He was neither terrified nor delighted, and merely from time to time, when he heard the history of the Gundasov family, said:

"Yes, it will be pleasant to have some one fresh to talk to."

My tutor was looked upon among us as an exceptional nature. He was a young man of twenty, with a pimply face, shaggy locks, a low forehead, and an unusually long nose. His nose was so big that when he wanted to look close at anything he had to put his head on one side like a bird. To our thinking, there was not a man in the province cleverer, more cultivated, or more stylish. He had left the high-school in the class next to the top, and had then entered a veterinary college, from which he was expelled before the end of the first half-year. The reason of his expulsion he carefully concealed, which enabled any one who wished to do so to look upon my instructor as an injured and to some extent a mysterious person. He spoke little, and only of intellectual subjects; he ate meat during the fasts, and looked with contempt and condescension on the life going on around him, which did not prevent him, however, from taking presents, such as suits of clothes, from my mother, and drawing funny faces with red teeth on my kites. Mother disliked him for his "pride," but stood in awe of his cleverness.

Our visitor did not keep us long waiting. At the beginning of May two wagon-loads of big boxes arrived from the station. These boxes looked so majestic that the drivers instinctively took off their hats as they lifted them down.

"There must be uniforms and gunpowder in those boxes," I thought.

Why "gunpowder"? Probably the conception of a general was closely connected in my mind with cannons and gunpowder.

When I woke up on the morning of the tenth of May, nurse told me in a whisper that "my uncle had come." I dressed rapidly, and, washing after a fashion, flew out of my bedroom without saying my prayers. In the vestibule I came upon a tall, solid gentleman with fashionable whiskers and a foppish-looking overcoat. Half dead with devout awe, I went up to him and, remembering the ceremonial mother had impressed upon me, I scraped my foot before him, made a very low bow, and craned forward to kiss his hand; but the gentleman did not allow me to kiss his hand: he informed me that he was not my uncle, but my uncle's footman, Pyotr. The appearance of this Pyotr, far better dressed than Pobyedimsky or me, excited in me the utmost astonishment, which, to tell the truth, has lasted to this day. Can such dignified, respectable people with stern and intellectual faces really be footmen? And what for?

Pyotr told me that my uncle was in the garden with my mother. I rushed into the garden.

Nature, knowing nothing of the history of the Gundasov family and the rank of my uncle, felt far more at ease and unconstrained than I. There was a clamour going on in the garden such as one only bears at fairs. Masses of starlings flitting through the air and hopping about the walks were noisily chattering as they hunted for cockchafers. There were swarms of sparrows in the lilac-bushes, which threw their tender, fragrant blossoms straight in one's face. Wherever one turned, from every direction came the note of the golden oriole and the shrill cry of the hoopoe and the red-legged falcon. At any other time I should have begun chasing dragon-flies or throwing stones at a crow which was sitting on a low mound under an aspen-tree, with his blunt beak turned away; but at that moment I was in no mood for mischief. My heart was throbbing, and I felt a cold sinking at my stomach; I was preparing myself to confront a gentleman with epaulettes, with a naked sword, and with terrible eyes!

But imagine my disappointment! A dapper little foppish gentleman in white silk trousers, with a white cap on his head, was walking beside my mother in the garden. With his hands behind him and his head thrown back, every now and then running on ahead of mother, he looked quite young. There was so much life and movement in his whole figure that I could only detect the treachery of age when I came close up behind and saw beneath his cap a fringe of close-cropped silver hair. Instead of the staid dignity and stolidity of a general, I saw an almost schoolboyish nimbleness; instead of a collar sticking up to his ears, an ordinary light blue necktie. Mother and my uncle were walking in the avenue talking together. I went softly up to them from behind, and waited for one of them to look round.

"What a delightful place you have here, Klavdia!" said my uncle. "How charming and lovely it is! Had I known before that you had such a charming place, nothing would have induced me to go abroad all these years."

My uncle stooped down rapidly and sniffed at a tulip. Everything he saw moved him to rapture and excitement, as though he had never been in a garden on a sunny day before. The queer man moved about as though he were on springs, and chattered incessantly, without allowing mother to utter a single word. All of a sudden Pobyedimsky came into sight from behind an elder-tree at the turn of the avenue. His appearance was so unexpected that my uncle positively started and stepped back a pace. On this occasion my tutor was attired in his best Inverness cape with sleeves, in which, especially back-view, he looked remarkably like a windmill. He had a solemn and majestic air. Pressing his hat to his bosom in Spanish style, he took a step towards my uncle and made a bow such as a marquis makes in a melodrama, bending forward, a little to one side.

"I have the honour to present myself to your high excellency," he said aloud: "the teacher and instructor of your nephew, formerly a pupil of the veterinary institute, and a nobleman by birth, Pobyedimsky!"

This politeness on the part of my tutor pleased my mother very much. She gave a smile, and waited in thrilled suspense to hear what clever thing he would say next; but my tutor, expecting his dignified address to be answered with equal dignity - that is, that my uncle would say "H'm!" like a general and hold out two fingers - was greatly confused and abashed when the latter laughed genially and shook hands with him. He muttered something incoherent, cleared his throat, and walked away.

"Come! isn't that charming?" laughed my uncle. "Just look! he has made his little flourish and thinks he's a very clever fellow! I do like that - upon my soul I do! What youthful aplomb, what life in that foolish flourish! And what boy is this?" he asked, suddenly turning and looking at me.

"That is my Andryushenka," my mother introduced me, flushing crimson. "My consolation. . ."

I made a scrape with my foot on the sand and dropped a low bow.

"A fine fellow . . . a fine fellow . . ." muttered my uncle, taking his hand from my lips and stroking me on the head. "So your name is Andrusha? Yes, yes. . . . H'm! . . . upon my soul! . . . Do you learn lessons?"

My mother, exaggerating and embellishing as all mothers do, began to describe my achievements in the sciences and the excellence of my behaviour, and I walked round my uncle and, following the ceremonial laid down for me, I continued making low bows. Then my mother began throwing out hints that with my remarkable abilities it would not be amiss for me to get a government nomination to the cadet school; but at the point when I was to have burst into tears and begged for my uncle's protection, my uncle suddenly stopped and flung up his hands in amazement.

"My goo-oodness! What's that?" he asked.

Tatyana Ivanovna, the wife of our bailiff, Fyodor Petrovna, was coming towards us. She was carrying a starched white petticoat and a long ironing-board. As she passed us she looked shyly at the visitor through her eyelashes and flushed crimson.

"Wonders will never cease . . ." my uncle filtered through his teeth, looking after her with friendly interest. "You have a fresh surprise at every step, sister . . . upon my soul!"

"She's a beauty . . ." said mother. "They chose her as a bride for Fyodor, though she lived over seventy miles from here. . . ."

Not every one would have called Tatyana a beauty. She was a plump little woman of twenty, with black eyebrows and a graceful figure, always rosy and attractive-looking, but in her face and in her whole person there was not one striking feature, not one bold line to catch the eye, as though nature had lacked inspiration and confidence when creating her. Tatyana Ivanovna was shy, bashful, and modest in her behaviour; she moved softly and smoothly, said little, seldom laughed, and her whole life was as regular as her face and as flat as her smooth, tidy hair. My uncle screwed up his eyes looking after her, and smiled. Mother looked intently at his smiling face and grew serious.

"And so, brother, you've never married!" she sighed.

"No; I've not married."

"Why not?" asked mother softly.

"How can I tell you? It has happened so. In my youth I was too hard at work, I had no time to live, and when I longed to live - I looked round - and there I had fifty years on my back already. I was too late! However, talking about it . . . is depressing."

My mother and my uncle both sighed at once and walked on, and I left them and flew off to find my tutor, that I might share my impressions with him. Pobyedimsky was standing in the middle of the yard, looking majestically at the heavens.

"One can see he is a man of culture!" he said, twisting his head round. "I hope we shall get on together."

An hour later mother came to us.

"I am in trouble, my dears!" she began, sighing. "You see brother has brought a valet with him, and the valet, God bless him, is not one you can put in the kitchen or in the hall; we must give him a room apart. I can't think what I am to do! I tell you what, children, couldn't you move out somewhere - to Fyodor's lodge, for instance - and give your room to the valet? What do you say?"

We gave our ready consent, for living in the lodge was a great deal more free than in the house, under mother's eye.

"It's a nuisance, and that's a fact!" said mother. "Brother says he won't have dinner in the middle of the day, but between six and seven, as they do in Petersburg. I am simply distracted with worry! By seven o'clock the dinner will be done to rags in the oven. Really, men don't understand anything about housekeeping, though they have so much intellect. Oh, dear! we shall have to cook two dinners every day! You will have dinner at midday as before, children, while your poor old mother has to wait till seven, for the sake of her brother."

Then my mother heaved a deep sigh, bade me try and please my uncle, whose coming was a piece of luck for me for which we must thank God, and hurried off to the kitchen. Pobyedimsky and I moved into the lodge the same day. We were installed in a room which formed the passage from the entry to the bailiff's bedroom.

Contrary to my expectations, life went on just as before, drearily and monotonously, in spite of my uncle's arrival and our move into new quarters. We were excused lessons "on account of the visitor. "Pobyedimsky, who never read anything or occupied himself in any way, spent most of his time sitting on his bed, with his long nose thrust into the air, thinking. Sometimes he would get up, try on his new suit, and sit down again to relapse into contemplation and silence. Only one thing worried him, the flies, which he used mercilessly to squash between his hands. After dinner he usually "rested," and his snores were a cause of annoyance to the whole household. I ran about the garden from morning to night, or sat in the lodge sticking my kites together. For the first two or three weeks we did not see my uncle often. For days together he sat in his own room working, in spite of the flies and the heat. His extraordinary capacity for sitting as though glued to his table produced upon us the effect of an inexplicable conjuring trick. To us idlers, knowing nothing of systematic work, his industry seemed simply miraculous. Getting up at nine, he sat down to his table, and did not leave it till dinner-time; after dinner he set to work again, and went on till late at night. Whenever I peeped through the keyhole I invariably saw the same thing: my uncle sitting at the table working. The work consisted in his writing with one hand while he turned over the leaves of a book with the other, and, strange to say, he kept moving all over - swinging his leg as though it were a pendulum, whistling, and nodding his head in time. He had an extremely careless and frivolous expression all the while, as though he were not working, but playing at noughts and crosses. I always saw him wearing a smart short jacket and a jauntily tied cravat, and he always smelt, even through the keyhole, of delicate feminine perfumery. He only left his room for dinner, but he ate little.

"I can't make brother out!" mother complained of him. "Every day we kill a turkey and pigeons on purpose for him, I make a *compote* with my own hands, and he eats a plateful of broth and a bit of meat the size of a finger and gets up from the table. I begin begging him to eat; he comes back and drinks a glass of milk. And what is there in that, in a glass of milk? It's no better than washing up water! You may die of a diet like that. . . . If I try to persuade him, he laughs and makes a joke of it. . . . No; he does not care for our fare, poor dear!"

We spent the evenings far more gaily than the days. As a rule, by the time the sun was setting and long shadows were lying across the yard, we - that is, Tatyana Ivanovna, Pobyedimsky, and I - were sitting on the steps of the lodge. We did not talk till it grew quite dusk. And, indeed, what is one to talk of when every subject has been talked over already? There was only one thing new, my uncle's arrival, and even that subject was soon exhausted. My tutor never took his eyes off Tatyana Ivanovna's face, and frequently heaved deep sighs. . . . At the time I did not understand those sighs, and did not try to fathom their significance; now they explain a great deal to me.

When the shadows merged into one thick mass of shade, the bailiff Fyodor would come in from shooting or from the field. This Fyodor gave me the impression of being a fierce and even a terrible man. The son of a Russianized gipsy from Izyumskoe, swarthy-faced and curly-headed, with big black eyes and a matted beard, he was never called among our Kotchuevko peasants by any name but "The Devil." And, indeed, there was a great deal of the gipsy about him apart from his appearance. He could not, for instance, stay at home, and went off for days together into the country or into the woods to shoot. He was gloomy, ill-humoured, taciturn, was afraid of nobody, and refused to recognize any authority. He was rude to mother, addressed me familiarly, and was contemptuous of Pobyedimsky's learning. All this we forgave him, looking upon him as a hot-tempered and nervous man; mother liked him because, in spite of his gipsy nature, he was ideally honest and industrious. He loved his Tatyana Ivanovna passionately, like a gipsy, but this love took in him a gloomy form, as though it cost him suffering. He was never affectionate to his wife in our presence, but simply rolled his eyes angrily at her and twisted his mouth.

When he came in from the fields he would noisily and angrily put down his gun, would come out to us on the steps, and sit down beside his wife. After resting a little, he would ask his wife a few questions about household matters, and then sink into silence.

"Let us sing," I would suggest.

My tutor would tune his guitar, and in a deep deacon's bass strike up "In the midst of the valley." We would begin singing. My tutor took the bass, Fyodor sang in a hardly audible tenor, while I sang soprano in unison with Tatyana Ivanovna.

When the whole sky was covered with stars and the frogs had left off croaking, they would bring in our supper from the kitchen. We went into the lodge and sat down to the meal. My tutor and the gipsy ate greedily, with such a sound that it was hard to tell whether it was the bones crunching or their jaws, and Tatyana Ivanovna and I scarcely succeeded in getting our share. After supper the lodge was plunged in deep sleep.

One evening, it was at the end of May, we were sitting on the steps, waiting for supper. A shadow suddenly fell across us, and Gundasov stood before us as though he had sprung out of the earth. He looked at us for a long time, then clasped his hands and laughed gaily.

"An idyll!" he said. "They sing and dream in the moonlight! It's charming, upon my soul! May I sit down and dream with you?"

We looked at one another and said nothing. My uncle sat down on the bottom step, yawned, and looked at the sky. A silence followed. Pobyedimsky, who had for a long time been wanting to talk to somebody fresh, was delighted at the opportunity, and was the first to break the silence. He had only one subject for intellectual conversation, the epizootic diseases. It sometimes happens that after one has been in an immense crowd, only some one countenance of the thousands remains long imprinted on the memory; in the same way, of all that Pobyedimsky had heard, during his six months at the veterinary institute, he remembered only one passage:

"The epizootics do immense damage to the stock of the country. It is the duty of society to work hand in hand with the government in waging war upon them."

Before saying this to Gundasov, my tutor cleared his throat three times, and several times, in his excitement, wrapped himself up in his Inverness. On hearing about the epizootics, my uncle looked intently at my tutor and made a sound between a snort and a laugh.

"Upon my soul, that's charming!" he said, scrutinizing us as though we were mannequins. "This is actually life. . . . This is really what reality is bound to be. Why are you silent, Pelagea Ivanovna?" he said, addressing Tatyana Ivanovna.

She coughed, overcome with confusion.

"Talk, my friends, sing . . . play! . . . Don't lose time. You know, time, the rascal, runs away and waits for no man! Upon my soul, before you have time to look round, old age is upon you. . . . Then it is too late to live! That's how it is, Pelagea Ivanovna. . . . We mustn't sit still and be silent. . . ."

At that point supper was brought out from the kitchen. Uncle went into the lodge with us, and to keep us company ate five curd fritters and the wing of a duck. He ate and looked at us. He was touched and delighted by us all. Whatever silly nonsense my precious tutor talked, and whatever Tatyana Ivanovna did, he thought charming and delightful. When after supper Tatyana Ivanovna sat quietly down and took up her knitting, he kept his eyes fixed on her fingers and chatted away without ceasing.

"Make all the haste you can to live, my friends. . ." he said."God forbid you should sacrifice the present for the future! There is youth, health, fire in the present; the future is smoke and deception! As soon as you are twenty begin to live."

Tatyana Ivanovna dropped a knitting-needle. My uncle jumped up, picked up the needle, and handed it to Tatyana Ivanovna with a bow, and for the first time in my life I learnt that there were people in the world more refined than Pobyedimsky.

"Yes . . ." my uncle went on, "love, marry, do silly things. Foolishness is a great deal more living and healthy than our straining and striving after rational life."

My uncle talked a great deal, so much that he bored us; I sat on a box listening to him and dropping to sleep. It distressed me that he did not once all the evening pay attention to me. He left the lodge at two o'clock, when, overcome with drowsiness, I was sound asleep.

From that time forth my uncle took to coming to the lodge every evening. He sang with us, had supper with us, and always stayed on till two o'clock in the morning, chatting incessantly, always about the same subject. His evening and night work was given up, and by the end of June, when the privy councillor had learned to eat mother's turkey and *compote*, his work by day was abandoned too. My uncle tore himself away from his table and plunged into "life." In the daytime he walked up and down the garden, he whistled to the workmen and hindered them from working, making them tell him their various histories. When his eye fell on Tatyana Ivanovna he ran up to her, and, if she were carrying anything, offered his assistance, which embarrassed her dreadfully.

As the summer advanced my uncle grew more and more frivolous, volatile, and careless. Pobyedimsky was completely disillusioned in regard to him.

"He is too one-sided," he said. "There is nothing to show that he is in the very foremost ranks of the service. And he doesn't even know how to talk. At every word it's 'upon my soul.' No, I don't like him!"

From the time that my uncle began visiting the lodge there was a noticeable change both in Fyodor and my tutor. Fyodor gave up going out shooting, came home early, sat more taciturn than ever, and stared with particular ill-humour at his wife. In my uncle's presence my tutor gave up talking about epizootics, frowned, and even laughed sarcastically.

"Here comes our little bantam cock!" he growled on one occasion when my uncle was coming into the lodge.

I put down this change in them both to their being offended with my uncle. My absent-minded uncle mixed up their names, and to the very day of his departure failed to distinguish which was my tutor and which was Tatyana Ivanovna's husband. Tatyana Ivanovna herself he sometimes called Nastasya, sometimes Pelagea, and sometimes Yevdokia. Touched and delighted by us, he laughed and behaved exactly as though in the company of small children. . . . All this, of course, might well offend young men. It was not a case of offended pride, however, but, as I realize now, subtler feelings.

I remember one evening I was sitting on the box struggling with sleep. My eyelids felt glued together and my body, tired out by running about all day, drooped sideways. But I struggled against sleep and tried to look on. It was about midnight. Tatyana Ivanovna, rosy and unassuming as always, was sitting at a little table sewing at her husband's shirt. Fyodor, sullen and gloomy, was staring at her from one corner, and in the other sat Pobyedimsky, snorting angrily and retreating into the high collar of his shirt. My uncle was walking up and down the room thinking. Silence reigned; nothing was to be heard but the rustling of the linen in Tatyana Ivanovna's hands. Suddenly my uncle stood still before Tatyana Ivanovna, and said:

"You are all so young, so fresh, so nice, you live so peacefully in this quiet place, that I envy you. I have become attached to your way of life here; my heart aches when I remember I have to go away. . . . You may believe in my sincerity!"

Sleep closed my eyes and I lost myself. When some sound waked me, my uncle was standing before Tatyana Ivanovna, looking at her with a softened expression. His cheeks were flushed.

"My life has been wasted," he said. "I have not lived! Your young face makes me think of my own lost youth, and I should be ready to sit here watching you to the day of my death. It would be a pleasure to me to take you with me to Petersburg."

"What for?" Fyodor asked in a husky voice.

"I should put her under a glass case on my work-table. I should admire her and show her to other people. You know, Pelagea Ivanovna, we have no women like you there. Among us there is wealth, distinction, sometimes beauty, but we have not this true sort of life, this healthy serenity. . . ."

My uncle sat down facing Tatyana Ivanovna and took her by the hand.

"So you won't come with me to Petersburg?" he laughed. "In that case give me your little hand. . . . A charming little hand! . . . You won't give it? Come, you miser! let me kiss it, anyway. . . ."

At that moment there was the scrape of a chair. Fyodor jumped up, and with heavy, measured steps went up to his wife. His face was pale, grey, and quivering. He brought his fist down on the table with a bang, and said in a hollow voice:

"I won't allow it!

At the same moment Pobyedimsky jumped up from his chair. He, too, pale and angry, went up to Tatyana Ivanovna, and he, too, struck the table with his fist.

"I . . . I won't allow it!" he said.

"What, what's the matter?" asked my uncle in surprise.

"I won't allow it!" repeated Fyodor, banging on the table.

My uncle jumped up and blinked nervously. He tried to speak, but in his amazement and alarm could not utter a word; with an embarrassed smile, he shuffled out of the lodge with the hurried step of an old man, leaving his hat behind. When, a little later, my mother ran into the lodge, Fyodor and Pobyedimsky were still hammering on the table like blacksmiths and repeating, "I won't allow it!"

"What has happened here?" asked mother. "Why has my brother been taken ill? What's the matter?"

Looking at Tatyana's pale, frightened face and at her infuriated husband, mother probably guessed what was the matter. She sighed and shook her head.

"Come! give over banging on the table!" she said. "Leave off, Fyodor! And why are you thumping, Yegor Alexyevitch? What have you got to do with it?"

Pobyedimsky was startled and confused. Fyodor looked intently at him, then at his wife, and began walking about the room. When mother had gone out of the lodge, I saw what for long afterwards I looked upon as a dream. I saw Fyodor seize my tutor, lift him up in the air, and thrust him out of the door.

When I woke up in the morning my tutor's bed was empty. To my question where he was nurse told me in a whisper that he had been taken off early in the morning to the hospital, as his arm was broken. Distressed at this intelligence and remembering the scene of the previous evening, I went out of doors. It was a grey day. The sky was covered with storm-clouds and there was a wind blowing dust, bits of paper, and feathers along the ground. . . . It felt as though rain were coming. There was a look of boredom in the servants and in the animals. When I went into the house I was told not to make such a noise with my feet, as mother was ill and in bed with a migraine. What was I to do? I went outside the gate, sat down on the little bench there, and fell to trying to discover the meaning of what I had seen and heard the day before. From our gate there was a road which, passing the forge and the pool which never dried up, ran into the main road. I looked at the telegraph-posts, about which clouds of dust were whirling, and at the sleepy birds sitting on the wires, and I suddenly felt so dreary that I began to cry.

A dusty wagonette crammed full of townspeople, probably going to visit the shrine, drove by along the main road. The wagonette was hardly out of sight when a light chaise with a pair of horses came into view. In it was Akim Nikititch, the police inspector, standing up and holding on to the coachman's belt. To my great surprise, the chaise turned into our road and flew by me in at the gate. While I was puzzling why the police inspector had come to see us, I heard a noise, and a carriage with three horses came into sight on the road. In the carriage stood the police captain, directing his coachman towards our gate.

"And why is he coming?" I thought, looking at the dusty police captain. "Most probably Pobyedimsky has complained of Fyodor to him, and they have come to take him to prison."

But the mystery was not so easily solved. The police inspector and the police captain were only the first instalment, for five minutes had scarcely passed when a coach drove in at our gate. It dashed by me so swiftly that I could only get a glimpse of a red beard.

Lost in conjecture and full of misgivings, I ran to the house. In the passage first of all I saw mother; she was pale and looking with horror towards the door, from which came the sounds of men's voices. The visitors had taken her by surprise in the very throes of migraine.

"Who has come, mother?" I asked.

"Sister," I heard my uncle's voice, "will you send in something to eat for the governor and me?"

"It is easy to say 'something to eat,' " whispered my mother, numb with horror. "What have I time to get ready now? I am put to shame in my old age!"

Mother clutched at her head and ran into the kitchen. The governor's sudden visit stirred and overwhelmed the whole household. A ferocious slaughter followed. A dozen fowls, five turkeys, eight ducks, were killed, and in the fluster the old gander, the progenitor of our whole flock of geese and a great favourite of mother's, was beheaded. The coachmen and the cook seemed frenzied, and slaughtered birds at random, without distinction of age or breed. For the sake of some wretched sauce a pair of valuable pigeons, as dear to me as the gander was to mother, were sacrificed. It was a long while before I could forgive the governor their death.

In the evening, when the governor and his suite, after a sumptuous dinner, had got into their carriages and driven away, I went into the house to look at the remains of the feast. Glancing into the drawing-room from the passage, I saw my uncle and my mother. My uncle, with his hands behind his back, was walking nervously up and down close to the wall, shrugging his shoulders. Mother, exhausted and looking much thinner, was sitting on the sofa and watching his movements with heavy eyes.

"Excuse me, sister, but this won't do at all," my uncle grumbled, wrinkling up his face. "I introduced the governor to you, and you didn't offer to shake hands. You covered him with confusion, poor fellow! No, that won't do. . . . Simplicity is a very good thing, but there must be limits to it. . . . Upon my soul! And then that dinner! How can one give people such things? What was that mess, for instance, that they served for the fourth course?"

"That was duck with sweet sauce . . ." mother answered softly.

"Duck! Forgive me, sister, but . . . but here I've got heartburn! I am ill!"

My uncle made a sour, tearful face, and went on:

"It was the devil sent that governor! As though I wanted his visit! Pff! . . . heartburn! I can't work or sleep . . . I am completely out of sorts. . . . And I can't understand how you can live here without anything to do . . . in this boredom! Here I've got a pain coming under my shoulder-blade! . . ."

My uncle frowned, and walked about more rapidly than ever.

"Brother," my mother inquired softly, "what would it cost to go abroad?"

"At least three thousand . . ." my uncle answered in a tearful voice. "I would go, but where am I to get it? I haven't a farthing. Pff! . . . heartburn!"

My uncle stopped to look dejectedly at the grey, overcast prospect from the window, and began pacing to and fro again.

A silence followed. . . . Mother looked a long while at the ikon, pondering something, then she began crying, and said:

"I'll give you the three thousand, brother. . . ."

Three days later the majestic boxes went off to the station, and the privy councillor drove off after them. As he said good-bye to mother he shed tears, and it was a long time before he took his lips from her hands, but when he got into his carriage his face beamed with childlike pleasure. . . . Radiant and happy, he settled himself comfortably, kissed his hand to my mother, who was crying, and all at once his eye was caught by me. A look of the utmost astonishment came into his face.

"What boy is this?" he asked.

My mother, who had declared my uncle's coming was a piece of luck for which I must thank God, was bitterly mortified at this question. I was in no mood for questions. I looked at my uncle's happy face, and for some reason I felt fearfully sorry for him. I could not resist jumping up to the carriage and hugging that frivolous man, weak as all men are. Looking into his face and wanting to say something pleasant, I asked:

"Uncle, have you ever been in a battle?"

"Ah, the dear boy . . ." laughed my uncle, kissing me. "A charming boy, upon my soul! How natural, how living it all is, upon my soul! . . ."

The carriage set off. . . . I looked after him, and long afterwards that farewell "upon my soul" was ringing in my ears.

# A DAY IN THE COUNTRY

Between eight and nine o'clock in the morning.

A dark leaden-coloured mass is creeping over the sky towards the sun. Red zigzags of lightning gleam here and there across it. There is a sound of far-away rumbling. A warm wind frolics over the grass, bends the trees, and stirs up the dust. In a minute there will be a spurt of May rain and a real storm will begin.

Fyokla, a little beggar-girl of six, is running through the village, looking for Terenty the cobbler. The white-haired, barefoot child is pale. Her eyes are wide-open, her lips are trembling.

"Uncle, where is Terenty?" she asks every one she meets. No one answers. They are all preoccupied with the approaching storm and take refuge in their huts. At last she meets Silanty Silitch, the sacristan, Terenty's bosom friend. He is coming along, staggering from the wind.

"Uncle, where is Terenty?"

"At the kitchen-gardens," answers Silanty.

The beggar-girl runs behind the huts to the kitchen-gardens and there finds Terenty; the tall old man with a thin, pock-marked face, very long legs, and bare feet, dressed in a woman's tattered jacket, is standing near the vegetable plots, looking with drowsy, drunken eyes at the dark storm-cloud. On his long crane-like legs he sways in the wind like a starling-cote.

"Uncle Terenty!" the white-headed beggar-girl addresses him. "Uncle, darling!"

Terenty bends down to Fyokla, and his grim, drunken face is overspread with a smile, such as come into people's faces when they look at something little, foolish, and absurd, but warmly loved.

"Ah! servant of God, Fyokla," he says, lisping tenderly, "where have you come from?"

"Uncle Terenty," says Fyokla, with a sob, tugging at the lapel of the cobbler's coat. "Brother Danilka has had an accident! Come along!"

"What sort of accident? Ough, what thunder! Holy, holy, holy. . . . What sort of accident?"

"In the count's copse Danilka stuck his hand into a hole in a tree, and he can't get it out. Come along, uncle, do be kind and pull his hand out!"

"How was it he put his hand in? What for?"

"He wanted to get a cuckoo's egg out of the hole for me."

"The day has hardly begun and already you are in trouble. . . ." Terenty shook his head and spat deliberately. "Well, what am I to do with you now? I must come . . . I must, may the wolf gobble you up, you naughty children! Come, little orphan!"

Terenty comes out of the kitchen-garden and, lifting high his long legs, begins striding down the village street. He walks quickly without stopping or looking from side to side, as though he were shoved from behind or afraid of pursuit. Fyokla can hardly keep up with him.

They come out of the village and turn along the dusty road towards the count's copse that lies dark blue in the distance. It is about a mile and a half away. The clouds have by now covered the sun, and soon afterwards there is not a speck of blue left in the sky. It grows dark.

"Holy, holy, holy . . ." whispers Fyokla, hurrying after Terenty. The first rain-drops, big and heavy, lie, dark dots on the dusty road. A big drop falls on Fyokla's cheek and glides like a tear down her chin.

"The rain has begun," mutters the cobbler, kicking up the dust with his bare, bony feet. "That's fine, Fyokla, old girl. The grass and the trees are fed by the rain, as we are by bread. And as for the thunder, don't you be frightened, little orphan. Why should it kill a little thing like you?"

As soon as the rain begins, the wind drops. The only sound is the patter of rain dropping like fine shot on the young rye and the parched road.

"We shall get soaked, Fyolka," mutters Terenty. "There won't be a dry spot left on us. . . . Ho-ho, my girl! It's run down my neck! But don't be frightened, silly. . . . The grass will be dry again, the earth will be dry again, and we shall be dry again. There is the same sun for us all."

A flash of lightning, some fourteen feet long, gleams above their heads. There is a loud peal of thunder, and it seems to Fyokla that something big, heavy, and round is rolling over the sky and tearing it open, exactly over her head.

"Holy, holy, holy . . ." says Terenty, crossing himself. "Don't be afraid, little orphan! It is not from spite that it thunders."

Terenty's and Fyokla's feet are covered with lumps of heavy, wet clay. It is slippery and difficult to walk, but Terenty strides on more and more rapidly. The weak little beggar-girl is breathless and ready to drop.

But at last they go into the count's copse. The washed trees, stirred by a gust of wind, drop a perfect waterfall upon them. Terenty stumbles over stumps and begins to slacken his pace.

"Whereabouts is Danilka?" he asks. "Lead me to him."

Fyokla leads him into a thicket, and, after going a quarter of a mile, points to Danilka. Her brother, a little fellow of eight, with hair as red as ochre and a pale sickly face, stands leaning against a tree, and, with his head on one side, looking sideways at the sky. In one hand he holds his shabby old cap, the other is hidden in an old lime tree. The boy is gazing at the stormy sky, and apparently not thinking of his trouble. Hearing footsteps and seeing the cobbler he gives a sickly smile and says:

"A terrible lot of thunder, Terenty. . . . I've never heard so much thunder in all my life."

"And where is your hand?"

"In the hole. . . . Pull it out, please, Terenty!"

The wood had broken at the edge of the hole and jammed Danilka's hand: he could push it farther in, but could not pull it out. Terenty snaps off the broken piece, and the boy's hand, red and crushed, is released.

"It's terrible how it's thundering," the boy says again, rubbing his hand. "What makes it thunder, Terenty?"

"One cloud runs against the other," answers the cobbler. The party come out of the copse, and walk along the edge of it towards the darkened road. The thunder gradually abates, and its rumbling is heard far away beyond the village.

"The ducks flew by here the other day, Terenty," says Danilka, still rubbing his hand. "They must be nesting in the Gniliya Zaimishtcha marshes. . . . Fyolka, would you like me to show you a nightingale's nest?"

"Don't touch it, you might disturb them," says Terenty, wringing the water out of his cap. "The nightingale is a singing-bird, without sin. He has had a voice given him in his throat, to praise God and gladden the heart of man. It's a sin to disturb him."

"What about the sparrow?"

"The sparrow doesn't matter, he's a bad, spiteful bird. He is like a pickpocket in his ways. He doesn't like man to be happy. When Christ was crucified it was the sparrow brought nails to the Jews, and called 'alive! alive!' "

A bright patch of blue appears in the sky.

"Look!" says Terenty. "An ant-heap burst open by the rain! They've been flooded, the rogues!"

They bend over the ant-heap. The downpour has damaged it; the insects are scurrying to and fro in the mud, agitated, and busily trying to carry away their drowned companions.

"You needn't be in such a taking, you won't die of it!" says Terenty, grinning. "As soon as the sun warms you, you'll come to your senses again. . . . It's a lesson to you, you stupids. You won't settle on low ground another time."

They go on.

"And here are some bees," cries Danilka, pointing to the branch of a young oak tree.

The drenched and chilled bees are huddled together on the branch. There are so many of them that neither bark nor leaf can be seen. Many of them are settled on one another.

"That's a swarm of bees," Terenty informs them. "They were flying looking for a home, and when the rain came down upon them they settled. If a swarm is flying, you need only sprinkle water on them to make them settle. Now if, say, you wanted to take the swarm, you would bend the branch with them into a sack and shake it, and they all fall in."

Little Fyokla suddenly frowns and rubs her neck vigorously. Her brother looks at her neck, and sees a big swelling on it.

"Hey-hey!" laughs the cobbler. "Do you know where you got that from, Fyokia, old girl? There are Spanish flies on some tree in the wood. The rain has trickled off them, and a drop has fallen on your neck - that's what has made the swelling."

The sun appears from behind the clouds and floods the wood, the fields, and the three friends with its warm light. The dark menacing cloud has gone far away and taken the storm with it. The air is warm and fragrant. There is a scent of bird-cherry, meadowsweet, and lilies-of-the-valley.

"That herb is given when your nose bleeds," says Terenty, pointing to a woolly-looking flower. "It does good."

They hear a whistle and a rumble, but not such a rumble as the storm-clouds carried away. A goods train races by before the eyes of Terenty, Danilka, and Fyokla. The engine, panting and puffing out black smoke, drags more than twenty vans after it. Its power is tremendous. The children are interested to know how an engine, not alive and without the help of horses, can move and drag such weights, and Terenty undertakes to explain it to them:

"It's all the steam's doing, children. . . . The steam does the work. . . . You see, it shoves under that thing near the wheels, and it . . . you see . . . it works. . . ."

They cross the railway line, and, going down from the embankment, walk towards the river. They walk not with any object, but just at random, and talk all the way. . . . Danilka asks questions, Terenty answers them. . . .

Terenty answers all his questions, and there is no secret in Nature which baffles him. He knows everything. Thus, for example, he knows the names of all the wild flowers, animals, and stones. He knows what herbs cure diseases, he has no difficulty in telling the age of a horse or a cow. Looking at the sunset, at the moon, or the birds, he can tell what sort of weather it will be next day. And indeed, it is not only Terenty who is so wise. Silanty Silitch, the innkeeper, the market-gardener, the shepherd, and all the villagers, generally speaking, know as much as he does. These people have learned not from books, but in the fields, in the wood, on the river bank. Their teachers have been the birds themselves, when they sang to them, the sun when it left a glow of crimson behind it at setting, the very trees, and wild herbs.

Danilka looks at Terenty and greedily drinks in every word. In spring, before one is weary of the warmth and the monotonous green of the fields, when everything is fresh and full of fragrance, who would not want to hear about the golden may-beetles, about the cranes, about the gurgling streams, and the corn mounting into ear?

The two of them, the cobbler and the orphan, walk about the fields, talk unceasingly, and are not weary. They could wander about the world endlessly. They walk, and in their talk of the beauty of the earth do not notice the frail little beggar-girl tripping after them. She is breathless and moves with a lagging step. There are tears in her eyes; she would be glad to stop these inexhaustible wanderers, but to whom and where can she go? She has no home or people of her own; whether she likes it or not, she must walk and listen to their talk.

Towards midday, all three sit down on the river bank. Danilka takes out of his bag a piece of bread, soaked and reduced to a mash, and they begin to eat. Terenty says a prayer when he has eaten the bread, then stretches himself on the sandy bank and falls asleep. While he is asleep, the boy gazes at the water, pondering. He has many different things to think of. He has just seen the storm, the bees, the ants, the train. Now, before his eyes, fishes are whisking about. Some are two inches long and more, others are no bigger than one's nail. A viper, with its head held high, is swimming from one bank to the other.

Only towards the evening our wanderers return to the village. The children go for the night to a deserted barn, where the corn of the commune used to be kept, while Terenty, leaving them, goes to the tavern. The children lie huddled together on the straw, dozing.

The boy does not sleep. He gazes into the darkness, and it seems to him that he is seeing all that he has seen in the day: the storm-clouds, the bright sunshine, the birds, the fish, lanky Terenty. The number of his impressions, together with exhaustion and hunger, are too much for him; he is as hot as though he were on fire, and tosses from, side to side. He longs to tell someone all that is haunting him now in the darkness and agitating his soul, but there is no one to tell. Fyokla is too little and could not understand.

"I'll tell Terenty to-morrow," thinks the boy.

The children fall asleep thinking of the homeless cobbler, and, in the night, Terenty comes to them, makes the sign of the cross over them, and puts bread under their heads. And no one sees his love. It is seen only by the moon which floats in the sky and peeps caressingly through the holes in the wall of the deserted barn.

# AT A SUMMER VILLA

"I love you. You are my life, my happiness - everything to me! Forgive the avowal, but I have not the strength to suffer and be silent. I ask not for love in return, but for sympathy. Be at the old arbour at eight o'clock this evening. . . . To sign my name is unnecessary I think, but do not be uneasy at my being anonymous. I am young, nice-looking . . . what more do you want?"

When Pavel Ivanitch Vyhodtsev, a practical married man who was spending his holidays at a summer villa, read this letter, he shrugged his shoulders and scratched his forehead in perplexity.

"What devilry is this?" he thought. "I'm a married man, and to send me such a queer . . . silly letter! Who wrote it?"

Pavel Ivanitch turned the letter over and over before his eyes, read it through again, and spat with disgust.

" 'I love you' " . . . he said jeeringly. "A nice boy she has pitched on! So I'm to run off to meet you in the arbour! . . . I got over all such romances and *fleurs d'amour* years ago, my girl. . . . Hm! She must be some reckless, immoral creature. . . . Well, these women are a set! What a whirligig - God forgive us! - she must be to write a letter like that to a stranger, and a married man, too! It's real demoralisation!"

In the course of his eight years of married life Pavel Ivanitch had completely got over all sentimental feeling, and he had received no letters from ladies except letters of congratulation, and so, although he tried to carry it off with disdain, the letter quoted above greatly intrigued and agitated him.

An hour after receiving it, he was lying on his sofa, thinking:

"Of course I am not a silly boy, and I am not going to rush off to this idiotic rendezvous; but yet it would be interesting to know who wrote it! Hm. . . . It is certainly a woman's writing. . . . The letter is written with genuine feeling, and so it can hardly be a joke. . . . Most likely it's some neurotic girl, or perhaps a widow . . . widows are frivolous and eccentric as a rule. Hm. . . . Who could it be?"

What made it the more difficult to decide the question was that Pavel Ivanitch had not one feminine acquaintance among all the summer visitors, except his wife.

"It is queer . . ." he mused. " 'I love you!'. . . When did she manage to fall in love? Amazing woman! To fall in love like this, apropos of nothing, without making any acquaintance and finding out what sort of man I am. . . . She must be extremely young and romantic if she is capable of falling in love after two or three looks at me. . . . But . . . who is she?"

Pavel Ivanitch suddenly recalled that when he had been walking among the summer villas the day before, and the day before that, he had several times been met by a fair young lady with a light blue hat and a turn-up nose. The fair charmer had kept looking at him, and when he sat down on a seat she had sat down beside him. . . .

"Can it be she?" Vyhodtsev wondered. "It can't be! Could a delicate ephemeral creature like that fall in love with a worn-out old eel like me? No, it's impossible!"

At dinner Pavel Ivanitch looked blankly at his wife while he meditated:

"She writes that she is young and nice-looking. . . . So she's not old. . . . Hm. . . . To tell the truth, honestly I am not so old and plain that no one could fall in love with me. My wife loves me! Besides, love is blind, we all know. . . ."

"What are you thinking about?" his wife asked him.

"Oh. . . my head aches a little. . ." Pavel Ivanitch said, quite untruly.

He made up his mind that it was stupid to pay attention to such a nonsensical thing as a love-letter, and laughed at it and at its authoress, but - alas! - powerful is the "dacha"enemy of mankind! After dinner, Pavel Ivanitch lay down on his bed, and instead of going to sleep, reflected:

"But there, I daresay she is expecting me to come! What a silly! I can just imagine what a nervous fidget she'll be in and how her *tournure* will quiver when she does not find me in the arbour! I shan't go, though. . . . Bother her!"

But, I repeat, powerful is the enemy of mankind.

"Though I might, perhaps, just out of curiosity. . ." he was musing, half an hour later. "I might go and look from a distance what sort of a creature she is. . . . It would be interesting to have a look at her! It would be fun, and that's all! After all, why shouldn't I have a little fun since such a chance has turned up?"

Pavel Ivanitch got up from his bed and began dressing. "What are you getting yourself up so smartly for?" his wife asked, noticing that he was putting on a clean shirt and a fashionable tie.

"Oh, nothing. . . . I must have a walk. . . . My head aches. . . . Hm."

Pavel Ivanitch dressed in his best, and waiting till eight o'clock, went out of the house. When the figures of gaily dressed summer visitors of both sexes began passing before his eyes against the bright green background, his heart throbbed.

"Which of them is it? . . ." he wondered, advancing irresolutely. "Come, what am I afraid of? Why, I am not going to the rendezvous! What . . . a fool! Go forward boldly! And what if I go into the arbour? Well, well . . . there is no reason I should."

Pavel Ivanitch's heart beat still more violently. . . . Involuntarily, with no desire to do so, he suddenly pictured to himself the half-darkness of the arbour. . . . A graceful fair girl with a little blue hat and a turn-up nose rose before his imagination. He saw her, abashed by her love and trembling all over, timidly approach him, breathing excitedly, and . . . suddenly clasping him in her arms.

"If I weren't married it would be all right . . ." he mused, driving sinful ideas out of his head. "Though . . . for once in my life, it would do no harm to have the experience, or else one will die without knowing what. . . . And my wife, what will it matter to her? Thank God, for eight years I've never moved one step away from her. . . . Eight years of irreproachable duty! Enough of her. . . . It's positively vexatious. . . . I'm ready to go to spite her!"

Trembling all over and holding his breath, Pavel Ivanitch went up to the arbour, wreathed with ivy and wild vine, and peeped into it. . . . A smell of dampness and mildew reached him. . . .

"I believe there's nobody . . ." he thought, going into the arbour, and at once saw a human silhouette in the corner.

The silhouette was that of a man. . . . Looking more closely, Pavel Ivanitch recognised his wife's brother, Mitya, a student, who was staying with them at the villa.

"Oh, it's you . . ." he growled discontentedly, as he took off his hat and sat down.

"Yes, it's I" . . . answered Mitya.

Two minutes passed in silence.

"Excuse me, Pavel Ivanitch," began Mitya: "but might I ask you to leave me alone?? . . . I am thinking over the dissertation for my degree and. . . and the presence of anybody else prevents my thinking."

"You had better go somewhere in a dark avenue. . ." Pavel Ivanitch observed mildly. "It's easier to think in the open air, and, besides, . . . er . . . I should like to have a little sleep here on this seat. . . It's not so hot here. . . ."

"You want to sleep, but it's a question of my dissertation . . ." Mitya grumbled. "The dissertation is more important."

Again there was a silence. Pavel Ivanitch, who had given the rein to his imagination and was continually hearing footsteps, suddenly leaped up and said in a plaintive voice:

"Come, I beg you, Mitya! You are younger and ought to consider me. . . . I am unwell and . . . I need sleep. . . . Go away!"

"That's egoism. . . . Why must you be here and not I? I won't go as a matter of principle."

"Come, I ask you to! Suppose I am an egoist, a despot and a fool . . . but I ask you to go! For once in my life I ask you a favour! Show some consideration!"

Mitya shook his head.

"What a beast! . . ." thought Pavel Ivanitch. "That can't be a rendezvous with him here! It's impossible with him here!"

"I say, Mitya," he said, "I ask you for the last time. . . . Show that you are a sensible, humane, and cultivated man!"

"I don't know why you keep on so!" . . . said Mitya, shrugging his shoulders. "I've said I won't go, and I won't. I shall stay here as a matter of principle. . . ."

At that moment a woman's face with a turn-up nose peeped into the arbour. . . .

Seeing Mitya and Pavel Ivanitch, it frowned and vanished.

"She is gone!" thought Pavel Ivanitch, looking angrily at Mitya. "She saw that blackguard and fled! It's all spoilt!"

After waiting a little longer, he got up, put on his hat and said:

"You're a beast, a low brute and a blackguard! Yes! A beast! It's mean . . . and silly! Everything is at an end between us!"

"Delighted to hear it!" muttered Mitya, also getting up and putting on his hat. "Let me tell you that by being here just now you've played me such a dirty trick that I'll never forgive you as long as I live."

Pavel Ivanitch went out of the arbour, and beside himself with rage, strode rapidly to his villa. Even the sight of the table laid for supper did not soothe him.

"Once in a lifetime such a chance has turned up," he thought in agitation; "and then it's been prevented! Now she is offended . . . crushed!"

At supper Pavel Ivanitch and Mitya kept their eyes on their plates and maintained a sullen silence. . . . They were hating each other from the bottom of their hearts.

"What are you smiling at?" asked Pavel Ivanitch, pouncing on his wife. "It's only silly fools who laugh for nothing!"

His wife looked at her husband's angry face, and went off into a peal of laughter.

"What was that letter you got this morning?" she asked.

"I? . . . I didn't get one. . . ." Pavel Ivanitch was overcome with confusion. "You are inventing. . . imagination."

"Oh, come, tell us! Own up, you did! Why, it was I sent you that letter! Honour bright, I did! Ha ha!"

Pavel Ivanitch turned crimson and bent over his plate. "Silly jokes," he growled.

"But what could I do? Tell me that. . . . We had to scrub the rooms out this evening, and how could we get you out of the house? There was no other way of getting you out. . . . But don't be angry, stupid. . . . I didn't want you to be dull in the arbour, so I sent the same letter to Mitya too! Mitya, have you been to the arbour?"

Mitya grinned and left off glaring with hatred at his rival.

# PANIC FEARS

During all the years I have been living in this world I have only three times been terrified.

The first real terror, which made my hair stand on end and made shivers run all over me, was caused by a trivial but strange phenomenon. It happened that, having nothing to do one July evening, I drove to the station for the newspapers. It was a still, warm, almost sultry evening, like all those monotonous evenings in July which, when once they have set in, go on for a week, a fortnight, or sometimes longer, in regular unbroken succession, and are suddenly cut short by a violent thunderstorm and a lavish downpour of rain that refreshes everything for a long time.

The sun had set some time before, and an unbroken gray dusk lay all over the land. The mawkishly sweet scents of the grass and flowers were heavy in the motionless, stagnant air.

I was driving in a rough trolley. Behind my back the gardener's son Pashka, a boy of eight years old, whom I had taken with me to look after the horse in case of necessity, was gently snoring, with his head on a sack of oats. Our way lay along a narrow by-road, straight as a ruler, which lay hid like a great snake in the tall thick rye. There was a pale light from the afterglow of sunset; a streak of light cut its way through a narrow, uncouth-looking cloud, which seemed sometimes like a boat and sometimes like a man wrapped in a quilt. . . .

I had driven a mile and a half, or two miles, when against the pale background of the evening glow there came into sight one after another some graceful tall poplars; a river glimmered beyond them, and a gorgeous picture suddenly, as though by magic, lay stretched before me. I had to stop the horse, for our straight road broke off abruptly and ran down a steep incline overgrown with bushes. We were standing on the hillside and beneath us at the bottom lay a huge hole full of twilight, of fantastic shapes, and of space. At the bottom of this hole, in a wide plain guarded by the poplars and caressed by the gleaming river, nestled a village. It was now sleeping. . . . Its huts, its church with the belfry, its trees, stood out against the gray twilight and were reflected darkly in the smooth surface of the river.

I waked Pashka for fear he should fall out and began cautiously going down.

"Have we got to Lukovo?" asked Pashka, lifting his head lazily.

"Yes. Hold the reins! . . ."

I led the horse down the hill and looked at the village. At the first glance one strange circumstance caught my attention: at the very top of the belfry, in the tiny window between the cupola and the bells, a light was twinkling. This light was like that of a smoldering lamp, at one moment dying down, at another flickering up. What could it come from?

Its source was beyond my comprehension. It could not be burning at the window, for there were neither ikons nor lamps in the top turret of the belfry; there was nothing there, as I knew, but beams, dust, and spiders' webs. It was hard to climb up into that turret, for the passage to it from the belfry was closely blocked up.

It was more likely than anything else to be the reflection of some outside light, but though I strained my eyes to the utmost, I could not see one other speck of light in the vast expanse that lay before me. There was no moon. The pale and, by now, quite dim streak of the afterglow could not have been reflected, for the window looked not to the west, but to the east. These and other similar considerations were straying through my mind all the while that I was going down the slope with the horse. At the bottom I sat down by the roadside and looked again at the light. As before it was glimmering and flaring up.

"Strange," I thought, lost in conjecture. "Very strange."

And little by little I was overcome by an unpleasant feeling. At first I thought that this was vexation at not being able to explain a simple phenomenon; but afterwards, when I suddenly turned away from the light in horror and caught hold of Pashka with one hand, it became clear that I was overcome with terror. . . .

I was seized with a feeling of loneliness, misery, and horror, as though I had been flung down against my will into this great hole full of shadows, where I was standing all alone with the belfry looking at me with its red eye.

"Pashka!" I cried, closing my eyes in horror.

"Well?"

"Pashka, what's that gleaming on the belfry?"

Pashka looked over my shoulder at the belfry and gave a yawn.

"Who can tell?"

This brief conversation with the boy reassured me for a little, but not for long. Pashka, seeing my uneasiness, fastened his big eyes upon the light, looked at me again, then again at the light. . . .

"I am frightened," he whispered.

At this point, beside myself with terror, I clutched the boy with one hand, huddled up to him, and gave the horse a violent lash.

"It's stupid!" I said to myself. "That phenomenon is only terrible because I don't understand it; everything we don't understand is mysterious."

I tried to persuade myself, but at the same time I did not leave off lashing the horse. When we reached the posting station I purposely stayed for a full hour chatting with the overseer, and read through two or three newspapers, but the feeling of uneasiness did not leave me. On the way back the light was not to be seen, but on the other hand the silhouettes of the huts, of the poplars, and of the hill up which I had to drive, seemed to me as though animated. And why the light was there I don't know to this day.

The second terror I experienced was excited by a circumstance no less trivial. . . . I was returning from a romantic interview. It was one o'clock at night, the time when nature is buried in the soundest, sweetest sleep before the dawn. That time nature was not sleeping, and one could not call the night a still one. Corncrakes, quails, nightingales, and woodcocks were calling, crickets and grasshoppers were chirruping. There was a light mist over the grass, and clouds were scurrying straight ahead across the sky near the moon. Nature was awake, as though afraid of missing the best moments of her life.

I walked along a narrow path at the very edge of a railway embankment. The moonlight glided over the lines which were already covered with dew. Great shadows from the clouds kept flitting over the embankment. Far ahead, a dim green light was glimmering peacefully.

"So everything is well," I thought, looking at them.

I had a quiet, peaceful, comfortable feeling in my heart. I was returning from a tryst, I had no need to hurry; I was not sleepy, and I was conscious of youth and health in every sigh, every step I took, rousing a dull echo in the monotonous hum of the night. I don't know what I was feeling then, but I remember I was happy, very happy.

I had gone not more than three-quarters of a mile when I suddenly heard behind me a monotonous sound, a rumbling, rather like the roar of a great stream. It grew louder and louder every second, and sounded nearer and nearer. I looked round; a hundred paces from me was the dark copse from which I had only just come; there the embankment turned to the right in a graceful curve and vanished among the trees. I stood still in perplexity and waited. A huge black body appeared at once at the turn, noisily darted towards me, and with the swiftness of a bird flew past me along the rails. Less than half a minute passed and the blur had vanished, the rumble melted away into the noise of the night.

It was an ordinary goods truck. There was nothing peculiar about it in itself, but its appearance without an engine and in the night puzzled me. Where could it have come from and what force sent it flying so rapidly along the rails? Where did it come from and where was it flying to?

If I had been superstitious I should have made up my mind it was a party of demons and witches journeying to a devils' sabbath, and should have gone on my way, but as it was, the phenomenon was absolutely inexplicable to me. I did not believe my eyes, and was entangled in conjectures like a fly in a spider's web. . . .

I suddenly realized that I was utterly alone on the whole vast plain; that the night, which by now seemed inhospitable, was peeping into my face and dogging my footsteps; all the sounds, the cries of the birds, the whisperings of the trees, seemed sinister, and existing simply to alarm my imagination. I dashed on like a madman, and without realizing what I was doing I ran, trying to run faster and faster. And at once I heard something to which I had paid no attention before: that is, the plaintive whining of the telegraph wires.

"This is beyond everything," I said, trying to shame myself. "It's cowardice! it's silly!"

But cowardice was stronger than common sense. I only slackened my pace when I reached the green light, where I saw a dark signal-box, and near it on the embankment the figure of a man, probably the signalman.

"Did you see it?" I asked breathlessly.

"See whom? What?"

"Why, a truck ran by."

"I saw it, . . ." the peasant said reluctantly. "It broke away from the goods train. There is an incline at the ninetieth mile . . .; the train is dragged uphill. The coupling on the last truck gave way, so it broke off and ran back. . . . There is no catching it now! . . ."

The strange phenomenon was explained and its fantastic character vanished. My panic was over and I was able to go on my way.

My third fright came upon me as I was going home from stand shooting in early spring. It was in the dusk of evening. The forest road was covered with pools from a recent shower of rain, and the earth squelched under one's feet. The crimson glow of sunset flooded the whole forest, coloring the white stems of the birches and the young leaves. I was exhausted and could hardly move.

Four or five miles from home, walking along the forest road, I suddenly met a big black dog of the water spaniel breed. As he ran by, the dog looked intently at me, straight in my face, and ran on.

"A nice dog!" I thought. "Whose is it?"

I looked round. The dog was standing ten paces off with his eyes fixed on me. For a minute we scanned each other in silence, then the dog, probably flattered by my attention, came slowly up to me and wagged his tail.

I walked on, the dog following me.

"Whose dog can it be?" I kept asking myself. "Where does he come from?"

I knew all the country gentry for twenty or thirty miles round, and knew all their dogs. Not one of them had a spaniel like that. How did he come to be in the depths of the forest, on a track used for nothing but carting timber? He could hardly have dropped behind someone passing through, for there was nowhere for the gentry to drive to along that road.

I sat down on a stump to rest, and began scrutinizing my companion. He, too, sat down, raised his head, and fastened upon me an intent stare. He gazed at me without blinking. I don't know whether it was the influence of the stillness, the shadows and sounds of the forest, or perhaps a result of exhaustion, but I suddenly felt uneasy under the steady gaze of his ordinary doggy eyes. I thought of Faust and his bulldog, and of the fact that nervous people sometimes when exhausted have hallucinations. That was enough to make me get up hurriedly and hurriedly walk on. The dog followed me.

"Go away!" I shouted.

The dog probably liked my voice, for he gave a gleeful jump and ran about in front of me.

"Go away!" I shouted again.

The dog looked round, stared at me intently, and wagged his tail good-humoredly. Evidently my threatening tone amused him. I ought to have patted him, but I could not get Faust's dog out of my head, and the feeling of panic grew more and more acute... Darkness was coming on, which completed my confusion, and every time the dog ran up to me and hit me with his tail, like a coward I shut my eyes. The same thing happened as with the light in the belfry and the truck on the railway: I could not stand it and rushed away.

At home I found a visitor, an old friend, who, after greeting me, began to complain that as he was driving to me he had lost his way in the forest, and a splendid valuable dog of his had dropped behind.

# THE CHEMIST'S WIFE

The little town of B - - , consisting of two or three crooked streets, was sound asleep. There was a complete stillness in the motionless air. Nothing could be heard but far away, outside the town no doubt, the barking of a dog in a thin, hoarse tenor. It was close upon daybreak.

Everything had long been asleep. The only person not asleep was the young wife of Tchernomordik, a qualified dispenser who kept a chemist's shop at B - - . She had gone to bed and got up again three times, but could not sleep, she did not know why. She sat at the open window in her nightdress and looked into the street. She felt bored, depressed, vexed . . . so vexed that she felt quite inclined to cry - again she did not know why. There seemed to be a lump in her chest that kept rising into her throat. . . . A few paces behind her Tchernomordik lay curled up close to the wall, snoring sweetly. A greedy flea was stabbing the bridge of his nose, but he did not feel it, and was positively smiling, for he was dreaming that every one in the town had a cough, and was buying from him the King of Denmark's cough-drops. He could not have been wakened now by pinpricks or by cannon or by caresses.

The chemist's shop was almost at the extreme end of the town, so that the chemist's wife could see far into the fields. She could see the eastern horizon growing pale by degrees, then turning crimson as though from a great fire. A big broad-faced moon peeped out unexpectedly from behind bushes in the distance. It was red (as a rule when the moon emerges from behind bushes it appears to be blushing).

Suddenly in the stillness of the night there came the sounds of footsteps and a jingle of spurs. She could hear voices.

"That must be the officers going home to the camp from the Police Captain's," thought the chemist's wife.

Soon afterwards two figures wearing officers' white tunics came into sight: one big and tall, the other thinner and shorter. . . . They slouched along by the fence, dragging one leg after the other and talking loudly together. As they passed the chemist's shop, they walked more slowly than ever, and glanced up at the windows.

"It smells like a chemist's," said the thin one. "And so it is! Ah, I remember. . . . I came here last week to buy some castor-oil. There's a chemist here with a sour face and the jawbone of an ass! Such a jawbone, my dear fellow! It must have been a jawbone like that Samson killed the Philistines with."

"M'yes," said the big one in a bass voice. "The pharmacist is asleep. And his wife is asleep too. She is a pretty woman, Obtyosov."

"I saw her. I liked her very much. . . . Tell me, doctor, can she possibly love that jawbone of an ass? Can she?"

"No, most likely she does not love him," sighed the doctor, speaking as though he were sorry for the chemist. "The little woman is asleep behind the window, Obtyosov, what? Tossing with the heat, her little mouth half open . . . and one little foot hanging out of bed. I bet that fool the chemist doesn't realise what a lucky fellow he is. . . . No doubt he sees no difference between a woman and a bottle of carbolic!"

"I say, doctor," said the officer, stopping. "Let us go into the shop and buy something. Perhaps we shall see her."

"What an idea - in the night!"

"What of it? They are obliged to serve one even at night. My dear fellow, let us go in!"

"If you like. . . ."

The chemist's wife, hiding behind the curtain, heard a muffled ring. Looking round at her husband, who was smiling and snoring sweetly as before, she threw on her dress, slid her bare feet into her slippers, and ran to the shop.

On the other side of the glass door she could see two shadows. The chemist's wife turned up the lamp and hurried to the door to open it, and now she felt neither vexed nor bored nor inclined to cry, though her heart was thumping. The big doctor and the slender Obtyosov walked in. Now she could get a view of them. The doctor was corpulent and swarthy; he wore a beard and was slow in his movements. At the slightest motion his tunic seemed as though it would crack, and perspiration came on to his face. The officer was rosy, clean-shaven, feminine-looking, and as supple as an English whip.

"What may I give you? asked the chemist's wife, holding her dress across her bosom.

"Give us . . . er-er . . . four pennyworth of peppermint lozenges!"

Without haste the chemist's wife took down a jar from a shelf and began weighing out lozenges. The customers stared fixedly at her back; the doctor screwed up his eyes like a well-fed cat, while the lieutenant was very grave.

"It's the first time I've seen a lady serving in a chemist's shop," observed the doctor.

"There's nothing out of the way in it," replied the chemist's wife, looking out of the corner of her eye at the rosy-cheeked officer. "My husband has no assistant, and I always help him."

"To be sure. . . . You have a charming little shop! What a number of different . . . jars! And you are not afraid of moving about among the poisons? Brrr!"

The chemist's wife sealed up the parcel and handed it to the doctor. Obtyosov gave her the money. Half a minute of silence followed. . . . The men exchanged glances, took a step towards the door, then looked at one another again.

"Will you give me two pennyworth of soda?" said the doctor.

Again the chemist's wife slowly and languidly raised her hand to the shelf.

"Haven't you in the shop anything . . . such as . . ." muttered Obtyosov, moving his fingers, "something, so to say, allegorical . . . revivifying . . . seltzer-water, for instance. Have you any seltzer-water?"

"Yes," answered the chemist's wife.

"Bravo! You're a fairy, not a woman! Give us three bottles!"

The chemist's wife hurriedly sealed up the soda and vanished through the door into the darkness.

"A peach!" said the doctor, with a wink. "You wouldn't find a pineapple like that in the island of Madeira! Eh? What do you say? Do you hear the snoring, though? That's his worship the chemist enjoying sweet repose."

A minute later the chemist's wife came back and set five bottles on the counter. She had just been in the cellar, and so was flushed and rather excited.

"Sh-sh! . . . quietly!" said Obtyosov when, after uncorking the bottles, she dropped the corkscrew. "Don't make such a noise; you'll wake your husband."

"Well, what if I do wake him?"

"He is sleeping so sweetly . . . he must be dreaming of you. . . . To your health!"

"Besides," boomed the doctor, hiccupping after the seltzer-water, "husbands are such a dull business that it would be very nice of them to be always asleep. How good a drop of red wine would be in this water!"

"What an idea!" laughed the chemist's wife.

"That would be splendid. What a pity they don't sell spirits in chemist's shops! Though you ought to sell wine as a medicine. Have you any *vinum gallicum rubrum?*"

"Yes."

"Well, then, give us some! Bring it here, damn it!"

"How much do you want?"

"*Quantum satis.* . . . Give us an ounce each in the water, and afterwards we'll see. . . . Obtyosov, what do you say? First with water and afterwards *per se.* . . ."

The doctor and Obtyosov sat down to the counter, took off their caps, and began drinking the wine.

"The wine, one must admit, is wretched stuff! *Vinum nastissimum!* Though in the presence of . . . er . . . it tastes like nectar. You are enchanting, madam! In imagination I kiss your hand."

"I would give a great deal to do so not in imagination," said Obtyosov. "On my honour, I'd give my life."

"That's enough," said Madame Tchernomordik, flushing and assuming a serious expression.

"What a flirt you are, though!" the doctor laughed softly, looking slyly at her from under his brows. "Your eyes seem to be firing shot: piff-paff! I congratulate you: you've conquered! We are vanquished!"

The chemist's wife looked at their ruddy faces, listened to their chatter, and soon she, too, grew quite lively. Oh, she felt so gay! She entered into the conversation, she laughed, flirted, and even, after repeated requests from the customers, drank two ounces of wine.

"You officers ought to come in oftener from the camp," she said; "it's awful how dreary it is here. I'm simply dying of it."

"I should think so!" said the doctor indignantly. "Such a peach, a miracle of nature, thrown away in the wilds! How well Griboyedov said, 'Into the wilds, to Saratov'! It's time for us to be off, though. Delighted to have made your acquaintance . . . very. How much do we owe you?"

The chemist's wife raised her eyes to the ceiling and her lips moved for some time.

"Twelve roubles forty-eight kopecks," she said.

Obtyosov took out of his pocket a fat pocket-book, and after fumbling for some time among the notes, paid.

"Your husband's sleeping sweetly . . . he must be dreaming," he muttered, pressing her hand at parting.

"I don't like to hear silly remarks. . . ."

"What silly remarks? On the contrary, it's not silly at all . . . even Shakespeare said: 'Happy is he who in his youth is young.' "

"Let go of my hand."

At last after much talk and after kissing the lady's hand at parting, the customers went out of the shop irresolutely, as though they were wondering whether they had not forgotten something.

She ran quickly into the bedroom and sat down in the same place. She saw the doctor and the officer, on coming out of the shop, walk lazily away a distance of twenty paces; then they stopped and began whispering together. What about? Her heart throbbed, there was a pulsing in her temples, and why she did not know. . . . Her heart beat violently as though those two whispering outside were deciding her fate.

Five minutes later the doctor parted from Obtyosov and walked on, while Obtyosov came back. He walked past the shop once and a second time. . . . He would stop near the door and then take a few steps again. At last the bell tinkled discreetly.

"What? Who is there?" the chemist's wife heard her husband's voice suddenly. "There's a ring at the bell, and you don't hear it," he said severely. "Is that the way to do things?"

He got up, put on his dressing-gown, and staggering, half asleep, flopped in his slippers to the shop.

"What . . . is it?" he asked Obtyosov.

"Give me . . . give me four pennyworth of peppermint lozenges."

Sniffing continually, yawning, dropping asleep as he moved, and knocking his knees against the counter, the chemist went to the shelf and reached down the jar.

Two minutes later the chemist's wife saw Obtyosov go out of the shop, and, after he had gone some steps, she saw him throw the packet of peppermints on the dusty road. The doctor came from behind a corner to meet him. . . . They met and, gesticulating, vanished in the morning mist.

"How unhappy I am!" said the chemist's wife, looking angrily at her husband, who was undressing quickly to get into bed again. "Oh, how unhappy I am!" she repeated, suddenly melting into bitter tears. "And nobody knows, nobody knows. . . ."

"I forgot fourpence on the counter," muttered the chemist, pulling the quilt over him. "Put it away in the till, please. . . ."

And at once he fell asleep again.

# NOT WANTED

Between six and seven o'clock on a July evening, a crowd of summer visitors - mostly fathers of families - burdened with parcels, portfolios, and ladies' hat-boxes, was trailing along from the little station of Helkovo, in the direction of the summer villas. They all looked exhausted, hungry, and ill-humoured, as though the sun were not shining and the grass were not green for them.

Trudging along among the others was Pavel Matveyitch Zaikin, a member of the Circuit Court, a tall, stooping man, in a cheap cotton dust-coat and with a cockade on his faded cap. He was perspiring, red in the face, and gloomy. . . .

"Do you come out to your holiday home every day?" said a summer visitor, in ginger-coloured trousers, addressing him.

"No, not every day," Zaikin answered sullenly. "My wife and son are staying here all the while, and I come down two or three times a week. I haven't time to come every day; besides, it is expensive."

"You're right there; it is expensive," sighed he of the ginger trousers. "In town you can't walk to the station, you have to take a cab; and then, the ticket costs forty-two kopecks; you buy a paper for the journey; one is tempted to drink a glass of vodka. It's all petty expenditure not worth considering, but, mind you, in the course of the summer it will run up to some two hundred roubles. Of course, to be in the lap of Nature is worth any money - I don't dispute it . . . idyllic and all the rest of it; but of course, with the salary an official gets, as you know yourself, every farthing has to be considered. If you waste a halfpenny you lie awake all night. . . . Yes. . . I receive, my dear sir - I haven't the honour of knowing your name - I receive a salary of very nearly two thousand roubles a year. I am a civil councillor, I smoke second-rate tobacco, and I haven't a rouble to spare to buy Vichy water, prescribed me by the doctor for gall-stones."

"It's altogether abominable," said Zaikin after a brief silence. "I maintain, sir, that summer holidays are the invention of the devil and of woman. The devil was actuated in the present instance by malice, woman by excessive frivolity. Mercy on us, it is not life at all; it is hard labour, it is hell! It's hot and stifling, you can hardly breathe, and you wander about like a lost soul and can find no refuge. In town there is no furniture, no servants. . . everything has been carried off to the villa: you eat what you can get; you go without your tea because there is no one to heat the samovar; you can't wash yourself; and when you come down here into this 'lap of Nature' you have to walk, if you please, through the dust and heat. . . . Phew! Are you married?"

"Yes. . . three children," sighs Ginger Trousers.

"It's abominable altogether. . . . It's a wonder we are still alive."

At last the summer visitors reached their destination. Zaikin said goodbye to Ginger Trousers and went into his villa. He found a death-like silence in the house. He could hear nothing but the buzzing of the gnats, and the prayer for help of a fly destined for the dinner of a spider. The windows were hung with muslin curtains, through which the faded flowers of the geraniums showed red. On the unpainted wooden walls near the oleographs flies were slumbering. There was not a soul in the passage, the kitchen, or the dining-room. In the room which was called indifferently the parlour or the drawing-room, Zaikin found his son Petya, a little boy of six. Petya was sitting at the table, and breathing loudly with his lower lip stuck out, was engaged in cutting out the figure of a knave of diamonds from a card.

"Oh, that's you, father!" he said, without turning round. "Good-evening."

"Good-evening. . . . And where is mother?"

"Mother? She is gone with Olga Kirillovna to a rehearsal of the play. The day after tomorrow they will have a performance. And they will take me, too. . . . And will you go?"

"H'm! . . . When is she coming back?"

"She said she would be back in the evening."

"And where is Natalya?"

"Mamma took Natalya with her to help her dress for the performance, and Akulina has gone to the wood to get mushrooms. Father, why is it that when gnats bite you their stomachs get red?"

"I don't know. . . . Because they suck blood. So there is no one in the house, then?"

"No one; I am all alone in the house."

Zaikin sat down in an easy-chair, and for a moment gazed blankly at the window.

"Who is going to get our dinner?" he asked.

"They haven't cooked any dinner today, father. Mamma thought you were not coming today, and did not order any dinner. She is going to have dinner with Olga Kirillovna at the rehearsal."

"Oh, thank you very much; and you, what have you to eat?"

"I've had some milk. They bought me six kopecks' worth of milk. And, father, why do gnats suck blood?"

Zaikin suddenly felt as though something heavy were rolling down on his liver and beginning to gnaw it. He felt so vexed, so aggrieved, and so bitter, that he was choking and tremulous; he wanted to jump up, to bang something on the floor, and to burst into loud abuse; but then he remembered that his doctor had absolutely forbidden him all excitement, so he got up, and making an effort to control himself, began whistling a tune from "Les Huguenots."

"Father, can you act in plays?" he heard Petya's voice.

"Oh, don't worry me with stupid questions!" said Zaikin, getting angry. "He sticks to one like a leaf in the bath! Here you are, six years old, and just as silly as you were three years ago. . . . Stupid, neglected child! Why are you spoiling those cards, for instance? How dare you spoil them?"

"These cards aren't yours," said Petya, turning round. "Natalya gave them me."

"You are telling fibs, you are telling fibs, you horrid boy!" said Zaikin, growing more and more irritated. "You are always telling fibs! You want a whipping, you horrid little pig! I will pull your ears!

Petya leapt up, and craning his neck, stared fixedly at his father's red and wrathful face. His big eyes first began blinking, then were dimmed with moisture, and the boy's face began working.

"But why are you scolding?" squealed Petya. "Why do you attack me, you stupid? I am not interfering with anybody; I am not naughty; I do what I am told, and yet . . . you are cross! Why are you scolding me?"

The boy spoke with conviction, and wept so bitterly that Zaikin felt conscience-stricken.

"Yes, really, why am I falling foul of him?" he thought. "Come, come," he said, touching the boy on the shoulder. "I am sorry, Petya . . . forgive me. You are my good boy, my nice boy, I love you."

Petya wiped his eyes with his sleeve, sat down, with a sigh, in the same place and began cutting out the queen. Zaikin went off to his own room. He stretched himself on the sofa, and putting his hands behind his head, sank into thought. The boy's tears had softened his anger, and by degrees the oppression on his liver grew less. He felt nothing but exhaustion and hunger.

"Father," he heard on the other side of the door, "shall I show you my collection of insects?"

"Yes, show me."

Petya came into the study and handed his father a long green box. Before raising it to his ear Zaikin could hear a despairing buzz and the scratching of claws on the sides of the box. Opening the lid, he saw a number of butterflies, beetles, grasshoppers, and flies fastened to the bottom of the box with pins. All except two or three butterflies were still alive and moving.

"Why, the grasshopper is still alive!" said Petya in surprise. "I caught him yesterday morning, and he is still alive!"

"Who taught you to pin them in this way?"

"Olga Kirillovna."

"Olga Kirillovna ought to be pinned down like that herself!" said Zaikin with repulsion. "Take them away! It's shameful to torture animals."

"My God! How horribly he is being brought up!" he thought, as Petya went out.

Pavel Matveyitch forgot his exhaustion and hunger, and thought of nothing but his boy's future. Meanwhile, outside the light was gradually fading. . . . He could hear the summer visitors trooping back from the evening bathe. Some one was stopping near the open dining-room window and shouting: "Do you want any mushrooms?" And getting no answer, shuffled on with bare feet. . . . But at last, when the dusk was so thick that the outlines of the geraniums behind the muslin curtain were lost, and whiffs of the freshness of evening were coming in at the window, the door of the passage was thrown open noisily, and there came a sound of rapid footsteps, talk, and laughter. . . .

"Mamma!" shrieked Petya.

Zaikin peeped out of his study and saw his wife, Nadyezhda Stepanovna, healthy and rosy as ever; with her he saw Olga Kirillovna, a spare woman with fair hair and heavy freckles, and two unknown men: one a lanky young man with curly red hair and a big Adam's apple; the other, a short stubby man with a shaven face like an actor's and a bluish crooked chin.

"Natalya, set the samovar," cried Nadyezhda Stepanovna, with a loud rustle of her skirts. "I hear Pavel Matveyitch is come. Pavel, where are you? Good-evening, Pavel!" she said, running into the study breathlessly. "So you've come. I am so glad. . . . Two of our amateurs have come with me. . . . Come, I'll introduce you. . . . Here, the taller one is Koromyslov . . . he sings splendidly; and the other, the little one . . . is called Smerkalov: he is a real actor . . . he recites magnificently. Oh, how tired I am! We have just had a rehearsal. . . . It goes splendidly. We are acting 'The Lodger with the Trombone' and 'Waiting for Him.' . . . The performance is the day after tomorrow. . . ."

"Why did you bring them?" asked Zaikin.

"I couldn't help it, Poppet; after tea we must rehearse our parts and sing something. . . . I am to sing a duet with Koromyslov. . . . Oh, yes, I was almost forgetting! Darling, send Natalya to get some sardines, vodka, cheese, and something else. They will most likely stay to supper. . . . Oh, how tired I am!"

"H'm! I've no money."

"You must, Poppet! It would be awkward! Don't make me blush."

Half an hour later Natalya was sent for vodka and savouries; Zaikin, after drinking tea and eating a whole French loaf, went to his bedroom and lay down on the bed, while Nadyezhda Stepanovna and her visitors, with much noise and laughter, set to work to rehearse their parts. For a long time Pavel Matveyitch heard Koromyslov's nasal reciting and Smerkalov's theatrical exclamations. . . . The rehearsal was followed by a long conversation, interrupted by the shrill laughter of Olga Kirillovna. Smerkalov, as a real actor, explained the parts with aplomb and heat. . . .

Then followed the duet, and after the duet there was the clatter of crockery. . . . Through his drowsiness Zaikin heard them persuading Smerkalov to read "The Woman who was a Sinner," and heard him, after affecting to refuse, begin to recite. He hissed, beat himself on the breast, wept, laughed in a husky bass. . . . Zaikin scowled and hid his head under the quilt.

"It's a long way for you to go, and it's dark," he heard Nadyezhda Stepanovna's voice an hour later. "Why shouldn't you stay the night here? Koromyslov can sleep here in the drawing-room on the sofa, and you, Smerkalov, in Petya's bed. . . . I can put Petya in my husband's study. . . . Do stay, really!"

At last when the clock was striking two, all was hushed, the bedroom door opened, and Nadyezhda Stepanovna appeared.

"Pavel, are you asleep?" she whispered.

"No; why?"

"Go into your study, darling, and lie on the sofa. I am going to put Olga Kirillovna here, in your bed. Do go, dear! I would put her to sleep in the study, but she is afraid to sleep alone. . . . Do get up!"

Zaikin got up, threw on his dressing-gown, and taking his pillow, crept wearily to the study. . . . Feeling his way to his sofa, he lighted a match, and saw Petya lying on the sofa. The boy was not asleep, and, looking at the match with wide-open eyes:

"Father, why is it gnats don't go to sleep at night?" he asked.

"Because . . . because . . . you and I are not wanted. . . . We have nowhere to sleep even."

"Father, and why is it Olga Kirillovna has freckles on her face?"

"Oh, shut up! I am tired of you."

After a moment's thought, Zaikin dressed and went out into the street for a breath of air. . . . He looked at the grey morning sky, at the motionless clouds, heard the lazy call of the drowsy corncrake, and began dreaming of the next day, when he would go to town, and coming back from the court would tumble into bed. . . . Suddenly the figure of a man appeared round the corner.

"A watchman, no doubt," thought Zaikin. But going nearer and looking more closely he recognized in the figure the summer visitor in the ginger trousers.

"You're not asleep?" he asked.

"No, I can't sleep," sighed Ginger Trousers. "I am enjoying Nature. . . . A welcome visitor, my wife's mother, arrived by the night train, you know. She brought with her our nieces . . . splendid girls! I was delighted to see them, although . . . it's very damp! And you, too, are enjoying Nature?"

"Yes," grunted Zaikin, "I am enjoying it, too. . . . Do you know whether there is any sort of tavern or restaurant in the neighbourhood?"

Ginger Trousers raised his eyes to heaven and meditated profoundly.

# THE CHORUS GIRL

One day when she was younger and better-looking, and when her voice was stronger, Nikolay Petrovitch Kolpakov, her adorer, was sitting in the outer room in her summer villa. It was intolerably hot and stifling. Kolpakov, who had just dined and drunk a whole bottle of inferior port, felt ill-humoured and out of sorts. Both were bored and waiting for the heat of the day to be over in order to go for a walk.

All at once there was a sudden ring at the door. Kolpakov, who was sitting with his coat off, in his slippers, jumped up and looked inquiringly at Pasha.

"It must be the postman or one of the girls," said the singer.

Kolpakov did not mind being found by the postman or Pasha's lady friends, but by way of precaution gathered up his clothes and went into the next room, while Pasha ran to open the door. To her great surprise in the doorway stood, not the postman and not a girl friend, but an unknown woman, young and beautiful, who was dressed like a lady, and from all outward signs was one.

The stranger was pale and was breathing heavily as though she had been running up a steep flight of stairs.

"What is it?" asked Pasha.

The lady did not at once answer. She took a step forward, slowly looked about the room, and sat down in a way that suggested that from fatigue, or perhaps illness, she could not stand; then for a long time her pale lips quivered as she tried in vain to speak.

"Is my husband here?" she asked at last, raising to Pasha her big eyes with their red tear-stained lids.

"Husband?" whispered Pasha, and was suddenly so frightened that her hands and feet turned cold. "What husband?" she repeated, beginning to tremble.

"My husband, . . . Nikolay Petrovitch Kolpakov."

"N . . . no, madam. . . . I . . . I don't know any husband."

A minute passed in silence. The stranger several times passed her handkerchief over her pale lips and held her breath to stop her inward trembling, while Pasha stood before her motionless, like a post, and looked at her with astonishment and terror.

"So you say he is not here?" the lady asked, this time speaking with a firm voice and smiling oddly.

"I . . . I don't know who it is you are asking about."

"You are horrid, mean, vile . . ." the stranger muttered, scanning Pasha with hatred and repulsion. "Yes, yes . . . you are horrid. I am very, very glad that at last I can tell you so!"

Pasha felt that on this lady in black with the angry eyes and white slender fingers she produced the impression of something horrid and unseemly, and she felt ashamed of her chubby red cheeks, the pock-mark on her nose, and the fringe on her forehead, which never could be combed back. And it seemed to her that if she had been thin, and had had no powder on her face and no fringe on her forehead, then she could have disguised the fact that she was not "respectable," and she would not have felt so frightened and ashamed to stand facing this unknown, mysterious lady.

"Where is my husband?" the lady went on. "Though I don't care whether he is here or not, but I ought to tell you that the money has been missed, and they are looking for Nikolay Petrovitch. . . . They mean to arrest him. That's your doing!"

The lady got up and walked about the room in great excitement. Pasha looked at her and was so frightened that she could not understand.

"He'll be found and arrested to-day," said the lady, and she gave a sob, and in that sound could be heard her resentment and vexation. "I know who has brought him to this awful position! Low, horrid creature! Loathsome, mercenary hussy!" The lady's lips worked and her nose wrinkled up with disgust. "I am helpless, do you hear, you low woman? . . . I am helpless; you are stronger than I am, but there is One to defend me and my children! God sees all! He is just! He will punish you for every tear I have shed, for all my sleepless nights! The time will come; you will think of me! . . ."

Silence followed again. The lady walked about the room and wrung her hands, while Pasha still gazed blankly at her in amazement, not understanding and expecting something terrible.

"I know nothing about it, madam," she said, and suddenly burst into tears.

"You are lying!" cried the lady, and her eyes flashed angrily at her. "I know all about it! I've known you a long time. I know that for the last month he has been spending every day with you!"

"Yes. What then? What of it? I have a great many visitors, but I don't force anyone to come. He is free to do as he likes."

"I tell you they have discovered that money is missing! He has embezzled money at the office! For the sake of such a . . . creature as you, for your sake he has actually committed a crime. Listen," said the lady in a resolute voice, stopping short, facing Pasha. "You can have no principles; you live simply to do harm - that's your object; but one can't imagine you have fallen so low that you have no trace of human feeling left! He has a wife, children. . . . If he is condemned and sent into exile we shall starve, the children and I. . . . Understand that! And yet there is a chance of saving him and us from destitution and disgrace. If I take them nine hundred roubles to-day they will let him alone. Only nine hundred roubles!"

"What nine hundred roubles?" Pasha asked softly. "I . . . I don't know. . . . I haven't taken it."

"I am not asking you for nine hundred roubles. . . . You have no money, and I don't want your money. I ask you for something else. . . . Men usually give expensive things to women like you. Only give me back the things my husband has given you!"

"Madam, he has never made me a present of anything!" Pasha wailed, beginning to understand.

"Where is the money? He has squandered his own and mine and other people's. . . . What has become of it all? Listen, I beg you! I was carried away by indignation and have said a lot of nasty things to you, but I apologize. You must hate me, I know, but if you are capable of

215

sympathy, put yourself in my position! I implore you to give me back the things!"

"H'm!" said Pasha, and she shrugged her shoulders. "I would with pleasure, but God is my witness, he never made me a present of anything. Believe me, on my conscience. However, you are right, though," said the singer in confusion, "he did bring me two little things. Certainly I will give them back, if you wish it."

Pasha pulled out one of the drawers in the toilet-table and took out of it a hollow gold bracelet and a thin ring with a ruby in it.

"Here, madam!" she said, handing the visitor these articles.

The lady flushed and her face quivered. She was offended.

"What are you giving me?" she said. "I am not asking for charity, but for what does not belong to you . . . what you have taken advantage of your position to squeeze out of my husband . . . that weak, unhappy man. . . . On Thursday, when I saw you with my husband at the harbour you were wearing expensive brooches and bracelets. So it's no use your playing the innocent lamb to me! I ask you for the last time: will you give me the things, or not?"

"You are a queer one, upon my word," said Pasha, beginning to feel offended. "I assure you that, except the bracelet and this little ring, I've never seen a thing from your Nikolay Petrovitch. He brings me nothing but sweet cakes."

"Sweet cakes!" laughed the stranger. "At home the children have nothing to eat, and here you have sweet cakes. You absolutely refuse to restore the presents?"

Receiving no answer, the lady sat, down and stared into space, pondering.

"What's to be done now?" she said. "If I don't get nine hundred roubles, he is ruined, and the children and I am ruined, too. Shall I kill this low woman or go down on my knees to her?"

The lady pressed her handkerchief to her face and broke into sobs.

"I beg you!" Pasha heard through the stranger's sobs. "You see you have plundered and ruined my husband. Save him. . . . You have no feeling for him, but the children . . . the children . . . What have the children done?"

Pasha imagined little children standing in the street, crying with hunger, and she, too, sobbed.

"What can I do, madam?" she said. "You say that I am a low woman and that I have ruined Nikolay Petrovitch, and I assure you . . . before God Almighty, I have had nothing from him whatever. . . . There is only one girl in our chorus who has a rich admirer; all the rest of us live from hand to mouth on bread and kvass. Nikolay Petrovitch is a highly educated, refined gentleman, so I've made him welcome. We are bound to make gentlemen welcome."

"I ask you for the things! Give me the things! I am crying. . . . I am humiliating myself. . . . If you like I will go down on my knees! If you wish it!"

Pasha shrieked with horror and waved her hands. She felt that this pale, beautiful lady who expressed herself so grandly, as though she were on the stage, really might go down on her knees to her, simply from pride, from grandeur, to exalt herself and humiliate the chorus girl.

"Very well, I will give you things!" said Pasha, wiping her eyes and bustling about. "By all means. Only they are not from Nikolay Petrovitch. . . . I got these from other gentlemen. As you please. . . ."

Pasha pulled out the upper drawer of the chest, took out a diamond brooch, a coral necklace, some rings and bracelets, and gave them all to the lady.

"Take them if you like, only I've never had anything from your husband. Take them and grow rich," Pasha went on, offended at the threat to go down on her knees. "And if you are a lady . . . his lawful wife, you should keep him to yourself. I should think so! I did not ask him to come; he came of himself."

Through her tears the lady scrutinized the articles given her and said.

"This isn't everything.... There won't be five hundred roubles' worth here."

Pasha impulsively flung out of the chest a gold watch, a cigar-case and studs, and said, flinging up her hands:

"I've nothing else left.... You can search!"

The visitor gave a sigh, with trembling hands twisted the things up in her handkerchief, and went out without uttering a word, without even nodding her head.

The door from the next room opened and Kolpakov walked in. He was pale and kept shaking his head nervously, as though he had swallowed something very bitter; tears were glistening in his eyes.

"What presents did you make me?" Pasha asked, pouncing upon him. "When did you, allow me to ask you?"

"Presents ... that's no matter!" said Kolpakov, and he tossed his head. "My God! She cried before you, she humbled herself...."

"I am asking you, what presents did you make me?" Pasha cried.

"My God! She, a lady, so proud, so pure.... She was ready to go down on her knees to ... to this wench! And I've brought her to this! I've allowed it!"

He clutched his head in his hands and moaned.

"No, I shall never forgive myself for this! I shall never forgive myself! Get away from me ... you low creature!" he cried with repulsion, backing away from Pasha, and thrusting her off with trembling hands. "She would have gone down on her knees, and ... and to you! Oh, my God!"

He rapidly dressed, and pushing Pasha aside contemptuously, made for the door and went out.

Pasha lay down and began wailing aloud. She was already regretting her things which she had given away so impulsively, and her feelings were hurt. She remembered how three years ago a merchant had beaten her for no sort of reason, and she wailed more loudly than ever.

# THE SCHOOLMASTER

Fyodor Lukitch Sysoev, the master of the factory school maintained at the expense of the firm of Kulikin, was getting ready for the annual dinner. Every year after the school examination the board of managers gave a dinner at which the inspector of elementary schools, all who had conducted the examinations, and all the managers and foremen of the factory were present. In spite of their official character, these dinners were always good and lively, and the guests sat a long time over them; forgetting distinctions of rank and recalling only their meritorious labours, they ate till they were full, drank amicably, chattered till they were all hoarse and parted late in the evening, deafening the whole factory settlement with their singing and the sound of their kisses. Of such dinners Sysoev had taken part in thirteen, as he had been that number of years master of the factory school.

Now, getting ready for the fourteenth, he was trying to make himself look as festive and correct as possible. He had spent a whole hour brushing his new black suit, and spent almost as long in front of a looking-glass while he put on a fashionable shirt; the studs would not go into the button-holes, and this circumstance called forth a perfect storm of complaints, threats, and reproaches addressed to his wife.

His poor wife, bustling round him, wore herself out with her efforts. And indeed he, too, was exhausted in the end. When his polished boots were brought him from the kitchen he had not strength to pull them on. He had to lie down and have a drink of water.

"How weak you have grown!" sighed his wife. "You ought not to go to this dinner at all."

"No advice, please!" the schoolmaster cut her short angrily.

He was in a very bad temper, for he had been much displeased with the recent examinations. The examinations had gone off splendidly; all the boys of the senior division had gained certificates and prizes; both the managers of the factory and the government officials were pleased with the results; but that was not enough for the schoolmaster. He was vexed that Babkin, a boy who never made a mistake in writing, had made three mistakes in the dictation; Sergeyev, another boy, had been so excited that he could not remember seventeen times thirteen; the inspector, a young and inexperienced man, had chosen a difficult article for dictation, and Lyapunov, the master of a neighbouring school, whom the inspector had asked to dictate, had not behaved like "a good comrade"; but in dictating had, as it were, swallowed the words and had not pronounced them as written.

After pulling on his boots with the assistance of his wife, and looking at himself once more in the looking-glass, the schoolmaster took his gnarled stick and set off for the dinner. Just before the factory manager's house, where the festivity was to take place, he had a little mishap. He was taken with a violent fit of coughing. . . . He was so shaken by it that the cap flew off his head and the stick dropped out of his hand; and when the school inspector and the teachers, hearing his cough, ran out of the house, he was sitting on the bottom step, bathed in perspiration.

"Fyodor Lukitch, is that you?" said the inspector, surprised. "You . . . have come?"

"Why not?"

"You ought to be at home, my dear fellow. You are not at all well to-day. . . ."

"I am just the same to-day as I was yesterday. And if my presence is not agreeable to you, I can go back."

"Oh, Fyodor Lukitch, you must not talk like that! Please come in. Why, the function is really in your honour, not ours. And we are delighted to see you. Of course we are! . . ."

Within, everything was ready for the banquet. In the big dining-room adorned with German oleographs and smelling of geraniums and varnish there were two tables, a larger one for the dinner and a smaller one for the hors-d'oeuvres. The hot light of midday faintly percolated through the lowered blinds. . . . The twilight of the room, the Swiss views on the blinds, the geraniums, the thin slices of sausage on the plates, all had a naïve, girlishly-sentimental air, and it was all in keeping with the master of the house, a good-natured little German with a round little stomach and affectionate, oily little eyes, Adolf Andreyitch Bruni (that was his name) was bustling round the table of hors-d'oeuvres as zealously as though it were a house on fire, filling up the wine-glasses, loading the plates, and trying in every way to please, to amuse, and to show his friendly feelings. He clapped people on the shoulder, looked into their eyes, chuckled, rubbed his hands, in fact was as ingratiating as a friendly dog.

"Whom do I behold? Fyodor Lukitch!" he said in a jerky voice, on seeing Sysoev. "How delightful! You have come in spite of your illness. Gentlemen, let me congratulate you, Fyodor Lukitch has come!"

The school-teachers were already crowding round the table and eating the hors-d'oeuvres. Sysoev frowned; he was displeased that his colleagues had begun to eat and drink without waiting for him. He noticed among them Lyapunov, the man who had dictated at the examination, and going up to him, began:

"It was not acting like a comrade! No, indeed! Gentlemanly people don't dictate like that!"

"Good Lord, you are still harping on it!" said Lyapunov, and he frowned. "Aren't you sick of it?"

"Yes, still harping on it! My Babkin has never made mistakes! I know why you dictated like that. You simply wanted my pupils to be floored, so that your school might seem better than mine. I know all about it! . . ."

"Why are you trying to get up a quarrel?" Lyapunov snarled. "Why the devil do you pester me?"

"Come, gentlemen," interposed the inspector, making a woebegone face. "Is it worth while to get so heated over a trifle? Three mistakes . . . not one mistake . . . does it matter?"

"Yes, it does matter. Babkin has never made mistakes."

"He won't leave off," Lyapunov went on, snorting angrily. "He takes advantage of his position as an invalid and worries us all to death. Well, sir, I am not going to consider your being ill."

"Let my illness alone!" cried Sysoev, angrily. "What is it to do with you? They all keep repeating it at me: illness! illness! illness! . . . As though I need your sympathy! Besides, where have you picked up the notion that I am ill? I was ill before the examinations, that's true, but now I have completely recovered, there is nothing left of it but weakness."

"You have regained your health, well, thank God," said the scripture teacher, Father Nikolay, a young priest in a foppish cinnamon-coloured cassock and trousers outside his boots. "You ought to rejoice, but you are irritable and so on."

"You are a nice one, too," Sysoev interrupted him. "Questions ought to be straightforward, clear, but you kept asking riddles. That's not the thing to do!"

By combined efforts they succeeded in soothing him and making him sit down to the table. He was a long time making up his mind what to drink, and pulling a wry face drank a wine-glass of some green liqueur; then he drew a bit of pie towards him, and sulkily picked out of the inside an egg with onion on it. At the first mouthful it seemed to him that there was no salt in it. He sprinkled salt on it and at once pushed it away as the pie was too salt.

At dinner Sysoev was seated between the inspector and Bruni. After the first course the toasts began, according to the old-established custom.

"I consider it my agreeable duty," the inspector began, "to propose a vote of thanks to the absent school wardens, Daniel Petrovitch and . . . and . . . and . . ."

"And Ivan Petrovitch," Bruni prompted him.

"And Ivan Petrovitch Kulikin, who grudge no expense for the school, and I propose to drink their health. . . ."

"For my part," said Bruni, jumping up as though he had been stung, "I propose a toast to the health of the honoured inspector of elementary schools, Pavel Gennadievitch Nadarov!"

Chairs were pushed back, faces beamed with smiles, and the usual clinking of glasses began.

The third toast always fell to Sysoev. And on this occasion, too, he got up and began to speak. Looking grave and clearing his throat, he first of all announced that he had not the gift of eloquence and that he was not prepared to make a speech. Further he said that during the fourteen years that he had been schoolmaster there had been many intrigues, many underhand attacks, and even secret reports on him to the authorities, and that he knew his enemies and those who had informed against him, and he would not mention their names, "for fear of spoiling somebody's appetite"; that in spite of these intrigues the Kulikin school held the foremost place in the whole province not only from a moral, but also from a material point of view."

"Everywhere else," he said, "schoolmasters get two hundred or three hundred roubles, while I get five hundred, and moreover my house has been redecorated and even furnished at the expense of the firm. And this year all the walls have been repapered...."

Further the schoolmaster enlarged on the liberality with which the pupils were provided with writing materials in the factory schools as compared with the Zemstvo and Government schools. And for all this the school was indebted, in his opinion, not to the heads of the firm, who lived abroad and scarcely knew of its existence, but to a man who, in spite of his German origin and Lutheran faith, was a Russian at heart.

Sysoev spoke at length, with pauses to get his breath and with pretensions to rhetoric, and his speech was boring and unpleasant. He several times referred to certain enemies of his, tried to drop hints, repeated himself, coughed, and flourished his fingers unbecomingly. At last he was exhausted and in a perspiration and he began talking jerkily, in a low voice as though to himself, and finished his speech not quite coherently: "And so I propose the health of Bruni, that is Adolf Andreyitch, who is here, among us . . . generally speaking . . . you understand . . ."

When he finished everyone gave a faint sigh, as though someone had sprinkled cold water and cleared the air. Bruni alone apparently had no unpleasant feeling. Beaming and rolling his sentimental eyes, the German shook Sysoev's hand with feeling and was again as friendly as a dog.

"Oh, I thank you," he said, with an emphasis on the *oh*, laying his left hand on his heart. "I am very happy that you understand me! I, with my whole heart, wish you all things good. But I ought only to observe; you exaggerate my importance. The school owes its flourishing condition only to you, my honoured friend, Fyodor Lukitch. But for you it would be in no way distinguished from other schools! You think the German is paying a compliment, the German is saying something polite. Ha-ha! No, my dear Fyodor Lukitch, I am an honest man and never make complimentary speeches. If we pay you five hundred roubles a year it is because you are valued by us. Isn't that so? Gentlemen, what I say is true, isn't it? We should not pay anyone else so much. . . . Why, a good school is an honour to the factory!"

"I must sincerely own that your school is really exceptional," said the inspector. "Don't think this is flattery. Anyway, I have never come across another like it in my life. As I sat at the examination I was full of admiration. . . . Wonderful children! They know a great deal and answer brightly, and at the same time they are somehow special, unconstrained, sincere. . . . One can see that they love you, Fyodor Lukitch. You are a schoolmaster to the marrow of your bones. You must have been born a teacher. You have all the gifts - innate vocation, long experience, and love for your work. . . . It's simply amazing, considering the weak state of your health, what energy, what understanding . . . what perseverance, do you understand, what confidence you have! Some one in the school committee said truly that you were a poet in your work. . . . Yes, a poet you are!"

And all present at the dinner began as one man talking of Sysoev's extraordinary talent. And as though a dam had been burst, there followed a flood of sincere, enthusiastic words such as men do not utter when they are restrained by prudent and cautious sobriety. Sysoev's speech and his intolerable temper and the horrid, spiteful expression on his face were all forgotten. Everyone talked freely, even the shy and silent new teachers, poverty-stricken, down-trodden youths who never spoke to the inspector without addressing him as "your honour." It was clear that in his own circle Sysoev was a person of consequence.

Having been accustomed to success and praise for the fourteen years that he had been schoolmaster, he listened with indifference to the noisy enthusiasm of his admirers.

It was Bruni who drank in the praise instead of the schoolmaster. The German caught every word, beamed, clapped his hands, and flushed modestly as though the praise referred not to the schoolmaster but to him.

"Bravo! bravo!" he shouted. "That's true! You have grasped my meaning! . . . Excellent! . . ." He looked into the schoolmaster's eyes as though he wanted to share his bliss with him. At last he could restrain himself no longer; he leapt up, and, overpowering all the other voices with his shrill little tenor, shouted:

"Gentlemen! Allow me to speak! Sh-h! To all you say I can make only one reply: the management of the factory will not be forgetful of what it owes to Fyodor Lukitch! . . ."

All were silent. Sysoev raised his eyes to the German's rosy face.

"We know how to appreciate it," Bruni went on, dropping his voice. "In response to your words I ought to tell you that . . . Fyodor Lukitch's family will be provided for and that a sum of money was placed in the bank a month ago for that object."

Sysoev looked enquiringly at the German, at his colleagues, as though unable to understand why his family should be provided for and not he himself. And at once on all the faces, in all the motionless eyes bent upon him, he read not the sympathy, not the commiseration which he could not endure, but something else, something soft, tender, but at the same time intensely sinister, like a terrible truth, something which in one instant turned him cold all over and filled his soul with unutterable despair. With a pale, distorted face he suddenly jumped up and clutched at his head. For a quarter of a minute he stood like that, stared with horror at a fixed point before him as though he saw the swiftly coming death of which Bruni was speaking, then sat down and burst into tears.

"Come, come! . . . What is it?" he heard agitated voices saying. "Water! drink a little water!"

A short time passed and the schoolmaster grew calmer, but the party did not recover their previous liveliness. The dinner ended in gloomy silence, and much earlier than on previous occasions.

When he got home Sysoev first of all looked at himself in the glass.

"Of course there was no need for me to blubber like that!" he thought, looking at his sunken cheeks and his eyes with dark rings under them. "My face is a much better colour to-day than yesterday. I am suffering from anemia and catarrh of the stomach, and my cough is only a stomach cough."

Reassured, he slowly began undressing, and spent a long time brushing his new black suit, then carefully folded it up and put it in the chest of drawers.

Then he went up to the table where there lay a pile of his pupils' exercise-books, and picking out Babkin's, sat down and fell to contemplating the beautiful childish handwriting. . . .

And meantime, while he was examining the exercise-books, the district doctor was sitting in the next room and telling his wife in a whisper that a man ought not to have been allowed to go out to dinner who had not in all probability more than a week to live.

# A TROUBLESOME VISITOR

In the low-pitched, crooked little hut of Artyom, the forester, two men were sitting under the big dark ikon - Artyom himself, a short and lean peasant with a wrinkled, aged-looking face and a little beard that grew out of his neck, and a well-grown young man in a new crimson shirt and big wading boots, who had been out hunting and come in for the night. They were sitting on a bench at a little three-legged table on which a tallow candle stuck into a bottle was lazily burning.

Outside the window the darkness of the night was full of the noisy uproar into which nature usually breaks out before a thunderstorm. The wind howled angrily and the bowed trees moaned miserably. One pane of the window had been pasted up with paper, and leaves torn off by the wind could be heard pattering against the paper.

"I tell you what, good Christian," said Artyom in a hoarse little tenor half-whisper, staring with unblinking, scared-looking eyes at the hunter. "I am not afraid of wolves or bears, or wild beasts of any sort, but I am afraid of man. You can save yourself from beasts with a gun or some other weapon, but you have no means of saving yourself from a wicked man."

"To be sure, you can fire at a beast, but if you shoot at a robber you will have to answer for it: you will go to Siberia."

"I've been forester, my lad, for thirty years, and I couldn't tell you what I have had to put up with from wicked men. There have been lots and lots of them here. The hut's on a track, it's a cart-road, and that brings them, the devils. Every sort of ruffian turns up, and without taking off his cap or making the sign of the cross, bursts straight in upon one with: 'Give us some bread, you old so-and-so.' And where am I to get bread for him? What claim has he? Am I a millionaire to feed every drunkard that passes? They are half-blind with spite. . . . They have no cross on them, the devils. . . . They'll give you a clout on the ear and not think twice about it: 'Give us bread! ' Well, one gives it. . . . One is not going to fight with them, the idols! Some of them are two yards across the shoulders, and a great fist as big as your boot, and you see the sort of figure I am. One of them could smash me with his little finger. . . . Well, one gives him bread and he gobbles it up, and stretches out full length across the hut with not a word of thanks. And there are some that ask for money. 'Tell me, where is your money?' As though I had money! How should I come by it?"

"A forester and no money!" laughed the hunter. "You get wages every month, and I'll be bound you sell timber on the sly."

Artyom took a timid sideway glance at his visitor and twitched his beard as a magpie twitches her tail.

"You are still young to say a thing like that to me," he said. "You will have to answer to God for those words. Whom may your people be? Where do you come from?"

"I am from Vyazovka. I am the son of Nefed the village elder."

"You have gone out for sport with your gun. I used to like sport, too, when I was young. H'm! Ah, our sins are grievous," said Artyom, with a yawn. "It's a sad thing! There are few good folks, but villains and murderers no end - God have mercy upon us."

"You seem to be frightened of me, too. . . ."

"Come, what next! What should I be afraid of you for? I see. . . . I understand. . . . You came in, and not just anyhow, but you made the sign of the cross, you bowed, all decent and proper. . . . I understand. . . . One can give you bread. . . . I am a widower, I don't heat the stove, I sold the samovar. . . . I am too poor to keep meat or anything else, but bread you are welcome to."

At that moment something began growling under the bench: the growl was followed by a hiss. Artyom started, drew up his legs, and looked enquiringly at the hunter.

"It's my dog worrying your cat," said the hunter. "You devils!" he shouted under the bench. "Lie down. You'll be beaten. I say, your cat's thin, mate! She is nothing but skin and bone."

"She is old, it is time she was dead. . . . So you say you are from Vyazovka?"

"I see you don't feed her. Though she's a cat she's a creature . . . every breathing thing. You should have pity on her!"

"You are a queer lot in Vyazovka," Artyom went on, as though not listening. "The church has been robbed twice in one year. . . To think that there are such wicked men! So they fear neither man nor God! To steal what is the Lord's! Hanging's too good for them! In old days the governors used to have such rogues flogged."

"However you punish, whether it is with flogging or anything else, it will be no good, you will not knock the wickedness out of a wicked man."

"Save and preserve us, Queen of Heaven!" The forester sighed abruptly. "Save us from all enemies and evildoers. Last week at Volovy Zaimishtchy, a mower struck another on the chest with his scythe . . . he killed him outright! And what was it all about, God bless me! One mower came out of the tavern . . . drunk. The other met him, drunk too."

The young man, who had been listening attentively, suddenly started, and his face grew tense as he listened.

"Stay," he said, interrupting the forester. "I fancy someone is shouting."

The hunter and the forester fell to listening with their eyes fixed on the window. Through the noise of the forest they could hear sounds such as the strained ear can always distinguish in every storm, so that it was difficult to make out whether people were calling for help or whether the wind was wailing in the chimney. But the wind tore at the roof, tapped at the paper on the window, and brought a distinct shout of "Help!"

"Talk of your murderers," said the hunter, turning pale and getting up. "Someone is being robbed!"

"Lord have mercy on us," whispered the forester, and he, too, turned pale and got up.

The hunter looked aimlessly out of window and walked up and down the hut.

"What a night, what a night!" he muttered. "You can't see your hand before your face! The very time for a robbery. Do you hear? There is a shout again."

The forester looked at the ikon and from the ikon turned his eyes upon the hunter, and sank on to the bench, collapsing like a man terrified by sudden bad news.

"Good Christian," he said in a tearful voice, "you might go into the passage and bolt the door. And we must put out the light."

"What for?"

"By ill-luck they may find their way here. . . . Oh, our sins!"

"We ought to be going, and you talk of bolting the door! You are a clever one! Are you coming?"

The hunter threw his gun over his shoulder and picked up his cap.

"Get ready, take your gun. Hey, Flerka, here," he called to his dog. "Flerka!"

A dog with long frayed ears, a mongrel between a setter and a house-dog, came out from under the bench. He stretched himself by his master's feet and wagged his tail.

"Why are you sitting there?" cried the hunter to the forester. "You mean to say you are not going?"

"Where?"

"To help!"

"How can I?" said the forester with a wave of his hand, shuddering all over. "I can't bother about it!"

"Why won't you come?"

"After talking of such dreadful things I won't stir a step into the darkness. Bless them! And what should I go for?"

"What are you afraid of? Haven't you got a gun? Let us go, please do. It's scaring to go alone; it will be more cheerful, the two of us. Do you hear? There was a shout again. Get up!"

"Whatever do you think of me, lad?" wailed the forester. "Do you think I am such a fool to go straight to my undoing?"

"So you are not coming?"

The forester did not answer. The dog, probably hearing a human cry, gave a plaintive whine.

"Are you coming, I ask you?" cried the hunter, rolling his eyes angrily.

"You do keep on, upon my word," said the forester with annoyance. "Go yourself."

"Ugh! . . . low cur," growled the hunter, turning towards the door. "Flerka, here!"

He went out and left the door open. The wind flew into the hut. The flame of the candle flickered uneasily, flared up, and went out.

As he bolted the door after the hunter, the forester saw the puddles in the track, the nearest pine-trees, and the retreating figure of his guest lighted up by a flash of lightning. Far away he heard the rumble of thunder.

"Holy, holy, holy," whispered the forester, making haste to thrust the thick bolt into the great iron rings. "What weather the Lord has sent us!"

Going back into the room, he felt his way to the stove, lay down, and covered himself from head to foot. Lying under the sheepskin and listening intently, he could no longer hear the human cry, but the peals of thunder kept growing louder and more prolonged. He could hear the big wind-lashed raindrops pattering angrily on the panes and on the paper of the window.

"He's gone on a fool's errand," he thought, picturing the hunter soaked with rain and stumbling over the tree-stumps. "I bet his teeth are chattering with terror!"

Not more than ten minutes later there was a sound of footsteps, followed by a loud knock at the door.

"Who's there?" cried the forester.

"It's I," he heard the young man's voice. "Unfasten the door."

The forester clambered down from the stove, felt for the candle, and, lighting it, went to the door. The hunter and his dog were drenched to the skin. They had come in for the heaviest of the downpour, and now the water ran from them as from washed clothes before they have been wrung out.

"What was it?" asked the forester.

"A peasant woman driving in a cart; she had got off the road . . ." answered the young man, struggling with his breathlessness. "She was caught in a thicket."

"Ah, the silly thing! She was frightened, then. . . . Well, did you put her on the road?"

"I don't care to talk to a scoundrel like you."

The young man flung his wet cap on the bench and went on:

"I know now that you are a scoundrel and the lowest of men. And you a keeper, too, getting a salary! You blackguard!"

The forester slunk with a guilty step to the stove, cleared his throat, and lay down. The young man sat on the bench, thought a little, and lay down on it full length. Not long afterwards he got up, put out the candle, and lay down again. During a particularly loud clap of thunder he turned over, spat on the floor, and growled out:

"He's afraid. . . . And what if the woman were being murdered? Whose business is it to defend her? And he an old man, too, and a Christian. . He's a pig and nothing else."

The forester cleared his throat and heaved a deep sigh. Somewhere in the darkness Flerka shook his wet coat vigorously, which sent drops of water flying about all over the room.

"So you wouldn't care if the woman were murdered? " the hunter went on. " Well - strike me, God - I had no notion you were that sort of man. . . ."

A silence followed. The thunderstorm was by now over and the thunder came from far away, but it was still raining.

"And suppose it hadn't been a woman but you shouting 'Help!'?" said the hunter, breaking the silence. "How would you feel, you beast, if no one ran to your aid? You have upset me with your meanness, plague take you!"

After another long interval the hunter said:

"You must have money to be afraid of people! A man who is poor is not likely to be afraid. . . ."

"For those words you will answer before God," Artyom said hoarsely from the stove. "I have no money."

"I dare say! Scoundrels always have money. . . . Why are you afraid of people, then? So you must have! I'd like to take and rob you for spite, to teach you a lesson! . . ."

Artyom slipped noiselessly from the stove, lighted a candle, and sat down under the holy image. He was pale and did not take his eyes off the hunter.

"Here, I'll rob you," said the hunter, getting up. "What do you think about it? Fellows like you want a lesson. Tell me, where is your money hidden?"

Artyom drew his legs up under him and blinked. "What are you wriggling for? Where is your money hidden? Have you lost your tongue, you fool? Why don't you answer?"

The young man jumped up and went up to the forester.

"He is blinking like an owl! Well? Give me your money, or I will shoot you with my gun."

"Why do you keep on at me?" squealed the forester, and big tears rolled from his eyes. "What's the reason of it? God sees all! You will have to answer, for every word you say, to God. You have no right whatever to ask for my money."

The young man looked at Artyom's tearful face, frowned, and walked up and down the hut, then angrily clapped his cap on his head and picked up his gun.

"Ugh! . . . ugh! . . . it makes me sick to look at you," he filtered through his teeth. "I can't bear the sight of you. I won't sleep in your house, anyway. Good-bye! Hey, Flerka!"

The door slammed and the troublesome visitor went out with his dog. . . . Artyom bolted the door after him, crossed himself, and lay down.

# THE HUSBAND

In the course of the manoeuvres the N - - cavalry regiment halted for a night at the district town of K - - . Such an event as the visit of officers always has the most exciting and inspiring effect on the inhabitants of provincial towns. The shopkeepers dream of getting rid of the rusty sausages and "best brand" sardines that have been lying for ten years on their shelves; the inns and restaurants keep open all night; the Military Commandant, his secretary, and the local garrison put on their best uniforms; the police flit to and fro like mad, while the effect on the ladies is beyond all description.

The ladies of K - - , hearing the regiment approaching, forsook their pans of boiling jam and ran into the street. Forgetting their morning *deshabille* and general untidiness, they rushed breathless with excitement to meet the regiment, and listened greedily to the band playing the march. Looking at their pale, ecstatic faces, one might have thought those strains came from some heavenly choir rather than from a military brass band.

"The regiment!" they cried joyfully. "The regiment is coming!"

What could this unknown regiment that came by chance to-day and would depart at dawn to-morrow mean to them?

Afterwards, when the officers were standing in the middle of the square, and, with their hands behind them, discussing the question of billets, all the ladies were gathered together at the examining magistrate's and vying with one another in their criticisms of the regiment. They already knew, goodness knows how, that the colonel was married, but not living with his wife; that the senior officer's wife had a baby born dead every year; that the adjutant was hopelessly in love with some countess, and had even once attempted suicide. They knew everything. When a pock-marked soldier in a red shirt darted past the windows, they knew for certain that it was Lieutenant Rymzov's orderly running about the town, trying to get some English bitter ale on tick for his master. They had only caught a passing glimpse of the officers' backs, but had already decided that there was not one handsome or interesting man among them. . . . Having talked to their hearts' content, they sent for the Military Commandant and the committee of the club, and instructed them at all costs to make arrangements for a dance.

Their wishes were carried out. At nine o'clock in the evening the military band was playing in the street before the club, while in the club itself the officers were dancing with the ladies of K - - . The ladies felt as though they were on wings. Intoxicated by the dancing, the music, and the clank of spurs, they threw themselves heart and soul into making the acquaintance of their new partners, and quite forgot their old civilian friends. Their fathers and husbands, forced temporarily into the background, crowded round the meagre refreshment table in the entrance hall. All these government cashiers, secretaries, clerks, and superintendents - stale, sickly-looking, clumsy figures - were perfectly well aware of their inferiority. They did not even enter the ball-room, but contented themselves with watching their wives and daughters in the distance dancing with the accomplished and graceful officers.

Among the husbands was Shalikov, the tax-collector - a narrow, spiteful soul, given to drink, with a big, closely cropped head, and thick, protruding lips. He had had a university education; there had been a time when he used to read progressive literature and sing students' songs, but now, as he said of himself, he was a tax-collector and nothing more.

He stood leaning against the doorpost, his eyes fixed on his wife, Anna Pavlovna, a little brunette of thirty, with a long nose and a pointed chin. Tightly laced, with her face carefully powdered, she danced without pausing for breath - danced till she was ready to drop exhausted. But though she was exhausted in body, her spirit was inexhaustible. . . . One could see as she danced that her thoughts were with the past, that faraway past when she used to dance at the "College for Young Ladies," dreaming of a life of luxury and gaiety, and never doubting that her husband was to be a prince or, at the worst, a baron.

The tax-collector watched, scowling with spite. . . .

It was not jealousy he was feeling. He was ill-humoured - first, because the room was taken up with dancing and there was nowhere he could play a game of cards; secondly, because he could not endure the sound of wind instruments; and, thirdly, because he fancied the officers treated the civilians somewhat too casually and disdainfully. But what above everything revolted him and moved him to indignation was the expression of happiness on his wife's face.

"It makes me sick to look at her!" he muttered. "Going on for forty, and nothing to boast of at any time, and she must powder her face and lace herself up! And frizzing her hair! Flirting and making faces, and fancying she's doing the thing in style! Ugh! you're a pretty figure, upon my soul!"

Anna Pavlovna was so lost in the dance that she did not once glance at her husband.

"Of course not! Where do we poor country bumpkins come in!" sneered the tax-collector.

"We are at a discount now. . . . We're clumsy seals, unpolished provincial bears, and she's the queen of the ball! She has kept enough of her looks to please even officers. . . They'd not object to making love to her, I dare say!"

During the mazurka the tax-collector's face twitched with spite. A black-haired officer with prominent eyes and Tartar cheekbones danced the mazurka with Anna Pavlovna. Assuming a stern expression, he worked his legs with gravity and feeling, and so crooked his knees that he looked like a jack-a-dandy pulled by strings, while Anna Pavlovna, pale and thrilled, bending her figure languidly and turning her eyes up, tried to look as though she scarcely touched the floor, and evidently felt herself that she was not on earth, not at the local club, but somewhere far, far away - in the clouds. Not only her face but her whole figure was expressive of beatitude. . . . The tax-collector could endure it no longer; he felt a desire to jeer at that beatitude, to make Anna Pavlovna feel that she had forgotten herself, that life was by no means so delightful as she fancied now in her excitement. . . .

"You wait; I'll teach you to smile so blissfully," he muttered. "You are not a boarding-school miss, you are not a girl. An old fright ought to realise she is a fright!"

Petty feelings of envy, vexation, wounded vanity, of that small, provincial misanthropy engendered in petty officials by vodka and a sedentary life, swarmed in his heart like mice. Waiting for the end of the mazurka, he went into the hall and walked up to his wife. Anna Pavlovna was sitting with her partner, and, flirting her fan and coquettishly dropping her eyelids, was describing how she used to dance in Petersburg (her lips were pursed up like a rosebud, and she pronounced "at home in Pütürsburg").

"Anyuta, let us go home," croaked the tax-collector.

Seeing her husband standing before her, Anna Pavlovna started as though recalling the fact that she had a husband; then she flushed all over: she felt ashamed that she had such a sickly-looking, ill-humoured, ordinary husband.

"Let us go home," repeated the tax-collector.

"Why? It's quite early!"

"I beg you to come home!" said the tax-collector deliberately, with a spiteful expression.

"Why? Has anything happened?" Anna Pavlovna asked in a flutter.

"Nothing has happened, but I wish you to go home at once. . . . I wish it; that's enough, and without further talk, please."

Anna Pavlovna was not afraid of her husband, but she felt ashamed on account of her partner, who was looking at her husband with surprise and amusement. She got up and moved a little apart with her husband.

"What notion is this?" she began. "Why go home? Why, it's not eleven o'clock."

"I wish it, and that's enough. Come along, and that's all about it."

"Don't be silly! Go home alone if you want to."

"All right; then I shall make a scene."

The tax-collector saw the look of beatitude gradually vanish from his wife's face, saw how ashamed and miserable she was - and he felt a little happier.

"Why do you want me at once?" asked his wife.

"I don't want you, but I wish you to be at home. I wish it, that's all."

At first Anna Pavlovna refused to hear of it, then she began entreating her husband to let her stay just another half-hour; then, without knowing why, she began to apologise, to protest - and all in a whisper, with a smile, that the spectators might not suspect that she was having a tiff with her husband. She began assuring him she would not stay long, only another ten minutes, only five minutes; but the tax-collector stuck obstinately to his point.

"Stay if you like," he said, "but I'll make a scene if you do."

And as she talked to her husband Anna Pavlovna looked thinner, older, plainer. Pale, biting her lips, and almost crying, she went out to the entry and began putting on her things.

"You are not going?" asked the ladies in surprise. "Anna Pavlovna, you are not going, dear?"

"Her head aches," said the tax-collector for his wife.

Coming out of the club, the husband and wife walked all the way home in silence. The tax-collector walked behind his wife, and watching her downcast, sorrowful, humiliated little figure, he recalled the look of beatitude which had so irritated him at the club, and the consciousness that the beatitude was gone filled his soul with triumph. He was pleased and satisfied, and at the same time he felt the lack of something; he would have liked to go back to the club and make every one feel dreary and miserable, so that all might know how stale and worthless life is when you walk along the streets in the dark and hear the slush of the mud under your feet, and when you know that you will wake up next morning with nothing to look forward to but vodka and cards. Oh, how awful it is!

And Anna Pavlovna could scarcely walk.... She was still under the influence of the dancing, the music, the talk, the lights, and the noise; she asked herself as she walked along why God had thus afflicted her. She felt miserable, insulted, and choking with hate as she listened to her husband's heavy footsteps. She was silent, trying to think of the most offensive, biting, and venomous word she could hurl at her husband, and at the same time she was fully aware that no word could penetrate her tax-collector's hide. What did he care for words? Her bitterest enemy could not have contrived for her a more helpless position.

And meanwhile the band was playing and the darkness was full of the most rousing, intoxicating dance-tunes.

# A MISFORTUNE

Sofya Petrovna, the wife of Lubyantsev the notary, a handsome young woman of five-and-twenty, was walking slowly along a track that had been cleared in the wood, with Ilyin, a lawyer who was spending the summer in the neighbourhood. It was five o'clock in the evening. Feathery-white masses of cloud stood overhead; patches of bright blue sky peeped out between them. The clouds stood motionless, as though they had caught in the tops of the tall old pine-trees. It was still and sultry.

Farther on, the track was crossed by a low railway embankment on which a sentinel with a gun was for some reason pacing up and down. Just beyond the embankment there was a large white church with six domes and a rusty roof.

"I did not expect to meet you here," said Sofya Petrovna, looking at the ground and prodding at the last year's leaves with the tip of her parasol, "and now I am glad we have met. I want to speak to you seriously and once for all. I beg you, Ivan Mihalovitch, if you really love and respect me, please make an end of this pursuit of me! You follow me about like a shadow, you are continually looking at me not in a nice way, making love to me, writing me strange letters, and . . . and I don't know where it's all going to end! Why, what can come of it?"

Ilyin said nothing. Sofya Petrovna walked on a few steps and continued:

"And this complete transformation in you all came about in the course of two or three weeks, after five years' friendship. I don't know you, Ivan Mihalovitch!"

Sofya Petrovna stole a glance at her companion. Screwing up his eyes, he was looking intently at the fluffy clouds. His face looked angry, ill-humoured, and preoccupied, like that of a man in pain forced to listen to nonsense.

"I wonder you don't see it yourself," Madame Lubyantsev went on, shrugging her shoulders. "You ought to realize that it's not a very nice part you are playing. I am married; I love and respect my husband. . . . I have a daughter . . . . Can you think all that means nothing? Besides, as an old friend you know my attitude to family life and my views as to the sanctity of marriage."

Ilyin cleared his throat angrily and heaved a sigh.

"Sanctity of marriage . . ." he muttered. "Oh, Lord!"

Yes, yes. . . . I love my husband, I respect him; and in any case I value the peace of my home. I would rather let myself be killed than be a cause of unhappiness to Andrey and his daughter. . . . And I beg you, Ivan Mihalovitch, for God's sake, leave me in peace! Let us be as good, true friends as we used to be, and give up these sighs and groans, which really don't suit you. It's settled and over! Not a word more about it. Let us talk of something else."

Sofya Petrovna again stole a glance at Ilyin's face. Ilyin was looking up; he was pale, and was angrily biting his quivering lips. She could not understand why he was angry and why he was indignant, but his pallor touched her.

"Don't be angry; let us be friends," she said affectionately. "Agreed? Here's my hand."

Ilyin took her plump little hand in both of his, squeezed it, and slowly raised it to his lips.

"I am not a schoolboy," he muttered. "I am not in the least tempted by friendship with the woman I love."

"Enough, enough! It's settled and done with. We have reached the seat; let us sit down."

Sofya Petrovna's soul was filled with a sweet sense of relief: the most difficult and delicate thing had been said, the painful question was settled and done with. Now she could breathe freely and look Ilyin straight in the face. She looked at him, and the egoistic feeling of the superiority of the woman over the man who loves her, agreeably flattered her. It pleased her to see this huge, strong man, with his manly, angry face and his big black beard - clever, cultivated, and, people said, talented - sit down obediently beside her and bow his head dejectedly. For two or three minutes they sat without speaking.

"Nothing is settled or done with," began Ilyin. "You repeat copy-book maxims to me. 'I love and respect my husband . . . the sanctity of marriage. . . .' I know all that without your help, and I could tell you more, too. I tell you truthfully and honestly that I consider the way I am behaving as criminal and immoral. What more can one say than that? But what's the good of saying what everybody knows? Instead of feeding nightingales with paltry words, you had much better tell me what I am to do."

"I've told you already - go away."

"As you know perfectly well, I have gone away five times, and every time I turned back on the way. I can show you my through tickets - I've kept them all. I have not will enough to run away from you! I am struggling. I am struggling horribly; but what the devil am I good for if I have no backbone, if I am weak, cowardly! I can't struggle with Nature! Do you understand? I cannot! I run away from here, and she holds on to me and pulls me back. Contemptible, loathsome weakness!"

Ilyin flushed crimson, got up, and walked up and down by the seat.

"I feel as cross as a dog," he muttered, clenching his fists. "I hate and despise myself! My God! like some depraved schoolboy, I am making love to another man's wife, writing idiotic letters, degrading myself . . . ugh!"

Ilyin clutched at his head, grunted, and sat down. "And then your insincerity!" he went on bitterly. "If you do dislike my disgusting behaviour, why have you come here? What drew you here? In my letters I only ask you for a direct, definite answer - yes or no; but instead of a direct answer, you contrive every day these 'chance' meetings with me and regale me with copy-book maxims!"

Madame Lubyantsev was frightened and flushed. She suddenly felt the awkwardness which a decent woman feels when she is accidentally discovered undressed.

"You seem to suspect I am playing with you," she muttered. "I have always given you a direct answer, and . . . only today I've begged you . . ."

"Ough! as though one begged in such cases! If you were to say straight out 'Get away,' I should have been gone long ago; but you've never said that. You've never once given me a direct answer. Strange indecision! Yes, indeed; either you are playing with me, or else . . ."

Ilyin leaned his head on his fists without finishing. Sofya Petrovna began going over in her own mind the way she had behaved from beginning to end. She remembered that not only in her actions, but even in her secret thoughts, she had always been opposed to Ilyin's love-making; but yet she felt there was a grain of truth in the lawyer's words. But not knowing exactly what the truth was, she could not find answers to make to Ilyin's complaint, however hard she thought. It was awkward to be silent, and, shrugging her shoulders, she said:

So I am to blame, it appears."

"I don't blame you for your insincerity," sighed Ilyin. "I did not mean that when I spoke of it. . . . Your insincerity is natural and in the order of things. If people agreed together and suddenly became sincere, everything would go to the devil."

Sofya Petrovna was in no mood for philosophical reflections, but she was glad of a chance to change the conversation, and asked:

"But why?"

"Because only savage women and animals are sincere. Once civilization has introduced a demand for such comforts as, for instance, feminine virtue, sincerity is out of place. . . ."

Ilyin jabbed his stick angrily into the sand. Madame Lubyantsev listened to him and liked his conversation, though a great deal of it she did not understand. What gratified her most was that she, an ordinary woman, was talked to by a talented man on "intellectual" subjects; it afforded her great pleasure, too, to watch the working of his mobile, young face, which was still pale and angry. She failed to understand a great deal that he said, but what was clear to her in his words was the attractive boldness with which the modern man without hesitation or doubt decides great questions and draws conclusive deductions.

She suddenly realized that she was admiring him, and was alarmed.

"Forgive me, but I don't understand," she said hurriedly. "What makes you talk of insincerity? I repeat my request again: be my good, true friend; let me alone! I beg you most earnestly!"

"Very good; I'll try again," sighed Ilyin. "Glad to do my best. . . . Only I doubt whether anything will come of my efforts. Either I shall put a bullet through my brains or take to drink in an idiotic way. I shall come to a bad end! There's a limit to everything - to struggles with Nature, too. Tell me, how can one struggle against madness? If you drink wine, how are you to struggle against intoxication? What am I to do if your image has grown into my soul, and day and night stands persistently before my eyes, like that pine there at this moment? Come, tell me, what hard and difficult thing can I do to get free from this abominable, miserable condition, in which all my thoughts, desires, and dreams are no longer my own, but belong to some demon who has taken possession of me? I love you, love you so much that I am completely thrown out of gear; I've given up my work and all who are dear to me; I've forgotten my God! I've never been in love like this in my life."

Sofya Petrovna, who had not expected such a turn to their conversation, drew away from Ilyin and looked into his face in dismay. Tears came into his eyes, his lips were quivering, and there was an imploring, hungry expression in his face.

"I love you!" he muttered, bringing his eyes near her big, frightened eyes. "You are so beautiful! I am in agony now, but I swear I would sit here all my life, suffering and looking in your eyes. But . . . be silent, I implore you!"

Sofya Petrovna, feeling utterly disconcerted, tried to think as quickly as possible of something to say to stop him. "I'll go away," she decided, but before she had time to make a movement to get up, Ilyin was on his knees before her. . . . He was clasping her knees, gazing into her face and speaking passionately, hotly, eloquently. In her terror and confusion she did not hear his words; for some reason now, at this dangerous moment, while her knees were being agreeably squeezed and felt as though they were in a warm bath, she was trying, with a sort of angry spite, to interpret her own sensations. She was angry that instead of brimming over with protesting virtue, she was entirely overwhelmed with weakness, apathy, and emptiness, like a drunken man utterly reckless; only at the bottom of her soul a remote bit of herself was malignantly taunting her: "Why don't you go? Is this as it should be? Yes?"

Seeking for some explanation, she could not understand how it was she did not pull away the hand to which Ilyin was clinging like a leech, and why, like Ilyin, she hastily glanced to right and to left to see whether any one was looking. The clouds and the pines stood motionless, looking at them severely, like old ushers seeing mischief, but bribed not to tell the school authorities. The sentry stood like a post on the embankment and seemed to be looking at the seat.

"Let him look," thought Sofya Petrovna.

"But . . . but listen," she said at last, with despair in her voice. "What can come of this? What will be the end of this?"

"I don't know, I don't know," he whispered, waving off the disagreeable questions.

They heard the hoarse, discordant whistle of the train. This cold, irrelevant sound from the everyday world of prose made Sofya Petrovna rouse herself.

"I can't stay . . . it's time I was at home," she said, getting up quickly. "The train is coming in. . . Andrey is coming by it! He will want his dinner."

Sofya Petrovna turned towards the embankment with a burning face. The engine slowly crawled by, then came the carriages. It was not the local train, as she had supposed, but a goods train. The trucks filed by against the background of the white church in a long string like the days of a man's life, and it seemed as though it would never end.

But at last the train passed, and the last carriage with the guard and a light in it had disappeared behind the trees. Sofya Petrovna turned round sharply, and without looking at Ilyin, walked rapidly back along the track. She had regained her self-possession. Crimson with shame, humiliated not by Ilyin - no, but by her own cowardice, by the shamelessness with which she, a chaste and high-principled woman, had allowed a man, not her husband, to hug her knees - she had only one thought now: to get home as quickly as possible to her villa, to her family. The lawyer could hardly keep pace with her. Turning from the clearing into a narrow path, she turned round and glanced at him so quickly that she saw nothing but the sand on his knees, and waved to him to drop behind.

Reaching home, Sofya Petrovna stood in the middle of her room for five minutes without moving, and looked first at the window and then at her writing-table.

"You low creature!" she said, upbraiding herself. "You low creature!"

To spite herself, she recalled in precise detail, keeping nothing back - she recalled that though all this time she had been opposed to Ilyin's lovemaking, something had impelled her to seek an interview with him; and what was more, when he was at her feet she had enjoyed it enormously. She recalled it all without sparing herself, and now, breathless with shame, she would have liked to slap herself in the face.

"Poor Andrey!" she said to herself, trying as she thought of her husband to put into her face as tender an expression as she could. "Varya, my poor little girl, doesn't know what a mother she has! Forgive me, my dear ones! I love you so much . . . so much!"

And anxious to prove to herself that she was still a good wife and mother, and that corruption had not yet touched that "sanctity of marriage" of which she had spoken to Ilyin, Sofya Petrovna ran to the kitchen and abused the cook for not having yet laid the table for Andrey Ilyitch. She tried to picture her husband's hungry and exhausted appearance, commiserated him aloud, and laid the table for him with her own hands, which she had never done before. Then she found her daughter Varya, picked her up in her arms and hugged her warmly; the child seemed to her cold and heavy, but she was unwilling to acknowledge this to herself, and she began explaining to the child how good, kind, and honourable her papa was.

But when Andrey Ilyitch arrived soon afterwards she hardly greeted him. The rush of false feeling had already passed off without proving anything to her, only irritating and exasperating her by its falsity. She was sitting by the window, feeling miserable and cross. It is only by being in trouble that people can understand how far from easy it is to be the master of one's feelings and thoughts. Sofya Petrovna said afterwards that there was a tangle within her which it was as difficult to unravel as to count a flock of sparrows rapidly flying by. From the fact that she was not overjoyed to see her husband, that she did not like his manner at dinner, she concluded all of a sudden that she was beginning to hate her husband

Andrey Ilyitch, languid with hunger and exhaustion, fell upon the sausage while waiting for the soup to be brought in, and ate it greedily, munching noisily and moving his temples.

"My goodness!" thought Sofya Petrovna. "I love and respect him, but . . . why does he munch so repulsively?"

The disorder in her thoughts was no less than the disorder in her feelings. Like all persons inexperienced in combating unpleasant ideas, Madame Lubyantsev did her utmost not to think of her trouble, and the harder she tried the more vividly Ilyin, the sand on his knees, the fluffy clouds, the train, stood out in her imagination.

"And why did I go there this afternoon like a fool?" she thought, tormenting herself. "And am I really so weak that I cannot depend upon myself?"

Fear magnifies danger. By the time Andrey Ilyitch was finishing the last course, she had firmly made up her mind to tell her husband everything and to flee from danger!

"I've something serious to say to you, Andrey," she began after dinner while her husband was taking off his coat and boots to lie down for a nap.

"Well?"

"Let us leave this place!"

" H'm! . . . Where shall we go? It's too soon to go back to town."

"No; for a tour or something of that sort.

"For a tour . . ." repeated the notary, stretching. "I dream of that myself, but where are we to get the money, and to whom am I to leave the office?"

And thinking a little he added:

"Of course, you must be bored. Go by yourself if you like."

Sofya Petrovna agreed, but at once reflected that Ilyin would be delighted with the opportunity, and would go with her in the same train, in the same compartment. . . . She thought and looked at her husband, now satisfied but still languid. For some reason her eyes rested on his feet - miniature, almost feminine feet, clad in striped socks; there was a thread standing out at the tip of each sock.

Behind the blind a bumble-bee was beating itself against the window-pane and buzzing. Sofya Petrovna looked at the threads on the socks, listened to the bee, and pictured how she would set off. . . . *vis-à-vis* Ilyin would sit, day and night, never taking his eyes off her, wrathful at his own weakness and pale with spiritual agony. He would call himself an immoral schoolboy, would abuse her, tear his hair, but when darkness came on and the passengers were asleep or got out at a station, he would seize the opportunity to kneel before her and embrace her knees as he had at the seat in the wood. . . .

She caught herself indulging in this day-dream.

"Listen. I won't go alone," she said. "You must come with me."

"Nonsense, Sofotchka!" sighed Lubyantsev. "One must be sensible and not want the impossible."

"You will come when you know all about it," thought Sofya Petrovna.

Making up her mind to go at all costs, she felt that she was out of danger. Little by little her ideas grew clearer; her spirits rose and she allowed herself to think about it all, feeling that however much she thought, however much she dreamed, she would go away. While her husband was asleep, the evening gradually came on. She sat in the drawing-room and played the piano. The greater liveliness out of doors, the sound of music, but above all the thought that she was a sensible person, that she had surmounted her difficulties, completely restored her spirits. Other women, her appeased conscience told her, would probably have been carried off their feet in her position, and would have lost their balance, while she had almost died of shame, had been miserable, and was now running out of the danger which perhaps did not exist! She was so touched by her own virtue and determination that she even looked at herself two or three times in the looking-glass.

When it got dark, visitors arrived. The men sat down in the dining-room to play cards; the ladies remained in the drawing-room and the verandah. The last to arrive was Ilyin. He was gloomy, morose, and looked ill. He sat down in the corner of the sofa and did not move the whole evening. Usually good-humoured and talkative, this time he remained silent, frowned, and rubbed his eyebrows. When he had to answer some question, he gave a forced smile with his upper lip only, and answered jerkily and irritably. Four or five times he made some jest, but his jests sounded harsh and cutting. It seemed to Sofya Petrovna that he was on the verge of hysterics. Only now, sitting at the piano, she recognized fully for the first time that this unhappy man was in deadly earnest, that his soul was sick, and that he could find no rest. For her sake he was wasting the best days of his youth and his career, spending the last of his money on a summer villa, abandoning his mother and sisters, and, worst of all, wearing himself out in an agonizing struggle with himself. From mere common humanity he ought to be treated seriously.

She recognized all this clearly till it made her heart ache, and if at that moment she had gone up to him and said to him, "No," there would have been a force in her voice hard to disobey. But she did not go up to him and did not speak - indeed, never thought of doing so. The pettiness and egoism of youth had never been more patent in her than that evening. She realized that Ilyin was unhappy, and that he was sitting on the sofa as though he were on hot coals; she felt sorry for him, but at the same time the presence of a man who loved her to distraction, filled her soul with triumph and a sense of her own power. She felt her youth, her beauty, and her unassailable virtue, and, since she had decided to go away, gave herself full licence for that evening. She flirted, laughed incessantly, sang with peculiar feeling and gusto. Everything delighted and amused her. She was amused at the memory of what had happened at the seat in the wood, of the sentinel who had looked on. She was amused by her guests, by Ilyin's cutting jests, by the pin in his cravat, which she had never noticed before. There was a red snake with diamond eyes on the pin; this snake struck her as so amusing that she could have kissed it on the spot.

Sofya Petrovna sang nervously, with defiant recklessness as though half intoxicated, and she chose sad, mournful songs which dealt with wasted hopes, the past, old age, as though in mockery of another's grief. " 'And old age comes nearer and nearer' . . ." she sang. And what was old age to her?

"It seems as though there is something going wrong with me," she thought from time to time through her laughter and singing.

The party broke up at twelve o'clock. Ilyin was the last to leave. Sofya Petrovna was still reckless enough to accompany him to the bottom step of the verandah. She wanted to tell him that she was going away with her husband, and to watch the effect this news would produce on him.

The moon was hidden behind the clouds, but it was light enough for Sofya Petrovna to see how the wind played with the skirts of his overcoat and with the awning of the verandah. She could see, too, how white Ilyin was, and how he twisted his upper lip in the effort to smile.

"Sonia, Sonitchka . . . my darling woman!" he muttered, preventing her from speaking. "My dear! my sweet!"

In a rush of tenderness, with tears in his voice, he showered caressing words upon her, that grew tenderer and tenderer, and even called her "thou," as though she were his wife or mistress. Quite unexpectedly he put one arm round her waist and with the other hand took hold of her elbow.

"My precious! my delight!" he whispered, kissing the nape of her neck; "be sincere; come to me at once!"

She slipped out of his arms and raised her head to give vent to her indignation and anger, but the indignation did not come off, and all her vaunted virtue and chastity was only sufficient to enable her to utter the phrase used by all ordinary women on such occasions:

"You must be mad."

"Come, let us go," Ilyin continued. "I felt just now, as well as at the seat in the wood, that you are as helpless as I am, Sonia. . . . You are in the same plight! You love me and are fruitlessly trying to appease your conscience. . . ."

Seeing that she was moving away, he caught her by her lace cuff and said rapidly:

"If not today, then tomorrow you will have to give in! Why, then, this waste of time? My precious, darling Sonia, the sentence is passed; why put off the execution? Why deceive yourself?"

Sofya Petrovna tore herself from him and darted in at the door. Returning to the drawing-room, she mechanically shut the piano, looked for a long time at the music-stand, and sat down. She could not stand up nor think. All that was left of her excitement and recklessness was a fearful weakness, apathy, and dreariness. Her conscience whispered to her that she had behaved badly, foolishly, that evening, like some madcap girl - that she had just been embraced on the verandah, and still had an uneasy feeling in her waist and her elbow. There was not a soul in the drawing-room; there was only one candle burning. Madame Lubyantsev sat on the round stool before the piano, motionless, as though expecting something. And as though taking advantage of the darkness and her extreme lassitude, an oppressive, overpowering desire began to assail her. Like a boa-constrictor it gripped her limbs and her soul, and grew stronger every second, and no longer menaced her as it had done, but stood clear before her in all its nakedness.

She sat for half an hour without stirring, not restraining herself from thinking of Ilyin, then she got up languidly and dragged herself to her bedroom. Andrey Ilyitch was already in bed. She sat down by the open window and gave herself up to desire. There was no "tangle" now in her head; all her thoughts and feelings were bent with one accord upon a single aim. She tried to struggle against it, but instantly gave it up. . . . She understood now how strong and relentless was the foe. Strength and fortitude were needed to combat him, and her birth, her education, and her life had given her nothing to fall back upon.

"Immoral wretch! Low creature!" she nagged at herself for her weakness. "So that's what you're like!"

Her outraged sense of propriety was moved to such indignation by this weakness that she lavished upon herself every term of abuse she knew, and told herself many offensive and humiliating truths. So, for instance, she told herself that she never had been moral, that she had not come to grief before simply because she had had no opportunity, that her inward conflict during that day had all been a farce. . . .

"And even if I have struggled," she thought, "what sort of struggle was it? Even the woman who sells herself struggles before she brings herself to it, and yet she sells herself. A fine struggle! Like milk, I've turned in a day! In one day!"

She convicted herself of being tempted, not by feeling, not by Ilyin personally, but by sensations which awaited her . . . an idle lady, having her fling in the summer holidays, like so many!

" 'Like an unfledged bird when the mother has been slain,' " sang a husky tenor outside the window.

"If I am to go, it's time," thought Sofya Petrovna. Her heart suddenly began beating violently.

"Andrey!" she almost shrieked. "Listen! we . . . we are going? Yes?"

"Yes, I've told you already: you go alone."

"But listen," she began. "If you don't go with me, you are in danger of losing me. I believe I am . . . in love already."

"With whom?" asked Andrey Ilyitch.

"It can't make any difference to you who it is!" cried Sofya Petrovna.

Andrey Ilyitch sat up with his feet out of bed and looked wonderingly at his wife's dark figure.

"It's a fancy!" he yawned.

He did not believe her, but yet he was frightened. After thinking a little and asking his wife several unimportant questions, he delivered himself of his opinions on the family, on infidelity . . . spoke listlessly for about ten minutes and got into bed again. His moralizing produced no effect. There are a great many opinions in the world, and a good half of them are held by people who have never been in trouble!

In spite of the late hour, summer visitors were still walking outside. Sofya Petrovna put on a light cape, stood a little, thought a little. . . . She still had resolution enough to say to her sleeping husband:

"Are you asleep? I am going for a walk. . . . Will you come with me?"

That was her last hope. Receiving no answer, she went out. . . . It was fresh and windy. She was conscious neither of the wind nor the darkness, but went on and on. . . . An overmastering force drove her on, and it seemed as though, if she had stopped, it would have pushed her in the back.

"Immoral creature!" she muttered mechanically. "Low wretch!"

She was breathless, hot with shame, did not feel her legs under her, but what drove her on was stronger than shame, reason, or fear.

# A PINK STOCKING

A dull, rainy day. The sky is completely covered with heavy clouds, and there is no prospect of the rain ceasing. Outside sleet, puddles, and drenched jackdaws. Indoors it is half dark, and so cold that one wants the stove heated.

Pavel Petrovitch Somov is pacing up and down his study, grumbling at the weather. The tears of rain on the windows and the darkness of the room make him depressed. He is insufferably bored and has nothing to do. . . . The newspapers have not been brought yet; shooting is out of the question, and it is not nearly dinner-time. . . .

Somov is not alone in his study. Madame Somov, a pretty little lady in a light blouse and pink stockings, is sitting at his writing table. She is eagerly scribbling a letter. Every time he passes her as he strides up and down, Ivan Petrovitch looks over her shoulder at what she is writing. He sees big sprawling letters, thin and narrow, with all sorts of tails and flourishes. There are numbers of blots, smears, and finger-marks. Madame Somov does not like ruled paper, and every line runs downhill with horrid wriggles as it reaches the margin. . . .

"Lidotchka, who is it you are writing such a lot to?" Somov inquires, seeing that his wife is just beginning to scribble the sixth page.

"To sister Varya."

"Hm . . . it's a long letter! I'm so bored - let me read it!"

"Here, you may read it, but there's nothing interesting in it."

Somov takes the written pages and, still pacing up and down, begins reading. Lidotchka leans her elbows on the back of her chair and watches the expression of his face. . . . After the first page his face lengthens and an expression of something almost like panic comes into it. . . . At the third page Somov frowns and scratches the back of his head. At the fourth he pauses, looks with a scared face at his wife, and seems to ponder. After thinking a little, he takes up the letter again with a sigh. . . . His face betrays perplexity and even alarm. . . ."

"Well, this is beyond anything!" he mutters, as he finishes reading the letter and flings the sheets on the table, "It's positively incredible!"

"What's the matter?" asks Lidotchka, flustered.

"What's the matter! You've covered six pages, wasted a good two hours scribbling, and there's nothing in it at all! If there were one tiny idea! One reads on and on, and one's brain is as muddled as though one were deciphering the Chinese wriggles on tea chests! Ough!"

"Yes, that's true, Vanya, . . ." says Lidotchka, reddening. "I wrote it carelessly. . . ."

"Queer sort of carelessness! In a careless letter there is some meaning and style - there is sense in it - while yours . . . excuse me, but I don't know what to call it! It's absolute twaddle! There are words and sentences, but not the slightest sense in them. Your whole letter is exactly like the conversation of two boys: 'We had pancakes to-day! And we had a soldier come to see us!' You say the same thing over and over again! You drag it out, repeat yourself. . . . The wretched ideas dance about like devils: there's no making out where anything begins, where anything ends. . . . How can you write like that?"

"If I had been writing carefully," Lidotchka says in self defence, "then there would not have been mistakes. . . ."

"Oh, I'm not talking about mistakes! The awful grammatical howlers! There's not a line that's not a personal insult to grammar! No stops nor commas - and the spelling . . . brrr! 'Earth' has an *a* in it!! And the writing! It's desperate! I'm not joking, Lida. . . . I'm surprised and appalled at your letter. . . . You mustn't be angry, darling, but, really, I had no idea you were such a duffer at grammar. . . . And yet you belong to a cultivated, well-educated circle: you are the wife of a University man, and the daughter of a general! Tell me, did you ever go to school?"

"What next! I finished at the Von Mebke's boarding school. . . ."

Somov shrugs his shoulders and continues to pace up and down, sighing. Lidotchka, conscious of her ignorance and ashamed of it, sighs too and casts down her eyes. . . . Ten minutes pass in silence.

"You know, Lidotchka, it really is awful!" says Somov, suddenly halting in front of her and looking into her face with horror. "You are a mother . . . do you understand? A mother! How can you teach your children if you know nothing yourself? You have a good brain, but what's the use of it if you have never mastered the very rudiments of knowledge? There - never mind about knowledge . . . the children will get that at school, but, you know, you are very shaky on the moral side too! You sometimes use such language that it makes my ears tingle!"

Somov shrugs his shoulders again, wraps himself in the folds of his dressing-gown and continues his pacing. . . . He feels vexed and injured, and at the same time sorry for Lidotchka, who does not protest, but merely blinks. . . . Both feel oppressed and miserable. . . . Absorbed in their woes, they do not notice how time is passing and the dinner hour is approaching.

Sitting down to dinner, Somov, who is fond of good eating and of eating in peace, drinks a large glass of vodka and begins talking about something else. Lidotchka listens and assents, but suddenly over the soup her eyes fill with tears and she begins whimpering.

"It's all mother's fault!" she says, wiping away her tears with her dinner napkin. "Everyone advised her to send me to the high school, and from the high school I should have been sure to go on to the University!"

"University . . . high school," mutters Somov. "That's running to extremes, my girl! What's the good of being a blue stocking! A blue stocking is the very deuce! Neither man nor woman, but just something midway: neither one thing nor another. . . I hate blue stockings! I would never have married a learned woman. . . ."

"There's no making you out . . .," says Lidotchka. "You are angry because I am not learned, and at the same time you hate learned women; you are annoyed because I have no ideas in my letter, and yet you yourself are opposed to my studying. . . ."

"You do catch me up at a word, my dear," yawns Somov, pouring out a second glass of vodka in his boredom.

Under the influence of vodka and a good dinner, Somov grows more good-humoured, lively, and soft. . . . He watches his pretty wife making the salad with an anxious face and a rush of affection for her, of indulgence and forgiveness comes over him.

"It was stupid of me to depress her, poor girl . . . ," he thought. "Why did I say such a lot of dreadful things? She is silly, that's true, uncivilised and narrow; but . . . there are two sides to the question, and *audiatur et altera pars*. . . . Perhaps people are perfectly right when they say that woman's shallowness rests on her very vocation. Granted that it is her vocation to love her husband, to bear children, and to mix salad, what the devil does she want with learning? No, indeed!"

At that point he remembers that learned women are usually tedious, that they are exacting, strict, and unyielding; and, on the other hand, how easy it is to get on with silly Lidotchka, who never pokes her nose into anything, does not understand so much, and never obtrudes her criticism. There is peace and comfort with Lidotchka, and no risk of being interfered with.

"Confound them, those clever and learned women! It's better and easier to live with simple ones," he thinks, as he takes a plate of chicken from Lidotchka.

He recollects that a civilised man sometimes feels a desire to talk and share his thoughts with a clever and well-educated woman. "What of it?" thinks Somov. "If I want to talk of intellectual subjects, I'll go to Natalya Andreyevna . . . or to Marya Frantsovna. . . . It's very simple! But no, I shan't go. One can discuss intellectual subjects with men," he finally decides.

# MARTYRS

Lizotchka Kudrinsky, a young married lady who had many admirers, was suddenly taken ill, and so seriously that her husband did not go to his office, and a telegram was sent to her mamma at Tver. This is how she told the story of her illness:

"I went to Lyesnoe to auntie's. I stayed there a week and then I went with all the rest to cousin Varya's. Varya's husband is a surly brute and a despot (I'd shoot a husband like that), but we had a very jolly time there. To begin with I took part in some private theatricals. It was *A Scandal in a Respectable Family*. Hrustalev acted marvellously! Between the acts I drank some cold, awfully cold, lemon squash, with the tiniest nip of brandy in it. Lemon squash with brandy in it is very much like champagne. . . . I drank it and I felt nothing. Next day after the performance I rode out on horseback with that Adolf Ivanitch. It was rather damp and there was a strong wind. It was most likely then that I caught cold. Three days later I came home to see how my dear, good Vassya was getting on, and while here to get my silk dress, the one that has little flowers on it. Vassya, of course, I did not find at home. I went into the kitchen to tell Praskovya to set the samovar, and there I saw on the table some pretty little carrots and turnips like playthings. I ate one little carrot and well, a turnip too. I ate very little, but only fancy, I began having a sharp pain at once - spasms . . . spasms . . . spasms . . . ah, I am dying. Vassya runs from the office. Naturally he clutches at his hair and turns white. They run for the doctor. . . . Do you understand, I am dying, dying."

The spasms began at midday, before three o'clock the doctor came, and at six Lizotchka fell asleep and slept soundly till two o'clock in the morning.

It strikes two. . . . The light of the little night lamp filters scantily through the pale blue shade. Lizotchka is lying in bed, her white lace cap stands out sharply against the dark background of the red cushion. Shadows from the blue lamp-shade lie in patterns on her pale face and her round plump shoulders. Vassily Stepanovitch is sitting at her feet. The poor fellow is happy that his wife is at home at last, and at the same time he is terribly alarmed by her illness.

"Well, how do you feel, Lizotchka?" he asks in a whisper, noticing that she is awake.

"I am better," moans Lizotchka. "I don't feel the spasms now, but there is no sleeping. . . . I can't get to sleep!"

"Isn't it time to change the compress, my angel?"

Lizotchka sits up slowly with the expression of a martyr and gracefully turns her head on one side. Vassily Stepanovitch with reverent awe, scarcely touching her hot body with his fingers, changes the compress. Lizotchka shrinks, laughs at the cold water which tickles her, and lies down again.

"You are getting no sleep, poor boy!" she moans.

"As though I could sleep!"

"It's my nerves, Vassya, I am a very nervous woman. The doctor has prescribed for stomach trouble, but I feel that he doesn't understand my illness. It's nerves and not the stomach, I swear that it is my nerves. There is only one thing I am afraid of, that my illness may take a bad turn."

"No, Lizotchka, no, to-morrow you will be all right!"

"Hardly likely! I am not afraid for myself. . . . I don't care, indeed, I shall be glad to die, but I am sorry for you! You'll be a widower and left all alone."

Vassitchka rarely enjoys his wife's society, and has long been used to solitude, but Lizotchka's words agitate him.

"Goodness knows what you are saying, little woman! Why these gloomy thoughts?"

"Well, you will cry and grieve, and then you will get used to it. You'll even get married again."

The husband clutches his head.

"There, there, I won't!" Lizotchka soothes him, "only you ought to be prepared for anything."

"And all of a sudden I shall die," she thinks, shutting her eyes.

And Lizotchka draws a mental picture of her own death, how her mother, her husband, her cousin Varya with her husband, her relations, the admirers of her "talent" press round her death bed, as she whispers her last farewell. All are weeping. Then when she is dead they dress her, interestingly pale and dark-haired, in a pink dress (it suits her) and lay her in a very expensive coffin on gold legs, full of flowers. There is a smell of incense, the candles splutter. Her husband never leaves the coffin, while the admirers of her talent cannot take their eyes off her, and say: "As though living! She is lovely in her coffin!" The whole town is talking of the life cut short so prematurely. But now they are carrying her to the church. The bearers are Ivan Petrovitch, Adolf Ivanitch, Varya's husband, Nikolay Semyonitch, and the black-eyed student who had taught her to drink lemon squash with brandy. It's only a pity there's no music playing. After the burial service comes the leave-taking. The church is full of sobs, they bring the lid with tassels, and . . . Lizotchka is shut off from the light of day forever, there is the sound of hammering nails. Knock, knock, knock.

Lizotchka shudders and opens her eyes.

"Vassya, are you here?" she asks. "I have such gloomy thoughts. Goodness, why am I so unlucky as not to sleep. Vassya, have pity, do tell me something!"

"What shall I tell you ?"

"Something about love," Lizotchka says languidly. "Or some anecdote about Jews. . . ."

Vassily Stepanovitch, ready for anything if only his wife will be cheerful and not talk about death, combs locks of hair over his ears, makes an absurd face, and goes up to Lizotchka.

"Does your vatch vant mending?" he asks.

"It does, it does," giggles Lizotchka, and hands him her gold watch from the little table. "Mend it."

Vassya takes the watch, examines the mechanism for a long time, and wriggling and shrugging, says: "She can not be mended . . . in vun veel two cogs are vanting. . . ."

This is the whole performance. Lizotchka laughs and claps her hands.

"Capital," she exclaims. "Wonderful. Do you know, Vassya, it's awfully stupid of you not to take part in amateur theatricals! You have a remarkable talent! You are much better than Sysunov. There was an amateur called Sysunov who played with us in *It's My Birthday*. A first-class comic talent, only fancy: a nose as thick as a parsnip, green eyes, and he walks like a crane. . . . We all roared; stay, I will show you how he walks."

Lizotchka springs out of bed and begins pacing about the floor, barefooted and without her cap.

"A very good day to you!" she says in a bass, imitating a man's voice. "Anything pretty? Anything new under the moon? Ha, ha, ha!" she laughs.

"Ha, ha, ha!" Vassya seconds her. And the young pair, roaring with laughter, forgetting the illness, chase one another about the room. The race ends in Vassya's catching his wife by her nightgown and eagerly showering kisses upon her. After one particularly passionate embrace Lizotchka suddenly remembers that she is seriously ill. . . .

"What silliness!" she says, making a serious face and covering herself with the quilt. "I suppose you have forgotten that I am ill! Clever, I must say!"

"Sorry . . ." falters her husband in confusion.

"If my illness takes a bad turn it will be your fault. Not kind! not good!"

Lizotchka closes her eyes and is silent. Her former languor and expression of martyrdom return again, there is a sound of gentle moans. Vassya changes the compress, and glad that his wife is at home and not gadding off to her aunt's, sits meekly at her feet. He does not sleep all night. At ten o'clock the doctor comes.

"Well, how are we feeling?" he asks as he takes her pulse. "Have you slept?"

"Badly," Lizotchka's husband answers for her, "very badly."

The doctor walks away to the window and stares at a passing chimney-sweep.

"Doctor, may I have coffee to-day?" asks Lizotchka.

"You may."

"And may I get up?"

"You might, perhaps, but . . . you had better lie in bed another day."

"She is awfully depressed," Vassya whispers in his ear, "such gloomy thoughts, such pessimism. I am dreadfully uneasy about her."

The doctor sits down to the little table, and rubbing his forehead, prescribes bromide of potassium for Lizotchka, then makes his bow, and promising to look in again in the evening, departs. Vassya does not go to the office, but sits all day at his wife's feet.

At midday the admirers of her talent arrive in a crowd. They are agitated and alarmed, they bring masses of flowers and French novels. Lizotchka, in a snow-white cap and a light dressing jacket, lies in bed with an enigmatic look, as though she did not believe in her own recovery. The admirers of her talent see her husband, but readily forgive his presence: they and he are united by one calamity at that bedside!

At six o'clock in the evening Lizotchka falls asleep, and again sleeps till two o'clock in the morning. Vassya as before sits at her feet, struggles with drowsiness, changes her compress, plays at being a Jew, and in the morning after a second night of suffering, Liza is prinking before the looking-glass and putting on her hat.

"Wherever are you going, my dear?" asks Vassya, with an imploring look at her.

"What?" says Lizotchka in wonder, assuming a scared expression, "don't you know that there is a rehearsal to-day at Marya Lvovna's?"

After escorting her there, Vassya having nothing to do to while away his boredom, takes his portfolio and goes to the office. His head aches so violently from his sleepless nights that his left eye shuts of itself and refuses to open. . . .

"What's the matter with you, my good sir?" his chief asks him. "What is it?"

Vassya waves his hand and sits down.

"Don't ask me, your Excellency," he says with a sigh. "What I have suffered in these two days, what I have suffered! Liza has been ill!"

"Good heavens," cried his chief in alarm. "Lizaveta Pavlovna, what is wrong with her?"

Vassily Stepanovitch merely throws up his hands and raises his eyes to the ceiling, as though he would say: "It's the will of Providence."

"Ah, my boy, I can sympathise with you with all my heart!" sighs his chief, rolling his eyes. "I've lost my wife, my dear, I understand. That is a loss, it is a loss! It's awful, awful! I hope Lizaveta Pavlovna is better now! What doctor is attending her?"

"Von Schterk."

"Von Schterk! But you would have been better to have called in Magnus or Semandritsky. But how very pale your face is. You are ill yourself! This is awful!"

"Yes, your Excellency, I haven't slept. What I have suffered, what I have been through!"

"And yet you came! Why you came I can't understand? One can't force oneself like that! One mustn't do oneself harm like that. Go home and stay there till you are well again! Go home, I command you! Zeal is a very fine thing in a young official, but you mustn't forget as the Romans used to say: 'mens sana in corpore sano,' that is, a healthy brain in a healthy body."

Vassya agrees, puts his papers back in his portfolio, and, taking leave of his chief, goes home to bed.

# THE FIRST CLASS PASSENGER

A first class passenger who had just dined at the station and drunk a little too much lay down on the velvet-covered seat, stretched himself out luxuriously, and sank into a doze. After a nap of no more than five minutes, he looked with oily eyes at his *vis-à-vis*, gave a smirk, and said:

"My father of blessed memory used to like to have his heels tickled by peasant women after dinner. I am just like him, with this difference, that after dinner I always like my tongue and my brains gently stimulated. Sinful man as I am, I like empty talk on a full stomach. Will you allow me to have a chat with you?"

"I shall be delighted," answered the *vis-à-vis*.

"After a good dinner the most trifling subject is sufficient to arouse devilishly great thoughts in my brain. For instance, we saw just now near the refreshment bar two young men, and you heard one congratulate the other on being celebrated. 'I congratulate you,' he said; 'you are already a celebrity and are beginning to win fame.' Evidently actors or journalists of microscopic dimensions. But they are not the point. The question that is occupying my mind at the moment, sir, is exactly what is to be understood by the word *fame* or *celebrity*. What do you think? Pushkin called fame a bright patch on a ragged garment; we all understand it as Pushkin does — that is, more or less subjectively — but no one has yet given a clear, logical definition of the word. . . . I would give a good deal for such a definition!"

"Why do you feel such a need for it?"

"You see, if we knew what fame is, the means of attaining it might also perhaps be known to us," said the first-class passenger, after a moment's thought. I must tell you, sir, that when I was younger I strove after celebrity with every fiber of my being. To be popular was my craze, so to speak. For the sake of it I studied, worked, sat up at night, neglected my meals. And I fancy, as far as I can judge without partiality, I had all the natural gifts for attaining it. To begin with, I am an engineer by profession. In the course of my life I have built in Russia some two dozen magnificent bridges, I have laid aqueducts for three towns; I have worked in Russia, in England, in Belgium. . . . Secondly, I am the author of several special treatises in my own line.

And thirdly, my dear sir, I have from a boy had a weakness for chemistry. Studying that science in my leisure hours, I discovered methods of obtaining certain organic acids, so that you will find my name in all the foreign manuals of chemistry. I have always been in the service, I have risen to the grade of actual civil councilor, and I have an unblemished record. I will not fatigue your attention by enumerating my works and my merits, I will only say that I have done far more than some celebrities. And yet here I am in my old age, I am getting ready for my coffin, so to say, and I am as celebrated as that black dog yonder running on the embankment."

"How can you tell? Perhaps you are celebrated."

"H'm! Well, we will test it at once. Tell me, have you ever heard the name Krikunov?"

The *vis-à-vis* raised his eyes to the ceiling, thought a minute, and laughed.

"No, I haven't heard it, . . ." he said.

"That is my surname. You, a man of education, getting on in years, have never heard of me - a convincing proof! It is evident that in my efforts to gain fame I have not done the right thing at all: I did not know the right way to set to work, and, trying to catch fame by the tail, got on the wrong side of her."

"What is the right way to set to work?"

"Well, the devil only knows! Talent, you say? Genius? Originality? Not a bit of it, sir!. . . People have lived and made a career side by side with me who were worthless, trivial, and even contemptible compared with me. They did not do one-tenth of the work I did, did not put themselves out, were not distinguished for their talents, and did not make an effort to be celebrated, but just look at them! Their names are continually in the newspapers and on men's lips! If you are not tired of listening I will illustrate it by an example. Some years ago I built a bridge in the town of K. I must tell you that the dullness of that scurvy little town was terrible. If it had not been for women and cards I believe I should have gone out of my mind. Well, it's an old story: I was so bored that I got into an affair with a singer. Everyone was enthusiastic about her, the devil only knows why; to my thinking she was - what shall I say? - an ordinary, commonplace creature, like lots of others. The hussy was empty-headed, ill-tempered, greedy, and what's more, she was a fool.

"She ate and drank a vast amount, slept till five o clock in the afternoon - and I fancy did nothing else. She was looked upon as a cocotte, and that was indeed her profession; but when people wanted to refer to her in a literary fashion, they called her an actress and a singer. I used to be devoted to the theatre, and therefore this fraudulent pretense of being an actress made me furiously indignant. My young lady had not the slightest right to call herself an actress or a singer. She was a creature entirely devoid of talent, devoid of feeling - a pitiful creature one may say. As far as I can judge she sang disgustingly. The whole charm of her 'art' lay in her kicking up her legs on every suitable occasion, and not being embarrassed when people walked into her dressing-room. She usually selected translated vaudevilles, with singing in them, and opportunities for disporting herself in male attire, in tights. In fact it was - ough! Well, I ask your attention. As I remember now, a public ceremony took place to celebrate the opening of the newly constructed bridge. There was a religious service, there were speeches, telegrams, and so on. I hung about my cherished creation, you know, all the while afraid that my heart would burst with the excitement of an author. Its an old story and there's no need for false modesty, and so I will tell you that my bridge was a magnificent work! It was not a bridge but a picture, a perfect delight! And who would not have been excited when the whole town came to the opening? 'Oh,' I thought, 'now the eyes of all the public will be on me! Where shall I hide myself?' Well, I need not have worried myself, sir - alas! Except the official personages, no one took the slightest notice of me. They stood in a crowd on the river-bank, gazed like sheep at the bridge, and did not concern themselves to know who had built it. And it was from that time, by the way, that I began to hate our estimable public - damnation take them! Well, to continue. All at once the public became agitated; a whisper ran through the crowd, . . a smile came on their faces, their shoulders began to move. 'They must have seen me,' I thought. A likely idea! I looked, and my singer, with a train of young scamps, was making her way through the crowd. The eyes of the crowd were hurriedly following this procession.

A whisper began in a thousand voices: 'That's so-and-so. . . . Charming! Bewitching!' Then it was they noticed me. . . . A couple of young milksops, local amateurs of the scenic art, I presume, looked at me, exchanged glances, and whispered: 'That's her lover!' How do you like that? And an unprepossessing individual in a top-hat, with a chin that badly needed shaving, hung round me, shifting from one foot to the other, then turned to me with the words:

"'Do you know who that lady is, walking on the other bank? That's so-and-so. . . . Her voice is beneath all criticism, but she has a most perfect mastery of it! . . .'

" 'Can you tell me,' I asked the unprepossessing individual, 'who built this bridge?'

" 'I really don't know,' answered the individual; some engineer, I expect.'

" 'And who built the cathedral in your town?' I asked again.

" 'I really can't tell you.'

"Then I asked him who was considered the best teacher in K., who the best architect, and to all my questions the unprepossessing individual answered that he did not know.

" 'And tell me, please,' I asked in conclusion, with whom is that singer living?'

" 'With some engineer called Krikunov.'

"Well, how do you like that, sir? But to proceed. There are no minnesingers or bards nowadays, and celebrity is created almost exclusively by the newspapers. The day after the dedication of the bridge, I greedily snatched up the local *Messenger*, and looked for myself in it. I spent a long time running my eyes over all the four pages, and at last there it was - hurrah! I began reading: 'Yesterday in beautiful weather, before a vast concourse of people, in the presence of His Excellency the Governor of the province, so-and-so, and other dignitaries, the ceremony of the dedication of the newly constructed bridge took place,' and so on. . . . Towards the end: Our talented actress so-and-so, the favorite of the K. public, was present at the dedication looking very beautiful. I need not say that her arrival created a sensation. The star was wearing . . .' and so on. They might have given me one word! Half a word. Petty as it seems, I actually cried with vexation!

"I consoled myself with the reflection that the provinces are stupid, and one could expect nothing of them and for celebrity one must go to the intellectual centers - to Petersburg and to Moscow. And as it happened, at that very time there was a work of mine in Petersburg which I had sent in for a competition. The date on which the result was to be declared was at hand.

"I took leave of K. and went to Petersburg. It is a long journey from K. to Petersburg, and that I might not be bored on the journey I took a reserved compartment and - well - of course, I took my singer. We set off, and all the way we were eating, drinking champagne, and - tra-la - la! But behold, at last we reach the intellectual center. I arrived on the very day the result was declared, and had the satisfaction, my dear sir, of celebrating my own success: my work received the first prize. Hurrah! Next day I went out along the Nevsky and spent seventy kopecks on various newspapers. I hastened to my hotel room, lay down on the sofa, and, controlling a quiver of excitement, made haste to read. I ran through one newspaper - nothing. I ran through a second - nothing either; my God! At last, in the fourth, I lighted upon the following paragraph: 'Yesterday the well-known provincial actress so-and-so arrived by express in Petersburg. We note with pleasure that the climate of the South has had a beneficial effect on our fair friend; her charming stage appearance. . .' and I don't remember the rest! Much lower down than that paragraph I found, printed in the smallest type: first prize in the competition was adjudged to an engineer called so-and-so.' That was all! And to make things better, they even misspelt my name: instead of Krikunov it was Kirkutlov. So much for your intellectual center! But that was not all. . . . By the time I left Petersburg, a month later, all the newspapers were vying with one another in discussing our incomparable, divine, highly talented actress, and my mistress was referred to, not by her surname, but by her Christian name and her father's. . . .

"Some years later I was in Moscow. I was summoned there by a letter, in the mayor's own handwriting, to undertake a work for which Moscow, in its newspapers, had been clamoring for over a hundred years. In the intervals of my work I delivered five public lectures, with a philanthropic object, in one of the museums there. One would have thought that was enough to make one known to the whole town for three days at least, wouldn't one? But, alas! not a single Moscow gazette said a word about me There was something about houses on fire, about an operetta, sleeping town councilors, drunken shop keepers - about everything; but about my work, my plans, my lectures - mum. And a nice set they are in Moscow! I got into a tram. . . . It was packed full; there were ladies and military men and students of both sexes, creatures of all sorts in couples.

" 'I am told the town council has sent for an engineer to plan such and such a work!' I said to my neighbor, so loudly that all the tram could hear. 'Do you know the name of the engineer?'

"My neighbor shook his head. The rest of the public took a cursory glance at me, and in all their eyes I read: 'I don't know.'

" 'I am told that there is someone giving lectures in such and such a museum?' I persisted, trying to get up a conversation. 'I hear it is interesting.'

"No one even nodded. Evidently they had not all of them heard of the lectures, and the ladies were not even aware of the existence of the museum. All that would not have mattered, but imagine, my dear sir, the people suddenly leaped to their feet and struggled to the windows. What was it? What was the matter?

" 'Look, look!' my neighbor nudged me. 'Do you see that dark man getting into that cab? That's the famous runner, King!'

"And the whole tram began talking breathlessly of the runner who was then absorbing the brains of Moscow.

"I could give you ever so many other examples, but I think that is enough. Now let us assume that I am mistaken about myself, that I am a wretchedly boastful and incompetent person; but apart from myself I might point to many of my contemporaries, men remarkable for their talent and industry, who have nevertheless died unrecognized. Are Russian navigators, chemists, physicists, mechanicians, and agriculturists popular with the public? Do our cultivated masses know anything of Russian artists, sculptors, and literary men? Some old literary hack, hard-working and talented, will wear away the doorstep of the publishers' offices for thirty-three years, cover reams of paper, be had up for libel twenty times, and yet not step beyond his ant-heap. Can you mention to me a single representative of our literature who would have become celebrated if the rumor had not been spread over the earth that he had been killed in a duel, gone out of his mind, been sent into exile, or had cheated at cards?"

The first-class passenger was so excited that he dropped his cigar out of his mouth and got up.

"Yes," he went on fiercely, "and side by side with these people I can quote you hundreds of all sorts of singers, acrobats, buffoons, whose names are known to every baby. Yes!"

The door creaked, there was a draught, and an individual of forbidding aspect, wearing an Inverness coat, a top-hat, and blue spectacles, walked into the carriage. The individual looked round at the seats, frowned, and went on further.

"Do you know who that is?" there came a timid whisper from the furthest corner of the compartment.

That is N. N., the famous Tula cardsharper who was had up in connection with the Y. bank affair."

"There you are!" laughed the first-class passenger. He knows a Tula cardsharper, but ask him whether he knows Semiradsky, Tchaykovsky, or Solovyov the philosopher - he'll shake his head. . . . It swinish!"

Three minutes passed in silence.

"Allow me in my turn to ask you a question," said the *vis-a-vis* timidly, clearing his throat. Do you know the name of Pushkov?"

"Pushkov? H'm! Pushkov. . . . No, I don't know it!"

273

"That is my name,..." said the *vis-à-vis*, overcome with embarrassment. "Then you don't know it? And yet I have been a professor at one of the Russian universities for thirty-five years, ... a member of the Academy of Sciences, ... have published more than one work...."

The first-class passenger and the *vis-à-vis* looked at each other and burst out laughing.

# TALENT

An artist called Yegor Savvitch, who was spending his summer holidays at the house of an officer's widow, was sitting on his bed, given up to the depression of morning. It was beginning to look like autumn out of doors. Heavy, clumsy clouds covered the sky in thick layers; there was a cold, piercing wind, and with a plaintive wail the trees were all bending on one side. He could see the yellow leaves whirling round in the air and on the earth. Farewell, summer! This melancholy of nature is beautiful and poetical in its own way, when it is looked at with the eyes of an artist, but Yegor Savvitch was in no humour to see beauty. He was devoured by ennui and his only consolation was the thought that by to-morrow he would not be there. The bed, the chairs, the tables, the floor, were all heaped up with cushions, crumpled bed-clothes, boxes. The floor had not been swept, the cotton curtains had been taken down from the windows. Next day he was moving, to town.

His landlady, the widow, was out. She had gone off somewhere to hire horses and carts to move next day to town. Profiting by the absence of her severe mamma, her daughter Katya, aged twenty, had for a long time been sitting in the young man's room. Next day the painter was going away, and she had a great deal to say to him. She kept talking, talking, and yet she felt that she had not said a tenth of what she wanted to say. With her eyes full of tears, she gazed at his shaggy head, gazed at it with rapture and sadness. And Yegor Savvitch was shaggy to a hideous extent, so that he looked like a wild animal. His hair hung down to his shoulder-blades, his beard grew from his neck, from his nostrils, from his ears; his eyes were lost under his thick overhanging brows. It was all so thick, so matted, that if a fly or a beetle had been caught in his hair, it would never have found its way out of this enchanted thicket. Yegor Savvitch listened to Katya, yawning. He was tired. When Katya began whimpering, he looked severely at her from his overhanging eyebrows, frowned, and said in a heavy, deep bass:

"I cannot marry."

"Why not?" Katya asked softly.

"Because for a painter, and in fact any man who lives for art, marriage is out of the question. An artist must be free."

"But in what way should I hinder you, Yegor Savvitch?"

"I am not speaking of myself, I am speaking in general. . . . Famous authors and painters have never married."

"And you, too, will be famous - I understand that perfectly. But put yourself in my place. I am afraid of my mother. She is stern and irritable. When she knows that you won't marry me, and that it's all nothing . . . she'll begin to give it to me. Oh, how wretched I am! And you haven't paid for your rooms, either! . . . ."

"Damn her! I'll pay."

Yegor Savvitch got up and began walking to and fro.

"I ought to be abroad!" he said. And the artist told her that nothing was easier than to go abroad. One need do nothing but paint a picture and sell it.

"Of course!" Katya assented. "Why haven't you painted one in the summer?"

"Do you suppose I can work in a barn like this?" the artist said ill-humouredly. "And where should I get models?"

Some one banged the door viciously in the storey below. Katya, who was expecting her mother's return from minute to minute, jumped up and ran away. The artist was left alone. For a long time he walked to and fro, threading his way between the chairs and the piles of untidy objects of all sorts. He heard the widow rattling the crockery and loudly abusing the peasants who had asked her two roubles for each cart. In his disgust Yegor Savvitch stopped before the cupboard and stared for a long while, frowning at the decanter of vodka.

"Ah, blast you!" he heard the widow railing at Katya. "Damnation take you!"

The artist drank a glass of vodka, and the dark cloud in his soul gradually disappeared, and he felt as though all his inside was smiling within him. He began dreaming. . . . His fancy pictured how he would become great. He could not imagine his future works but he could see distinctly how the papers would talk of him, how the shops would sell his photographs, with what envy his friends would look after him. He tried to picture himself in a magnificent drawing-room surrounded by pretty and adoring women; but the picture was misty, vague, as he had never in his life seen a drawing-room. The pretty and adoring women were not a success either, for, except Katya, he knew no adoring woman, not even one respectable girl. People who know nothing about life usually picture life from books, but Yegor Savvitch knew no books either. He had tried to read Gogol, but had fallen asleep on the second page.

"It won't burn, drat the thing!" the widow bawled down below, as she set the samovar. "Katya, give me some charcoal!"

The dreamy artist felt a longing to share his hopes and dreams with some one. He went downstairs into the kitchen, where the stout widow and Katya were busy about a dirty stove in the midst of charcoal fumes from the samovar. There he sat down on a bench close to a big pot and began:

"It's a fine thing to be an artist! I can go just where I like, do what I like. One has not to work in an office or in the fields. I've no superiors or officers over me. . . . I'm my own superior. And with all that I'm doing good to humanity!"

And after dinner he composed himself for a " rest." He usually slept till the twilight of evening. But this time soon after dinner he felt that some one was pulling at his leg. Some one kept laughing and shouting his name. He opened his eyes and saw his friend Ukleikin, the landscape painter, who had been away all the summer in the Kostroma district.

"Bah!" he cried, delighted. "What do I see?"

There followed handshakes, questions.

"Well, have you brought anything? I suppose you've knocked off hundreds of sketches?" said Yegor Savvitch, watching Ukleikin taking his belongings out of his trunk.

"H'm! . . . Yes. I have done something. And how are you getting on? Have you been painting anything?"

Yegor Savvitch dived behind the bed, and crimson in the face, extracted a canvas in a frame covered with dust and spider webs.

"See here. . . . A girl at the window after parting from her betrothed. In three sittings. Not nearly finished yet."

The picture represented Katya faintly outlined sitting at an open window, from which could be seen a garden and lilac distance. Ukleikin did not like the picture.

"H'm! . . . There is air and . . . and there is expression," he said. "There's a feeling of distance, but . . . but that bush is screaming . . . screaming horribly!"

The decanter was brought on to the scene.

Towards evening Kostyliov, also a promising beginner, an historical painter, came in to see Yegor Savvitch. He was a friend staying at the next villa, and was a man of five-and-thirty. He had long hair, and wore a blouse with a Shakespeare collar, and had a dignified manner. Seeing the vodka, he frowned, complained of his chest, but yielding to his friends' entreaties, drank a glass.

"I've thought of a subject, my friends," he began, getting drunk. "I want to paint some new . . . Herod or Clepentian, or some blackguard of that description, you understand, and to contrast with him the idea of Christianity. On the one side Rome, you understand, and on the other Christianity. . . . I want to represent the spirit, you understand? The spirit!"

And the widow downstairs shouted continually:

"Katya, give me the cucumbers! Go to Sidorov's and get some kvass, you jade!"

Like wolves in a cage, the three friends kept pacing to and fro from one end of the room to the other. They talked without ceasing, talked, hotly and genuinely; all three were excited, carried away. To listen to them it would seem they had the future, fame, money, in their hands. And it never occurred to either of them that time was passing, that every day life was nearing its close, that they had lived at other people's expense a great deal and nothing yet was accomplished; that they were all bound by the inexorable law by which of a hundred promising beginners only two or three rise to any position and all the others draw blanks in the lottery, perish playing the part of flesh for the cannon. . . . They were gay and happy, and looked the future boldly in the face!

At one o'clock in the morning Kostyliov said good-bye, and smoothing out his Shakespeare collar, went home. The landscape painter remained to sleep at Yegor Savvitch's. Before going to bed, Yegor Savvitch took a candle and made his way into the kitchen to get a drink of water. In the dark, narrow passage Katya was sitting, on a box, and, with her hands clasped on her knees, was looking upwards. A blissful smile was straying on her pale, exhausted face, and her eyes were beaming.

"Is that you? What are you thinking about?" Yegor Savvitch asked her.

"I am thinking of how you'll be famous," she said in a half-whisper. "I keep fancying how you'll become a famous man. . . . I overheard all your talk. . . . I keep dreaming and dreaming. . . ."

Katya went off into a happy laugh, cried, and laid her hands reverently on her idol's shoulders.

# THE DEPENDENTS

Mihail Petrovitch Zotov, a decrepit and solitary old man of seventy, belonging to the artisan class, was awakened by the cold and the aching in his old limbs. It was dark in his room, but the little lamp before the ikon was no longer burning. Zotov raised the curtain and looked out of the window. The clouds that shrouded the sky were beginning to show white here and there, and the air was becoming transparent, so it must have been nearly five, not more.

Zotov cleared his throat, coughed, and shrinking from the cold, got out of bed. In accordance with years of habit, he stood for a long time before the ikon, saying his prayers. He repeated "Our Father," "Hail Mary," the Creed, and mentioned a long string of names. To whom those names belonged he had forgotten years ago, and he only repeated them from habit. From habit, too, he swept his room and entry, and set his fat little four-legged copper samovar. If Zotov had not had these habits he would not have known how to occupy his old age.

The little samovar slowly began to get hot, and all at once, unexpectedly, broke into a tremulous bass hum.

"Oh, you've started humming!" grumbled Zotov. "Hum away then, and bad luck to you!"

At that point the old man appropriately recalled that, in the preceding night, he had dreamed of a stove, and to dream of a stove is a sign of sorrow.

Dreams and omens were the only things left that could rouse him to reflection; and on this occasion he plunged with a special zest into the considerations of the questions: What the samovar was humming for? and what sorrow was foretold by the stove? The dream seemed to come true from the first. Zotov rinsed out his teapot and was about to make his tea, when he found there was not one teaspoonful left in the box.

"What an existence!" he grumbled, rolling crumbs of black bread round in his mouth. "It's a dog's life. No tea! And it isn't as though I were a simple peasant: I'm an artisan and a house-owner. The disgrace!"

Grumbling and talking to himself, Zotov put on his overcoat, which was like a crinoline, and, thrusting his feet into huge clumsy galosh-boots (made in the year 1867 by a bootmaker called Prohoritch), went out into the yard. The air was grey, cold, and sullenly still. The big yard, full of tufts of burdock and strewn with yellow leaves, was faintly silvered with autumn frost. Not a breath of wind nor a sound. The old man sat down on the steps of his slanting porch, and at once there happened what happened regularly every morning: his dog Lyska, a big, mangy, decrepit-looking, white yard-dog, with black patches, came up to him with its right eye shut. Lyska came up timidly, wriggling in a frightened way, as though her paws were not touching the earth but a hot stove, and the whole of her wretched figure was expressive of abjectness. Zotov pretended not to notice her, but when she faintly wagged her tail, and, wriggling as before, licked his galosh, he stamped his foot angrily.

"Be off! The plague take you!" he cried. "Con-found-ed bea-east!"

Lyska moved aside, sat down, and fixed her solitary eye upon her master.

"You devils!" he went on. "You are the last straw on my back, you Herods."

And he looked with hatred at his shed with its crooked, overgrown roof; there from the door of the shed a big horse's head was looking out at him. Probably flattered by its master's attention, the head moved, pushed forward, and there emerged from the shed the whole horse, as decrepit as Lyska, as timid and as crushed, with spindly legs, grey hair, a pinched stomach, and a bony spine. He came out of the shed and stood still, hesitating as though overcome with embarrassment.

"Plague take you," Zotov went on. "Shall I ever see the last of you, you jail-bird Pharaohs! . . . I wager you want your breakfast!" he jeered, twisting his angry face into a contemptuous smile. "By all means, this minute! A priceless steed like you must have your fill of the best oats! Pray begin! This minute! And I have something to give to the magnificent, valuable dog! If a precious dog like you does not care for bread, you can have meat."

Zotov grumbled for half an hour, growing more and more irritated. In the end, unable to control the anger that boiled up in him, he jumped up, stamped with his goloshes, and growled out to be heard all over the yard:

"I am not obliged to feed you, you loafers! I am not some millionaire for you to eat me out of house and home! I have nothing to eat myself, you cursed carcases, the cholera take you! I get no pleasure or profit out of you; nothing but trouble and ruin, Why don't you give up the ghost? Are you such personages that even death won't take you? You can live, damn you! but I don't want to feed you! I have had enough of you! I don't want to!"

Zotov grew wrathful and indignant, and the horse and the dog listened. Whether these two dependents understood that they were being reproached for living at his expense, I don't know, but their stomachs looked more pinched than ever, and their whole figures shrivelled up, grew gloomier and more abject than before. . . . Their submissive air exasperated Zotov more than ever.

"Get away!" he shouted, overcome by a sort of inspiration. "Out of my house! Don't let me set eyes on you again! I am not obliged to keep all sorts of rubbish in my yard! Get away!"

The old man moved with little hurried steps to the gate, opened it, and picking up a stick from the ground, began driving out his dependents. The horse shook its head, moved its shoulder-blades, and limped to the gate; the dog followed him. Both of them went out into the street, and, after walking some twenty paces, stopped at the fence.

"I'll give it you!" Zotov threatened them.

When he had driven out his dependents he felt calmer, and began sweeping the yard. From time to time he peeped out into the street: the horse and the dog were standing like posts by the fence, looking dejectedly towards the gate.

"Try how you can do without me," muttered the old man, feeling as though a weight of anger were being lifted from his heart. "Let somebody else look after you now! I am stingy and ill-tempered. . . . It's nasty living with me, so you try living with other people. . . . Yes. . . ."

After enjoying the crushed expression of his dependents, and grumbling to his heart's content, Zotov went out of the yard, and, assuming a ferocious air, shouted:

"Well, why are you standing there? Whom are you waiting for? Standing right across the middle of the road and preventing the public from passing! Go into the yard!"

The horse and the dog with drooping heads and a guilty air turned towards the gate. Lyska, probably feeling she did not deserve forgiveness, whined piteously.

"Stay you can, but as for food, you'll get nothing from me! You may die, for all I care!"

Meanwhile the sun began to break through the morning mist; its slanting rays gilded over the autumn frost. There was a sound of steps and voices. Zotov put back the broom in its place, and went out of the yard to see his crony and neighbour, Mark Ivanitch, who kept a little general shop. On reaching his friend's shop, he sat down on a folding-stool, sighed sedately, stroked his beard, and began about the weather. From the weather the friends passed to the new deacon, from the deacon to the choristers; and the conversation lengthened out. They did not notice as they talked how time was passing, and when the shop-boy brought in a big teapot of boiling water, and the friends proceeded to drink tea, the time flew as quickly as a bird. Zotov got warm and felt more cheerful.

"I have a favour to ask of you, Mark Ivanitch," he began, after the sixth glass, drumming on the counter with his fingers. "If you would just be so kind as to give me a gallon of oats again to-day. . . ."

From behind the big tea-chest behind which Mark Ivanitch was sitting came the sound of a deep sigh.

"Do be so good," Zotov went on; "never mind tea - don't give it me to-day, but let me have some oats. . . . I am ashamed to ask you, I have wearied you with my poverty, but the horse is hungry."

"I can give it you," sighed the friend - "why not? But why the devil do you keep those carcases? - tfool    Tell me that, please. It would be all right if it were a useful horse, but - tfoo! - one is ashamed to look at it. . . . And the dog's nothing but a skeleton! Why the devil do you keep them?"

"What am I to do with them?"

"You know. Take them to Ignat the slaughterer - that is all there is to do. They ought to have been there long ago. It's the proper place for them."

"To be sure, that is so! . . . I dare say! . . ."

"You live like a beggar and keep animals," the friend went on. "I don't grudge the oats. . . . God bless you. But as to the future, brother . . . I can't afford to give regularly every day! There is no end to your poverty! One gives and gives, and one doesn't know when there will be an end to it all."

The friend sighed and stroked his red face.

"If you were dead that would settle it," he said. "You go on living, and you don't know what for. . . . Yes, indeed! But if it is not the Lord's will for you to die, you had better go somewhere into an almshouse or a refuge."

"What for? I have relations. I have a great-niece. . . ."

And Zotov began telling at great length of his great-niece Glasha, daughter of his niece Katerina, who lived somewhere on a farm.

"She is bound to keep me!" he said. "My house will be left to her, so let her keep me; I'll go to her. It's Glasha, you know . . . Katya's daughter; and Katya, you know, was my brother Panteley's stepdaughter. . . . You understand? The house will come to her. . . . Let her keep me!"

"To be sure; rather than live, as you do, a beggar, I should have gone to her long ago."

"I will go! As God's above, I will go. It's her duty."

When an hour later the old friends were drinking a glass of vodka, Zotov stood in the middle of the shop and said with enthusiasm:

"I have been meaning to go to her for a long time; I will go this very day."

"To be sure; rather than hanging about and dying of hunger, you ought to have gone to the farm long ago."

"I'll go at once! When I get there, I shall say: Take my house, but keep me and treat me with respect. It's your duty! If you don't care to, then there is neither my house, nor my blessing for you! Good-bye, Ivanitch!"

Zotov drank another glass, and, inspired by the new idea, hurried home. The vodka had upset him and his head was reeling, but instead of lying down, he put all his clothes together in a bundle, said a prayer, took his stick, and went out. Muttering and tapping on the stones with his stick, he walked the whole length of the street without looking back, and found himself in the open country. It was eight or nine miles to the farm. He walked along the dry road, looked at the town herd lazily munching the yellow grass, and pondered on the abrupt change in his life which he had only just brought about so resolutely. He thought, too, about his dependents. When he went out of the house, he had not locked the gate, and so had left them free to go whither they would.

He had not gone a mile into the country when he heard steps behind him. He looked round and angrily clasped his hands. The horse and Lyska, with their heads drooping and their tails between their legs, were quietly walking after him.

"Go back!" he waved to them.

They stopped, looked at one another, looked at him. He went on, they followed him. Then he stopped and began ruminating. It was impossible to go to his great-niece Glasha, whom he hardly knew, with these creatures; he did not want to go back and shut them up, and, indeed, he could not shut them up, because the gate was no use.

"To die of hunger in the shed," thought Zotov. "Hadn't I really better take them to Ignat?"

Ignat's hut stood on the town pasture-ground, a hundred paces from the flagstaff. Though he had not quite made up his mind, and did not know what to do, he turned towards it. His head was giddy and there was a darkness before his eyes. . . .

He remembers little of what happened in the slaughterer's yard. He has a memory of a sickening, heavy smell of hides and the savoury steam of the cabbage-soup Ignat was sipping when he went in to him. As in a dream he saw Ignat, who made him wait two hours, slowly preparing something, changing his clothes, talking to some women about corrosive sublimate; he remembered the horse was put into a stand, after which there was the sound of two dull thuds, one of a blow on the skull, the other of the fall of a heavy body. When Lyska, seeing the death of her friend, flew at Ignat, barking shrilly, there was the sound of a third blow that cut short the bark abruptly. Further, Zotov remembers that in his drunken foolishness, seeing the two corpses, he went up to the stand, and put his own forehead ready for a blow.

And all that day his eyes were dimmed by a haze, and he could not even see his own fingers.

# THE JEUNE PREMIER

Yevgeny Alexeyitch Podzharov, the *jeune premier*, a graceful, elegant young man with an oval face and little bags under his eyes, had come for the season to one of the southern towns of Russia, and tried at once to make the acquaintance of a few of the leading families of the place. "Yes, signor," he would often say, gracefully swinging his foot and displaying his red socks, "an artist ought to act upon the masses, both directly and indirectly; the first aim is attained by his work on the stage, the second by an acquaintance with the local inhabitants. On my honour, *parole d'honneur*, I don't understand why it is we actors avoid making acquaintance with local families. Why is it? To say nothing of dinners, name-day parties, feasts, *soirées fixes*, to say nothing of these entertainments, think of the moral influence we may have on society! Is it not agreeable to feel one has dropped a spark in some thick skull? The types one meets! The women! *Mon Dieu*, what women! they turn one's head! One penetrates into some huge merchant's house, into the sacred retreats, and picks out some fresh and rosy little peach - it's heaven, *parole d'honneur!*"

In the southern town, among other estimable families he made the acquaintance of that of a manufacturer called Zybaev. Whenever he remembers that acquaintance now he frowns contemptuously, screws up his eyes, and nervously plays with his watch-chain.

One day - it was at a name-day party at Zybaev's - the actor was sitting in his new friends' drawing-room and holding forth as usual. Around him "types" were sitting in armchairs and on the sofa, listening affably; from the next room came feminine laughter and the sounds of evening tea. . . . Crossing his legs, after each phrase sipping tea with rum in it, and trying to assume an expression of careless boredom, he talked of his stage triumphs.

"I am a provincial actor principally," he said, smiling condescendingly, "but I have played in Petersburg and Moscow too. . . . By the way, I will describe an incident which illustrates pretty well the state of mind of to-day. At my benefit in Moscow the young people brought me such a mass of laurel wreaths that I swear by all I hold sacred I did not know where to put them! *Parole d'honneur!* Later on, at a moment when funds were short, I took the laurel wreaths to the shop, and . . . guess what they weighed. Eighty pounds altogether. Ha, ha! you can't think how useful the money was. Artists, indeed, are often hard up. To-day I have hundreds, thousands, tomorrow nothing. . . . To-day I haven't a crust of bread, to-morrow I have oysters and anchovies, hang it all!"

The local inhabitants sipped their glasses decorously and listened. The well-pleased host, not knowing how to make enough of his cultured and interesting visitor, presented to him a distant relative who had just arrived, one Pavel Ignatyevitch Klimov, a bulky gentleman about forty, wearing a long frock-coat and very full trousers.

"You ought to know each other," said Zybaev as he presented Klimov; "he loves theatres, and at one time used to act himself. He has an estate in the Tula province."

Podzharov and Klimov got into conversation. It appeared, to the great satisfaction of both, that the Tula landowner lived in the very town in which the *jeune premier* had acted for two seasons in succession. Enquiries followed about the town, about common acquaintances, and about the theatre. . . .

"Do you know, I like that town awfully," said the *jeune premier*, displaying his red socks. "What streets, what a charming park, and what society! Delightful society!"

"Yes, delightful society," the landowner assented.

"A commercial town, but extremely cultured. . . . For instance, er-er-er . . . the head master of the high school, the public prosecutor . . . the officers. . . . The police captain, too, was not bad, a man, as the French say, *enchanté*, and the women, Allah, what women!"

"Yes, the women . . . certainly. . . ."

"Perhaps I am partial; the fact is that in your town, I don't know why, I was devilishly lucky with the fair sex! I could write a dozen novels. To take this episode, for instance. . . . I was staying in Yegoryevsky Street, in the very house where the Treasury is. . . ."

"The red house without stucco?"

"Yes, yes . . . without stucco. . . . Close by, as I remember now, lived a local beauty, Varenka. . . ."

"Not Varvara Nikolayevna?" asked Klimov, and he beamed with satisfaction. "She really is a beauty . . . the most beautiful girl in the town."

"The most beautiful girl in the town! A classic profile, great black eyes . . . . and hair to her waist! She saw me in 'Hamlet,' she wrote me a letter *à la* Pushkin's 'Tatyana.' . . . I answered, as you may guess. . . ."

Podzharov looked round, and having satisfied himself that there were no ladies in the room, rolled his eyes, smiled mournfully, and heaved a sigh.

"I came home one evening after a performance," he whispered, "and there she was, sitting on my sofa. There followed tears, protestations of love, kisses. . . . Oh, that was a marvellous, that was a divine night! Our romance lasted two months, but that night was never repeated. It was a night, *parole d'honneur!Ê*"

"Excuse me, what's that?" muttered Klimov, turning crimson and gazing open-eyed at the actor. "I know Varvara Nikolayevna well: she's my niece."

Podzharov was embarrassed, and he, too, opened his eyes wide.

"How's this?" Klimov went on, throwing up his hands. "I know the girl, and . . . and . . . I am surprised. . . ."

"I am very sorry this has come up," muttered the actor, getting up and rubbing something out of his left eye with his little finger. "Though, of course . . . of course, you as her uncle . . ."

The other guests, who had hitherto been listening to the actor with pleasure and rewarding him with smiles, were embarrassed and dropped their eyes.

"Please, do be so good . . . take your words back . . ." said Klimov in extreme embarrassment. "I beg you to do so!"

"If . . . er-er-er . . . it offends you, certainly," answered the actor, with an undefined movement of his hand.

"And confess you have told a falsehood."

"I, no . . . er-er-er. . . . It was not a lie, but I greatly regret having spoken too freely. . . . And, in fact . . . I don't understand your tone!"

Klimov walked up and down the room in silence, as though in uncertainty and hesitation. His fleshy face grew more and more crimson, and the veins in his neck swelled up. After walking up and down for about two minutes he went up to the actor and said in a tearful voice:

"No, do be so good as to confess that you told a lie about Varenka! Have the goodness to do so!"

"It's queer," said the actor, with a strained smile, shrugging his shoulders and swinging his leg. "This is positively insulting!"

"So you will not confess it?"

"I do-on't understand!"

"You will not? In that case, excuse me . . . I shall have to resort to unpleasant measures. Either, sir, I shall insult you at once on the spot, or . . . if you are an honourable man, you will kindly accept my challenge to a duel. . . . We will fight!"

"Certainly!" rapped out the *jeune premier*, with a contemptuous gesture. "Certainly."

Extremely perturbed, the guests and the host, not knowing what to do, drew Klimov aside and began begging him not to get up a scandal. Astonished feminine countenances appeared in the doorway. . . . The *jeune premier* turned round, said a few words, and with an air of being unable to remain in a house where he was insulted, took his cap and made off without saying good-bye.

On his way home the *jeune premier* smiled contemptuously and shrugged his shoulders, but when he reached his hotel room and stretched himself on his sofa he felt exceedingly uneasy.

"The devil take him!" he thought. "A duel does not matter, he won't kill me, but the trouble is the other fellows will hear of it, and they know perfectly well it was a yarn. It's abominable! I shall be disgraced all over Russia. . . ."

Podzharov thought a little, smoked, and to calm himself went out into the street.

"I ought to talk to this bully, ram into his stupid noddle that he is a blockhead and a fool, and that I am not in the least afraid of him. . . ."

The *jeune premier* stopped before Zybaev's house and looked at the windows. Lights were still burning behind the muslin curtains and figures were moving about.

"I'll wait for him!" the actor decided.

It was dark and cold. A hateful autumn rain was drizzling as though through a sieve. Podzharov leaned his elbow on a lamp-post and abandoned himself to a feeling of uneasiness.

He was wet through and exhausted.

At two o'clock in the night the guests began coming out of Zybaev's house. The landowner from Tula was the last to make his appearance. He heaved a sigh that could be heard by the whole street and scraped the pavement with his heavy overboots.

"Excuse me!" said the *jeune premier*, overtaking him. "One minute."

Klimov stopped. The actor gave a smile, hesitated, and began, stammering: "I . . . I confess . . . I told a lie."

"No, sir, you will please confess that publicly," said Klimov, and he turned crimson again. "I can't leave it like that. . . ."

"But you see I am apologizing! I beg you . . . don't you understand? I beg you because you will admit a duel will make talk, and I am in a position. . . . My fellow-actors . . . goodness knows what they may think. . . ."

The *jeune premier* tried to appear unconcerned, to smile, to stand erect, but his body would not obey him, his voice trembled, his eyes blinked guiltily, and his head drooped. For a good while he went on muttering something. Klimov listened to him, thought a little, and heaved a sigh.

"Well, so be it," he said. "May God forgive you. Only don't lie in future, young man. Nothing degrades a man like lying . . . yes, indeed! You are a young man, you have had a good education. . . ."

The landowner from Tula, in a benignant, fatherly way, gave him a lecture, while the *jeune premier* listened and smiled meekly. . . . When it was over he smirked, bowed, and with a guilty step and a crestfallen air set off for his hotel.

As he went to bed half an hour later he felt that he was out of danger and was already in excellent spirits. Serene and satisfied that the misunderstanding had ended so satisfactorily, he wrapped himself in the bedclothes, soon fell asleep, and slept soundly till ten o'clock next morning.

# IN THE DARK

A fly of medium size made its way into the nose of the assistant procurator, Gagin. It may have been impelled by curiosity, or have got there through frivolity or accident in the dark; anyway, the nose resented the presence of a foreign body and gave the signal for a sneeze. Gagin sneezed, sneezed impressively and so shrilly and loudly that the bed shook and the springs creaked. Gagin's wife, Marya Mihalovna, a full, plump, fair woman, started, too, and woke up. She gazed into the darkness, sighed, and turned over on the other side. Five minutes afterwards she turned over again and shut her eyes more firmly but she could not get to sleep again. After sighing and tossing from side to side for a time, she got up, crept over her husband, and putting on her slippers, went to the window.

It was dark outside. She could see nothing but the outlines of the trees and the roof of the stables. There was a faint pallor in the east, but this pallor was beginning to be clouded over. There was perfect stillness in the air wrapped in slumber and darkness. Even the watchman, paid to disturb the stillness of night, was silent; even the corncrake - the only wild creature of the feathered tribe that does not shun the proximity of summer visitors - was silent.

The stillness was broken by Marya Mihalovna herself. Standing at the window and gazing into the yard, she suddenly uttered a cry. She fancied that from the flower garden with the gaunt, clipped poplar, a dark figure was creeping towards the house. For the first minute she thought it was a cow or a horse, then, rubbing her eyes, she distinguished clearly the outlines of a man.

Then she fancied the dark figure approached the window of the kitchen and, standing still a moment, apparently undecided, put one foot on the window ledge and disappeared into the darkness of the window.

"A burglar!" flashed into her mind and a deathly pallor overspread her face.

And in one instant her imagination had drawn the picture so dreaded by lady visitors in country places - a burglar creeps into the kitchen, from the kitchen into the dining-room . . . the silver in the cupboard . .

. next into the bedroom . . . an axe . . . the face of a brigand . . . jewelry. . . . Her knees gave way under her and a shiver ran down her back.

"Vassya!" she said, shaking her husband, "*Basile!* Vassily Prokovitch! Ah! mercy on us, he might be dead! Wake up, *Basile,* I beseech you!"

"W-well?" grunted the assistant procurator, with a deep inward breath and a munching sound.

"For God's sake, wake up! A burglar has got into the kitchen! I was standing at the window looking out and someone got in at the window. He will get into the dining-room next . . . the spoons are in the cupboard! *Basile!* They broke into Mavra Yegorovna's last year."

"Wha - what's the matter?"

"Heavens! he does not understand. Do listen, you stupid! I tell you I've just seen a man getting in at the kitchen window! Pelagea will be frightened and . . . and the silver is in the cupboard!"

"Stuff and nonsense!"

"*Basile,* this is unbearable! I tell you of a real danger and you sleep and grunt! What would you have? Would you have us robbed and murdered?"

The assistant procurator slowly got up and sat on the bed, filling the air with loud yawns.

"Goodness knows what creatures women are! he muttered. "Can't leave one in peace even at night! To wake a man for such nonsense!"

"But, *Basile,* I swear I saw a man getting in at the window!"

"Well, what of it? Let him get in. . . . That's pretty sure to be Pelagea's sweetheart, the fireman."

"What! what did you say?"

"I say it's Pelagea's fireman come to see her."

"Worse than ever!" shrieked Marya Mihalovna. "That's worse than a burglar! I won't put up with cynicism in my house!"

"Hoity-toity! We are virtuous! . . . Won't put up with cynicism? As though it were cynicism! What's the use of firing off those foreign words? My dear girl, it's a thing that has happened ever since the world began, sanctified by tradition. What's a fireman for if not to make love to the cook?"

"No, *Basile!* It seems you don't know me! I cannot face the idea of such a . . . such a . . . in my house. You must go this minute into the kitchen and tell him to go away! This very minute! And to-morrow I'll tell Pelagea that she must not dare to demean herself by such proceedings! When I am dead you may allow immorality in your house, but you shan't do it now! . . . Please go!"

"Damn it," grumbled Gagin, annoyed. "Consider with your microscopic female brain, what am I to go for?"

"*Basile,* I shall faint! . . ."

Gagin cursed, put on his slippers, cursed again, and set off to the kitchen. It was as dark as the inside of a barrel, and the assistant procurator had to feel his way. He groped his way to the door of the nursery and waked the nurse.

"Vassilissa," he said, "you took my dressing-gown to brush last night - where is it?"

"I gave it to Pelagea to brush, sir."

"What carelessness! You take it away and don't put it back - now I've to go without a dressing-gown!"

On reaching the kitchen, he made his way to the corner in which on a box under a shelf of saucepans the cook slept.

"Pelagea," he said, feeling her shoulder and giving it a shake, "Pelagea! Why are you pretending? You are not asleep! Who was it got in at your window just now?"

"Mm . . . m . . . good morning! Got in at the window? Who could get in?"

"Oh come, it's no use your trying to keep it up! You'd better tell your scamp to clear out while he can! Do you hear? He's no business to be here!"

"Are you out of your senses, sir, bless you? Do you think I'd be such a fool? Here one's running about all day long, never a minute to sit down and then spoken to like this at night! Four roubles a month . . . and to find my own tea and sugar and this is all the credit I get for it! I used to live in a tradesman's house, and never met with such insult there!"

"Come, come - no need to go over your grievances! This very minute your grenadier must turn out! Do you understand?"

"You ought to be ashamed, sir," said Pelagea, and he could hear the tears in her voice. "Gentlefolks . . . educated, and yet not a notion that with our hard lot . . . in our life of toil" - she burst into tears. "It's easy to insult us. There's no one to stand up for us."

"Come, come . . . I don't mind! Your mistress sent me. You may let a devil in at the window for all I care!"

There was nothing left for the assistant procurator but to acknowledge himself in the wrong and go back to his spouse.

"I say, Pelagea," he said, "you had my dressing-gown to brush. Where is it?"

"Oh, I am so sorry, sir; I forgot to put it on your chair. It's hanging on a peg near the stove."

Gagin felt for the dressing-gown by the stove, put it on, and went quietly back to his room.

When her husband went out Marya Mihalovna got into bed and waited. For the first three minutes her mind was at rest, but after that she began to feel uneasy.

"What a long time he's gone," she thought. "It's all right if he is there . . . that immoral man . . . but if it's a burglar?"

And again her imagination drew a picture of her husband going into the dark kitchen . . . a blow with an axe . . . dying without uttering a single sound . . . a pool of blood! . . .

Five minutes passed . . . five and a half . . . at last six. . . . A cold sweat came out on her forehead.

"*Basile!*" she shrieked, "*Basile!*"

"What are you shouting for? I am here." She heard her husband's voice and steps. "Are you being murdered?"

The assistant procurator went up to the bedstead and sat down on the edge of it.

"There's nobody there at all," he said. "It was your fancy, you queer creature. . . . You can sleep easy, your fool of a Pelagea is as virtuous as her mistress. What a coward you are! What a . . . ."

And the deputy procurator began teasing his wife. He was wide awake now and did not want to go to sleep again.

"You are a coward!" he laughed. "You'd better go to the doctor tomorrow and tell him about your hallucinations. You are a neurotic!"

"What a smell of tar," said his wife - "tar or something . . . onion . . . cabbage soup!"

"Y-yes! There is a smell . . . I am not sleepy. I say, I'll light the candle. . . . Where are the matches? And, by the way, I'll show you the photograph of the procurator of the Palace of Justice. He gave us all a photograph when he said good-bye to us yesterday, with his autograph."

Gagin struck a match against the wall and lighted a candle. But before he had moved a step from the bed to fetch the photographs he heard behind him a piercing, heartrending shriek. Looking round, he saw his wife's large eyes fastened upon him, full of amazement, horror, and wrath. . . .

"You took your dressing-gown off in the kitchen?" she said, turning pale.

"Why?"

"Look at yourself!"

The deputy procurator looked down at himself, and gasped.

Flung over his shoulders was not his dressing-gown, but the fireman's overcoat. How had it come on his shoulders? While he was settling that question, his wife's imagination was drawing another picture, awful and impossible: darkness, stillness, whispering, and so on, and so on.

# A TRIVIAL INCIDENT

It was a sunny August midday as, in company with a Russian prince who had come down in the world, I drove into the immense so-called Shabelsky pine-forest where we were intending to look for woodcocks. In virtue of the part he plays in this story my poor prince deserves a detailed description. He was a tall, dark man, still youngish, though already somewhat battered by life; with long moustaches like a police captain's; with prominent black eyes, and with the manners of a retired army man. He was a man of Oriental type, not very intelligent, but straightforward and honest, not a bully, not a fop, and not a rake - virtues which, in the eyes of the general public, are equivalent to a certificate of being a nonentity and a poor creature. People generally did not like him (he was never spoken of in the district, except as "the illustrious duffer"). I personally found the poor prince extremely nice with his misfortunes and failures, which made up indeed his whole life. First of all he was poor. He did not play cards, did not drink, had no occupation, did not poke his nose into anything, and maintained a perpetual silence but yet he had somehow succeeded in getting through thirty to forty thousand roubles left him at his father's death. God only knows what had become of the money. All that I can say is that owing to lack of supervision a great deal was stolen by stewards, bailiffs, and even footmen; a great deal went on lending money, giving bail, and standing security. There were few landowners in the district who did not owe him money. He gave to all who asked, and not so much from good nature or confidence in people as from exaggerated gentlemanliness as though he would say: "Take it and feel how *comme il faut* I am!" By the time I made his acquaintance he had got into debt himself, had learned what it was like to have a second mortgage on his land, and had sunk so deeply into difficulties that there was no chance of his ever getting out of them again. There were days when he had no dinner, and went about with an empty cigar-holder, but he was always seen clean and fashionably dressed, and always smelt strongly of ylang-ylang.

The prince's second misfortune was his absolute solitariness. He was not married, he had no friends nor relations. His silent and reserved character and his *comme il faut* deportment, which became the more conspicuous the more anxious he was to conceal his poverty, prevented him from becoming intimate with people. For love affairs he was too heavy, spiritless, and cold, and so rarely got on with women. . . .

When we reached the forest this prince and I got out of the chaise and walked along a narrow woodland path which was hidden among huge ferns. But before we had gone a hundred paces a tall, lank figure with a long oval face, wearing a shabby reefer jacket, a straw hat, and patent leather boots, rose up from behind a young fir-tree some three feet high, as though he had sprung out of the ground. The stranger held in one hand a basket of mushrooms, with the other he playfully fingered a cheap watch-chain on his waistcoat. On seeing us he was taken aback, smoothed his waistcoat, coughed politely, and gave an agreeable smile, as though he were delighted to see such nice people as us. Then, to our complete surprise, he came up to us, scraping with his long feet on the grass, bending his whole person, and, still smiling agreeably, lifted his hat and pronounced in a sugary voice with the intonations of a whining dog:

"Aie, aie . . . gentlemen, painful as it is, it is my duty to warn you that shooting is forbidden in this wood. Pardon me for venturing to disturb you, though unacquainted, but . . . allow me to present myself. I am Grontovsky, the head clerk on Madame Kandurin's estate."

"Pleased to make your acquaintance, but why can't we shoot?"

"Such is the wish of the owner of this forest!"

The prince and I exchanged glances. A moment passed in silence. The prince stood looking pensively at a big fly agaric at his feet, which he had crushed with his stick. Grontovsky went on smiling agreeably. His whole face was twitching, exuding honey, and even the watch-chain on his waistcoat seemed to be smiling and trying to impress us all with its refinement. A shade of embarrassment passed over us like an angel passing; all three of us felt awkward.

"Nonsense!" I said. "Only last week I was shooting here!"

"Very possible!" Grontovsky sniggered through his teeth. "As a matter of fact everyone shoots here regardless of the prohibition. But once I have met you, it is my duty . . . my sacred duty to warn you. I am a man in a dependent position. If the forest were mine, on the word of honour of a Grontovsky, I should not oppose your agreeable pleasure. But whose fault is it that I am in a dependent position?"

The lanky individual sighed and shrugged his shoulders. I began arguing, getting hot and protesting, but the more loudly and impressively I spoke the more mawkish and sugary Grontovsky's face became. Evidently the consciousness of a certain power over us afforded him the greatest gratification. He was enjoying his condescending tone, his politeness, his manners, and with peculiar relish pronounced his sonorous surname, of which he was probably very fond. Standing before us he felt more than at ease, but judging from the confused sideway glances he cast from time to time at his basket, only one thing was spoiling his satisfaction - the mushrooms, womanish, peasantish, prose, derogatory to his dignity.

"We can't go back!" I said. "We have come over ten miles!"

"What's to be done?" sighed Grontovsky. "If you had come not ten but a hundred thousand miles, if the king even had come from America or from some other distant land, even then I should think it my duty . . . sacred, so to say, obligation . . ."

"Does the forest belong to Nadyezhda Lvovna?" asked the prince.

"Yes, Nadyezhda Lvovna . . ."

"Is she at home now?"

"Yes . . . I tell you what, you go to her, it is not more than half a mile from here; if she gives you a note, then I. . . . I needn't say! Ha ha . . . he he - !"

"By all means," I agreed. "It's much nearer than to go back. . . . You go to her, Sergey Ivanitch," I said, addressing the prince. "You know her."

The prince, who had been gazing the whole time at the crushed agaric, raised his eyes to me, thought a minute, and said:

"I used to know her at one time, but . . . it's rather awkward for me to go to her. Besides, I am in shabby clothes. . . . You go, you don't know her. . . . It's more suitable for you to go."

I agreed. We got into our chaise and, followed by Grontovsky's smiles, drove along the edge of the forest to the manor house. I was not acquainted with Nadyezhda Lvovna Kandurin, née Shabelsky. I had never seen her at close quarters, and knew her only by hearsay. I knew that she was incredibly wealthy, richer than anyone else in the province. After the death of her father, Shabelsky, who was a landowner with no other children, she was left with several estates, a stud farm, and a lot of money. I had heard that, though she was only twenty-five or twenty-six, she was ugly, uninteresting, and as insignificant as anybody, and was only distinguished from the ordinary ladies of the district by her immense wealth.

It has always seemed to me that wealth is felt, and that the rich must have special feelings unknown to the poor. Often as I passed by Nadyezhda Lvovna's big fruit garden, in which stood the large, heavy house with its windows always curtained, I thought: "What is she thinking at this moment? Is there happiness behind those blinds?" and so on. Once I saw her from a distance in a fine light cabriolet, driving a handsome white horse, and, sinful man that I am, I not only envied her, but even thought that in her poses, in her movements, there was something special, not to be found in people who are not rich, just as persons of a servile nature succeed in discovering "good family" at the first glance in people of the most ordinary exterior, if they are a little more distinguished than themselves. Nadyezhda Lvovna's inner life was only known to me by scandal. It was said in the district that five or six years ago, before she was married, during her father's lifetime, she had been passionately in love with Prince Sergey Ivanitch, who was now beside me in the chaise. The prince had been fond of visiting her father, and used to spend whole days in his billiard room, where he played pyramids indefatigably till his arms and legs ached. Six months before the old man's death he had suddenly given up visiting the Shabelskys. The gossip of the district having no positive facts to go upon explained this abrupt change in their relations in various ways. Some said that the prince, having observed the plain daughter's feeling for him and being unable to reciprocate it, considered it the duty of a gentleman to cut short his visits. Others maintained that old Shabelsky had discovered why his daughter was pining away, and had proposed to the poverty-stricken prince that he should marry her; the prince, imagining in his narrow-minded way that they were trying to buy him together with his title, was indignant, said foolish things, and quarrelled with them. What was true and what was false in this nonsense was difficult to say. But that there was a portion of truth in it was evident, from the fact that the prince always avoided conversation about Nadyezhda Lvovna.

I knew that soon after her father's death Nadyezhda Lvovna had married one Kandurin, a bachelor of law, not wealthy, but adroit, who had come on a visit to the neighbourhood. She married him not from love, but because she was touched by the love of the legal gentleman who, so it was said, had cleverly played the love-sick swain. At the time I am describing, Kandurin was for some reason living in Cairo, and writing thence to his friend, the marshal of the district, "Notes of Travel," while she sat languishing behind lowered blinds, surrounded by idle parasites, and whiled away her dreary days in petty philanthropy.

On the way to the house the prince fell to talking.

"It's three days since I have been at home," he said in a half whisper, with a sidelong glance at the driver. "I am not a child, nor a silly woman, and I have no prejudices, but I can't stand the bailiffs. When I see a bailiff in my house I turn pale and tremble, and even have a twitching in the calves of my legs. Do you know Rogozhin refused to honour my note?"

The prince did not, as a rule, like to complain of his straitened circumstances; where poverty was concerned he was reserved and exceedingly proud and sensitive, and so this announcement surprised me. He stared a long time at the yellow clearing, warmed by the sun, watched a long string of cranes float in the azure sky, and turned facing me.

"And by the sixth of September I must have the money ready for the bank . . . the interest for my estate," he said aloud, by now regardless of the coachman. "And where am I to get it? Altogether, old man, I am in a tight fix! An awfully tight fix!"

The prince examined the cock of his gun, blew on it for some reason, and began looking for the cranes which by now were out of sight.

"Sergey Ivanitch," I asked, after a minute's silence, "imagine if they sell your Shatilovka, what will you do?"

"I? I don't know! Shatilovka can't be saved, that's clear as daylight, but I cannot imagine such a calamity. I can't imagine myself without my daily bread secure. What can I do? I have had hardly any education; I have not tried working yet; for government service it is late to begin, . . . Besides, where could I serve? Where could I be of use? Admitting that no great cleverness is needed for serving in our Zemstvo, for example, yet I suffer from . . . the devil knows what, a sort of faintheartedness, I haven't a ha'p'orth of pluck. If I went into the Service I should always feel I was not in my right place. I am not an idealist; I am not a Utopian; I haven't any special principles; but am simply, I suppose, stupid and thoroughly incompetent, a neurotic and a coward. Altogether not like other people. All other people are like other people, only I seem to be something . . . a poor thing. . . . I met Naryagin last Wednesday - you know him? - drunken, slovenly . . . doesn't pay his debts, stupid" (the prince frowned and tossed his head) . . . "a horrible person! He said to me, staggering: 'I'm being balloted for as a justice of the peace!' Of course, they won't elect him, but, you see, he believes he is fit to be a justice of the peace and considers that position within his capacity. He has boldness and self-confidence. I went to see our investigating magistrate too. The man gets two hundred and fifty roubles a month, and does scarcely anything. All he can do is to stride backwards and forwards for days together in nothing but his underclothes, but, ask him, he is convinced he is doing his work and honourably performing his duty. I couldn't go on like that! I should be ashamed to look the clerk in the face."

At that moment Grontovsky, on a chestnut horse, galloped by us with a flourish. On his left arm the basket bobbed up and down with the mushrooms dancing in it. As he passed us he grinned and waved his hand, as though we were old friends.

"Blockhead!" the prince filtered through his teeth, looking after him. "It's wonderful how disgusting it sometimes is to see satisfied faces. A stupid, animal feeling due to hunger, I expect. . . . What was I saying? Oh, yes, about going into the Service, . . . I should be ashamed to take the salary, and yet, to tell the truth, it is stupid. If one looks at it from a broader point of view, more seriously, I am eating what isn't mine now.

Am I not? But why am I not ashamed of that. . . . It is a case of habit, I suppose . . . and not being able to realize one's true position. . . . But that position is most likely awful. . ."

I looked at him, wondering if the prince were showing off. But his face was mild and his eyes were mournfully following the movements of the chestnut horse racing away, as though his happiness were racing away with it.

Apparently he was in that mood of irritation and sadness when women weep quietly for no reason, and men feel a craving to complain of themselves, of life, of God. . . .

When I got out of the chaise at the gates of the house the prince said to me:

"A man once said, wanting to annoy me, that I have the face of a cardsharper. I have noticed that cardsharpers are usually dark. Do you know, it seems that if I really had been born a cardsharper I should have remained a decent person to the day of my death, for I should never have had the boldness to do wrong. I tell you frankly I have had the chance once in my life of getting rich if I had told a lie, a lie to myself and one woman . . . and one other person whom I know would have forgiven me for lying; I should have put into my pocket a million. But I could not. I hadn't the pluck!"

From the gates we had to go to the house through the copse by a long road, level as a ruler, and planted on each side with thick, lopped lilacs. The house looked somewhat heavy, tasteless, like a façade on the stage. It rose clumsily out of a mass of greenery, and caught the eye like a great stone thrown on the velvety turf. At the chief entrance I was met by a fat old footman in a green swallow-tail coat and big silver-rimmed spectacles; without making any announcement, only looking contemptuously at my dusty figure, he showed me in. As I mounted the soft carpeted stairs there was, for some reason, a strong smell of india-rubber. At the top I was enveloped in an atmosphere found only in museums, in signorial mansions and old-fashioned merchant houses; it seemed like the smell of something long past, which had once lived and died and had left its soul in the rooms. I passed through three or four rooms on my way from the entry to the drawing room. I remember bright yellow, shining floors, lustres wrapped in stiff muslin, narrow, striped rugs which stretched not straight from door to door, as they usually do, but along the walls, so that not venturing to touch the bright floor with my muddy boots I had to describe a rectangle in each room. In the drawing-room, where the footman left me, stood old-fashioned ancestral furniture in white covers, shrouded in twilight. It looked surly and elderly, and, as though out of respect for its repose, not a sound was audible.

Even the clock was silent . . . it seemed as though the Princess Tarakanov had fallen asleep in the golden frame, and the water and the rats were still and motionless through magic. The daylight, afraid of disturbing the universal tranquillity, scarcely pierced through the lowered blinds, and lay on the soft rugs in pale, slumbering streaks.

Three minutes passed and a big, elderly woman in black, with her cheek bandaged up, walked noiselessly into the drawing-room. She bowed to me and pulled up the blinds. At once, enveloped in the bright sunlight, the rats and water in the picture came to life and movement, Princess Tarakanov was awakened, and the old chairs frowned gloomily.

"Her honour will be here in a minute, sir . . ." sighed the old lady, frowning too.

A few more minutes of waiting and I saw Nadyezhda Lvovna. What struck me first of all was that she certainly was ugly, short, scraggy, and round-shouldered. Her thick, chestnut hair was magnificent; her face, pure and with a look of culture in it, was aglow with youth; there was a clear and intelligent expression in her eyes; but the whole charm of her head was lost through the thickness of her lips and the over-acute facial angle.

I mentioned my name, and announced the object of my visit.

"I really don't know what I am to say!" she said, in hesitation, dropping her eyes and smiling. "I don't like to refuse, and at the same time. . . ."

"Do, please," I begged.

Nadyezhda Lvovna looked at me and laughed. I laughed too. She was probably amused by what Grontovsky had so enjoyed - that is, the right of giving or withholding permission; my visit suddenly struck me as queer and strange.

"I don't like to break the long-established rules," said Madame Kandurin. "Shooting has been forbidden on our estate for the last six years. No!" she shook her head resolutely. "Excuse me, I must refuse you. If I allow you I must allow others. I don't like unfairness. Either let all or no one."

"I am sorry!" I sighed. "It's all the sadder because we have come more than ten miles. I am not alone," I added, "Prince Sergey Ivanitch is with me."

I uttered the prince's name with no *arrière pensée*, not prompted by any special motive or aim; I simply blurted it out without thinking, in the simplicity of my heart. Hearing the familiar name Madame Kandurin started, and bent a prolonged gaze upon me. I noticed her nose turn pale.

"That makes no difference . . ." she said, dropping her eyes.

As I talked to her I stood at the window that looked out on the shrubbery. I could see the whole shrubbery with the avenues and the ponds and the road by which I had come. At the end of the road, beyond the gates, the back of our chaise made a dark patch. Near the gate, with his back to the house, the prince was standing with his legs apart, talking to the lanky Grontovsky.

Madame Kandurin had been standing all the time at the other window. She looked from time to time towards the shrubbery, and from the moment I mentioned the prince's name she did not turn away from the window.

"Excuse me," she said, screwing up her eyes as she looked towards the road and the gate, "but it would be unfair to allow you only to shoot.... And, besides, what pleasure is there in shooting birds? What's it for? Are they in your way?"

A solitary life, immured within four walls, with its indoor twilight and heavy smell of decaying furniture, disposes people to sentimentality. Madame Kandurin's idea did her credit, but I could not resist saying:

"If one takes that line one ought to go barefoot. Boots are made out of the leather of slaughtered animals."

"One must distinguish between a necessity and a caprice," Madame Kandurin answered in a toneless voice.

She had by now recognized the prince, and did not take her eyes off his figure. It is hard to describe the delight and the suffering with which her ugly face was radiant! Her eyes were smiling and shining, her lips were quivering and laughing, while her face craned closer to the panes. Keeping hold of a flower-pot with both hands, with bated breath and with one foot slightly lifted, she reminded me of a dog pointing and waiting with passionate impatience for "Fetch it!"

I looked at her and at the prince who could not tell a lie once in his life, and I felt angry and bitter against truth and falsehood, which play such an elemental part in the personal happiness of men.

The prince started suddenly, took aim and fired. A hawk, flying over him, fluttered its wings and flew like an arrow far away.

"He aimed too high!" I said. "And so, Nadyezhda Lvovna," I sighed, moving away from the window, "you will not permit . . ." - Madame Kandurin was silent.

"I have the honour to take my leave," I said, "and I beg you to forgive my disturbing you. . ."

Madame Kandurin would have turned facing me, and had already moved through a quarter of the angle, when she suddenly hid her face behind the hangings, as though she felt tears in her eyes that she wanted to conceal.

"Good-bye. . . . Forgive me . . ." she said softly.

I bowed to her back, and strode away across the bright yellow floors, no longer keeping to the carpet. I was glad to get away from this little domain of gilded boredom and sadness, and I hastened as though anxious to shake off a heavy, fantastic dream with its twilight, its enchanted princess, its lustres. . . .

At the front door a maidservant overtook me and thrust a note into my hand: "Shooting is permitted on showing this. N. K.," I read.

# A TRIPPING TONGUE

Natalya Mihalovna, a young married lady who had arrived in the morning from Yalta, was having her dinner, and in a never-ceasing flow of babble was telling her husband of all the charms of the Crimea. Her husband, delighted, gazed tenderly at her enthusiastic face, listened, and from time to time put in a question.

"But they say living is dreadfully expensive there?" he asked, among other things.

"Well, what shall I say? To my thinking this talk of its being so expensive is exaggerated, hubby. The devil is not as black as he is painted. Yulia Petrovna and I, for instance, had very decent and comfortable rooms for twenty roubles a day. Everything depends on knowing how to do things, my dear. Of course if you want to go up into the mountains . . . to Aie-Petri for instance . . . if you take a horse, a guide, then of course it does come to something. It's awful what it comes to! But, Vassitchka, the mountains there! Imagine high, high mountains, a thousand times higher than the church. . . . At the top - mist, mist, mist. . . . At the bottom - enormous stones, stones, stones. . . . And pines. . . . Ah, I can't bear to think of it!"

"By the way, I read about those Tatar guides there, in some magazine while you were away . . . . such abominable stories! Tell me is there really anything out of the way about them?"

Natalya Mihalovna made a little disdainful grimace and shook her head.

"Just ordinary Tatars, nothing special . . ." she said, "though indeed I only had a glimpse of them in the distance. They were pointed out to me, but I did not take much notice of them. You know, hubby, I always had a prejudice against all such Circassians, Greeks . . . Moors!"

"They are said to be terrible Don Juans."

"Perhaps! There are shameless creatures who . . . ."

Natalya Mihalovna suddenly jumped up from her chair, as though she had thought of something dreadful; for half a minute she looked with frightened eyes at her husband and said, accentuating each word:

"Vassitchka, I say, the im-mo-ral women there are in the world! Ah, how immoral! And it's not as though they were working-class or middle-class people, but aristocratic ladies, priding themselves on their *bon-ton!* It was simply awful, I could not believe my own eyes! I shall remember it as long as I live! To think that people can forget themselves to such a point as . . . ach, Vassitchka, I don't like to speak of it! Take my companion, Yulia Petrovna, for example. . . . Such a good husband, two children . . . she moves in a decent circle, always poses as a saint - and all at once, would you believe it. . . . Only, hubby, of course this is *entre nous*. . . . Give me your word of honour you won't tell a soul?"

"What next! Of course I won't tell."

"Honour bright? Mind now! I trust you. . . ."

The little lady put down her fork, assumed a mysterious air, and whispered:

"Imagine a thing like this. . . . That Yulia Petrovna rode up into the mountains . . . . It was glorious weather! She rode on ahead with her guide, I was a little behind. We had ridden two or three miles, all at once, only fancy, Vassitchka, Yulia cried out and clutched at her bosom. Her Tatar put his arm round her waist or she would have fallen off the saddle. . . . I rode up to her with my guide. . . . 'What is it? What is the matter?' 'Oh,' she cried, 'I am dying! I feel faint! I can't go any further' Fancy my alarm! 'Let us go back then,' I said. 'No, *Natalie*,' she said, 'I can't go back! I shall die of pain if I move another step! I have spasms.' And she prayed and besought my Sulciman and me to ride back to the town and fetch her some of her drops which always do her good."

"Stay. . . . I don't quite understand you," muttered the husband, scratching his forehead. "You said just now that you had only seen those Tatars from a distance, and now you are talking of some Suleiman."

"There, you are finding fault again," the lady pouted, not in the least disconcerted. " I can't endure suspiciousness! I can't endure it! It's stupid, stupid!"

"I am not finding fault, but . . . why say what is not true? If you rode about with Tatars, so be it, God bless you, but . . . why shuffle about it?"

"H'm! . . . you are a queer one!" cried the lady, revolted. "He is jealous of Suleiman! as though one could ride up into the mountains without a guide! I should like to see you do it! If you don't know the ways there, if you don't understand, you had better hold your tongue! Yes, hold your tongue. You can't take a step there without a guide."

"So it seems!"

"None of your silly grins, if you please! I am not a Yulia. . . . I don't justify her but I . . . ! Though I don't pose as a saint, I don't forget myself to that degree. My Suleiman never overstepped the limits. . . . No-o! Mametkul used to be sitting at Yulia's all day long, but in my room as soon as it struck eleven: 'Suleiman, march! Off you go!' And my foolish Tatar boy would depart. I made him mind his p's and q's, hubby! As soon as he began grumbling about money or anything, I would say 'How? Wha-at? Wha-a-a-t?' And his heart would be in his mouth directly. . . . Ha-ha-ha! His eyes, you know, Vassitchka, were as black, as black, like coals, such an amusing little Tatar face, so funny and silly! I kept him in order, didn't I just!"

"I can fancy . . ." mumbled her husband, rolling up pellets of bread.

"That's stupid, Vassitchka! I know what is in your mind! I know what you are thinking . . . But I assure you even when we were on our expeditions I never let him overstep the limits. For instance, if we rode to the mountains or to the U-Chan-Su waterfall, I would always say to him, 'Suleiman, ride behind! Do you hear!' And he always rode behind, poor boy. . . . Even when we . . . even at the most dramatic moments I would say to him, 'Still, you must not forget that you are only a Tatar and I am the wife of a civil councillor!' Ha-ha. . . ."

The little lady laughed, then, looking round her quickly and assuming an alarmed expression, whispered:

But Yulia! Oh, that Yulia! I quite see, Vassitchka, there is no reason why one shouldn't have a little fun, a little rest from the emptiness of conventional life! That's all right, have your fling by all means - no one will blame you, but to take the thing seriously, to get up scenes . . . no, say what you like, I cannot understand that! Just fancy, she was jealous! Wasn't that silly? One day Mametkul, her *grande passion*, came to see her . . . she was not at home. . . . Well, I asked him into my room . . . there was conversation, one thing and another . . . they're awfully amusing, you know! The evening passed without our noticing it. . . . All at once Yulia rushed in. . . . She flew at me and at Mametkul - made such a scene . . . fi! I can't understand that sort of thing, Vassitchka."

Vassitchka cleared his throat, frowned, and walked up and down the room.

"You had a gay time there, I must say," he growled with a disdainful smile.

"How stu-upid that is!" cried Natalya Mihalovna, offended. "I know what you are thinking about! You always have such horrid ideas! I won't tell you anything! No, I won't!"

The lady pouted and said no more.

# A TRIFLE FROM LIFE

A well-fed, red-cheeked young man called Nikolay Ilyitch Belyaev, of thirty-two, who was an owner of house property in Petersburg, and a devotee of the race-course, went one evening to see Olga Ivanovna Irnin, with whom he was living, or, to use his own expression, was dragging out a long, wearisome romance. And, indeed, the first interesting and enthusiastic pages of this romance had long been perused; now the pages dragged on, and still dragged on, without presenting anything new or of interest.

Not finding Olga Ivanovna at home, my hero lay down on the lounge chair and proceeded to wait for her in the drawing-room.

"Good-evening, Nikolay Ilyitch!" he heard a child's voice. "Mother will be here directly. She has gone with Sonia to the dressmaker's."

Olga Ivanovna's son, Alyosha - a boy of eight who looked graceful and very well cared for, who was dressed like a picture, in a black velvet jacket and long black stockings - was lying on the sofa in the same room. He was lying on a satin cushion and, evidently imitating an acrobat he had lately seen at the circus, stuck up in the air first one leg and then the other. When his elegant legs were exhausted, he brought his arms into play or jumped up impulsively and went on all fours, trying to stand with his legs in the air. All this he was doing with the utmost gravity, gasping and groaning painfully as though he regretted that God had given him such a restless body.

"Ah, good-evening, my boy," said Belyaev. "It's you! I did not notice you. Is your mother well?"

Alyosha, taking hold of the tip of his left toe with his right hand and falling into the most unnatural attitude, turned over, jumped up, and peeped at Belyaev from behind the big fluffy lampshade.

"What shall I say?" he said, shrugging his shoulders. "In reality mother's never well. You see, she is a woman, and women, Nikolay Ilyitch, have always something the matter with them."

Belyaev, having nothing better to do, began watching Alyosha's face. He had never before during the whole of his intimacy with Olga

Ivanovna paid any attention to the boy, and had completely ignored his existence; the boy had been before his eyes, but he had not cared to think why he was there and what part he was playing.

In the twilight of the evening, Alyosha's face, with his white forehead and black, unblinking eyes, unexpectedly reminded Belyaev of Olga Ivanovna as she had been during the first pages of their romance. And he felt disposed to be friendly to the boy.

"Come here, insect," he said; "let me have a closer look at you."

The boy jumped off the sofa and skipped up to Belyaev.

"Well," began Nikolay Ilyitch, putting a hand on the boy's thin shoulder. "How are you getting on?"

"How shall I say! We used to get on a great deal better."

"Why?"

"It's very simple. Sonia and I used only to learn music and reading, and now they give us French poetry to learn. Have you been shaved lately?"

"Yes."

"Yes, I see you have. Your beard is shorter. Let me touch it. . . . Does that hurt?"

"No."

"Why is it that if you pull one hair it hurts, but if you pull a lot at once it doesn't hurt a bit? Ha, ha! And, you know, it's a pity you don't have whiskers. Here ought to be shaved . . . but here at the sides the hair ought to be left. . . ."

The boy nestled up to Belyaev and began playing with his watch chain.

"When I go to the high-school," he said, "mother is going to buy me a watch. I shall ask her to buy me a watch-chain like this. . . . Wh-at a lo-ket! Father's got a locket like that, only yours has little bars on it and his has letters. . . . There's mother's portrait in the middle of his. Father has a different sort of chain now, not made with rings, but like ribbon. . . ."

"How do you know? Do you see your father?"

"I? M'm . . . no . . . I . . ."

Alyosha blushed, and in great confusion, feeling caught in a lie, began zealously scratching the locket with his nail. . . . Belyaev looked steadily into his face and asked:

"Do you see your father?"

"N-no!"

"Come, speak frankly, on your honour. . . . I see from your face you are telling a fib. Once you've let a thing slip out it's no good wriggling about it. Tell me, do you see him? Come, as a friend."

Alyosha hesitated.

"You won't tell mother?" he said.

"As though I should!"

"On your honour?"

"On my honour."

"Do you swear?"

"Ah, you provoking boy! What do you take me for?"

Alyosha looked round him, then with wide-open eyes, whispered to him:

"Only, for goodness' sake, don't tell mother. . . . Don't tell any one at all, for it is a secret. I hope to goodness mother won't find out, or we should all catch it - Sonia, and I, and Pelagea. . . . Well, listen. . . Sonia and I see father every Tuesday and Friday. When Pelagea takes us for a walk before dinner we go to the Apfel Restaurant, and there is father waiting for us. . . . He is always sitting in a room apart, where you know there's a marble table and an ash-tray in the shape of a goose without a back. . . ."

"What do you do there?"

"Nothing! First we say how-do-you-do, then we all sit round the table, and father treats us with coffee and pies. You know Sonia eats the meat-pies, but I can't endure meat-pies! I like the pies made of cabbage and eggs. We eat such a lot that we have to try hard to eat as much as we can at dinner, for fear mother should notice."

"What do you talk about?"

"With father? About anything. He kisses us, he hugs us, tells us all sorts of amusing jokes. Do you know, he says when we are grown up he is going to take us to live with him. Sonia does not want to go, but I agree. Of course, I should miss mother; but, then, I should write her letters! It's a queer idea, but we could come and visit her on holidays - couldn't we? Father says, too, that he will buy me a horse. He's an awfully kind man! I can't understand why mother does not ask him to come and live with us, and why she forbids us to see him. You know he loves mother very much. He is always asking us how she is and what she is doing. When she was ill he clutched his head like this, and . . . and kept running about. He always tells us to be obedient and respectful to her. Listen. Is it true that we are unfortunate?"

"H'm! . . . Why?"

"That's what father says. 'You are unhappy children,' he says. It's strange to hear him, really. 'You are unhappy,' he says, 'I am unhappy, and mother's unhappy. You must pray to God,' he says; 'for yourselves and for her.'"

Alyosha let his eyes rest on a stuffed bird and sank into thought.

"So . . ." growled Belyaev. "So that's how you are going on. You arrange meetings at restaurants. And mother does not know?"

"No-o. . . . How should she know? Pelagea would not tell her for anything, you know. The day before yesterday he gave us some pears. As sweet as jam! I ate two."

"H'm! . . . Well, and I say . . Listen. Did father say anything about me?"

"About you? What shall I say?"

Alyosha looked searchingly into Belyaev's face and shrugged his shoulders.

"He didn't say anything particular."

"For instance, what did he say?"

"You won't be offended?"

"What next? Why, does he abuse me?"

"He doesn't abuse you, but you know he is angry with you. He says mother's unhappy owing to you . . . and that you have ruined mother. You know he is so queer! I explain to him that you are kind, that you never scold mother; but he only shakes his head."

"So he says I have ruined her?"

"Yes; you mustn't be offended, Nikolay Ilyitch."

Belyaev got up, stood still a moment, and walked up and down the drawing-room.

"That's strange and . . . ridiculous!" he muttered, shrugging his shoulders and smiling sarcastically. "He's entirely to blame, and I have ruined her, eh? An innocent lamb, I must say. So he told you I ruined your mother?"

"Yes, but . . . you said you would not be offended, you know."

"I am not offended, and . . . and it's not your business. Why, it's . . . why, it's positively ridiculous! I have been thrust into it like a chicken in the broth, and now it seems I'm to blame!"

A ring was heard. The boy sprang up from his place and ran out. A minute later a lady came into the room with a little girl; this was Olga Ivanovna, Alyosha's mother. Alyosha followed them in, skipping and jumping, humming aloud and waving his hands. Belyaev nodded, and went on walking up and down.

"Of course, whose fault is it if not mine?" he muttered with a snort. "He is right! He is an injured husband."

"What are you talking about?" asked Olga Ivanovna.

"What about? . . . Why, just listen to the tales your lawful spouse is spreading now! It appears that I am a scoundrel and a villain, that I have ruined you and the children. All of you are unhappy, and I am the only happy one! Wonderfully, wonderfully happy!"

"I don't understand, Nikolay. What's the matter?"

"Why, listen to this young gentleman!" said Belyaev, pointing to Alyosha.

Alyosha flushed crimson, then turned pale, and his whole face began working with terror.

"Nikolay Ilyitch," he said in a loud whisper. "Sh-sh!"

Olga Ivanovna looked in surprise at Alyosha, then at Belyaev, then at Alyosha again.

"Just ask him," Belyaev went on. "Your Pelagea, like a regular fool, takes them about to restaurants and arranges meetings with their papa. But that's not the point: the point is that their dear papa is a victim, while I'm a wretch who has broken up both your lives. . ."

"Nikolay Ilyitch," moaned Alyosha. "Why, you promised on your word of honour!"

"Oh, get away!" said Belyaev, waving him off. "This is more important than any word of honour. It's the hypocrisy revolts me, the lying! . . ."

"I don't understand it," said Olga Ivanovna, and tears glistened in her eyes. "Tell me, Alyosha," she turned to her son. "Do you see your father?"

Alyosha did not hear her; he was looking with horror at Belyaev.

"It's impossible," said his mother; "I will go and question Pelagea."

Olga Ivanovna went out.

"I say, you promised on your word of honour!" said Alyosha, trembling all over.

Belyaev dismissed him with a wave of his hand, and went on walking up and down. He was absorbed in his grievance and was oblivious of the boy's presence, as he always had been. He, a grownup, serious person, had no thought to spare for boys. And Alyosha sat down in the corner and told Sonia with horror how he had been deceived. He was trembling, stammering, and crying. It was the first time in his life that he had been brought into such coarse contact with lying; till then he had not known that there are in the world, besides sweet pears, pies, and expensive watches, a great many things for which the language of children has no expression.

# DIFFICULT PEOPLE

Yevgraf Ivanovitch Shiryaev, a small farmer, whose father, a parish priest, now deceased, had received a gift of three hundred acres of land from Madame Kuvshinnikov, a general's widow, was standing in a corner before a copper washing-stand, washing his hands. As usual, his face looked anxious and ill-humoured, and his beard was uncombed.

"What weather!" he said. "It's not weather, but a curse laid upon us. It's raining again!"

He grumbled on, while his family sat waiting at table for him to have finished washing his hands before beginning dinner. Fedosya Semyonovna, his wife, his son Pyotr, a student, his eldest daughter Varvara, and three small boys, had been sitting waiting a long time. The boys - Kolka, Vanka, and Arhipka - grubby, snub-nosed little fellows with chubby faces and tousled hair that wanted cutting, moved their chairs impatiently, while their elders sat without stirring, and apparently did not care whether they ate their dinner or waited....

As though trying their patience, Shiryaev deliberately dried his hands, deliberately said his prayer, and sat down to the table without hurrying himself. Cabbage-soup was served immediately. The sound of carpenters' axes (Shiryaev was having a new barn built) and the laughter of Fomka, their labourer, teasing the turkey, floated in from the courtyard.

Big, sparse drops of rain pattered on the window.

Pyotr, a round-shouldered student in spectacles, kept exchanging glances with his mother as he ate his dinner. Several times he laid down his spoon and cleared his throat, meaning to begin to speak, but after an intent look at his father he fell to eating again. At last, when the porridge had been served, he cleared his throat resolutely and said:

"I ought to go tonight by the evening train. I out to have gone before; I have missed a fortnight as it is. The lectures begin on the first of September."

"Well, go," Shiryaev assented; "why are you lingering on here? Pack up and go, and good luck to you."

A minute passed in silence.

"He must have money for the journey, Yevgraf Ivanovitch," the mother observed in a low voice.

"Money? To be sure, you can't go without money. Take it at once, since you need it. You could have had it long ago!"

The student heaved a faint sigh and looked with relief at his mother. Deliberately Shiryaev took a pocket-book out of his coat-pocket and put on his spectacles.

"How much do you want?" he asked.

"The fare to Moscow is eleven roubles forty-two kopecks...."

"Ah, money, money!" sighed the father. (He always sighed when he saw money, even when he was receiving it.) "Here are twelve roubles for you. You will have change out of that which will be of use to you on the journey."

"Thank you."

After waiting a little, the student said:

"I did not get lessons quite at first last year. I don't know how it will be this year; most likely it will take me a little time to find work. I ought to ask you for fifteen roubles for my lodging and dinner."

Shiryaev thought a little and heaved a sigh.

"You will have to make ten do," he said. "Here, take it."

The student thanked him. He ought to have asked him for something more, for clothes, for lecture fees, for books, but after an intent look at his father he decided not to pester him further.

The mother, lacking in diplomacy and prudence, like all mothers, could not restrain herself, and said:

"You ought to give him another six roubles, Yevgraf Ivanovitch, for a pair of boots. Why, just see, how can he go to Moscow in such wrecks?"

"Let him take my old ones; they are still quite good."

"He must have trousers, anyway; he is a disgrace to look at."

And immediately after that a storm-signal showed itself, at the sight of which all the family trembled.

Shiryaev's short, fat neck turned suddenly red as a beetroot. The colour mounted slowly to his ears, from his ears to his temples, and by degrees suffused his whole face. Yevgraf Ivanovitch shifted in his chair and unbuttoned his shirt-collar to save himself from choking. He was evidently struggling with the feeling that was mastering him. A deathlike silence followed. The children held their breath. Fedosya Semyonovna, as though she did not grasp what was happening to her husband, went on:

"He is not a little boy now, you know; he is ashamed to go about without clothes."

Shiryaev suddenly jumped up, and with all his might flung down his fat pocket-book in the middle of the table, so that a hunk of bread flew off a plate. A revolting expression of anger, resentment, avarice - all mixed together - flamed on his face.

"Take everything!" he shouted in an unnatural voice; "plunder me! Take it all! Strangle me!"

He jumped up from the table, clutched at his head, and ran staggering about the room.

"Strip me to the last thread!" he shouted in a shrill voice. "Squeeze out the last drop! Rob me! Wring my neck!"

The student flushed and dropped his eyes. He could not go on eating. Fedosya Semyonovna, who had not after twenty-five years grown used to her husband's difficult character, shrank into herself and muttered something in self-defence. An expression of amazement and dull terror came into her wasted and birdlike face, which at all times looked dull and scared. The little boys and the elder daughter Varvara, a girl in her teens, with a pale ugly face, laid down their spoons and sat mute.

Shiryaev, growing more and more ferocious, uttering words each more terrible than the one before, dashed up to the table and began shaking the notes out of his pocket-book.

"Take them!" he muttered, shaking all over. "You've eaten and drunk your fill, so here's money for you too! I need nothing! Order yourself new boots and uniforms!"

The student turned pale and got up.

"Listen, papa," he began, gasping for breath. "I . . . I beg you to end this, for . . ."

"Hold your tongue!" the father shouted at him, and so loudly that the spectacles fell off his nose; "hold your tongue!"

"I used . . . I used to be able to put up with such scenes, but . . . but now I have got out of the way of it. Do you understand? I have got out of the way of it!"

"Hold your tongue!" cried the father, and he stamped with his feet. "You must listen to what I say! I shall say what I like, and you hold your tongue. At your age I was earning my living, while you . . . Do you know what you cost me, you scoundrel? I'll turn you out! Wastrel!"

"Yevgraf Ivanovitch," muttered Fedosya Semyonovna, moving her fingers nervously; "you know he. . . you know Petya . . . !"

"Hold your tongue!" Shiryaev shouted out to her, and tears actually came into his eyes from anger. "It is you who have spoilt them - you! It's all your fault! He has no respect for us, does not say his prayers, and earns nothing! I am only one against the ten of you! I'll turn you out of the house!"

The daughter Varvara gazed fixedly at her mother with her mouth open, moved her vacant-looking eyes to the window, turned pale, and, uttering a loud shriek, fell back in her chair. The father, with a curse and a wave of the hand, ran out into the yard.

This was how domestic scenes usually ended at the Shiryaevs'. But on this occasion, unfortunately, Pyotr the student was carried away by overmastering anger. He was just as hasty and ill-tempered as his father and his grandfather the priest, who used to beat his parishioners about the head with a stick. Pale and clenching his fists, he went up to his mother and shouted in the very highest tenor note his voice could reach:

"These reproaches are loathsome! sickening to me! I want nothing from you! Nothing! I would rather die of hunger than eat another mouthful at your expense! Take your nasty money back! take it!"

The mother huddled against the wall and waved her hands, as though it were not her son, but some phantom before her. "What have I done?" she wailed. "What?"

Like his father, the boy waved his hands and ran into the yard. Shiryaev's house stood alone on a ravine which ran like a furrow for four miles along the steppe. Its sides were overgrown with oak saplings and alders, and a stream ran at the bottom. On one side the house looked towards the ravine, on the other towards the open country, there were no fences nor hurdles. Instead there were farm-buildings of all sorts close to one another, shutting in a small space in front of the house which was regarded as the yard, and in which hens, ducks, and pigs ran about.

Going out of the house, the student walked along the muddy road towards the open country. The air was full of a penetrating autumn dampness. The road was muddy, puddles gleamed here and there, and in the yellow fields autumn itself seemed looking out from the grass, dismal, decaying, dark. On the right-hand side of the road was a vegetable-garden cleared of its crops and gloomy-looking, with here and there sunflowers standing up in it with hanging heads already black.

Pyotr thought it would not be a bad thing to walk to Moscow on foot; to walk just as he was, with holes in his boots, without a cap, and without a farthing of money. When he had gone eighty miles his father, frightened and aghast, would overtake him, would begin begging him to turn back or take the money, but he would not even look at him, but would go on and on. . . . Bare forests would be followed by desolate fields, fields by forests again; soon the earth would be white with the first snow, and the streams would be coated with ice. . . . Somewhere near Kursk or near Serpuhovo, exhausted and dying of hunger, he would sink down and die. His corpse would be found, and there would be a paragraph in all the papers saying that a student called Shiryaev had died of hunger. . . .

A white dog with a muddy tail who was wandering about the vegetable-garden looking for something gazed at him and sauntered after him.

He walked along the road and thought of death, of the grief of his family, of the moral sufferings of his father, and then pictured all sorts of adventures on the road, each more marvellous than the one before - picturesque places, terrible nights, chance encounters. He imagined a string of pilgrims, a hut in the forest with one little window shining in the darkness; he stands before the window, begs for a night's lodging. . . . They let him in, and suddenly he sees that they are robbers. Or, better still, he is taken into a big manor-house, where, learning who he is, they give him food and drink, play to him on the piano, listen to his complaints, and the daughter of the house, a beauty, falls in love with him.

Absorbed in his bitterness and such thoughts, young Shiryaev walked on and on. Far, far ahead he saw the inn, a dark patch against the grey background of cloud. Beyond the inn, on the very horizon, he could see a little hillock; this was the railway-station. That hillock reminded him of the connection existing between the place where he was now standing and Moscow, where street-lamps were burning and carriages were rattling in the streets, where lectures were being given. And he almost wept with depression and impatience. The solemn landscape, with its order and beauty, the deathlike stillness all around, revolted him and moved him to despair and hatred!

"Look out!" He heard behind him a loud voice.

An old lady of his acquaintance, a landowner of the neighbourhood, drove past him in a light, elegant landau. He bowed to her, and smiled all over his face. And at once he caught himself in that smile, which was so out of keeping with his gloomy mood. Where did it come from if his whole heart was full of vexation and misery? And he thought nature itself had given man this capacity for lying, that even in difficult moments of spiritual strain he might be able to hide the secrets of his nest as the fox and the wild duck do. Every family has its joys and its horrors, but however great they may be, it's hard for an outsider's eye to see them; they are a secret. The father of the old lady who had just driven by, for instance, had for some offence lain for half his lifetime under the ban of the wrath of Tsar Nicolas I.; her husband had been a gambler; of her four sons, not one had turned out well. One could imagine how many terrible scenes there must have been in her life, how many tears must have been shed. And yet the old lady seemed happy and satisfied, and she had answered his smile by smiling too. The student thought of his comrades, who did not like talking about their families; he thought of his mother, who almost always lied when she had to speak of her husband and children. . . .

Pyotr walked about the roads far from home till dusk, abandoning himself to dreary thoughts. When it began to drizzle with rain he turned homewards. As he walked back he made up his mind at all costs to talk to his father, to explain to him, once and for all, that it was dreadful and oppressive to live with him.

He found perfect stillness in the house. His sister Varvara was lying behind a screen with a headache, moaning faintly. His mother, with a look of amazement and guilt upon her face, was sitting beside her on a box, mending Arhipka's trousers. Yevgraf Ivanovitch was pacing from one window to another, scowling at the weather. From his walk, from the way he cleared his throat, and even from the back of his head, it was evident he felt himself to blame.

"I suppose you have changed your mind about going today?" he asked.

The student felt sorry for him, but immediately suppressing that feeling, he said:

"Listen . . . I must speak to you seriously. . . yes, seriously. I have always respected you, and . . . and have never brought myself to speak to you in such a tone, but your behaviour . . . your last action . . ."

The father looked out of the window and did not speak. The student, as though considering his words, rubbed his forehead and went on in great excitement:

"Not a dinner or tea passes without your making an uproar. Your bread sticks in our throat... nothing is more bitter, more humiliating, than bread that sticks in one's throat.... Though you are my father, no one, neither God nor nature, has given you the right to insult and humiliate us so horribly, to vent your ill-humour on the weak. You have worn my mother out and made a slave of her, my sister is hopelessly crushed, while I . . ."

"It's not your business to teach me," said his father.

"Yes, it is my business! You can quarrel with me as much as you like, but leave my mother in peace! I will not allow you to torment my mother!" the student went on, with flashing eyes. "You are spoilt because no one has yet dared to oppose you. They tremble and are mute towards you, but now that is over! Coarse, ill-bred man! You are coarse . . . do you understand? You are coarse, ill-humoured, unfeeling. And the peasants can't endure you!"

The student had by now lost his thread, and was not so much speaking as firing off detached words. Yevgraf Ivanovitch listened in silence, as though stunned; but suddenly his neck turned crimson, the colour crept up his face, and he made a movement.

"Hold your tongue!" he shouted.

"That's right!" the son persisted; "you don't like to hear the truth! Excellent! Very good! begin shouting! Excellent!"

"Hold your tongue, I tell you!" roared Yevgraf Ivanovitch.

Fedosya Semyonovna appeared in the doorway, very pale, with an astonished face; she tried to say something, but she could not, and could only move her fingers.

"It's all your fault!" Shiryaev shouted at her. "You have brought him up like this!"

"I don't want to go on living in this house!" shouted the student, crying, and looking angrily at his mother. "I don't want to live with you!"

Varvara uttered a shriek behind the screen and broke into loud sobs. With a wave of his hand, Shiryaev ran out of the house.

The student went to his own room and quietly lay down. He lay till midnight without moving or opening his eyes. He felt neither anger nor shame, but a vague ache in his soul. He neither blamed his father nor pitied his mother, nor was he tormented by stings of conscience; he realized that every one in the house was feeling the same ache, and God only knew which was most to blame, which was suffering most...

At midnight he woke the labourer, and told him to have the horse ready at five o'clock in the morning for him to drive to the station; he undressed and got into bed, but could not get to sleep. He heard how his father, still awake, paced slowly from window to window, sighing, till early morning. No one was asleep; they spoke rarely, and only in whispers. Twice his mother came to him behind the screen. Always with the same look of vacant wonder, she slowly made the cross over him, shaking nervously.

At five o'clock in the morning he said good-bye to them all affectionately, and even shed tears. As he passed his father's room, he glanced in at the door. Yevgraf Ivanovitch, who had not taken off his clothes or gone to bed, was standing by the window, drumming on the panes.

"Good-bye; I am going," said his son.

"Good-bye . . . the money is on the round table . . ." his father answered, without turning round.

A cold, hateful rain was falling as the labourer drove him to the station. The sunflowers were drooping their heads still lower, and the grass seemed darker than ever.

# IN THE COURT

At the district town of N. in the cinnamon-coloured government house in which the Zemstvo, the sessional meetings of the justices of the peace, the Rural Board, the Liquor Board, the Military Board, and many others sit by turns, the Circuit Court was in session on one of the dull days of autumn. Of the above-mentioned cinnamon-coloured house a local official had wittily observed:

"Here is Justitia, here is Policia, here is Militia - a regular boarding school of high-born young ladies."

But, as the saying is, "Too many cooks spoil the broth," and probably that is why the house strikes, oppresses, and overwhelms a fresh unofficial visitor with its dismal barrack-like appearance, its decrepit condition, and the complete absence of any kind of comfort, external or internal. Even on the brightest spring days it seems wrapped in a dense shade, and on clear moonlight nights, when the trees and the little dwelling-houses merged in one blur of shadow seem plunged in quiet slumber, it alone absurdly and inappropriately towers, an oppressive mass of stone, above the modest landscape, spoils the general harmony, and keeps sleepless vigil as though it could not escape from burdensome memories of past unforgiven sins. Inside it is like a barn and extremely unattractive. It is strange to see how readily these elegant lawyers, members of committees, and marshals of nobility, who in their own homes will make a scene over the slightest fume from the stove, or stain on the floor, resign themselves here to whirring ventilation wheels, the disgusting smell of fumigating candles, and the filthy, forever perspiring walls.

The sitting of the circuit court began between nine and ten. The programme of the day was promptly entered upon, with noticeable haste. The cases came on one after another and ended quickly, like a church service without a choir, so that no mind could form a complete picture of all this parti-coloured mass of faces, movements, words, misfortunes, true sayings and lies, all racing by like a river in flood. . . . By two o'clock a great deal had been done: two prisoners had been sentenced to service in convict battalions, one of the privileged class had been sentenced to deprivation of rights and imprisonment, one had been acquitted, one case had been adjourned.

At precisely two o'clock the presiding judge announced that the case "of the peasant Nikolay Harlamov, charged with the murder of his wife," would next be heard. The composition of the court remained the same as it had been for the preceding case, except that the place of the defending counsel was filled by a new personage, a beardless young graduate in a coat with bright buttons. The president gave the order - "Bring in the prisoner!"

But the prisoner, who had been got ready beforehand, was already walking to his bench. He was a tall, thick-set peasant of about fifty-five, completely bald, with an apathetic, hairy face and a big red beard. He was followed by a frail-looking little soldier with a gun.

Just as he was reaching the bench the escort had a trifling mishap. He stumbled and dropped the gun out of his hands, but caught it at once before it touched the ground, knocking his knee violently against the butt end as he did so. A faint laugh was audible in the audience. Either from the pain or perhaps from shame at his awkwardness the soldier flushed a dark red.

After the customary questions to the prisoner, the shuffling of the jury, the calling over and swearing in of the witnesses, the reading of the charge began. The narrow-chested, pale-faced secretary, far too thin for his uniform, and with sticking plaster on his cheek, read it in a low, thick bass, rapidly like a sacristan, without raising or dropping his voice, as though afraid of exerting his lungs; he was seconded by the ventilation wheel whirring indefatigably behind the judge's table, and the result was a sound that gave a drowsy, narcotic character to the stillness of the hall.

The president, a short-sighted man, not old but with an extremely exhausted face, sat in his armchair without stirring and held his open hand near his brow as though screening his eyes from the sun. To the droning of the ventilation wheel and the secretary he meditated. When the secretary paused for an instant to take breath on beginning a new page, he suddenly started and looked round at the court with lustreless eyes, then bent down to the ear of the judge next to him and asked with a sigh:

"Are you putting up at Demyanov's, Matvey Petrovitch?"

"Yes, at Demyanov's," answered the other, starting too.

"Next time I shall probably put up there too. It's really impossible to put up at Tipyakov's! There's noise and uproar all night! Knocking, coughing, children crying. . . . It's impossible!"

The assistant prosecutor, a fat, well-nourished, dark man with gold spectacles, with a handsome, well-groomed beard, sat motionless as a statue, with his cheek propped on his fist, reading Byron's "Cain." His eyes were full of eager attention and his eyebrows rose higher and higher with wonder. . . . From time to time he dropped back in his chair, gazed without interest straight before him for a minute, and then buried himself in his reading again. The council for the defence moved the blunt end of his pencil about the table and mused with his head on one side. . . . His youthful face expressed nothing but the frigid, immovable boredom which is commonly seen on the face of schoolboys and men on duty who are forced from day to day to sit in the same place, to see the same faces, the same walls. He felt no excitement about the speech he was to make, and indeed what did that speech amount to? On instructions from his superiors in accordance with long-established routine he would fire it off before the jurymen, without passion or ardour, feeling that it was colourless and boring, and then - gallop through the mud and the rain to the station, thence to the town, shortly to receive instructions to go off again to some district to deliver another speech. . . . It was a bore!

At first the prisoner turned pale and coughed nervously into his sleeve, but soon the stillness, the general monotony and boredom infected him too. He looked with dull-witted respectfulness at the judges' uniforms, at the weary faces of the jurymen, and blinked calmly. The surroundings and procedure of the court, the expectation of which had so weighed on his soul while he was awaiting them in prison, now had the most soothing effect on him. What he met here was not at all what he could have expected. The charge of murder hung over him, and yet here he met with neither threatening faces nor indignant looks nor loud phrases about retribution nor sympathy for his extraordinary fate; not one of those who were judging him looked at him with interest or for long. . . . The dingy windows and walls, the voice of the secretary, the attitude of the prosecutor were all saturated with official indifference and produced an atmosphere of frigidity, as though the murderer were simply an official property, or as though he were not being judged by living men, but by some unseen machine, set going, goodness knows how or by whom. . . .

The peasant, reassured, did not understand that the men here were as accustomed to the dramas and tragedies of life and were as blunted by the sight of them as hospital attendants are at the sight of death, and that the whole horror and hopelessness of his position lay just in this mechanical indifference. It seemed that if he were not to sit quietly but to get up and begin beseeching, appealing with tears for their mercy, bitterly repenting, that if he were to die of despair - it would all be shattered against blunted nerves and the callousness of custom, like waves against a rock.

When the secretary finished, the president for some reason passed his hands over the table before him, looked for some time with his eyes screwed up towards the prisoner, and then asked, speaking languidly:

"Prisoner at the bar, do you plead guilty to having murdered your wife on the evening of the ninth of June?"

"No, sir," answered the prisoner, getting up and holding his gown over his chest.

After this the court proceeded hurriedly to the examination of witnesses. Two peasant women and five men and the village policeman who had made the enquiry were questioned. All of them, mud-bespattered, exhausted with their long walk and waiting in the witnesses' room, gloomy and dispirited, gave the same evidence. They testified that Harlamov lived "well" with his old woman, like anyone else; that he never beat her except when he had had a drop; that on the ninth of June when the sun was setting the old woman had been found in the porch with her skull broken; that beside her in a pool of blood lay an axe. When they looked for Nikolay to tell him of the calamity he was not in his hut or in the streets. They ran all over the village, looking for him. They went to all the pothouses and huts, but could not find him. He had disappeared, and two days later came of his own accord to the police office, pale, with his clothes torn, trembling all over. He was bound and put in the lock-up.

"Prisoner," said the president, addressing Harlamov, "cannot you explain to the court where you were during the three days following the murder?"

"I was wandering about the fields. . . . Neither eating nor drinking. . . ."

"Why did you hide yourself, if it was not you that committed the murder?"

"I was frightened. . . . I was afraid I might be judged guilty. . . ."

"Aha! . . . Good, sit down!"

The last to be examined was the district doctor who had made a post-mortem on the old woman. He told the court all that he remembered of his report at the post-mortem and all that he had succeeded in thinking of on his way to the court that morning. The president screwed up his eyes at his new glossy black suit, at his foppish cravat, at his moving lips; he listened and in his mind the languid thought seemed to spring up of itself:

"Everyone wears a short jacket nowadays, why has he had his made long? Why long and not short?"

The circumspect creak of boots was audible behind the president's back. It was the assistant prosecutor going up to the table to take some papers.

"Mihail Vladimirovitch," said the assistant prosecutor, bending down to the president's ear, "amazingly slovenly the way that Koreisky conducted the investigation. The prisoner's brother was not examined, the village elder was not examined, there's no making anything out of his description of the hut. . . ."

"It can't be helped, it can't be helped," said the president, sinking back in his chair. "He's a wreck . . . dropping to bits!"

"By the way," whispered the assistant prosecutor, "look at the audience, in the front row, the third from the right . . . a face like an actor's . . . that's the local Croesus. He has a fortune of something like fifty thousand."

"Really? You wouldn't guess it from his appearance. . . . Well, dear boy, shouldn't we have a break?"

"We will finish the case for the prosecution, and then. . . ."

"As you think best. . . . Well?" the president raised his eyes to the doctor. "So you consider that death was instantaneous?"

"Yes, in consequence of the extent of the injury to the brain substance. . . ."

When the doctor had finished, the president gazed into the space between the prosecutor and the counsel for the defence and suggested:

"Have you any questions to ask?"

The assistant prosecutor shook his head negatively, without lifting his eyes from "Cain"; the counsel for the defence unexpectedly stirred and, clearing his throat, asked:

"Tell me, doctor, can you from the dimensions of the wound form any theory as to . . . as to the mental condition of the criminal? That is, I mean, does the extent of the injury justify the supposition that the accused was suffering from temporary aberration?"

The president raised his drowsy indifferent eyes to the counsel for the defence. The assistant prosecutor tore himself from "Cain," and looked at the president. They merely looked, but there was no smile, no surprise, no perplexity-their faces expressed nothing.

"Perhaps," the doctor hesitated, "if one considers the force with which . . . er - er - er . . . the criminal strikes the blow. . . . However, excuse me, I don't quite understand your question. . . ."

The counsel for the defence did not get an answer to his question, and indeed he did not feel the necessity of one. It was clear even to himself that that question had strayed into his mind and found utterance simply through the effect of the stillness, the boredom, the whirring ventilator wheels.

When they had got rid of the doctor the court rose to examine the "material evidences." The first thing examined was the full-skirted coat,

335

upon the sleeve of which there was a dark brownish stain of blood. Harlamov on being questioned as to the origin of the stain stated:

"Three days before my old woman's death Penkov bled his horse. I was there; I was helping to be sure, and . . . and got smeared with it. . . ."

"But Penkov has just given evidence that he does not remember that you were present at the bleeding. . . ."

"I can't tell about that."

"Sit down."

They proceeded to examine the axe with which the old woman had been murdered.

"That's not my axe," the prisoner declared.

"Whose is it, then?"

"I can't tell . . . I hadn't an axe. . . ."

"A peasant can't get on for a day without an axe. And your neighbour Ivan Timofeyitch, with whom you mended a sledge, has given evidence that it is your axe. . . ."

"I can't say about that, but I swear before God (Harlamov held out his hand before him and spread out the fingers), before the living God. And I don't remember how long it is since I did have an axe of my own. I did have one like that only a bit smaller, but my son Prohor lost it. Two years before he went into the army, he drove off to fetch wood, got drinking with the fellows, and lost it. . . ."

"Good, sit down."

This systematic distrust and disinclination to hear him probably irritated and offended Harlamov. He blinked and red patches came out on his cheekbones.

"I swear in the sight of God," he went on, craning his neck forward. "If you don't believe me, be pleased to ask my son Prohor. Proshka, what did you do with the axe?" he suddenly asked in a rough voice, turning abruptly to the soldier escorting him. "Where is it?"

It was a painful moment! Everyone seemed to wince and as it were shrink together. The same fearful, incredible thought flashed like lightning through every head in the court, the thought of possibly fatal coincidence, and not one person in the court dared to look at the soldier's face. Everyone refused to trust his thought and believed that he had heard wrong.

"Prisoner, conversation with the guards is forbidden . . ." the president made haste to say.

No one saw the escort's face, and horror passed over the hall unseen as in a mask. The usher of the court got up quietly from his place and tiptoeing with his hand held out to balance himself went out of the court. Half a minute later there came the muffled sounds and footsteps that accompany the change of guard.

All raised their heads and, trying to look as though nothing had happened, went on with their work. . . .

# A PECULIAR MAN

Between twelve and one at night a tall gentleman, wearing a top-hat and a coat with a hood, stops before the door of Marya Petrovna Koshkin, a midwife and an old maid. Neither face nor hand can be distinguished in the autumn darkness, but in the very manner of his coughing and the ringing of the bell a certain solidity, positiveness, and even impressiveness can be discerned. After the third ring the door opens and Marya Petrovna herself appears. She has a man's overcoat flung on over her white petticoat. The little lamp with the green shade which she holds in her hand throws a greenish light over her sleepy, freckled face, her scraggy neck, and the lank, reddish hair that strays from under her cap.

"Can I see the midwife?" asks the gentleman.

"I am the midwife. What do you want?"

The gentleman walks into the entry and Marya Petrovna sees facing her a tall, well-made man, no longer young, but with a handsome, severe face and bushy whiskers.

"I am a collegiate assessor, my name is Kiryakov," he says. "I came to fetch you to my wife. Only please make haste."

"Very good . . ." the midwife assents. I'll dress at once, and I must trouble you to wait for me in the parlour."

Kiryakov takes off his overcoat and goes into the parlour. The greenish light of the lamp lies sparsely on the cheap furniture in patched white covers, on the pitiful flowers and the posts on which ivy is trained. . . . There is a smell of geranium and carbolic. The little clock on the wall ticks timidly, as though abashed at the presence of a strange man.

"I am ready," says Marya Petrovna, coming into the room five minutes later, dressed, washed, and ready for action. "Let us go."

"Yes, you must make haste," says Kiryakov. "And, by the way, it is not out of place to enquire - what do you ask for your services?"

"I really don't know . . ." says Marya Petrovna with an embarrassed smile. "As much as you will give."

"No, I don't like that," says Kiryakov, looking coldly and steadily at the midwife. "An arrangement beforehand is best. I don't want to take advantage of you and you don't want to take advantage of me. To avoid misunderstandings it is more sensible for us to make an arrangement beforehand."

"I really don't know - there is no fixed price."

"I work myself and am accustomed to respect the work of others. I don't like injustice. It will be equally unpleasant to me if I pay you too little, or if you demand from me too much, and so I insist on your naming your charge."

"Well, there are such different charges."

"H'm. In view of your hesitation, which I fail to understand, I am constrained to fix the sum myself. I can give you two roubles."

"Good gracious! . . . Upon my word! . . ." says Marya Petrovna, turning crimson and stepping back. "I am really ashamed. Rather than take two roubles I will come for nothing . . . . Five roubles, if you like."

"Two roubles, not a kopeck more. I don't want to take advantage of you, but I do not intend to be overcharged."

"As you please, but I am not coming for two roubles. . . ."

"But by law you have not the right to refuse."

"Very well, I will come for nothing."

"I won't have you for nothing. All work ought to receive remuneration. I work myself and I understand that. . . ."

"I won't come for two roubles," Marya Petrovna answers mildly. "I'll come for nothing if you like."

"In that case I regret that I have troubled you for nothing. I have the honour to wish you good-bye."

"Well, you are a man!" says Marya Petrovna, seeing him into the entry. "I will come for three roubles if that will satisfy you."

339

Kiryakov frowns and ponders for two full minutes, looking with concentration on the floor, then he says resolutely, "No," and goes out into the street. The astonished and disconcerted midwife fastens the door after him and goes back into her bedroom.

"He's good-looking, respectable, but how queer, God bless the man!. . ." she thinks as she gets into bed.

But in less than half an hour she hears another ring; she gets up and sees the same Kiryakov again.

"Extraordinary the way things are mismanaged. Neither the chemist, nor the police, nor the house-porters can give me the address of a midwife, and so I am under the necessity of assenting to your terms. I will give you three roubles, but . . . I warn you beforehand that when I engage servants or receive any kind of services, I make an arrangement beforehand in order that when I pay there may be no talk of extras, tips, or anything of the sort. Everyone ought to receive what is his due."

Marya Petrovna has not listened to Kiryakov for long, but already she feels that she is bored and repelled by him, that his even, measured speech lies like a weight on her soul. She dresses and goes out into the street with him. The air is still but cold, and the sky is so overcast that the light of the street lamps is hardly visible. The sloshy snow squelches under their feet. The midwife looks intently but does not see a cab.

"I suppose it is not far?" she asks.

"No, not far," Kiryakov answers grimly.

They walk down one turning, a second, a third. . . . Kiryakov strides along, and even in his step his respectability and positiveness is apparent.

"What awful weather!" the midwife observes to him.

But he preserves a dignified silence, and it is noticeable that he tries to step on the smooth stones to avoid spoiling his goloshes. At last after a long walk the midwife steps into the entry; from which she can see a big decently furnished drawing-room. There is not a soul in the rooms, even in the bedroom where the woman is lying in labour. . . . The old women and relations who flock in crowds to every confinement are not to be seen. The cook rushes about alone, with a scared and vacant face. There is a sound of loud groans.

Three hours pass. Marya Petrovna sits by the mother's bedside and whispers to her. The two women have already had time to make friends, they have got to know each other, they gossip, they sigh together. . . .

"You mustn't talk," says the midwife anxiously, and at the same time she showers questions on her.

Then the door opens and Kiryakov himself comes quietly and stolidly into the room. He sits down in the chair and strokes his whiskers. Silence reigns. Marya Petrovna looks timidly at his handsome, passionless, wooden face and waits for him to begin to talk, but he remains absolutely silent and absorbed in thought. After waiting in vain, the midwife makes up her mind to begin herself, and utters a phrase commonly used at confinements.

"Well now, thank God, there is one human being more in the world!"

"Yes, that's agreeable," said Kiryakov, preserving the wooden expression of his face, "though indeed, on the other hand, to have more children you must have more money. The baby is not born fed and clothed."

A guilty expression comes into the mother's face, as though she had brought a creature into the world without permission or through idle caprice. Kiryakov gets up with a sigh and walks with solid dignity out of the room.

"What a man, bless him!" says the midwife to the mother. "He's so stern and does not smile."

The mother tells her that *he* is always like that. He is honest, fair, prudent, sensibly economical, but all that to such an exceptional degree that simple mortals feel suffocated by it. His relations have parted from him, the servants will not stay more than a month; they have no friends; his wife and children are always on tenterhooks from terror over every step they take. He does not shout at them nor beat them, his virtues are far more numerous than his defects, but when he goes out of the house they all feel better, and more at ease. Why it is so the woman herself cannot say.

"The basins must be properly washed and put away in the store cupboard," says Kiryakov, coming into the bedroom. "These bottles must be put away too: they may come in handy."

What he says is very simple and ordinary, but the midwife for some reason feels flustered. She begins to be afraid of the man and shudders every time she hears his footsteps. In the morning as she is preparing to depart she sees Kiryakov's little son, a pale, close-cropped schoolboy, in the dining-room drinking his tea. . . . Kiryakov is standing opposite him, saying in his flat, even voice:

"You know how to eat, you must know how to work too. You have just swallowed a mouthful but have not probably reflected that that mouthful costs money and money is obtained by work. You must eat and reflect. . . ."

The midwife looks at the boy's dull face, and it seems to her as though the very air is heavy, that a little more and the very walls will fall, unable to endure the crushing presence of the peculiar man. Beside herself with terror, and by now feeling a violent hatred for the man, Marya Petrovna gathers up her bundles and hurriedly departs.

Half-way home she remembers that she has forgotten to ask for her three roubles, but after stopping and thinking for a minute, with a wave of her hand, she goes on.

# MIRE

## I

Gracefully swaying in the saddle, a young man wearing the snow-white tunic of an officer rode into the great yard of the vodka distillery belonging to the heirs of M. E. Rothstein. The sun smiled carelessly on the lieutenant's little stars, on the white trunks of the birch-trees, on the heaps of broken glass scattered here and there in the yard. The radiant, vigorous beauty of a summer day lay over everything, and nothing hindered the snappy young green leaves from dancing gaily and winking at the clear blue sky. Even the dirty and soot-begrimed appearance of the bricksheds and the stifling fumes of the distillery did not spoil the general good impression. The lieutenant sprang gaily out of the saddle, handed over his horse to a man who ran up, and stroking with his finger his delicate black moustaches, went in at the front door. On the top step of the old but light and softly carpeted staircase he was met by a maidservant with a haughty, not very youthful face. The lieutenant gave her his card without speaking.

As she went through the rooms with the card, the maid could see on it the name "Alexandr Grigoryevitch Sokolsky." A minute later she came back and told the lieutenant that her mistress could not see him, as she was not feeling quite well. Sokolsky looked at the ceiling and thrust out his lower lip.

"How vexatious!" he said. "Listen, my dear," he said eagerly. "Go and tell Susanna Moiseyevna, that it is very necessary for me to speak to her - very. I will only keep her one minute. Ask her to excuse me."

The maid shrugged one shoulder and went off languidly to her mistress.

"Very well!" she sighed, returning after a brief interval. "Please walk in!"

The lieutenant went with her through five or six large, luxuriously furnished rooms and a corridor, and finally found himself in a large and lofty square room, in which from the first step he was impressed by the abundance of flowers and plants and the sweet, almost revoltingly heavy fragrance of jasmine. Flowers were trained to trellis-work along the walls, screening the windows, hung from the ceiling, and were wreathed over the corners, so that the room was more like a greenhouse than a place to live in. Tits, canaries, and goldfinches chirruped among the green leaves and fluttered against the window-panes.

"Forgive me for receiving you here," the lieutenant heard in a mellow feminine voice with a burr on the letter *r* which was not without charm. "Yesterday I had a sick headache, and I'm trying to keep still to prevent its coming on again. What do you want?"

Exactly opposite the entrance, he saw sitting in a big low chair, such as old men use, a woman in an expensive Chinese dressing-gown, with her head wrapped up, leaning back on a pillow. Nothing could be seen behind the woollen shawl in which she was muffled but a pale, long, pointed, somewhat aquiline nose, and one large dark eye. Her ample dressing-gown concealed her figure, but judging from her beautiful hand, from her voice, her nose, and her eye, she might be twenty-six or twenty-eight.

"Forgive me for being so persistent . . ." began the lieutenant, clinking his spurs. "Allow me to introduce myself: Sokolsky! I come with a message from my cousin, your neighbour, Alexey Ivanovitch Kryukov, who . . ."

"I know!" interposed Susanna Moiseyevna. "I know Kryukov. Sit down; I don't like anything big standing before me."

"My cousin charges me to ask you a favour," the lieutenant went on, clinking his spurs once more and sitting down. "The fact is, your late father made a purchase of oats from my cousin last winter, and a small sum was left owing. The payment only becomes due next week, but my cousin begs you most particularly to pay him - if possible, to-day."

As the lieutenant talked, he stole side-glances about him.

"Surely I'm not in her bedroom?" he thought.

In one corner of the room, where the foliage was thickest and tallest, under a pink awning like a funeral canopy, stood a bed not yet made, with the bedclothes still in disorder. Close by on two arm-chairs lay heaps of crumpled feminine garments. Petticoats and sleeves with rumpled lace and flounces were trailing on the carpet, on which here and there lay bits of white tape, cigarette-ends, and the papers of caramels. . . . Under the bed the toes, pointed and square, of slippers of all kinds peeped out in a long row. And it seemed to the lieutenant that the scent of the jasmine came not from the flowers, but from the bed and the slippers.

"And what is the sum owing?" asked Susanna Moiseyevna.

"Two thousand three hundred."

"Oho!" said the Jewess, showing another large black eye. "And you call that - a small sum! However, it's just the same paying it to-day or paying it in a week, but I've had so many payments to make in the last two months since my father's death. . . . Such a lot of stupid business, it makes my head go round! A nice idea! I want to go abroad, and they keep forcing me to attend to these silly things. Vodka, oats . . ." she muttered, half closing her eyes, "oats, bills, percentages, or, as my head-clerk says, 'percentage.' . . . It's awful. Yesterday I simply turned the excise officer out. He pesters me with his Tralles. I said to him: 'Go to the devil with your Tralles! I can't see any one!' He kissed my hand and went away. I tell you what: can't your cousin wait two or three months?"

"A cruel question!" laughed the lieutenant. "My cousin can wait a year, but it's I who cannot wait! You see, it's on my own account I'm acting, I ought to tell you. At all costs I must have money, and by ill-luck my cousin hasn't a rouble to spare. I'm forced to ride about and collect debts. I've just been to see a peasant, our tenant; here I'm now calling on you; from here I shall go on to somewhere else, and keep on like that until I get together five thousand roubles. I need money awfully!"

"Nonsense! What does a young man want with money? Whims, mischief. Why, have you been going in for dissipation? Or losing at cards? Or are you getting married?"

"You've guessed!" laughed the lieutenant, and rising slightly from his seat, he clinked his spurs. "I really am going to be married."

Susanna Moiseyevna looked intently at her visitor, made a wry face, and sighed.

"I can't make out what possesses people to get married!" she said, looking about her for her pocket-handkerchief. "Life is so short, one has so little freedom, and they must put chains on themselves!"

"Every one has his own way of looking at things...."

"Yes, yes, of course; every one has his own way of looking at things.... But, I say, are you really going to marry some one poor? Are you passionately in love? And why must you have five thousand? Why won't four do, or three?"

"What a tongue she has!" thought the lieutenant, and answered: "The difficulty is that an officer is not allowed by law to marry till he is twenty-eight; if you choose to marry, you have to leave the Service or else pay a deposit of five thousand."

"Ah, now I understand. Listen. You said just now that every one has his own way of looking at things.... Perhaps your fiancée is some one special and remarkable, but ... but I am utterly unable to understand how any decent man can live with a woman. I can't for the life of me understand it. I have lived, thank the Lord, twenty-seven years, and I have never yet seen an endurable woman. They're all affected minxes, immoral, liars.... The only ones I can put up with are cooks and housemaids, but so-called ladies I won't let come within shooting distance of me. But, thank God, they hate me and don't force themselves on me! If one of them wants money she sends her husband, but nothing will induce her to come herself, not from pride - no, but from cowardice; she's afraid of my making a scene. Oh, I understand their hatred very well! Rather! I openly display what they do their very utmost to conceal from God and man. How can they help hating me? No doubt you've heard bushels of scandal about me already...."

"I only arrived here so lately ..."

"Tut, tut, tut! ... I see from your eyes! But your brother's wife, surely she primed you for this expedition? Think of letting a young man come to see such an awful woman without warning him - how could she? Ha, ha! ... But tell me, how is your brother? He's a fine fellow, such a handsome man! . . . I've seen him several times at mass. Why do you look at me like that? I very often go to church! We all have the same God. To an educated person externals matter less than the idea. . . . That's so, isn't it?"

"Yes, of course . . ." smiled the lieutenant.

"Yes, the idea. . . . But you are not a bit like your brother. You are handsome, too, but your brother is a great deal better-looking. There's wonderfully little likeness!"

"That's quite natural; he's not my brother, but my cousin."

"Ah, to be sure! So you must have the money to-day? Why to-day?"

"My furlough is over in a few days."

"Well, what's to be done with you!" sighed Susanna Moiseyevna. "So be it. I'll give you the money, though I know you'll abuse me for it afterwards. You'll quarrel with your wife after you are married, and say: 'If that mangy Jewess hadn't given me the money, I should perhaps have been as free as a bird to-day!' Is your fiancée pretty?"

"Oh yes. . . ."

"H'm! . . . Anyway, better something, if it's only beauty, than nothing. Though however beautiful a woman is, it can never make up to her husband for her silliness."

"That's original!" laughed the lieutenant. "You are a woman yourself, and such a woman hater!"

"A woman . . ." smiled Susanna. "It's not my fault that God has cast me into this mould, is it? I'm no more to blame for it than you are for having moustaches. The violin is not responsible for the choice of its case. I am very fond of myself, but when any one reminds me that I am a woman, I begin to hate myself. Well, you can go away, and I'll dress. Wait for me in the drawing-room."

The lieutenant went out, and the first thing he did was to draw a deep breath, to get rid of the heavy scent of jasmine, which had begun to irritate his throat and to make him feel giddy.

"What a strange woman!" he thought, looking about him. "She talks fluently, but . . . far too much, and too freely. She must be neurotic."

The drawing-room, in which he was standing now, was richly furnished, and had pretensions to luxury and style. There were dark bronze dishes with patterns in relief, views of Nice and the Rhine on the tables, old-fashioned sconces, Japanese statuettes, but all this striving after luxury and style only emphasised the lack of taste which was glaringly apparent in the gilt cornices, the gaudy wall-paper, the bright velvet table-cloths, the common oleographs in heavy frames. The bad taste of the general effect was the more complete from the lack of finish and the overcrowding of the room, which gave one a feeling that something was lacking, and that a great deal should have been thrown away. It was evident that the furniture had not been bought all at once, but had been picked up at auctions and other favourable opportunities.

Heaven knows what taste the lieutenant could boast of, but even he noticed one characteristic peculiarity about the whole place, which no luxury or style could efface - a complete absence of all trace of womanly, careful hands, which, as we all know, give a warmth, poetry, and snugness to the furnishing of a room. There was a chilliness about it such as one finds in waiting-rooms at stations, in clubs, and foyers at the theatres.

There was scarcely anything in the room definitely Jewish, except, perhaps, a big picture of the meeting of Jacob and Esau. The lieutenant looked round about him, and, shrugging his shoulders, thought of his strange, new acquaintance, of her free-and-easy manners, and her way of talking. But then the door opened, and in the doorway appeared the lady herself, in a long black dress, so slim and tightly laced that her figure looked as though it had been turned in a lathe. Now the lieutenant saw not only the nose and eyes, but also a thin white face, a head black and as curly as lamb's-wool. She did not attract him, though she did not strike him as ugly. He had a prejudice against un-Russian faces in general, and he considered, too, that the lady's white face, the whiteness of which for some reason suggested the cloying scent of jasmine, did not go well with her little black curls and thick eyebrows; that her nose and ears were astoundingly white, as though they belonged to a corpse, or had been moulded out of transparent wax.

When she smiled she showed pale gums as well as her teeth, and he did not like that either.

"Anæmic debility . . ." he thought; "she's probably as nervous as a turkey."

"Here I am! Come along!" she said, going on rapidly ahead of him and pulling off the yellow leaves from the plants as she passed.

"I'll give you the money directly, and if you like I'll give you some lunch. Two thousand three hundred roubles! After such a good stroke of business you'll have an appetite for your lunch. Do you like my rooms? The ladies about here declare that my rooms always smell of garlic. With that culinary gibe their stock of wit is exhausted. I hasten to assure you that I've no garlic even in the cellar. And one day when a doctor came to see me who smelt of garlic, I asked him to take his hat and go and spread his fragrance elsewhere. There is no smell of garlic here, but the place does smell of drugs. My father lay paralyzed for a year and a half, and the whole house smelt of medicine. A year and a half! I was sorry to lose him, but I'm glad he's dead: he suffered so!"

She led the officer through two rooms similar to the drawing-room, through a large reception hall, and came to a stop in her study, where there was a lady's writing-table covered with little knick-knacks. On the carpet near it several books lay strewn about, opened and folded back. Through a small door leading from the study he saw a table laid for lunch.

Still chatting, Susanna took out of her pocket a bunch of little keys and unlocked an ingeniously made cupboard with a curved, sloping lid. When the lid was raised the cupboard emitted a plaintive note which made the lieutenant think of an Æolian harp. Susanna picked out another key and clicked another lock.

"I have underground passages here and secret doors," she said, taking out a small morocco portfolio. "It's a funny cupboard, isn't it? And in this portfolio I have a quarter of my fortune. Look how podgy it is! You won't strangle me, will you?"

Susanna raised her eyes to the lieutenant and laughed good-naturedly. The lieutenant laughed too.

"She's rather jolly," he thought, watching the keys flashing between her fingers.

"Here it is," she said, picking out the key of the portfolio. "Now, Mr. Creditor, trot out the IOU. What a silly thing money is really! How paltry it is, and yet how women love it! I am a Jewess, you know, to the marrow of my bones. I am passionately fond of Shmuls and Yankels, but how I loathe that passion for gain in our Semitic blood. They hoard and they don't know what they are hoarding for. One ought to live and enjoy oneself, but they're afraid of spending an extra farthing. In that way I am more like an hussar than a Shmul. I don't like money to be kept long in one place. And altogether I fancy I'm not much like a Jewess. Does my accent give me away much, eh?"

"What shall I say?" mumbled the lieutenant. "You speak good Russian, but you do roll your *r's*."

Susanna laughed and put the little key in the lock of the portfolio. The lieutenant took out of his pocket a little roll of IOUs and laid them with a notebook on the table.

"Nothing betrays a Jew as much as his accent," Susanna went on, looking gaily at the lieutenant. "However much he twists himself into a Russian or a Frenchman, ask him to say 'feather' and he will say 'fedder' ... but I pronounce it correctly: 'Feather! feather! feather!' "

Both laughed.

"By Jove, she's very jolly!" thought Sokolsky.

Susanna put the portfolio on a chair, took a step towards the lieutenant, and bringing her face close to his, went on gaily:

"Next to the Jews I love no people so much as the Russian and the French. I did not do much at school and I know no history, but it seems to me that the fate of the world lies in the hands of those two nations. I lived a long time abroad. . . . I spent six months in Madrid. . . . I've gazed my fill at the public, and the conclusion I've come to is that there are no decent peoples except the Russian and the French. Take the languages, for instance. . . . The German language is like the neighing of horses; as for the English . . . you can't imagine anything stupider. Fight - feet - foot! Italian is only pleasant when they speak it slowly. If you listen to Italians gabbling, you get the effect of the Jewish jargon. And the Poles? Mercy on us! There's no language so disgusting! 'Nie pieprz, Pietrze, pieprzem wieprza bo mozeoz przepieprzyé wieprza pieprzem.' That means: 'Don't pepper a sucking pig with pepper, Pyotr, or perhaps you'll over-pepper the sucking pig with pepper.' Ha, ha, ha!"

Susanna Moiseyevna rolled her eyes and broke into such a pleasant, infectious laugh that the lieutenant, looking at her, went off into a loud and merry peal of laughter. She took the visitor by the button, and went on:

"You don't like Jews, of course . . . they've many faults, like all nations. I don't dispute that. But are the Jews to blame for it? No, it's not the Jews who are to blame, but the Jewish women! They are narrow-minded, greedy; there's no sort of poetry about them, they're dull. . . . You have never lived with a Jewess, so you don't know how charming it is!" Susanna Moiseyevna pronounced the last words with deliberate emphasis and with no eagerness or laughter. She paused as though frightened at her own openness, and her face was suddenly distorted in a strange, unaccountable way. Her eyes stared at the lieutenant without blinking, her lips parted and showed clenched teeth. Her whole face, her throat, and even her bosom, seemed quivering with a spiteful, catlike expression. Still keeping her eyes fixed on her visitor, she rapidly bent to one side, and swiftly, like a cat, snatched something from the table. All this was the work of a few seconds. Watching her movements, the lieutenant saw five fingers crumple up his IOUs and caught a glimpse of the white rustling paper as it disappeared in her clenched fist. Such an extraordinary transition from good-natured laughter to crime so appalled him that he turned pale and stepped back. . . .

And she, still keeping her frightened, searching eyes upon him, felt along her hip with her clenched fist for her pocket. Her fist struggled convulsively for the pocket, like a fish in the net, and could not find the opening. In another moment the IOUs would have vanished in the recesses of her feminine garments, but at that point the lieutenant uttered a faint cry, and, moved more by instinct than reflection, seized the Jewess by her arm above the clenched fist. Showing her teeth more than ever, she struggled with all her might and pulled her hand away. Then Sokolsky put his right arm firmly round her waist, and the other round her chest and a struggle followed. Afraid of outraging her sex or hurting her, he tried only to prevent her moving, and to get hold of the fist with the IOUs; but she wriggled like an eel in his arms with her supple, flexible body, struck him in the chest with her elbows, and scratched him, so that he could not help touching her all over, and was forced to hurt her and disregard her modesty.

"How unusual this is! How strange!" he thought, utterly amazed, hardly able to believe his senses, and feeling rather sick from the scent of jasmine.

In silence, breathing heavily, stumbling against the furniture, they moved about the room. Susanna was carried away by the struggle. She flushed, closed her eyes, and forgetting herself, once even pressed her face against the face of the lieutenant, so that there was a sweetish taste left on his lips. At last he caught hold of her clenched hand. . . . Forcing it open, and not finding the papers in it, he let go the Jewess. With flushed faces and dishevelled hair, they looked at one another, breathing hard. The spiteful, catlike expression on the Jewess's face was gradually replaced by a good-natured smile. She burst out laughing, and turning on one foot, went towards the room where lunch was ready. The lieutenant moved slowly after her. She sat down to the table, and, still flushed and breathing hard, tossed off half a glass of port.

"Listen" - the lieutenant broke the silence - "I hope you are joking?"

"Not a bit of it," she answered, thrusting a piece of bread into her mouth.

"H'm! . . . How do you wish me to take all this?"

"As you choose. Sit down and have lunch!"

"But . . . it's dishonest!"

"Perhaps. But don't trouble to give me a sermon; I have my own way of looking at things."

"Won't you give them back?"

"Of course not! If you were a poor unfortunate man, with nothing to eat, then it would be a different matter. But - he wants to get married!"

"It's not my money, you know; it's my cousin's!"

"And what does your cousin want with money? To get fashionable clothes for his wife? But I really don't care whether your *belle-sœur* has dresses or not."

The lieutenant had ceased to remember that he was in a strange house with an unknown lady, and did not trouble himself with decorum. He strode up and down the room, scowled and nervously fingered his waistcoat. The fact that the Jewess had lowered herself in his eyes by her dishonest action, made him feel bolder and more free-and-easy.

"The devil knows what to make of it!" he muttered. "Listen. I shan't go away from here until I get the IOUs!"

"Ah, so much the better," laughed Susanna. "If you stay here for good, it will make it livelier for me."

Excited by the struggle, the lieutenant looked at Susanna's laughing, insolent face, at her munching mouth, at her heaving bosom, and grew bolder and more audacious. Instead of thinking about the IOU he began for some reason recalling with a sort of relish his cousin's stories of the Jewess's romantic adventures, of her free way of life, and these reminiscences only provoked him to greater audacity. Impulsively he sat down beside the Jewess and thinking no more of the IOUs began to eat. . . .

"Will you have vodka or wine?" Susanna asked with a laugh. "So you will stay till you get the IOUs? Poor fellow! How many days and nights you will have to spend with me, waiting for those IOUs! Won't your fiancée have something to say about it?"

## II

Five hours had passed. The lieutenant's cousin, Alexey Ivanovitch Kryukov was walking about the rooms of his country-house in his dressing-gown and slippers, and looking impatiently out of window. He was a tall, sturdy man, with a large black beard and a manly face; and as the Jewess had truly said, he was handsome, though he had reached the age when men are apt to grow too stout, puffy, and bald. By mind and temperament he was one of those natures in which the Russian intellectual classes are so rich: warm-hearted, good-natured, well-bred, having some knowledge of the arts and sciences, some faith, and the most chivalrous notions about honour, but indolent and lacking in depth. He was fond of good eating and drinking, was an ideal whist-player, was a connoisseur in women and horses, but in other things he was apathetic and sluggish as a seal, and to rouse him from his lethargy something extraordinary and quite revolting was needed, and then he would forget everything in the world and display intense activity; he would fume and talk of a duel, write a petition of seven pages to a Minister, gallop at breakneck speed about the district, call some one publicly "a scoundrel," would go to law, and so on.

"How is it our Sasha's not back yet?" he kept asking his wife, glancing out of window. "Why, it's dinner-time!"

After waiting for the lieutenant till six o'clock, they sat down to dinner. When supper-time came, however, Alexey Ivanovitch was listening to every footstep, to every sound of the door, and kept shrugging his shoulders.

"Strange!" he said. "The rascally dandy must have stayed on at the tenant's."

As he went to bed after supper, Kryukov made up his mind that the lieutenant was being entertained at the tenant's, where after a festive evening he was staying the night.

Alexandr Grigoryevitch only returned next morning. He looked extremely crumpled and confused.

"I want to speak to you alone . . ." he said mysteriously to his cousin.

They went into the study. The lieutenant shut the door, and he paced for a long time up and down before he began to speak.

"Something's happened, my dear fellow," he began, "that I don't know how to tell you about. You wouldn't believe it . . ."

And blushing, faltering, not looking at his cousin, he told what had happened with the IOUs. Kryukov, standing with his feet wide apart and his head bent, listened and frowned.

"Are you joking?" he asked.

"How the devil could I be joking? It's no joking matter!"

"I don't understand!" muttered Kryukov, turning crimson and flinging up his hands. "It's positively . . . immoral on your part. Before your very eyes a hussy is up to the devil knows what, a serious crime, plays a nasty trick, and you go and kiss her!"

"But I can't understand myself how it happened!" whispered the lieutenant, blinking guiltily. "Upon my honour, I don't understand it! It's the first time in my life I've come across such a monster! It's not her beauty that does for you, not her mind, but that . . . you understand . . . insolence, cynicism. . . ."

"Insolence, cynicism . . . it's unclean! If you've such a longing for insolence and cynicism, you might have picked a sow out of the mire and have devoured her alive. It would have been cheaper, anyway! Instead of two thousand three hundred!"

"You do express yourself elegantly!" said the lieutenant, frowning. "I'll pay you back the two thousand three hundred!"

"I know you'll pay it back, but it's not a question of money! Damn the money! What revolts me is your being such a limp rag . . . such filthy feebleness! And engaged! With a fiancée!"

"Don't speak of it . . . ," said the lieutenant, blushing. "I loathe myself as it is. I should like to sink into the earth. It's sickening and vexatious that I shall have to bother my aunt for that five thousand. . . ."

Kryukov continued for some time longer expressing his indignation and grumbling, then, as he grew calmer, he sat down on the sofa and began to jeer at his cousin.

"You young officers!" he said with contemptuous irony. "Nice bridegrooms."

Suddenly he leapt up as though he had been stung, stamped his foot, and ran about the study.

"No, I'm not going to leave it like that!" he said, shaking his fist. "I will have those IOUs, I will! I'll give it her! One doesn't beat women, but I'll break every bone in her body. . . . I'll pound her to a jelly! I'm not a lieutenant! You won't touch me with insolence or cynicism! No-o-o, damn her! Mishka!" he shouted, "run and tell them to get the racing droshky out for me!"

Kryukov dressed rapidly, and, without heeding the agitated lieutenant, got into the droshky, and with a wave of his hand resolutely raced off to Susanna Moiseyevna. For a long time the lieutenant gazed out of window at the clouds of dust that rolled after his cousin's droshky, stretched, yawned, and went to his own room. A quarter of an hour later he was sound asleep.

At six o'clock he was waked up and summoned to dinner.

"How nice this is of Alexey!" his cousin's wife greeted him in the dining-room. "He keeps us waiting for dinner."

"Do you mean to say he's not come back yet?" yawned the lieutenant. "H'm! . . . he's probably gone round to see the tenant."

But Alexey Ivanovitch was not back by supper either. His wife and Sokolsky decided that he was playing cards at the tenant's and would most likely stay the night there. What had happened was not what they had supposed, however.

Kryukov returned next morning, and without greeting any one, without a word, dashed into his study.

"Well?" whispered the lieutenant, gazing at him round-eyed.

Kryukov waved his hand and gave a snort.

"Why, what's the matter? What are you laughing at?"

Kryukov flopped on the sofa, thrust his head in the pillow, and shook with suppressed laughter. A minute later he got up, and looking at the surprised lieutenant, with his eyes full of tears from laughing, said:

"Close the door. Well . . . she *is* a fe-e-male, I beg to inform you!"

"Did you get the IOUs?"

Kryukov waved his hand and went off into a peal of laughter again.

"Well! she is a female!" he went on. "*Merci* for the acquaintance, my boy! She's a devil in petticoats. I arrived; I walked in like such an avenging Jove, you know, that I felt almost afraid of myself. . . . I frowned, I scowled, even clenched my fists to be more awe-inspiring. . . . 'Jokes don't pay with me, madam!' said I, and more in that style. And I threatened her with the law and with the Governor. To begin with she burst into tears, said she'd been joking with you, and even took me to the cupboard to give me the money. Then she began arguing that the future of Europe lies in the hands of the French, and the Russians, swore at women. . . . Like you, I listened, fascinated, ass that I was. . . . She kept singing the praises of my beauty, patted me on the arm near the shoulder, to see how strong I was, and . . . and as you see, I've only just got away from her! Ha, ha! She's enthusiastic about you!"

"You're a nice fellow!" laughed the lieutenant. "A married man! highly respected. . . . Well, aren't you ashamed? Disgusted? Joking apart though, old man, you've got your Queen Tamara in your own neighbourhood. . . ."

"In my own neighbourhood! Why, you wouldn't find another such chameleon in the whole of Russia! I've never seen anything like it in my life, though I know a good bit about women, too. I have known regular devils in my time, but I never met anything like this. It is, as you say, by insolence and cynicism she gets over you. What is so attractive in her is the diabolical suddenness, the quick transitions, the swift shifting hues. . . . Brrr! And the IOU - phew! Write it off for lost. We are both great sinners, we'll go halves in our sin. I shall put down to you not two thousand three hundred, but half of it. Mind, tell my wife I was at the tenant's."

Kryukov and the lieutenant buried their heads in the pillows, and broke into laughter; they raised their heads, glanced at one another, and again subsided into their pillows.

"Engaged! A lieutenant!" Kryukov jeered.

"Married!" retorted Sokolsky. "Highly respected! Father of a family!"

At dinner they talked in veiled allusions, winked at one another, and, to the surprise of the others, were continually gushing with laughter into their dinner-napkins. After dinner, still in the best of spirits, they dressed up as Turks, and, running after one another with guns, played at soldiers with the children. In the evening they had a long argument. The lieutenant maintained that it was mean and contemptible to accept a dowry with your wife, even when there was passionate love on both sides. Kryukov thumped the table with his fists and declared that this was absurd, and that a husband who did not like his wife to have property of her own was an egoist and a despot. Both shouted, boiled over, did not understand each other, drank a good deal, and in the end, picking up the skirts of their dressing-gowns, went to their bedrooms. They soon fell asleep and slept soundly.

Life went on as before, even, sluggish and free from sorrow. The shadows lay on the earth, thunder pealed from the clouds, from time to time the wind moaned plaintively, as though to prove that nature, too, could lament, but nothing troubled the habitual tranquillity of these people. Of Susanna Moiseyevna and the IOUs they said nothing. Both of them felt, somehow, ashamed to speak of the incident aloud. Yet they remembered it and thought of it with pleasure, as of a curious farce, which life had unexpectedly and casually played upon them, and which it would be pleasant to recall in old age.

On the sixth or seventh day after his visit to the Jewess, Kryukov was sitting in his study in the morning writing a congratulatory letter to his aunt. Alexandr Grigoryevitch was walking to and fro near the table in silence. The lieutenant had slept badly that night; he woke up depressed, and now he felt bored. He paced up and down, thinking of the end of his furlough, of his fiancée, who was expecting him, of how people could live all their lives in the country without feeling bored. Standing at the window, for a long time he stared at the trees, smoked three cigarettes one after another, and suddenly turned to his cousin.

"I have a favour to ask you, Alyosha," he said. "Let me have a saddle-horse for the day...."

Kryukov looked searchingly at him and continued his writing with a frown.

"You will, then?" asked the lieutenant.

Kryukov looked at him again, then deliberately drew out a drawer in the table, and taking out a thick roll of notes, gave it to his cousin.

"Here's five thousand . . ." he said. "Though it's not my money, yet, God bless you, it's all the same. I advise you to send for post-horses at once and go away. Yes, really!"

The lieutenant in his turn looked searchingly at Kryukov and laughed.

"You've guessed right, Alyosha," he said, reddening. "It was to her I meant to ride. Yesterday evening when the washerwoman gave me that damned tunic, the one I was wearing then, and it smelt of jasmine, why . . . I felt I must go!"

"You must go away."

"Yes, certainly. And my furlough's just over. I really will go to-day! Yes, by Jove! However long one stays, one has to go in the end. . . . I'm going!"

The post-horses were brought after dinner the same day; the lieutenant said good-bye to the Kryukovs and set off, followed by their good wishes.

Another week passed. It was a dull but hot and heavy day. From early morning Kryukov walked aimlessly about the house, looking out of window, or turning over the leaves of albums, though he was sick of the sight of them already. When he came across his wife or children, he began grumbling crossly. It seemed to him, for some reason that day, that his children's manners were revolting, that his wife did not know how to look after the servants, that their expenditure was quite disproportionate to their income. All this meant that "the master" was out of humour.

After dinner, Kryukov, feeling dissatisfied with the soup and the roast meat he had eaten, ordered out his racing droshky. He drove slowly out of the courtyard, drove at a walking pace for a quarter of a mile, and stopped.

"Shall I . . . drive to her . . . that devil?" he thought, looking at the leaden sky.

And Kryukov positively laughed, as though it were the first time that day he had asked himself that question. At once the load of boredom was lifted from his heart, and there rose a gleam of pleasure in his lazy eyes. He lashed the horse. . . .

All the way his imagination was picturing how surprised the Jewess would be to see him, how he would laugh and chat, and come home feeling refreshed. . . .

"Once a month one needs something to brighten one up . . . something out of the common round," he thought, "something that would give the stagnant organism a good shaking up, a reaction . . . whether it's a drinking bout, or . . . Susanna. One can't get on without it."

It was getting dark when he drove into the yard of the vodka distillery. From the open windows of the owner's house came sounds of laughter and singing:

" 'Brighter than lightning, more burning than flame. . . .' "

sang a powerful, mellow, bass voice.

"Aha! she has visitors," thought Kryukov.

And he was annoyed that she had visitors.

"Shall I go back?" he thought with his hand on the bell, but he rang all the same, and went up the familiar staircase. From the entry he glanced into the reception hall. There were about five men there - all landowners and officials of his acquaintance; one, a tall, thin gentleman, was sitting at the piano, singing, and striking the keys with his long, thin fingers. The others were listening and grinning with enjoyment. Kryukov looked himself up and down in the looking-glass, and was about to go into the hall, when Susanna Moiseyevna herself darted into the entry, in high spirits and wearing the same black dress. .

. . Seeing Kryukov, she was petrified for an instant, then she uttered a little scream and beamed with delight.

"Is it you?" she said, clutching his hand. "What a surprise!"

"Here she is!" smiled Kryukov, putting his arm round her waist. "Well! Does the destiny of Europe still lie in the hands of the French and the Russians?"

"I'm so glad," laughed the Jewess, cautiously removing his arm. "Come, go into the hall; they're all friends there. . . . I'll go and tell them to bring you some tea. Your name's Alexey, isn't it? Well, go in, I'll come directly. . . ."

She blew him a kiss and ran out of the entry, leaving behind her the same sickly smell of jasmine. Kryukov raised his head and walked into the hall. He was on terms of friendly intimacy with all the men in the room, but scarcely nodded to them; they, too, scarcely responded, as though the places in which they met were not quite decent, and as though they were in tacit agreement with one another that it was more suitable for them not to recognise one another.

From the hall Kryukov walked into the drawing-room, and from it into a second drawing-room. On the way he met three or four other guests, also men whom he knew, though they barely recognised him. Their faces were flushed with drink and merriment. Alexey Ivanovitch glanced furtively at them and marvelled that these men, respectable heads of families, who had known sorrow and privation, could demean themselves to such pitiful, cheap gaiety! He shrugged his shoulders, smiled, and walked on.

"There are places," he reflected, "where a sober man feels sick, and a drunken man rejoices. I remember I never could go to the operetta or the gipsies when I was sober: wine makes a man more good-natured and reconciles him with vice. . . ."

Suddenly he stood still, petrified, and caught hold of the door-post with both hands. At the writing-table in Susanna's study was sitting Lieutenant Alexandr Grigoryevitch. He was discussing something in an undertone with a fat, flabby looking Jew, and seeing his cousin, flushed crimson and looked down at an album.

The sense of decency was stirred in Kryukov and the blood rushed to his head. Overwhelmed with amazement, shame, and anger, he walked up to the table without a word. Sokolsky's head sank lower than ever. His face worked with an expression of agonising shame.

"Ah, it's you, Alyosha!" he articulated, making a desperate effort to raise his eyes and to smile. "I called here to say good-bye, and, as you see. . . . But to-morrow I am certainly going."

"What can I say to him? What?" thought Alexey Ivanovitch. "How can I judge him since I'm here myself?"

And clearing his throat without uttering a word, he went out slowly.

" 'Call her not heavenly, and leave her on earth. . . .' "

The bass was singing in the hall. A little while after, Kryukov's racing droshky was bumping along the dusty road.

# DREAMS

Two peasant constables - one a stubby, black-bearded individual with such exceptionally short legs that if you looked at him from behind it seemed as though his legs began much lower down than in other people; the other, long, thin, and straight as a stick, with a scanty beard of dark reddish colour - were escorting to the district town a tramp who refused to remember his name. The first waddled along, looking from side to side, chewing now a straw, now his own sleeve, slapping himself on the haunches and humming, and altogether had a careless and frivolous air; the other, in spite of his lean face and narrow shoulders, looked solid, grave, and substantial; in the lines and expression of his whole figure he was like the priests among the Old Believers, or the warriors who are painted on old-fashioned ikons. "For his wisdom God had added to his forehead" - that is, he was bald - which increased the resemblance referred to. The first was called Andrey Ptaha, the second Nikandr Sapozhnikov.

The man they were escorting did not in the least correspond with the conception everyone has of a tramp. He was a frail little man, weak and sickly-looking, with small, colourless, and extremely indefinite features. His eyebrows were scanty, his expression mild and submissive; he had scarcely a trace of a moustache, though he was over thirty. He walked along timidly, bent forward, with his hands thrust into his sleeves. The collar of his shabby cloth overcoat, which did not look like a peasant's, was turned up to the very brim of his cap, so that only his little red nose ventured to peep out into the light of day. He spoke in an ingratiating tenor, continually coughing. It was very, very difficult to believe that he was a tramp concealing his surname. He was more like an unsuccessful priest's son, stricken by God and reduced to beggary; a clerk discharged for drunkenness; a merchant's son or nephew who had tried his feeble powers in a theatrical career, and was now going home to play the last act in the parable of the prodigal son; perhaps, judging by the dull patience with which he struggled with the hopeless autumn mud, he might have been a fanatical monk, wandering from one Russian monastery to another, continually seeking "a peaceful life, free from sin," and not finding it. . . .

The travellers had been a long while on their way, but they seemed to be always on the same small patch of ground. In front of them there stretched thirty feet of muddy black-brown mud, behind them the same, and wherever one looked further, an impenetrable wall of white fog. They went on and on, but the ground remained the same, the wall was no nearer, and the patch on which they walked seemed still the same patch. They got a glimpse of a white, clumsy-looking stone, a small ravine, or a bundle of hay dropped by a passer-by, the brief glimmer of a great muddy puddle, or, suddenly, a shadow with vague outlines would come into view ahead of them; the nearer they got to it the smaller and darker it became; nearer still, and there stood up before the wayfarers a slanting milestone with the number rubbed off, or a wretched birch-tree drenched and bare like a wayside beggar. The birch-tree would whisper something with what remained of its yellow leaves, one leaf would break off and float lazily to the ground. . . . And then again fog, mud, the brown grass at the edges of the road. On the grass hung dingy, unfriendly tears. They were not the tears of soft joy such as the earth weeps at welcoming the summer sun and parting from it, and such as she gives to drink at dawn to the corncrakes, quails, and graceful, long-beaked crested snipes. The travellers' feet stuck in the heavy, clinging mud. Every step cost an effort.

Andrey Ptaha was somewhat excited. He kept looking round at the tramp and trying to understand how a live, sober man could fail to remember his name.

"You are an orthodox Christian, aren't you?" he asked.

"Yes," the tramp answered mildly.

"H'm. . . then you've been christened?"

"Why, to be sure! I'm not a Turk. I go to church and to the sacrament, and do not eat meat when it is forbidden. And I observe my religious duties punctually. . . ."

"Well, what are you called, then?"

"Call me what you like, good man."

Ptaha shrugged his shoulders and slapped himself on the haunches in extreme perplexity. The other constable, Nikandr Sapozhnikov, maintained a staid silence. He was not so naïve as Ptaha, and apparently knew very well the reasons which might induce an orthodox Christian to conceal his name from other people. His expressive face was cold and stern. He walked apart and did not condescend to idle chatter with his companions, but, as it were, tried to show everyone, even the fog, his sedateness and discretion.

"God knows what to make of you," Ptaha persisted in addressing the tramp. "Peasant you are not, and gentleman you are not, but some sort of a thing between. . . . The other day I was washing a sieve in the pond and caught a reptile - see, as long as a finger, with gills and a tail. The first minute I thought it was a fish, then I looked - and, blow it! if it hadn't paws. It was not a fish, it was a viper, and the deuce only knows what it was. . . . So that's like you. . . . What's your calling?"

"I am a peasant and of peasant family," sighed the tramp. "My mamma was a house serf. I don't look like a peasant, that's true, for such has been my lot, good man. My mamma was a nurse with the gentry, and had every comfort, and as I was of her flesh and blood, I lived with her in the master's house. She petted and spoiled me, and did her best to take me out of my humble class and make a gentleman of me. I slept in a bed, every day I ate a real dinner, I wore breeches and shoes like a gentleman's child. What my mamma ate I was fed on, too; they gave her stuffs as a present, and she dressed me up in them. . . . We lived well! I ate so many sweets and cakes in my childish years that if they could be sold now it would be enough to buy a good horse. Mamma taught me to read and write, she instilled the fear of God in me from my earliest years, and she so trained me that now I can't bring myself to utter an unrefined peasant word. And I don't drink vodka, my lad, and am neat in my dress, and know how to behave with decorum in good society. If she is still living, God give her health; and if she is dead, then, O Lord, give her soul peace in Thy Kingdom, wherein the just are at rest."

The tramp bared his head with the scanty hair standing up like a brush on it, turned his eyes upward and crossed himself twice.

"Grant her, O Lord, a verdant and peaceful resting-place," he said in a drawling voice, more like an old woman's than a man's. "Teach Thy servant Xenia Thy justifications, O Lord! If it had not been for my beloved mamma I should have been a peasant with no sort of understanding! Now, young man, ask me about anything and I understand it all: the holy Scriptures and profane writings, and every prayer and catechism. I live according to the Scriptures. . . . I don't injure anyone, I keep my flesh in purity and continence, I observe the fasts, I eat at fitting times. Another man will take no pleasure in anything but vodka and lewd talk, but when I have time I sit in a corner and read a book. I read and I weep and weep."

"What do you weep for?"

"They write so pathetically! For some books one gives but a five-kopeck piece, and yet one weeps and sighs exceedingly over it."

"Is your father dead?" asked Ptaha.

"I don't know, good man. I don't know my parent; it is no use concealing it. I judge that I was mamma's illegitimate son. My mamma lived all her life with the gentry, and did not want to marry a simple peasant. . . ."

"And so she fell into the master's hands," laughed Ptaha.

"She did transgress, that's true. She was pious, God-fearing, but she did not keep her maiden purity. It is a sin, of course, a great sin, there's no doubt about it, but to make up for it there is, maybe, noble blood in me. Maybe I am only a peasant by class, but in nature a noble gentleman."

The "noble gentleman" uttered all this in a soft, sugary tenor, wrinkling up his narrow forehead and emitting creaking sounds from his red, frozen little nose. Ptaha listened and looked askance at him in wonder, continually shrugging his shoulders.

After going nearly five miles the constables and the tramp sat down on a mound to rest.

"Even a dog knows his name," Ptaha muttered. "My name is Andryushka, his is Nikandr; every man has his holy name, and it can't be forgotten. Nohow."

"Who has any need to know my name?" sighed the tramp, leaning his cheek on his fist. "And what advantage would it be to me if they did know it? If I were allowed to go where I would - but it would only make things worse. I know the law, Christian brothers. Now I am a tramp who doesn't remember his name, and it's the very most if they send me to Eastern Siberia and give me thirty or forty lashes; but if I were to tell them my real name and description they would send me back to hard labour, I know!"

"Why, have you been a convict?"

"I have, dear friend. For four years I went about with my head shaved and fetters on my legs."

"What for?"

"For murder, my good man! When I was still a boy of eighteen or so, my mamma accidentally poured arsenic instead of soda and acid into my master's glass. There were boxes of all sorts in the storeroom, numbers of them; it was easy to make a mistake over them."

The tramp sighed, shook his head, and said:

"She was a pious woman, but, who knows? another man's soul is a slumbering forest! It may have been an accident, or maybe she could not endure the affront of seeing the master prefer another servant. . . . Perhaps she put it in on purpose, God knows! I was young then, and did not understand it all . . . now I remember that our master had taken another mistress and mamma was greatly disturbed. Our trial lasted nearly two years. . . . Mamma was condemned to penal servitude for twenty years, and I, on account of my youth, only to seven."

"And why were you sentenced?"

"As an accomplice. I handed the glass to the master. That was always the custom. Mamma prepared the soda and I handed it to him. Only I tell you all this as a Christian, brothers, as I would say it before God. Don't you tell anybody. . . ."

"Oh, nobody's going to ask us," said Ptaha. "So you've run away from prison, have you?"

"I have, dear friend. Fourteen of us ran away. Some folks, God bless them! ran away and took me with them. Now you tell me, on your conscience, good man, what reason have I to disclose my name? They will send me back to penal servitude, you know! And I am not fit for penal servitude! I am a refined man in delicate health. I like to sleep and eat in cleanliness. When I pray to God I like to light a little lamp or a candle, and not to have a noise around me. When I bow down to the ground I like the floor not to be dirty or spat upon. And I bow down forty times every morning and evening, praying for mamma."

The tramp took off his cap and crossed himself.

"And let them send me to Eastern Siberia," he said; "I am not afraid of that."

"Surely that's no better?"

"It is quite a different thing. In penal servitude you are like a crab in a basket: crowding, crushing, jostling, there's no room to breathe; it's downright hell - such hell, may the Queen of Heaven keep us from it! You are a robber and treated like a robber - worse than any dog. You can't sleep, you can't eat or even say your prayers. But it's not like that in a settlement. In a settlement I shall be a member of a commune like other people. The authorities are bound by law to give me my share . . . ye-es! They say the land costs nothing, no more than snow; you can take what you like! They will give me corn land and building land and garden. . . . I shall plough my fields like other people, sow seed. I shall have cattle and stock of all sorts, bees, sheep, and dogs. . . . A Siberian cat, that rats and mice may not devour my goods. . . . I will put up a house, I shall buy ikons. . . . Please God, I'll get married, I shall have children. . . ."

The tramp muttered and looked, not at his listeners, but away into the distance. Naïve as his dreams were, they were uttered in such a genuine and heartfelt tone that it was difficult not to believe in them. The tramp's little mouth was screwed up in a smile. His eyes and little nose and his whole face were fixed and blank with blissful anticipation of happiness in the distant future. The constables listened and looked at him gravely, not without sympathy. They, too, believed in his dreams.

"I am not afraid of Siberia," the tramp went on muttering. "Siberia is just as much Russia and has the same God and Tsar as here. They are just as orthodox Christians as you and I. Only there is more freedom there and people are better off. Everything is better there. Take the rivers there, for instance; they are far better than those here. There's no end of fish; and all sorts of wild fowl. And my greatest pleasure, brothers, is fishing. Give me no bread to eat, but let me sit with a fishhook. Yes, indeed! I fish with a hook and with a wire line, and set creels, and when the ice comes I catch with a net. I am not strong to draw up the net, so I shall hire a man for five kopecks. And, Lord, what a pleasure it is! You catch an eel-pout or a roach of some sort and are as pleased as though you had met your own brother. And would you believe it, there's a special art for every fish: you catch one with a live bait, you catch another with a grub, the third with a frog or a grasshopper. One has to understand all that, of course! For example, take the eel-pout. It is not a delicate fish - it will take a perch; and a pike loves a gudgeon, the *shilishper* likes a butterfly. If you fish for a roach in a rapid stream there is no greater pleasure. You throw the line of seventy feet without lead, with a butterfly or a beetle, so that the bait floats on the surface; you stand in the water without your trousers and let it go with the current, and tug! the roach pulls at it! Only you have got to be artful that he doesn't carry off the bait, the damned rascal. As soon as he tugs at your line you must whip it up; it's no good waiting. It's wonderful what a lot of fish I've caught in my time. When we were running away the other convicts would sleep in the forest; I could not sleep, but I was off to the river. The rivers there are wide and rapid, the banks are steep - awfully! It's all slumbering forests on the bank. The trees are so tall that if you look to the top it makes you dizzy. Every pine would be worth ten roubles by the prices here."

In the overwhelming rush of his fancies, of artistic images of the past and sweet presentiments of happiness in the future, the poor wretch sank into silence, merely moving his lips as though whispering to himself. The vacant, blissful smile never left his lips. The constables were silent. They were pondering with bent heads. In the autumn stillness, when the cold, sullen mist that rises from the earth lies like a weight on the heart, when it stands like a prison wall before the eyes, and reminds man of the limitation of his freedom, it is sweet to think of the broad, rapid rivers, with steep banks wild and luxuriant, of the impenetrable forests, of the boundless steppes. Slowly and quietly the fancy pictures how early in the morning, before the flush of dawn has left the sky, a man makes his way along the steep deserted bank like a tiny speck: the ancient, mast-like pines rise up in terraces on both sides of the torrent, gaze sternly at the free man and murmur menacingly; rocks, huge stones, and thorny bushes bar his way, but he is strong in body and bold in spirit, and has no fear of the pine-trees, nor stones, nor of his solitude, nor of the reverberating echo which repeats the sound of every footstep that he takes.

The peasants called up a picture of a free life such as they had never lived; whether they vaguely recalled the images of stories heard long ago or whether notions of a free life had been handed down to them with their flesh and blood from far-off free ancestors, God knows!

The first to break the silence was Nikandr Sapozhnikov, who had not till then let fall a single word. Whether he envied the tramp's transparent happiness, or whether he felt in his heart that dreams of happiness were out of keeping with the grey fog and the dirty brown mud - anyway, he looked sternly at the tramp and said:

"It's all very well, to be sure, only you won't reach those plenteous regions, brother. How could you? Before you'd gone two hundred miles you'd give up your soul to God. Just look what a weakling you are! Here you've hardly gone five miles and you can't get your breath."

The tramp turned slowly toward Nikandr, and the blissful smile vanished from his face. He looked with a scared and guilty air at the peasant's staid face, apparently remembered something, and bent his head. A silence followed again. . . . All three were pondering. The peasants were racking their brains in the effort to grasp in their imagination what can be grasped by none but God - that is, the vast expanse dividing them from the land of freedom. Into the tramp's mind thronged clear and distinct pictures more terrible than that expanse. Before him rose vividly the picture of the long legal delays and procrastinations, the temporary and permanent prisons, the convict boats, the wearisome stoppages on the way, the frozen winters, illnesses, deaths of companions. . . .

The tramp blinked guiltily, wiped the tiny drops of sweat from his forehead with his sleeve, drew a deep breath as though he had just leapt out of a very hot bath, then wiped his forehead with the other sleeve and looked round fearfully.

"That's true; you won't get there!" Ptaha agreed. "You are not much of a walker! Look at you - nothing but skin and bone! You'll die, brother!"

"Of course he'll die! What could he do?" said Nikandr. "He's fit for the hospital now. . . . For sure!"

The man who had forgotten his name looked at the stern, unconcerned faces of his sinister companions, and without taking off his cap, hurriedly crossed himself, staring with wide-open eyes. . . . He trembled, his head shook, and he began twitching all over, like a caterpillar when it is stepped upon. . . .

"Well, it's time to go," said Nikandr, getting up; "we've had a rest."

A minute later they were stepping along the muddy road. The tramp was more bent than ever, and he thrust his hands further up his sleeves. Ptaha was silent.

# HUSH!

Ivan Yegoritch Krasnyhin, a fourth-rate journalist, returns home late at night, grave and careworn, with a peculiar air of concentration. He looks like a man expecting a police-raid or contemplating suicide. Pacing about his rooms he halts abruptly, ruffles up his hair, and says in the tone in which Laertes announces his intention of avenging his sister:

"Shattered, soul-weary, a sick load of misery on the heart . . . and then to sit down and write. And this is called life! How is it nobody has described the agonizing discord in the soul of a writer who has to amuse the crowd when his heart is heavy or to shed tears at the word of command when his heart is light? I must be playful, coldly unconcerned, witty, but what if I am weighed down with misery, what if I am ill, or my child is dying or my wife in anguish!"

He says this, brandishing his fists and rolling his eyes. . . . Then he goes into the bedroom and wakes his wife.

"Nadya," he says, "I am sitting down to write. . . . Please don't let anyone interrupt me. I can't write with children crying or cooks snoring. . . . See, too, that there's tea and . . . steak or something. . . . You know that I can't write without tea. . . . Tea is the one thing that gives me the energy for my work."

Returning to his room he takes off his coat, waistcoat, and boots. He does this very slowly; then, assuming an expression of injured innocence, he sits down to his table.

There is nothing casual, nothing ordinary on his writing-table, down to the veriest trifle everything bears the stamp of a stern, deliberately planned programme. Little busts and photographs of distinguished writers, heaps of rough manuscripts, a volume of Byelinsky with a page turned down, part of a skull by way of an ash-tray, a sheet of newspaper folded carelessly, but so that a passage is uppermost, boldly marked in blue pencil with the word "disgraceful." There are a dozen sharply-pointed pencils and several penholders fitted with new nibs, put in readiness that no accidental breaking of a pen may for a single second interrupt the flight of his creative fancy.

Ivan Yegoritch throws himself back in his chair, and closing his eyes concentrates himself on his subject. He hears his wife shuffling about in her slippers and splitting shavings to heat the samovar. She is hardly awake, that is apparent from the way the knife and the lid of the samovar keep dropping from her hands. Soon the hissing of the samovar and the spluttering of the frying meat reaches him. His wife is still splitting shavings and rattling with the doors and blowers of the stove.

All at once Ivan Yegoritch starts, opens frightened eyes, and begins to sniff the air.

"Heavens! the stove is smoking!" he groans, grimacing with a face of agony. "Smoking! That insufferable woman makes a point of trying to poison me! How, in God's Name, am I to write in such surroundings, kindly tell me that?"

He rushes into the kitchen and breaks into a theatrical wail. When a little later, his wife, stepping cautiously on tiptoe, brings him in a glass of tea, he is sitting in an easy chair as before with his eyes closed, absorbed in his article. He does not stir, drums lightly on his forehead with two fingers, and pretends he is not aware of his wife's presence. . . . His face wears an expression of injured innocence.

Like a girl who has been presented with a costly fan, he spends a long time coquetting, grimacing, and posing to himself before he writes the title. . . . He presses his temples, he wriggles, and draws his legs up under his chair as though he were in pain, or half closes his eyes languidly like a cat on the sofa. At last, not without hesitation, he stretches out his hand towards the inkstand, and with an expression as though he were signing a death-warrant, writes the title. . . .

"Mammy, give me some water!" he hears his son's voice.

"Hush!" says his mother. "Daddy's writing! Hush!"

Daddy writes very, very quickly, without corrections or pauses, he has scarcely time to turn over the pages. The busts and portraits of celebrated authors look at his swiftly racing pen and, keeping stock still, seem to be thinking: "Oh my, how you are going it!"

"Sh!" squeaks the pen.

"Sh!" whisper the authors, when his knee jolts the table and they are set trembling.

All at once Krasnyhin draws himself up, lays down his pen and listens. . . . He hears an even monotonous whispering. . . . It is Foma Nikolaevitch, the lodger in the next room, saying his prayers.

"I say!" cries Krasnyhin. "Couldn't you, please, say your prayers more quietly? You prevent me from writing!"

"Very sorry. . . ." Foma Nikolaevitch answers timidly.

After covering five pages, Krasnyhin stretches and looks at his watch.

"Goodness, three o'clock already," he moans. "Other people are asleep while I . . . I alone must work!"

Shattered and exhausted he goes, with his head on one side, to the bedroom to wake his wife, and says in a languid voice:

"Nadya, get me some more tea! I . . . feel weak."

He writes till four o'clock and would readily have written till six if his subject had not been exhausted. Coquetting and posing to himself and the inanimate objects about him, far from any indiscreet, critical eye, tyrannizing and domineering over the little anthill that fate has put in his power are the honey and the salt of his existence. And how different is this despot here at home from the humble, meek, dull-witted little man we are accustomed to see in the editor's offices!

"I am so exhausted that I am afraid I shan't sleep . . ." he says as he gets into bed. "Our work, this cursed, ungrateful hard labour, exhausts the soul even more than the body. . . . I had better take some bromide. . . . God knows, if it were not for my family I'd throw up the work. . . . To write to order! It is awful."

He sleeps till twelve or one o'clock in the day, sleeps a sound, healthy sleep. . . . Ah! how he would sleep, what dreams he would have, how he would spread himself if he were to become a well-known writer, an editor, or even a sub-editor!

"He has been writing all night," whispers his wife with a scared expression on her face. "Sh!"

No one dares to speak or move or make a sound. His sleep is something sacred, and the culprit who offends against it will pay dearly for his fault.

"Hush!" floats over the flat. "Hush!"

# EXCELLENT PEOPLE

Once upon a time there lived in Moscow a man called Vladimir Semyonitch Liadovsky. He took his degree at the university in the faculty of law and had a post on the board of management of some railway; but if you had asked him what his work was, he would look candidly and openly at you with his large bright eyes through his gold pincenez, and would answer in a soft, velvety, lisping baritone:

"My work is literature."

After completing his course at the university, Vladimir Semyonitch had had a paragraph of theatrical criticism accepted by a newspaper. From this paragraph he passed on to reviewing, and a year later he had advanced to writing a weekly article on literary matters for the same paper. But it does not follow from these facts that he was an amateur, that his literary work was of an ephemeral, haphazard character. Whenever I saw his neat spare figure, his high forehead and long mane of hair, when I listened to his speeches, it always seemed to me that his writing, quite apart from what and how he wrote, was something organically part of him, like the beating of his heart, and that his whole literary programme must have been an integral part of his brain while he was a baby in his mother's womb. Even in his walk, his gestures, his manner of shaking off the ash from his cigarette, I could read this whole programme from A to Z, with all its claptrap, dulness, and honourable sentiments. He was a literary man all over when with an inspired face he laid a wreath on the coffin of some celebrity, or with a grave and solemn face collected signatures for some address; his passion for making the acquaintance of distinguished literary men, his faculty for finding talent even where it was absent, his perpetual enthusiasm, his pulse that went at one hundred and twenty a minute, his ignorance of life, the genuinely feminine flutter with which he threw himself into concerts and literary evenings for the benefit of destitute students, the way in which he gravitated towards the young - all this would have created for him the reputation of a writer even if he had not written his articles.

He was one of those writers to whom phrases like, "We are but few," or "What would life be without strife? Forward!" were pre-eminently becoming, though he never strove with any one and never did go forward. It did not even sound mawkish when he fell to discoursing of ideals. Every anniversary of the university, on St. Tatiana's Day, he got drunk, chanted *Gaudeamus* out of tune, and his beaming and perspiring countenance seemed to say: "See, I'm drunk; I'm keeping it up!" But even that suited him.

Vladimir Semyonitch had genuine faith in his literary vocation and his whole programme. He had no doubts, and was evidently very well pleased with himself. Only one thing grieved him - the paper for which he worked had a limited circulation and was not very influential. But Vladimir Semyonitch believed that sooner or later he would succeed in getting on to a solid magazine where he would have scope and could display himself - and what little distress he felt on this score was pale beside the brilliance of his hopes.

Visiting this charming man, I made the acquaintance of his sister, Vera Semyonovna, a woman doctor. At first sight, what struck me about this woman was her look of exhaustion and extreme ill-health. She was young, with a good figure and regular, rather large features, but in comparison with her agile, elegant, and talkative brother she seemed angular, listless, slovenly, and sullen. There was something strained, cold, apathetic in her movements, smiles, and words; she was not liked, and was thought proud and not very intelligent.

In reality, I fancy, she was resting.

"My dear friend," her brother would often say to me, sighing and flinging back his hair in his picturesque literary way, "one must never judge by appearances! Look at this book: it has long ago been read. It is warped, tattered, and lies in the dust uncared for; but open it, and it will make you weep and turn pale. My sister is like that book. Lift the cover and peep into her soul, and you will be horror-stricken. Vera passed in some three months through experiences that would have been ample for a whole lifetime!"

Vladimir Semyonitch looked round him, took me by the sleeve, and began to whisper:

"You know, after taking her degree she married, for love, an architect. It's a complete tragedy! They had hardly been married a month when - whew — her husband died of typhus. But that was not all. She caught typhus from him, and when, on her recovery, she learnt that her Ivan was dead, she took a good dose of morphia. If it had not been for vigorous measures taken by her friends, my Vera would have been by now in Paradise. Tell me, isn't it a tragedy? And is not my sister like an *ingénue*, who has played already all the five acts of her life? The audience may stay for the farce, but the *ingénue* must go home to rest."

After three months of misery Vera Semyonovna had come to live with her brother. She was not fitted for the practice of medicine, which exhausted her and did not satisfy her; she did not give one the impression of knowing her subject, and I never once heard her say anything referring to her medical studies.

She gave up medicine, and, silent and unoccupied, as though she were a prisoner, spent the remainder of her youth in colourless apathy, with bowed head and hanging hands. The only thing to which she was not completely indifferent, and which brought some brightness into the twilight of her life, was the presence of her brother, whom she loved. She loved him himself and his programme, she was full of reverence for his articles; and when she was asked what her brother was doing, she would answer in a subdued voice as though afraid of waking or distracting him: "He is writing. . . ." Usually when he was at his work she used to sit beside him, her eyes fixed on his writing hand. She used at such moments to look like a sick animal warming itself in the sun. . . .

One winter evening Vladimir Semyonitch was sitting at his table writing a critical article for his newspaper: Vera Semyonovna was sitting beside him, staring as usual at his writing hand. The critic wrote rapidly, without erasures or corrections. The pen scratched and squeaked. On the table near the writing hand there lay open a freshly-cut volume of a thick magazine, containing a story of peasant life, signed with two initials. Vladimir Semyonitch was enthusiastic; he thought the author was admirable in his handling of the subject, suggested Turgenev in his descriptions of nature, was truthful, and had an excellent knowledge of the life of the peasantry. The critic himself knew nothing of peasant life except from books and hearsay, but his feelings and his inner convictions forced him to believe the story. He foretold a brilliant future for the author, assured him he should await the conclusion of the story with great impatience, and so on.

"Fine story!" he said, flinging himself back in his chair and closing his eyes with pleasure. "The tone is extremely good."

Vera Semyonovna looked at him, yawned aloud, and suddenly asked an unexpected question. In the evening she had a habit of yawning nervously and asking short, abrupt questions, not always relevant.

"Volodya," she asked, "what is the meaning of non-resistance to evil?"

"Non-resistance to evil!" repeated her brother, opening his eyes.

"Yes. What do you understand by it?"

"You see, my dear, imagine that thieves or brigands attack you, and you, instead of . . ."

"No, give me a logical definition.

"A logical definition? Um! Well." Vladimir Semyonitch pondered. "Non-resistance to evil means an attitude of non-interference with regard to all that in the sphere of mortality is called evil."

Saying this, Vladimir Semyonitch bent over the table and took up a novel. This novel, written by a woman, dealt with the painfulness of the irregular position of a society lady who was living under the same roof with her lover and her illegitimate child. Vladimir Semyonitch was pleased with the excellent tendency of the story, the plot and the presentation of it. Making a brief summary of the novel, he selected the best passages and added to them in his account: "How true to reality, how living, how picturesque! The author is not merely an artist; he is also a subtle psychologist who can see into the hearts of his characters. Take, for example, this vivid description of the emotions of the heroine on meeting her husband," and so on.

"Volodya," Vera Semyonovna interrupted his critical effusions, "I've been haunted by a strange idea since yesterday. I keep wondering where we should all be if human life were ordered on the basis of non-resistance to evil?"

"In all probability, nowhere. Non-resistance to evil would give the full rein to the criminal will, and, to say nothing of civilisation, this would leave not one stone standing upon another anywhere on earth."

"What would be left?"

"Bashi-Bazouke and brothels. In my next article I'll talk about that perhaps. Thank you for reminding me."

And a week later my friend kept his promise. That was just at the period - in the eighties - when people were beginning to talk and write of non-resistance, of the right to judge, to punish, to make war; when some people in our set were beginning to do without servants, to retire into the country, to work on the land, and to renounce animal food and carnal love.

After reading her brother's article, Vera Semyonovna pondered and hardly perceptibly shrugged her shoulders.

"Very nice!" she said. "But still there's a great deal I don't understand. For instance, in Leskov's story 'Belonging to the Cathedral' there is a queer gardener who sows for the benefit of all - for customers, for beggars, and any who care to steal. Did he behave sensibly?"

From his sister's tone and expression Vladimir Semyonitch saw that she did not like his article, and, almost for the first time in his life, his vanity as an author sustained a shock. With a shade of irritation he answered:

"Theft is immoral. To sow for thieves is to recognise the right of thieves to existence. What would you think if I were to establish a newspaper and, dividing it into sections, provide for blackmailing as well as for liberal ideas? Following the example of that gardener, I ought, logically, to provide a section for blackmailers, the intellectual scoundrels? Yes."

Vera Semyonovna made no answer. She got up from the table, moved languidly to the sofa and lay down.

"I don't know, I know nothing about it," she said musingly. "You are probably right, but it seems to me, I feel somehow, that there's something false in our resistance to evil, as though there were something concealed or unsaid. God knows, perhaps our methods of resisting evil belong to the category of prejudices which have become so deeply rooted in us, that we are incapable of parting with them, and therefore cannot form a correct judgment of them."

"How do you mean?"

"I don't know how to explain to you. Perhaps man is mistaken in thinking that he is obliged to resist evil and has a right to do so, just as he is mistaken in thinking, for instance, that the heart looks like an ace of hearts. It is very possible in resisting evil we ought not to use force, but to use what is the very opposite of force - if you, for instance, don't want this picture stolen from you, you ought to give it away rather than lock it up...."

"That's clever, very clever! If I want to marry a rich, vulgar woman, she ought to prevent me from such a shabby action by hastening to make me an offer herself!"

The brother and sister talked till midnight without understanding each other. If any outsider had overheard them he would hardly have been able to make out what either of them was driving at.

They usually spent the evening at home. There were no friends' houses to which they could go, and they felt no need for friends; they only went to the theatre when there was a new play - such was the custom in literary circles - they did not go to concerts, for they did not care for music.

"You may think what you like," Vera Semyonovna began again the next day, "but for me the question is to a great extent settled. I am firmly convinced that I have no grounds for resisting evil directed against me personally. If they want to kill me, let them. My defending myself will not make the murderer better. All I have now to decide is the second half of the question: how I ought to behave to evil directed against my neighbours?"

"Vera, mind you don't become rabid! "said Vladimir Semyonitch, laughing. " I see non-resistance is becoming your *idée fixe!*"

He wanted to turn off these tedious conversations with a jest, but somehow it was beyond a jest; his smile was artificial and sour. His sister gave up sitting beside his table and gazing reverently at his writing hand, and he felt every evening that behind him on the sofa lay a person who did not agree with him. And his back grew stiff and numb, and there was a chill in his soul. An author's vanity is vindictive, implacable, incapable of forgiveness, and his sister was the first and only person who had laid bare and disturbed that uneasy feeling, which is like a big box of crockery, easy to unpack but impossible to pack up again as it was before.

Weeks and months passed by, and his sister clung to her ideas, and did not sit down by the table. One spring evening Vladimir Semyonitch was sitting at his table writing an article. He was reviewing a novel which described how a village schoolmistress refused the man whom she loved and who loved her, a man both wealthy and intellectual, simply because marriage made her work as a schoolmistress impossible. Vera Semyonovna lay on the sofa and brooded.

"My God, how slow it is!" she said, stretching. "How insipid and empty life is! I don't know what to do with myself, and you are wasting your best years in goodness knows what. Like some alchemist, you are rummaging in old rubbish that nobody wants. My God!"

Vladimir Semyonitch dropped his pen and slowly looked round at his sister.

"It's depressing to look at you!" said his sister. "Wagner in 'Faust' dug up worms, but he was looking for a treasure, anyway, and you are looking for worms for the sake of the worms."

"That's vague!"

"Yes, Volodya; all these days I've been thinking, I've been thinking painfully for a long time, and I have come to the conclusion that you are hopelessly reactionary and conventional. Come, ask yourself what is the object of your zealous, conscientious work? Tell me, what is it? Why, everything has long ago been extracted that can be extracted from that rubbish in which you are always rummaging. You may pound water in a mortar and analyse it as long as you like, you'll make nothing more of it than the chemists have made already...."

"Indeed!" drawled Vladimir Semyonitch, getting up. "Yes, all this is old rubbish because these ideas are eternal; but what do you consider new, then?"

"You undertake to work in the domain of thought; it is for you to think of something new. It's not for me to teach you."

"Me - an alchemist!" the critic cried in wonder and indignation, screwing up his eyes ironically. "Art, progress - all that is alchemy?"

"You see, Volodya, it seems to me that if all you thinking people had set yourselves to solving great problems, all these little questions that you fuss about now would solve themselves by the way. If you go up in a balloon to see a town, you will incidentally, without any effort, see the fields and the villages and the rivers as well. When stearine is manufactured, you get glycerine as a by-product. It seems to me that contemporary thought has settled on one spot and stuck to it. It is prejudiced, apathetic, timid, afraid to take a wide titanic flight, just as you and I are afraid to climb on a high mountain; it is conservative."

Such conversations could not but leave traces. The relations of the brother and sister grew more and more strained every day. The brother became unable to work in his sister's presence, and grew irritable when he knew his sister was lying on the sofa, looking at his back; while the sister frowned nervously and stretched when, trying to bring back the past, he attempted to share his enthusiasms with her. Every evening she complained of being bored, and talked about independence of mind and those who are in the rut of tradition. Carried away by her new ideas, Vera Semyonovna proved that the work that her brother was so engrossed in was conventional, that it was a vain effort of conservative minds to preserve what had already served its turn and was vanishing from the scene of action. She made no end of comparisons. She compared her brother at one time to an alchemist, then to a musty old Believer who would sooner die than listen to reason. By degrees there was a perceptible change in her manner of life, too. She was capable of lying on the sofa all day long doing nothing but think, while her face wore a cold, dry expression such as one sees in one-sided people of strong faith. She began to refuse the attentions of the servants, swept and tidied her own room, cleaned her own boots and brushed her own clothes. Her brother could not help looking with irritation and even hatred at her cold face when she went about her menial work. In that work, which was always performed with a certain solemnity, he saw something strained and false, he saw something both pharisaical and affected. And knowing he could not touch her by persuasion, he carped at her and teased her like a schoolboy.

"You won't resist evil, but you resist my having servants!" he taunted her. "If servants are an evil, why do you oppose it? That's inconsistent!"

He suffered, was indignant and even ashamed. He felt ashamed when his sister began doing odd things before strangers.

"It's awful, my dear fellow," he said to me in private, waving his hands in despair. "It seems that our *ingénue* has remained to play a part in the farce, too. She's become morbid to the marrow of her bones! I've washed my hands of her, let her think as she likes; but why does she talk, why does she excite me? She ought to think what it means for me to listen to her. What I feel when in my presence she has the effrontery to support her errors by blasphemously quoting the teaching of Christ! It chokes me! It makes me hot all over to hear my sister propounding her doctrines and trying to distort the Gospel to suit her, when she purposely refrains from mentioning how the moneychangers were driven out of the Temple. That's, my dear fellow, what comes of being half educated, undeveloped! That's what comes of medical studies which provide no general culture!"

One day on coming home from the office, Vladimir Semyonitch found his sister crying. She was sitting on the sofa with her head bowed, wringing her hands, and tears were flowing freely down her cheeks. The critic's good heart throbbed with pain. Tears fell from his eyes, too, and he longed to pet his sister, to forgive her, to beg her forgiveness, and to live as they used to before. . . . He knelt down and kissed her head, her hands, her shoulders. . . . She smiled, smiled bitterly, unaccountably, while he with a cry of joy jumped up, seized the magazine from the table and said warmly:

"Hurrah! We'll live as we used to, Verotchka! With God's blessing! And I've such a surprise for you here! Instead of celebrating the occasion with champagne, let us read it together! A splendid, wonderful thing!"

"Oh, no, no!" cried Vera Semyonovna, pushing away the book in alarm. "I've read it already! I don't want it, I don't want it!"

"When did you read it?"

"A year . . . two years ago. . . . I read it long ago, and I know it, I know it!"

"H'm! . . . You're a fanatic!" her brother said coldly, flinging the magazine on to the table.

"No, you are a fanatic, not I! You!" And Vera Semyonovna dissolved into tears again. Her brother stood before her, looked at her quivering shoulders, and thought. He thought, not of the agonies of loneliness endured by any one who begins to think in a new way of their own, not of the inevitable sufferings of a genuine spiritual revolution, but of the outrage of his programme, the outrage to his author's vanity.

From this time he treated his sister coldly, with careless irony, and he endured her presence in the room as one endures the presence of old women that are dependent on one. For her part, she left off disputing with him and met all his arguments, jeers, and attacks with a condescending silence which irritated him more than ever.

One summer morning Vera Semyonovna, dressed for travelling with a satchel over her shoulder, went in to her brother and coldly kissed him on the forehead.

"Where are you going?" he asked with surprise.

"To the province of N. to do vaccination work." Her brother went out into the street with her.

"So that's what you've decided upon, you queer girl," he muttered. "Don't you want some money?"

"No, thank you. Good-bye."

The sister shook her brother's hand and set off.

"Why don't you have a cab?" cried Vladimir Semyonitch.

She did not answer. Her brother gazed after her, watched her rusty-looking waterproof, the swaying of her figure as she slouched along, forced himself to sigh, but did not succeed in rousing a feeling of regret. His sister had become a stranger to him. And he was a stranger to her. Anyway, she did not once look round.

Going back to his room, Vladimir Semyonitch at once sat down to the table and began to work at his article.

I never saw Vera Semyonovna again. Where she is now I do not know. And Vladimir Semyonitch went on writing his articles, laying wreaths on coffins, singing *Gaudeamus*, busying himself over the Mutual Aid Society of Moscow Journalists.

He fell ill with inflammation of the lungs; he was ill in bed for three months - at first at home, and afterwards in the Golitsyn Hospital. An abscess developed in his knee. People said he ought to be sent to the Crimea, and began getting up a collection for him. But he did not go to the Crimea - he died. We buried him in the Vagankovsky Cemetery, on the left side, where artists and literary men are buried.

One day we writers were sitting in the Tatars' restaurant. I mentioned that I had lately been in the Vagankovsky Cemetery and had seen Vladimir Semyonitch's grave there. It was utterly neglected and almost indistinguishable from the rest of the ground, the cross had fallen; it was necessary to collect a few roubles to put it in order.

But they listened to what I said unconcernedly, made no answer, and I could not collect a farthing. No one remembered Vladimir Semyonitch. He was utterly forgotten.

## AN INCIDENT

Morning. Brilliant sunshine is piercing through the frozen lacework on the window-panes into the nursery. Vanya, a boy of six, with a cropped head and a nose like a button, and his sister Nina, a short, chubby, curly-headed girl of four, wake up and look crossly at each other through the bars of their cots.

"Oo-oo-oo! naughty children!" grumbles their nurse. "Good people have had their breakfast already, while you can't get your eyes open."

The sunbeams frolic over the rugs, the walls, and nurse's skirts, and seem inviting the children to join in their play, but they take no notice. They have woken up in a bad humour. Nina pouts, makes a grimace, and begins to whine:

"Brea-eakfast, nurse, breakfast!"

Vanya knits his brows and ponders what to pitch upon to howl over. He has already begun screwing up his eyes and opening his mouth, but at that instant the voice of mamma reaches them from the drawing-room, saying: "Don't forget to give the cat her milk, she has a family now!"

The children's puckered countenances grow smooth again as they look at each other in astonishment. Then both at once begin shouting, jump out of their cots, and filling the air with piercing shrieks, run barefoot, in their nightgowns, to the kitchen.

"The cat has puppies!" they cry. "The cat has got puppies!"

Under the bench in the kitchen there stands a small box, the one in which Stepan brings coal when he lights the fire. The cat is peeping out of the box. There is an expression of extreme exhaustion on her grey face; her green eyes, with their narrow black pupils, have a languid, sentimental look. From her face it is clear that the only thing lacking to complete her happiness is the presence in the box of "him," the father of her children, to whom she had abandoned herself so recklessly! She wants to mew, and opens her mouth wide, but nothing but a hiss comes from her throat; the squealing of the kittens is audible.

The children squat on their heels before the box, and, motionless, holding their breath, gaze at the cat. . . . They are surprised, impressed, and do not hear nurse grumbling as she pursues them. The most genuine delight shines in the eyes of both.

Domestic animals play a scarcely noticed but undoubtedly beneficial part in the education and life of children. Which of us does not remember powerful but magnanimous dogs, lazy lapdogs, birds dying in captivity, dull-witted but haughty turkeys, mild old tabby cats, who forgave us when we trod on their tails for fun and caused them agonising pain? I even fancy, sometimes, that the patience, the fidelity, the readiness to forgive, and the sincerity which are characteristic of our domestic animals have a far stronger and more definite effect on the mind of a child than the long exhortations of some dry, pale Karl Karlovitch, or the misty expositions of a governess, trying to prove to children that water is made up of hydrogen and oxygen.

"What little things!" says Nina, opening her eyes wide and going off into a joyous laugh. "They are like mice!"

"One, two, three," Vanya counts. "Three kittens. So there is one for you, one for me, and one for somebody else, too."

"Murrm . . . murrm . . ." purrs the mother, flattered by their attention. "Murrm."

After gazing at the kittens, the children take them from under the cat, and begin squeezing them in their hands, then, not satisfied with this, they put them in the skirts of their nightgowns, and run into the other rooms.

"Mamma, the cat has got pups!" they shout.

Mamma is sitting in the drawing-room with some unknown gentleman. Seeing the children unwashed, undressed, with their nightgowns held up high, she is embarrassed, and looks at them severely.

"Let your nightgowns down, disgraceful children," she says. "Go out of the room, or I will punish you."

But the children do not notice either mamma's threats or the presence of a stranger. They put the kittens down on the carpet, and go off into deafening squeals. The mother walks round them, mewing imploringly. When, a little afterwards, the children are dragged off to the nursery, dressed, made to say their prayers, and given their breakfast, they are full of a passionate desire to get away from these prosaic duties as quickly as possible, and to run to the kitchen again.

Their habitual pursuits and games are thrown completely into the background.

The kittens throw everything into the shade by making their appearance in the world, and supply the great sensation of the day. If Nina or Vanya had been offered forty pounds of sweets or ten thousand kopecks for each kitten, they would have rejected such a barter without the slightest hesitation. In spite of the heated protests of the nurse and the cook, the children persist in sitting by the cat's box in the kitchen, busy with the kittens till dinner-time. Their faces are earnest and concentrated and express anxiety. They are worried not so much by the present as by the future of the kittens. They decide that one kitten shall remain at home with the old cat to be a comfort to her mother, while the second shall go to their summer villa, and the third shall live in the cellar, where there are ever so many rats.

"But why don't they look at us?" Nina wondered. "Their eyes are blind like the beggars'."

Vanya, too, is perturbed by this question. He tries to open one kitten's eyes, and spends a long time puffing and breathing hard over it, but his operation is unsuccessful. They are a good deal troubled, too, by the circumstance that the kittens obstinately refuse the milk and the meat that is offered to them. Everything that is put before their little noses is eaten by their grey mamma.

"Let's build the kittens little houses," Vanya suggests. "They shall live in different houses, and the cat shall come and pay them visits."

Cardboard hat-boxes are put in the different corners of the kitchen and the kittens are installed in them. But this division turns out to be premature; the cat, still wearing an imploring and sentimental expression on her face, goes the round of all the hat-boxes, and carries off her children to their original position.

"The cat's their mother," observed Vanya, "but who is their father?"

"Yes, who is their father? " repeats Nina.

"They must have a father."

Vanya and Nina are a long time deciding who is to be the kittens' father, and, in the end, their choice falls on a big dark-red horse without a tail, which is lying in the store-cupboard under the stairs, together with other relics of toys that have outlived their day. They drag him up out of the store-cupboard and stand him by the box.

"Mind now!" they admonish him, "stand here and see they behave themselves properly."

All this is said and done in the gravest way, with an expression of anxiety on their faces. Vanya and Nina refuse to recognise the existence of any world but the box of kittens. Their joy knows no bounds. But they have to pass through bitter, agonising moments, too.

Just before dinner, Vanya is sitting in his father's study, gazing dreamily at the table. A kitten is moving about by the lamp, on stamped note paper. Vanya is watching its movements, and thrusting first a pencil, then a match into its little mouth. . . . All at once, as though he has sprung out of the floor, his father is beside the table.

"What's this?" Vanya hears, in an angry voice.

"It's . . . it's the kitty, papa. . . ."

"I'll give it you; look what you have done, you naughty boy! You've dirtied all my paper!"

To Vanya's great surprise his papa does not share his partiality for the kittens, and, instead of being moved to enthusiasm and delight, he pulls Vanya's ear and shouts:

"Stepan, take away this horrid thing."

At dinner, too, there is a scene. . . . During the second course there is suddenly the sound of a shrill mew. They begin to investigate its origin, and discover a kitten under Nina's pinafore.

"Nina, leave the table!" cries her father angrily. "Throw the kittens in the cesspool! I won't have the nasty things in the house! . . ."

Vanya and Nina are horrified. Death in the cesspool, apart from its cruelty, threatens to rob the cat and the wooden horse of their children, to lay waste the cat's box, to destroy their plans for the future, that fair future in which one cat will be a comfort to its old mother, another will live in the country, while the third will catch rats in the cellar. The children begin to cry and entreat that the kittens may be spared. Their father consents, but on the condition that the children do not go into the kitchen and touch the kittens.

After dinner, Vanya and Nina slouch about the rooms, feeling depressed. The prohibition of visits to the kitchen has reduced them to dejection. They refuse sweets, are naughty, and are rude to their mother. When their uncle Petrusha comes in the evening, they draw him aside, and complain to him of their father, who wanted to throw the kittens into the cesspool.

"Uncle Petrusha, tell mamma to have the kittens taken to the nursery," the children beg their uncle, "do-o tell her."

"There, there . . . very well," says their uncle, waving them off. "All right."

Uncle Petrusha does not usually come alone. He is accompanied by Nero, a big black dog of Danish breed, with drooping ears, and a tail as hard as a stick. The dog is silent, morose, and full of a sense of his own dignity. He takes not the slightest notice of the children, and when he passes them hits them with his tail as though they were chairs. The children hate him from the bottom of their hearts, but on this occasion, practical considerations override sentiment.

"I say, Nina," says Vanya, opening his eyes wide. "Let Nero be their father, instead of the horse! The horse is dead and he is alive, you see."

They are waiting the whole evening for the moment when papa will sit down to his cards and it will be possible to take Nero to the kitchen without being observed. . . . At last, papa sits down to cards, mamma is busy with the samovar and not noticing the children. . . .

The happy moment arrives.

"Come along!" Vanya whispers to his sister.

But, at that moment, Stepan comes in and, with a snigger, announces:

"Nero has eaten the kittens, madam."

Nina and Vanya turn pale and look at Stepan with horror.

"He really has . . ." laughs the footman, "he went to the box and gobbled them up."

The children expect that all the people in the house will be aghast and fall upon the miscreant Nero. But they all sit calmly in their seats, and only express surprise at the appetite of the huge dog. Papa and mamma laugh. Nero walks about by the table, wags his tail, and licks his lips complacently . . . the cat is the only one who is uneasy. With her tail in the air she walks about the rooms, looking suspiciously at people and mewing plaintively.

Children, it's past nine," cries mamma, "it's bedtime."

Vanya and Nina go to bed, shed tears, and spend a long time thinking about the injured cat, and the cruel, insolent, and unpunished Nero.

# THE ORATOR

One fine morning the collegiate assessor, Kirill Ivanovitch Babilonov, who had died of the two afflictions so widely spread in our country, a bad wife and alcoholism, was being buried. As the funeral procession set off from the church to the cemetery, one of the deceased's colleagues, called Poplavsky, got into a cab and galloped off to find a friend, one Grigory Petrovitch Zapoikin, a man who though still young had acquired considerable popularity. Zapoikin, as many of my readers are aware, possesses a rare talent for impromptu speechifying at weddings, jubilees, and funerals. He can speak whenever he likes: in his sleep, on an empty stomach, dead drunk or in a high fever. His words flow smoothly and evenly, like water out of a pipe, and in abundance; there are far more moving words in his oratorical dictionary than there are beetles in any restaurant. He always speaks eloquently and at great length, so much so that on some occasions, particularly at merchants' weddings, they have to resort to assistance from the police to stop him.

"I have come for you, old man!" began Poplavsky, finding him at home. "Put on your hat and coat this minute and come along. One of our fellows is dead, we are just sending him off to the other world, so you must do a bit of palavering by way of farewell to him. . . . You are our only hope. If it had been one of the smaller fry it would not have been worth troubling you, but you see it's the secretary . . . a pillar of the office, in a sense. It's awkward for such a whopper to be buried without a speech."

"Oh, the secretary!" yawned Zapoikin. "You mean the drunken one?"

"Yes. There will be pancakes, a lunch . . . you'll get your cab-fare. Come along, dear chap. You spout out some rigmarole like a regular Cicero at the grave and what gratitude you will earn!"

Zapoikin readily agreed. He ruffled up his hair, cast a shade of melancholy over his face, and went out into the street with Poplavsky.

"I know your secretary," he said, as he got into the cab. "A cunning rogue and a beast - the kingdom of heaven be his - such as you don't often come across."

"Come, Grisha, it is not the thing to abuse the dead."

"Of course not, *aut mortuis nihil bene,* but still he was a rascal."

The friends overtook the funeral procession and joined it. The coffin was borne along slowly so that before they reached the cemetery they were able three times to drop into a tavern and imbibe a little to the health of the departed.

In the cemetery came the service by the graveside. The mother-in-law, the wife, and the sister-in-law in obedience to custom shed many tears. When the coffin was being lowered into the grave the wife even shrieked "Let me go with him!" but did not follow her husband into the grave probably recollecting her pension. Waiting till everything was quiet again Zapoikin stepped forward, turned his eyes on all present, and began:

"Can I believe my eyes and ears? Is it not a terrible dream this grave, these tear-stained faces, these moans and lamentations? Alas, it is not a dream and our eyes do not deceive us! He whom we have only so lately seen, so full of courage, so youthfully fresh and pure, who so lately before our eyes like an unwearying bee bore his honey to the common hive of the welfare of the state, he who . . . he is turned now to dust, to inanimate mirage. Inexorable death has laid his bony hand upon him at the time when, in spite of his bowed age, he was still full of the bloom of strength and radiant hopes. An irremediable loss! Who will fill his place for us? Good government servants we have many, but Prokofy Osipitch was unique. To the depths of his soul he was devoted to his honest duty; he did not spare his strength but worked late at night, and was disinterested, impervious to bribes. . . . How he despised those who to the detriment of the public interest sought to corrupt him, who by the seductive goods of this life strove to draw him to betray his duty! Yes, before our eyes Prokofy Osipitch would divide his small salary between his poorer colleagues, and you have just heard yourselves the lamentations of the widows and orphans who lived upon his alms. Devoted to good works and his official duty, he gave up the joys of this life and even renounced the happiness of domestic existence; as you are aware, to the end of his days he was a bachelor. And who will replace him as a comrade? I can see now the kindly, shaven face turned to us with a gentle smile, I can hear now his soft friendly voice. Peace to thine ashes, Prokofy Osipitch! Rest, honest, noble toiler!"

Zapoikin continued while his listeners began whispering together. His speech pleased everyone and drew some tears, but a good many things in it seemed strange. In the first place they could not make out why the orator called the deceased Prokofy Osipitch when his name was Kirill Ivanovitch. In the second, everyone knew that the deceased had spent his whole life quarelling with his lawful wife, and so consequently could not be called a bachelor; in the third, he had a thick red beard and had never been known to shave, and so no one could understand why the orator spoke of his shaven face. The listeners were perplexed; they glanced at each other and shrugged their shoulders.

"Prokofy Osipitch," continued the orator, looking with an air of inspiration into the grave, "your face was plain, even hideous, you were morose and austere, but we all know that under that outer husk there beat an honest, friendly heart!"

Soon the listeners began to observe something strange in the orator himself. He gazed at one point, shifted about uneasily and began to shrug his shoulders too. All at once he ceased speaking, and gaping with astonishment, turned to Poplavsky.

"I say! he's alive," he said, staring with horror.

"Who's alive?"

"Why, Prokofy Osipitch, there he stands, by that tombstone!"

"He never died! It's Kirill Ivanovitch who's dead."

"But you told me yourself your secretary was dead."

"Kirill Ivanovitch was our secretary. You've muddled it, you queer fish. Prokofy Osipitch was our secretary before, that's true, but two years ago he was transferred to the second division as head clerk."

"How the devil is one to tell?"

"Why are you stopping? Go on, it's awkward."

Zapoikin turned to the grave, and with the same eloquence continued his interrupted speech. Prokofy Osipitch, an old clerk with a clean-shaven face, was in fact standing by a tombstone. He looked at the orator and frowned angrily.

"Well, you have put your foot into it, haven't you!" laughed his fellow-clerks as they returned from the funeral with Zapoikin. "Burying a man alive!"

"It's unpleasant, young man," grumbled Prokofy Osipitch. "Your speech may be all right for a dead man, but in reference to a living one it is nothing but sarcasm! Upon my soul what have you been saying? Disinterested, incorruptible, won't take bribes! Such things can only be said of the living in sarcasm. And no one asked you, sir, to expatiate on my face. Plain, hideous, so be it, but why exhibit my countenance in that public way! It's insulting."

# A WORK OF ART

Sasha Smirnov, the only son of his mother, holding under his arm, something wrapped up in No. 223 of the *Financial News*, assumed a sentimental expression, and went into Dr. Koshelkov's consulting-room.

"Ah, dear lad!" was how the doctor greeted him. "Well! how are we feeling? What good news have you for me?"

Sasha blinked, laid his hand on his heart and said in an agitated voice: "Mamma sends her greetings to you, Ivan Nikolaevitch, and told me to thank you. . . . I am the only son of my mother and you have saved my life . . . you have brought me through a dangerous illness and . . . we do not know how to thank you."

"Nonsense, lad!" said the doctor, highly delighted. "I only did what anyone else would have done in my place."

"I am the only son of my mother . . . we are poor people and cannot of course repay you, and we are quite ashamed, doctor, although, however, mamma and I . . . the only son of my mother, earnestly beg you to accept in token of our gratitude . . . this object, which . . . An object of great value, an antique bronze. . . . A rare work of art."

"You shouldn't!" said the doctor, frowning. "What's this for!"

"No, please do not refuse," Sasha went on muttering as he unpacked the parcel. "You will wound mamma and me by refusing. . . . It's a fine thing . . . an antique bronze. . . . It was left us by my deceased father and we have kept it as a precious souvenir. My father used to buy antique bronzes and sell them to connoisseurs . . . Mamma and I keep on the business now."

Sasha undid the object and put it solemnly on the table. It was a not very tall candelabra of old bronze and artistic workmanship. It consisted of a group: on the pedestal stood two female figures in the costume of Eve and in attitudes for the description of which I have neither the courage nor the fitting temperament. The figures were smiling coquettishly and altogether looked as though, had it not been for the necessity of supporting the candlestick, they would have skipped off the pedestal and have indulged in an orgy such as is improper for the reader even to imagine.

Looking at the present, the doctor slowly scratched behind his ear, cleared his throat and blew his nose irresolutely.

"Yes, it certainly is a fine thing," he muttered, "but . . . how shall I express it? . . . it's . . . h'm . . . it's not quite for family reading. It's not simply decolleté but beyond anything, dash it all. . . ."

"How do you mean?"

"The serpent-tempter himself could not have invented anything worse. . . . Why, to put such a phantasmagoria on the table would be defiling the whole flat."

"What a strange way of looking at art, doctor!" said Sasha, offended. "Why, it is an artistic thing, look at it! There is so much beauty and elegance that it fills one's soul with a feeling of reverence and brings a lump into one's throat! When one sees anything so beautiful one forgets everything earthly. . . . Only look, how much movement, what an atmosphere, what expression!"

"I understand all that very well, my dear boy," the doctor interposed, "but you know I am a family man, my children run in here, ladies come in."

"Of course if you look at it from the point of view of the crowd," said Sasha, "then this exquisitely artistic work may appear in a certain light. . . . But, doctor, rise superior to the crowd, especially as you will wound mamma and me by refusing it. I am the only son of my mother, you have saved my life. . . . We are giving you the thing most precious to us and . . . and I only regret that I have not the pair to present to you. . . ."

"Thank you, my dear fellow, I am very grateful . . . Give my respects to your mother but really consider, my children run in here, ladies come. . . . However, let it remain! I see there's no arguing with you."

"And there is nothing to argue about," said Sasha, relieved. "Put the candlestick here, by this vase. What a pity we have not the pair to it! It is a pity! Well, good-bye, doctor."

After Sasha's departure the doctor looked for a long time at the candelabra, scratched behind his ear and meditated.

"It's a superb thing, there's no denying it," he thought, "and it would be a pity to throw it away.... But it's impossible for me to keep it.... H'm!... Here's a problem! To whom can I make a present of it, or to what charity can I give it?"

After long meditation he thought of his good friend, the lawyer Uhov, to whom he was indebted for the management of legal business.

"Excellent," the doctor decided, "it would be awkward for him as a friend to take money from me, and it will be very suitable for me to present him with this. I will take him the devilish thing! Luckily he is a bachelor and easy-going."

Without further procrastination the doctor put on his hat and coat, took the candelabra and went off to Uhov's.

"How are you, friend!" he said, finding the lawyer at home. "I've come to see you ... to thank you for your efforts.... You won't take money so you must at least accept this thing here.... See, my dear fellow.... The thing is magnificent!"

On seeing the bronze the lawyer was moved to indescribable delight.

"What a specimen!" he chuckled. "Ah, deuce take it, to think of them imagining such a thing, the devils! Exquisite! Ravishing! Where did you get hold of such a delightful thing?"

After pouring out his ecstasies the lawyer looked timidly towards the door and said: "Only you must carry off your present, my boy.... I can't take it...."

"Why?" cried the doctor, disconcerted.

"Why ... because my mother is here at times, my clients ... besides I should be ashamed for my servants to see it."

"Nonsense! Nonsense! Don't you dare to refuse!" said the doctor, gesticulating. "It's piggish of you! It's a work of art!... What movement... what expression! I won't even talk of it! You will offend me!"

"If one could plaster it over or stick on fig-leaves..."

But the doctor gesticulated more violently than before, and dashing out of the flat went home, glad that he had succeeded in getting the present off his hands.

When he had gone away the lawyer examined the candelabra, fingered it all over, and then, like the doctor, racked his brains over the question what to do with the present.

"It's a fine thing," he mused, "and it would be a pity to throw it away and improper to keep it. The very best thing would be to make a present of it to someone.... I know what! I'll take it this evening to Shashkin, the comedian. The rascal is fond of such things, and by the way it is his benefit tonight."

No sooner said than done. In the evening the candelabra, carefully wrapped up, was duly carried to Shashkin's. The whole evening the comic actor's dressing-room was besieged by men coming to admire the present; the dressing-room was filled with the hum of enthusiasm and laughter like the neighing of horses. If one of the actresses approached the door and asked: "May I come in?" the comedian's husky voice was heard at once: "No, no, my dear, I am not dressed!"

After the performance the comedian shrugged his shoulders, flung up his hands and said: "Well what am I to do with the horrid thing? Why, I live in a private flat! Actresses come and see me! It's not a photograph that you can put in a drawer!"

"You had better sell it, sir," the hairdresser who was disrobing the actor advised him. "There's an old woman living about here who buys antique bronzes. Go and enquire for Madame Smirnov... everyone knows her."

The actor followed his advice.... Two days later the doctor was sitting in his consulting-room, and with his finger to his brow was meditating on the acids of the bile. All at once the door opened and Sasha Smirnov flew into the room. He was smiling, beaming, and his whole figure was radiant with happiness. In his hands he held something wrapped up in newspaper.

"Doctor!" he began breathlessly, "imagine my delight! Happily for you we have succeeded in picking up the pair to your candelabra! Mamma is so happy.... I am the only son of my mother, you saved my life..."

And Sasha, all of a tremor with gratitude, set the candelabra before the doctor. The doctor opened his mouth, tried to say something, but said nothing: he could not speak.

## WHO WAS TO BLAME?

As my uncle Pyotr Demyanitch, a lean, bilious collegiate councillor, exceedingly like a stale smoked fish with a stick through it, was getting ready to go to the high school, where he taught Latin, he noticed that the corner of his grammar was nibbled by mice.

"I say, Praskovya," he said, going into the kitchen and addressing the cook, "how is it we have got mice here? Upon my word! yesterday my top hat was nibbled, to-day they have disfigured my Latin grammar.... At this rate they will soon begin eating my clothes!

"What can I do? I did not bring them in!" answered Praskovya.

"We must do something! You had better get a cat, hadn't you?"

"I've got a cat, but what good is it?"

And Praskovya pointed to the corner where a white kitten, thin as a match, lay curled up asleep beside a broom.

"Why is it no good?" asked Pyotr Demyanitch.

"It's young yet, and foolish. It's not two months old yet."

"H'm.... Then it must be trained. It had much better be learning instead of lying there."

Saying this, Pyotr Demyanitch sighed with a careworn air and went out of the kitchen. The kitten raised his head, looked lazily after him, and shut his eyes again.

The kitten lay awake thinking. Of what? Unacquainted with real life, having no store of accumulated impressions, his mental processes could only be instinctive, and he could but picture life in accordance with the conceptions that he had inherited, together with his flesh and blood, from his ancestors, the tigers (*vide* Darwin). His thoughts were of the nature of day-dreams. His feline imagination pictured something like the Arabian desert, over which flitted shadows closely resembling Praskovya, the stove, the broom. In the midst of the shadows there suddenly appeared a saucer of milk; the saucer began to grow paws, it began moving and displayed a tendency to run; the kitten made a bound, and with a thrill of blood-thirsty sensuality thrust his claws into it.

When the saucer had vanished into obscurity a piece of meat appeared, dropped by Praskovya; the meat ran away with a cowardly squeak, but the kitten made a bound and got his claws into it. . . . Everything that rose before the imagination of the young dreamer had for its starting-point leaps, claws, and teeth. . . The soul of another is darkness, and a cat's soul more than most, but how near the visions just described are to the truth may be seen from the following fact: under the influence of his day-dreams the kitten suddenly leaped up, looked with flashing eyes at Praskovya, ruffled up his coat, and making one bound, thrust his claws into the cook's skirt. Obviously he was born a mouse catcher, a worthy son of his bloodthirsty ancestors. Fate had destined him to be the terror of cellars, store-rooms and cornbins, and had it not been for education . . . we will not anticipate, however.

On his way home from the high school, Pyotr Demyanitch went into a general shop and bought a mouse-trap for fifteen kopecks. At dinner he fixed a little bit of his rissole on the hook, and set the trap under the sofa, where there were heaps of the pupils' old exercise-books, which Praskovya used for various domestic purposes. At six o'clock in the evening, when the worthy Latin master was sitting at the table correcting his pupils' exercises, there was a sudden "klop!" so loud that my uncle started and dropped his pen. He went at once to the sofa and took out the trap. A neat little mouse, the size of a thimble, was sniffing the wires and trembling with fear.

"Aha," muttered Pyotr Demyanitch, and he looked at the mouse malignantly, as though he were about to give him a bad mark. "You are cau - aught, wretch! Wait a bit! I'll teach you to eat my grammar!"

Having gloated over his victim, Poytr Demyanitch put the mouse-trap on the floor and called:

"Praskovya, there's a mouse caught! Bring the kitten here!"

"I'm coming," responded Praskovya, and a minute later she came in with the descendant of tigers in her arms.

"Capital!" said Pyotr Demyanitch, rubbing his hands. "We will give him a lesson. . . . Put him down opposite the mouse-trap . . . that's it. . . . Let him sniff it and look at it. . . . That's it. . . ."

The kitten looked wonderingly at my uncle, at his arm-chair, sniffed the mouse-trap in bewilderment, then, frightened probably by the glaring lamplight and the attention directed to him, made a dash and ran in terror to the door.

"Stop!" shouted my uncle, seizing him by the tail, "stop, you rascal! He's afraid of a mouse, the idiot! Look! It's a mouse! Look! Well? Look, I tell you!"

Pyotr Demyanitch took the kitten by the scruff of the neck and pushed him with his nose against the mouse-trap.

"Look, you carrion! Take him and hold him, Praskovya. . . . Hold him opposite the door of the trap. . . . When I let the mouse out, you let him go instantly. . . . Do you hear? . . . Instantly let go! Now!"

My uncle assumed a mysterious expression and lifted the door of the trap. . . . The mouse came out irresolutely, sniffed the air, and flew like an arrow under the sofa. . . . The kitten on being released darted under the table with his tail in the air.

"It has got away! got away!" cried Pyotr Demyanitch, looking ferocious. "Where is he, the scoundrel? Under the table? You wait. . ."

My uncle dragged the kitten from under the table and shook him in the air.

"Wretched little beast," he muttered, smacking him on the ear. "Take that, take that! Will you shirk it next time? Wr-r-r-etch. . . ."

Next day Praskovya heard again the summons.

"Praskovya, there is a mouse caught! Bring the kitten here!"

After the outrage of the previous day the kitten had taken refuge under the stove and had not come out all night. When Praskovya pulled him out and, carrying him by the scruff of the neck into the study, set him down before the mouse-trap, he trembled all over and mewed piteously.

"Come, let him feel at home first," Pyotr Demyanitch commanded. "Let him look and sniff. Look and learn! Stop, plague take you!" he shouted, noticing that the kitten was backing away from the mouse-trap. "I'll thrash you! Hold him by the ear! That's it. . . . Well now, set him down before the trap. . . ."

My uncle slowly lifted the door of the trap . . . the mouse whisked under the very nose of the kitten, flung itself against Praskovya's hand and fled under the cupboard; the kitten, feeling himself free, took a desperate bound and retreated under the sofa.

"He's let another mouse go!" bawled Pyotr Demyanitch. "Do you call that a cat? Nasty little beast! Thrash him! thrash him by the mousetrap!"

When the third mouse had been caught, the kitten shivered all over at the sight of the mousetrap and its inmate, and scratched Praskovya's hand. . . . After the fourth mouse my uncle flew into a rage, kicked the kitten, and said:

"Take the nasty thing away! Get rid of it! Chuck it away! It's no earthly use!"

A year passed, the thin, frail kitten had turned into a solid and sagacious tom-cat. One day he was on his way by the back yards to an amatory interview. He had just reached his destination when he suddenly heard a rustle, and thereupon caught sight of a mouse which ran from a water-trough towards a stable; my hero's hair stood on end, he arched his back, hissed, and trembling all over, took to ignominious flight.

Alas! sometimes I feel myself in the ludicrous position of the flying cat. Like the kitten, I had in my day the honour of being taught Latin by my uncle. Now, whenever I chance to see some work of classical antiquity, instead of being moved to eager enthusiasm, I begin recalling, *ut consecutivum*, the irregular verbs, the sallow grey face of my uncle, the ablative absolute. . . . I turn pale, my hair stands up on my head, and, like the cat, I take to ignominious flight.

# VANKA

Vanka Zhukov, a boy of nine, who had been for three months apprenticed to Alyahin the shoemaker, was sitting up on Christmas Eve. Waiting till his master and mistress and their workmen had gone to the midnight service, he took out of his master's cupboard a bottle of ink and a pen with a rusty nib, and, spreading out a crumpled sheet of paper in front of him, began writing. Before forming the first letter he several times looked round fearfully at the door and the windows, stole a glance at the dark ikon, on both sides of which stretched shelves full of lasts, and heaved a broken sigh. The paper lay on the bench while he knelt before it.

"Dear grandfather, Konstantin Makaritch," he wrote, "I am writing you a letter. I wish you a happy Christmas, and all blessings from God Almighty. I have neither father nor mother, you are the only one left me."

Vanka raised his eyes to the dark ikon on which the light of his candle was reflected, and vividly recalled his grandfather, Konstantin Makaritch, who was night watchman to a family called Zhivarev. He was a thin but extraordinarily nimble and lively little old man of sixty-five, with an everlastingly laughing face and drunken eyes. By day he slept in the servants' kitchen, or made jokes with the cooks; at night, wrapped in an ample sheepskin, he walked round the grounds and tapped with his little mallet. OldKashtanka and Eel, so-called on account of his dark colour and his long body like a weasel's, followed him with hanging heads. This Eel was exceptionally polite and affectionate, and looked with equal kindness on strangers and his own masters, but had not a very good reputation. Under his politeness and meekness was hidden the most Jesuitical cunning. No one knew better how to creep up on occasion and snap at one's legs, to slip into the store-room, or steal a hen from a peasant. His hind legs had been nearly pulled off more than once, twice he had been hanged, every week he was thrashed till he was half dead, but he always revived.

At this moment grandfather was, no doubt, standing at the gate, screwing up his eyes at the red windows of the church, stamping with his high felt boots, and joking with the servants. His little mallet was hanging on his belt. He was clasping his hands, shrugging with the cold, and, with an aged chuckle, pinching first the housemaid, then the cook.

"How about a pinch of snuff?" he was saying, offering the women his snuff-box.

The women would take a sniff and sneeze. Grandfather would be indescribably delighted, go off into a merry chuckle, and cry:

"Tear it off, it has frozen on!"

They give the dogs a sniff of snuff too. Kashtanka sneezes, wriggles her head, and walks away offended. Eel does not sneeze, from politeness, but wags his tail. And the weather is glorious. The air is still, fresh, and transparent. The night is dark, but one can see the whole village with its white roofs and coils of smoke coming from the chimneys, the trees silvered with hoar frost, the snowdrifts. The whole sky spangled with gay twinkling stars, and the Milky Way is as distinct as though it had been washed and rubbed with snow for a holiday....

Vanka sighed, dipped his pen, and went on writing:

"And yesterday I had a wigging. The master pulled me out into the yard by my hair, and whacked me with a boot-stretcher because I accidentally fell asleep while I was rocking their brat in the cradle. And a week ago the mistress told me to clean a herring, and I began from the tail end, and she took the herring and thrust its head in my face. The workmen laugh at me and send me to the tavern for vodka, and tell me to steal the master's cucumbers for them, and the master beats me with anything that comes to hand. And there is nothing to eat. In the morning they give me bread, for dinner, porridge, and in the evening, bread again; but as for tea, or soup, the master and mistress gobble it all up themselves. And I am put to sleep in the passage, and when their wretched brat cries I get no sleep at all, but have to rock the cradle. Dear grandfather, show the divine mercy, take me away from here, home to the village. It's more than I can bear. I bow down to your feet, and will pray to God for you forever, take me away from here or I shall die."

Vanka's mouth worked, he rubbed his eyes with his black fist, and gave a sob.

"I will powder your snuff for you," he went on. "I will pray for you, and if I do anything you can thrash me like Sidor's goat. And if you think I've no job, then I will beg the steward for Christ's sake to let me clean his boots, or I'll go for a shepherd-boy instead of Fedka. Dear grandfather, it is more than I can bear, it's simply no life at all. I wanted to run away to the village, but I have no boots, and I am afraid of the frost. When I grow up big I will take care of you for this, and not let anyone annoy you, and when you die I will pray for the rest of your soul, just as for my mammy's.

Moscow is a big town. It's all gentlemen's houses, and there are lots of horses, but there are no sheep, and the dogs are not spiteful. The lads here don't go out with thestar, and they don't let anyone go into the choir, and once I saw in a shop window fishing-hooks for sale, fitted ready with the line and for all sorts of fish, awfully good ones, there was even one hook that would hold a forty-pound sheat-fish. And I have seen shops where there are guns of all sorts, after the pattern of the master's guns at home, so that I shouldn't wonder if they are a hundred roubles each. . . . And in the butchers' shops there are grouse and woodcocks and fish and hares, but the shopmen don't say where they shoot them.

"Dear grandfather, when they have the Christmas tree at the big house, get me a gilt walnut, and put it away in the green trunk. Ask the young lady Olga Ignatyevna, say it's for Vanka."

Vanka gave a tremulous sigh, and again stared at the window. He remembered how his grandfather always went into the forest to get the Christmas tree for his master's family, and took his grandson with him. It was a merry time! Grandfather made a noise in his throat, the forest crackled with the frost, and looking at them Vanka chortled too. Before chopping down the Christmas tree, grandfather would smoke a pipe, slowly take a pinch of snuff, and laugh at frozen Vanka. . . . The young fir trees, covered with hoar frost, stood motionless, waiting to see which of them was to die. Wherever one looked, a hare flew like an arrow over the snowdrifts. . . . Grandfather could not refrain from shouting: "Hold him, hold him . . . hold him! Ah, the bob-tailed devil!"

When he had cut down the Christmas tree, grandfather used to drag it to the big house, and there set to work to decorate it. . . . The young lady, who was Vanka's favourite, Olga Ignatyevna, was the busiest of all. When Vanka's mother Pelageya was alive, and a servant in the big house, Olga Ignatyevna used to give him goodies, and having nothing better to do, taught him to read and write, to count up to a hundred, and even to dance a quadrille. When Pelageya died, Vanka had been transferred to the servants' kitchen to be with his grandfather, and from the kitchen to the shoemaker's in Moscow.

"Do come, dear grandfather," Vanka went on with his letter. "For Christ's sake, I beg you, take me away. Have pity on an unhappy orphan like me; here everyone knocks me about, and I am fearfully hungry; I can't tell you what misery it is, I am always crying. And the other day the master hit me on the head with a last, so that I fell down. My life is wretched, worse than any dog's. . . . I send greetings to Alyona, one-eyed Yegorka, and the coachman, and don't give my concertina to anyone. I remain, your grandson, Ivan Zhukov. Dear grandfather, do come."

Vanka folded the sheet of writing-paper twice, and put it into an envelope he had bought the day before for a kopeck. . . . After thinking a little, he dipped the pen and wrote the address:

*To grandfather in the village.*

Then he scratched his head, thought a little, and added: *Konstantin Makaritch*. Glad that he had not been prevented from writing, he put on his cap and, without putting on his little greatcoat, ran out into the street as he was in his shirt. . . .

The shopmen at the butcher's, whom he had questioned the day before, told him that letters were put in post-boxes, and from the boxes were carried about all over the earth in mailcarts with drunken drivers and ringing bells. Vanka ran to the nearest post-box, and thrust the precious letter in the slit. . . .

An hour later, lulled by sweet hopes, he was sound asleep. . . . He dreamed of the stove. On the stove was sitting his grandfather, swinging his bare legs, and reading the letter to the cooks. . . .

By the stove was Eel, wagging his tail.

# ON THE ROAD

*"Upon the breast of a gigantic crag,*
*A golden cloudlet rested for one night."*

LERMONTOV.

IN the room which the tavern keeper, the Cossack Semyon Tchistopluy, called the "travellers' room," that is kept exclusively for travellers, a tall, broad-shouldered man of forty was sitting at the big unpainted table. He was asleep with his elbows on the table and his head leaning on his fist. An end of tallow candle, stuck into an old pomatum pot, lighted up his light brown beard, his thick, broad nose, his sunburnt cheeks, and the thick, black eyebrows overhanging his closed eyes. . . . The nose and the cheeks and the eyebrows, all the features, each taken separately, were coarse and heavy, like the furniture and the stove in the "travellers' room," but taken all together they gave the effect of something harmonious and even beautiful. Such is the lucky star, as it is called, of the Russian face: the coarser and harsher its features the softer and more good-natured it looks. The man was dressed in a gentleman's reefer jacket, shabby, but bound with wide new braid, a plush waistcoat, and full black trousers thrust into big high boots.

On one of the benches, which stood in a continuous row along the wall, a girl of eight, in a brown dress and long black stockings, lay asleep on a coat lined with fox. Her face was pale, her hair was flaxen, her shoulders were narrow, her whole body was thin and frail, but her nose stood out as thick and ugly a lump as the man's. She was sound asleep, and unconscious that her semi-circular comb had fallen off her head and was cutting her cheek.

The "travellers' room" had a festive appearance. The air was full of the smell of freshly scrubbed floors, there were no rags hanging as usual on the line that ran diagonally across the room, and a little lamp was burning in the corner over the table, casting a patch of red light on the ikon of St. George the Victorious. From the ikon stretched on each side of the corner a row of cheap oleographs, which maintained a strict and careful gradation in the transition from the sacred to the profane. In the dim light of the candle end and the red ikon lamp the pictures looked like one continuous stripe, covered with blurs of black. When the tiled stove, trying to sing in unison with the weather, drew in the air with a howl, while the logs, as though waking up, burst into bright flame and hissed angrily, red patches began dancing on the log walls, and over the head of the sleeping man could be seen first the Elder Seraphim, then the Shah Nasir-ed-Din, then a fat, brown baby with goggle eyes, whispering in the ear of a young girl with an extraordinarily blank, and indifferent face. . . .

Outside a storm was raging. Something frantic and wrathful, but profoundly unhappy, seemed to be flinging itself about the tavern with the ferocity of a wild beast and trying to break in. Banging at the doors, knocking at the windows and on the roof, scratching at the walls, it alternately threatened and besought, then subsided for a brief interval, and then with a gleeful, treacherous howl burst into the chimney, but the wood flared up, and the fire, like a chained dog, flew wrathfully to meet its foe, a battle began, and after it - sobs, shrieks, howls of wrath. In all of this there was the sound of angry misery and unsatisfied hate, and the mortified impatience of something accustomed to triumph.

Bewitched by this wild, inhuman music the "travellers' room" seemed spellbound forever, but all at once the door creaked and the potboy, in a new print shirt, came in. Limping on one leg, and blinking his sleepy eyes, he snuffed the candle with his fingers, put some more wood on the fire and went out. At once from the church, which was three hundred paces from the tavern, the clock struck midnight. The wind played with the chimes as with the snowflakes; chasing the sounds of the clock it whirled them round and round over a vast space, so that some strokes were cut short or drawn out in long, vibrating notes, while others were completely lost in the general uproar. One stroke sounded as distinctly in the room as though it had chimed just under the window. The child, sleeping on the fox-skin, started and raised her head. For a minute she stared blankly at the dark window, at Nasir-ed-Din over whom a crimson glow from the fire flickered at that moment, then she turned her eyes upon the sleeping man.

"Daddy," she said.

But the man did not move. The little girl knitted her brow angrily, lay down, and curled up her legs. Someone in the tavern gave a loud, prolonged yawn. Soon afterwards there was the squeak of the swing door and the sound of indistinct voices. Someone came in, shaking the snow off, and stamping in felt boots which made a muffled thud.

"What is it?" a woman s voice asked languidly.

"Mademoiselle Ilovaisky has come, . . . ." answered a bass voice.

Again there was the squeak of the swing door. Then came the roar of the wind rushing in. Someone, probably the lame boy, ran to the door leading to the "travellers' room," coughed deferentially, and lifted the latch.

"This way, lady, please," said a woman's voice in dulcet tones. "It's clean in here, my beauty. . . ."

The door was opened wide and a peasant with a beard appeared in the doorway, in the long coat of a coachman, plastered all over with snow from head to foot, and carrying a big trunk on his shoulder. He was followed into the room by a feminine figure, scarcely half his height, with no face and no arms, muffled and wrapped up like a bundle and also covered with snow. A damp chill, as from a cellar, seemed to come to the child from the coachman and the bundle, and the fire and the candles flickered.

"What nonsense!" said the bundle angrily, "We could go perfectly well. We have only nine more miles to go, mostly by the forest, and we should not get lost. . . ."

"As for getting lost, we shouldn't, but the horses can't go on, lady!" answered the coachman. "And it is Thy Will, O Lord! As though I had done it on purpose!"

"God knows where you have brought me. . . . Well, be quiet. . . . There are people asleep here, it seems. You can go. . . ."

The coachman put the portmanteau on the floor, and as he did so, a great lump of snow fell off his shoulders. He gave a sniff and went out.

Then the little girl saw two little hands come out from the middle of the bundle, stretch upwards and begin angrily disentangling the network of shawls, kerchiefs, and scarves. First a big shawl fell on the ground, then a hood, then a white knitted kerchief. After freeing her head, the traveller took off her pelisse and at once shrank to half the size. Now she was in a long, grey coat with big buttons and bulging pockets. From one pocket she pulled out a paper parcel, from the other a bunch of big, heavy keys, which she put down so carelessly that the sleeping man started and opened his eyes. For some time he looked blankly round him as though he didn't know where he was, then he shook his head, went to the corner and sat down. . . . The newcomer took off her great coat, which made her shrink to half her size again, she took off her big felt boots, and sat down, too.

By now she no longer resembled a bundle: she was a thin little brunette of twenty, as slim as a snake, with a long white face and curly hair. Her nose was long and sharp, her chin, too, was long and sharp, her eyelashes were long, the corners of her mouth were sharp, and, thanks to this general sharpness, the expression of her face was biting. Swathed in a closely fitting black dress with a mass of lace at her neck and sleeves, with sharp elbows and long pink fingers, she recalled the portraits of mediæval English ladies. The grave concentration of her face increased this likeness.

The lady looked round at the room, glanced sideways at the man and the little girl, shrugged her shoulders, and moved to the window. The dark windows were shaking from the damp west wind. Big flakes of snow glistening in their whiteness, lay on the window frame, but at once disappeared, borne away by the wind. The savage music grew louder and louder. . . .

After a long silence the little girl suddenly turned over, and said angrily, emphasizing each word:

"Oh, goodness, goodness, how unhappy I am! Unhappier than anyone!"

The man got up and moved with little steps to the child with a guilty air, which was utterly out of keeping with his huge figure and big beard.

"You are not asleep, dearie?" he said, in an apologetic voice. "What do you want?"

"I don't want anything, my shoulder aches! You are a wicked man, Daddy, and God will punish you! You'll see He will punish you."

"My darling, I know your shoulder aches, but what can I do, dearie?" said the man, in the tone in which men who have been drinking excuse themselves to their stern spouses. "It's the journey has made your shoulder ache, Sasha. To-morrow we shall get there and rest, and the pain will go away. . . ."

"To-morrow, to-morrow. . . . Every day you say to-morrow. We shall be going on another twenty days."

"But we shall arrive to-morrow, dearie, on your father's word of honour. I never tell a lie, but if we are detained by the snowstorm it is not my fault."

"I can't bear any more, I can't, I can't!"

Sasha jerked her leg abruptly and filled the room with an unpleasant wailing. Her father made a despairing gesture, and looked hopelessly towards the young lady. The latter shrugged her shoulders, and hesitatingly went up to Sasha.

"Listen, my dear," she said, "it is no use crying. It's really naughty; if your shoulder aches it can't be helped."

"You see, Madam," said the man quickly, as though defending himself, "we have not slept for two nights, and have been travelling in a revolting conveyance. Well, of course, it is natural she should be ill and miserable, . . . and then, you know, we had a drunken driver, our portmanteau has been stolen . . . the snowstorm all the time, but what's the use of crying, Madam? I am exhausted, though, by sleeping in a sitting position, and I feel as though I were drunk. Oh, dear! Sasha, and I feel sick as it is, and then you cry!"

The man shook his head, and with a gesture of despair sat down.

"Of course you mustn't cry," said the young lady. "It's only little babies cry. If you are ill, dear, you must undress and go to sleep. . . . Let us take off your things!"

When the child had been undressed and pacified a silence reigned again. The young lady seated herself at the window, and looked round wonderingly at the room of the inn, at the ikon, at the stove. . . . Apparently the room and the little girl with the thick nose, in her short boy's nightgown, and the child's father, all seemed strange to her. This strange man was sitting in a corner; he kept looking about him helplessly, as though he were drunk, and rubbing his face with the palm of his hand. He sat silent, blinking, and judging from his guilty-looking figure it was difficult to imagine that he would soon begin to speak. Yet he was the first to begin. Stroking his knees, he gave a cough, laughed, and said:

"It's a comedy, it really is. . . . I look and I cannot believe my eyes: for what devilry has destiny driven us to this accursed inn? What did she want to show by it? Life sometimes performs such *'salto mortale,'* one can only stare and blink in amazement. Have you come from far, Madam?"

"No, not from far," answered the young lady. "I am going from our estate, fifteen miles from here, to our farm, to my father and brother. My name is Ilovaisky, and the farm is called Ilovaiskoe. It's nine miles away. What unpleasant weather!"

"It couldn't be worse."

The lame boy came in and stuck a new candle in the pomatum pot.

"You might bring us the samovar, boy," said the man, addressing him.

"Who drinks tea now?" laughed the boy. "It is a sin to drink tea before mass. . . ."

"Never mind boy, you won't burn in hell if we do. . . ."

Over the tea the new acquaintances got into conversation.

Mlle. Ilovaisky learned that her companion was called Grigory Petrovitch Liharev, that he was the brother of the Liharev who was

Marshal of Nobility in one of the neighbouring districts, and he himself had once been a landowner, but had "run through everything in his time." Liharev learned that her name was Marya Mihailovna, that her father had a huge estate, but that she was the only one to look after it as her father and brother looked at life through their fingers, were irresponsible, and were too fond of harriers.

"My father and brother are all alone at the farm," she told him, brandishing her fingers (she had the habit of moving her fingers before her pointed face as she talked, and after every sentence moistened her lips with her sharp little tongue). "They, I mean men, are an irresponsible lot, and don't stir a finger for themselves. I can fancy there will be no one to give them a meal after the fast! We have no mother, and we have such servants that they can't lay the tablecloth properly when I am away. You can imagine their condition now! They will be left with nothing to break their fast, while I have to stay here all night. How strange it all is."

She shrugged her shoulders, took a sip from her cup, and said:

"There are festivals that have a special fragrance: at Easter, Trinity and Christmas there is a peculiar scent in the air. Even unbelievers are fond of those festivals. My brother, for instance, argues that there is no God, but he is the first to hurry to Matins at Easter."

Liharev raised his eyes to Mlle. Ilovaisky and laughed.

"They argue that there is no God," she went on, laughing too, "but why is it, tell me, all the celebrated writers, the learned men, clever people generally, in fact, believe towards the end of their life?"

"If a man does not know how to believe when he is young, Madam, he won't believe in his old age if he is ever so much of a writer."

Judging from Liharev's cough he had a bass voice, but, probably from being afraid to speak aloud, or from exaggerated shyness, he spoke in a tenor. After a brief pause he heaved a sign and said:

"The way I look at it is that faith is a faculty of the spirit. It is just the same as a talent, one must be born with it. So far as I can judge by myself, by the people I have seen in my time, and by all that is done around us, this faculty is present in Russians in its highest degree. Russian life presents us with an uninterrupted succession of convictions and aspirations, and if you care to know, it has not yet the faintest notion of lack of faith or scepticism. If a Russian does not believe in God, it means he believes in something else."

Liharev took a cup of tea from Mlle. Ilovaisky, drank off half in one gulp, and went on:

"I will tell you about myself. Nature has implanted in my breast an extraordinary faculty for belief. Whisper it not to the night, but half my life I was in the ranks of the Atheists and Nihilists, but there was not one hour in my life in which I ceased to believe. All talents, as a rule, show themselves in early childhood, and so my faculty showed itself when I could still walk upright under the table. My mother liked her children to eat a great deal, and when she gave me food she used to say: 'Eat! Soup is the great thing in life!' I believed, and ate the soup ten times a day, ate like a shark, ate till I was disgusted and stupefied. My nurse used to tell me fairy tales, and I believed in house-spirits, in wood-elves, and in goblins of all kinds. I used sometimes to steal corrosive sublimate from my father, sprinkle it on cakes, and carry them up to the attic that the house-spirits, you see, might eat them and be killed. And when I was taught to read and understand what I read, then there was a fine to-do. I ran away to America and went off to join the brigands, and wanted to go into a monastery, and hired boys to torture me for being a Christian. And note that my faith was always active, never dead. If I was running away to America I was not alone, but seduced someone else, as great a fool as I was, to go with me, and was delighted when I was nearly frozen outside the town gates and when I was thrashed; if I went to join the brigands I always came back with my face battered. A most restless childhood, I assure you! And when they sent me to the high school and pelted me with all sorts of truths - that is, that the earth goes round the sun, or that white light is not white, but is made up of seven colours - my poor little head began to go round! Everything was thrown into a whirl in me; Navin who made the sun stand still, and my mother who in the name of the Prophet Elijah disapproved of lightning conductors, and my father who was indifferent to the truths I had learned. My enlightenment inspired me. I wandered about the house and stables like one possessed, preaching my truths, was horrified by ignorance, glowed with hatred for anyone who saw in white light nothing but white light. . . . But all that's nonsense and childishness. Serious, so to speak, manly enthusiasms began only at the university. You have, no doubt, Madam, taken your degree somewhere?"

"I studied at Novotcherkask at the Don Institute."

"Then you have not been to a university? So you don't know what science means. All the sciences in the world have the same passport, without which they regard themselves as meaningless . . . the striving towards truth! Every one of them, even pharmacology, has for its aim not utility, not the alleviation of life, but truth. It's remarkable! When you set to work to study any science, what strikes you first of all is its beginning. I assure you there is nothing more attractive and grander, nothing is so staggering, nothing takes a man's breath away like the beginning of any science. From the first five or six lectures you are soaring on wings of the brightest hopes, you already seem to yourself to be welcoming truth with open arms. And I gave myself up to science, heart and soul, passionately, as to the woman one loves. I was its slave; I found it the sun of my existence, and asked for no other. I studied day and night without rest, ruined myself over books, wept when before my eyes men exploited science for their own personal ends. But my enthusiasm did not last long. The trouble is that every science has a beginning but not an end, like a recurring decimal. Zoology has discovered 35,000 kinds of insects, chemistry reckons 60 elements. If in time tens of noughts can be written after these figures. Zoology and chemistry will be just as far from their end as now, and all contemporary scientific work consists in increasing these numbers. I saw through this trick when I discovered the 35,001-st and felt no satisfaction. Well, I had no time to suffer from disillusionment, as I was soon possessed by a new faith. I plunged into Nihilism, with its manifestoes, its 'black divisions,' and all the rest of it. I 'went to the people,' worked in factories, worked as an oiler, as a barge hauler. Afterwards, when wandering over Russia, I had a taste of Russian life, I turned into a fervent devotee of that life. I loved the Russian people with poignant intensity; I loved their God and believed in Him, and in their language, their creative genius. . . . And so on, and so on. . . . I have been a Slavophile in my time, I used to pester Aksakov with letters, and I was a Ukrainophile, and an archæologist, and a collector of specimens of peasant art. . . . I was enthusiastic over ideas, people, events, places . . . my enthusiasm was endless! Five years ago I was working for the abolition of private property; my last creed was non-resistance to evil."

Sasha gave an abrupt sigh and began moving. Liharev got up and went to her.

"Won't you have some tea, dearie?" he asked tenderly.

"Drink it yourself," the child answered rudely. Liharev was disconcerted, and went back to the table with a guilty step.

"Then you have had a lively time," said Mlle. Ilovaisky; "you have something to remember."

"Well, yes, it's all very lively when one sits over tea and chatters to a kind listener, but you should ask what that liveliness has cost me! What price have I paid for the variety of my life? You see, Madam, I have not held my convictions like a German doctor of philosophy, *zierlichmännerlich*, I have not lived in solitude, but every conviction I have had has bound my back to the yoke, has torn my body to pieces. Judge, for yourself. I was wealthy like my brothers, but now I am a beggar. In the delirium of my enthusiasm I smashed up my own fortune and my wife's - a heap of other people's money. Now I am forty-two, old age is close upon me, and I am homeless, like a dog that has dropped behind its waggon at night. All my life I have not known what peace meant, my soul has been in continual agitation, distressed even by its hopes . . . I have been wearied out with heavy irregular work, have endured privation, have five times been in prison, have dragged myself across the provinces of Archangel and of Tobolsk . . . it's painful to think of it! I have lived, but in my fever I have not even been conscious of the process of life itself. Would you believe it, I don't remember a single spring, I never noticed how my wife loved me, how my children were born. What more can I tell you? I have been a misfortune to all who have loved me. . . . My mother has worn mourning for me all these fifteen years, while my proud brothers, who have had to wince, to blush, to bow their heads, to waste their money on my account, have come in the end to hate me like poison."

Liharev got up and sat down again.

"If I were simply unhappy I should thank God," he went on without looking at his listener. "My personal unhappiness sinks into the background when I remember how often in my enthusiasms I have been absurd, far from the truth, unjust, cruel, dangerous! How often I have hated and despised those whom I ought to have loved, and *vice versa*, I have changed a thousand times. One day I believe, fall down and worship, the next I flee like a coward from the gods and friends of yesterday, and swallow in silence the 'scoundrel!' they hurl after me. God alone has seen how often I have wept and bitten my pillow in shame for my enthusiasms. Never once in my life have I intentionally lied or done evil, but my conscience is not clear! I cannot even boast, Madam, that I have no one's life upon my conscience, for my wife died before my eyes, worn out by my reckless activity. Yes, my wife! I tell you they have two ways of treating women nowadays. Some measure women's skulls to prove woman is inferior to man, pick out her defects to mock at her, to look original in her eyes, and to justify their sensuality. Others do their utmost to raise women to their level, that is, force them to learn by heart the 35,000 species, to speak and write the same foolish things as they speak and write themselves."

Liharev's face darkened.

"I tell you that woman has been and always will be the slave of man," he said in a bass voice, striking his fist on the table. "She is the soft, tender wax which a man always moulds into anything he likes. . . . My God! for the sake of some trumpery masculine enthusiasm she will cut off her hair, abandon her family, die among strangers! . . . among the ideas for which she has sacrificed herself there is not a single feminine one. . . . An unquestioning, devoted slave! I have not measured skulls, but I say this from hard, bitter experience: the proudest, most independent women, if I have succeeded in communicating to them my enthusiasm, have followed me without criticism, without question, and done anything I chose; I have turned a nun into a Nihilist who, as I heard afterwards, shot a gendarme; my wife never left me for a minute in my wanderings, and like a weathercock changed her faith in step with my changing enthusiasms."

Liharev jumped up and walked up and down the room.

"A noble, sublime slavery!" he said, clasping his hands. "It is just in it that the highest meaning of woman's life lies! Of all the fearful medley of thoughts and impressions accumulated in my brain from my association with women my memory, like a filter, has retained no ideas, no clever saying, no philosophy, nothing but that extraordinary, resignation to fate, that wonderful mercifulness, forgiveness of everything."

Liharev clenched his fists, stared at a fixed point, and with a sort of passionate intensity, as though he were savouring each word as he uttered it, hissed through his clenched teeth:

"That . . . that great-hearted fortitude, faithfulness unto death, poetry of the heart. . . . The meaning of life lies in just that unrepining martyrdom, in the tears which would soften a stone, in the boundless, all-forgiving love which brings light and warmth into the chaos of life. . . ."

Mlle. Ilovaisky got up slowly, took a step towards Liharev, and fixed her eyes upon his face. From the tears that glittered on his eyelashes, from his quivering, passionate voice, from the flush on his cheeks, it was clear to her that women were not a chance, not a simple subject of conversation. They were the object of his new enthusiasm, or, as he said himself, his new faith! For the first time in her life she saw a man carried away, fervently believing. With his gesticulations, with his flashing eyes he seemed to her mad, frantic, but there was a feeling of such beauty in the fire of his eyes, in his words, in all the movements of his huge body, that without noticing what she was doing she stood facing him as though rooted to the spot, and gazed into his face with delight.

"Take my mother," he said, stretching out his hand to her with an imploring expression on his face, "I poisoned her existence, according to her ideas disgraced the name of Liharev, did her as much harm as the most malignant enemy, and what do you think? My brothers give her little sums for holy bread and church services, and outraging her religious feelings, she saves that money and sends it in secret to her erring Grigory. This trifle alone elevates and ennobles the soul far more than all the theories, all the clever sayings and the 35,000 species. I can give you thousands of instances. Take you, even, for instance! With tempest and darkness outside you are going to your father and your brother to cheer them with your affection in the holiday, though very likely they have forgotten and are not thinking of you. And, wait a bit, and you will love a man and follow him to the North Pole. You would, wouldn't you?"

"Yes, if I loved him."

"There, you see," cried Liharev delighted, and he even stamped with his foot. "Oh dear! How glad I am that I have met you! Fate is kind to me, I am always meeting splendid people. Not a day passes but one makes acquaintance with somebody one would give one's soul for. There are ever so many more good people than bad in this world. Here, see, for instance, how openly and from our hearts we have been talking as though we had known each other a hundred years. Sometimes, I assure you, one restrains oneself for ten years and holds one's tongue, is reserved with one's friends and one's wife, and meets some cadet in a train and babbles one's whole soul out to him. It is the first time I have the honour of seeing you, and yet I have confessed to you as I have never confessed in my life. Why is it?"

Rubbing his hands and smiling good-humouredly Liharev walked up and down the room, and fell to talking about women again. Meanwhile they began ringing for matins.

"Goodness," wailed Sasha. "He won't let me sleep with his talking!"

"Oh, yes!" said Liharev, startled. "I am sorry, darling, sleep, sleep. . . . I have two boys besides her," he whispered. "They are living with their uncle, Madam, but this one can't exist a day without her father. She's wretched, she complains, but she sticks to me like a fly to honey. I have been chattering too much, Madam, and it would do you no harm to sleep. Wouldn't you like me to make up a bed for you?"

Without waiting for permission he shook the wet pelisse, stretched it on a bench, fur side upwards, collected various shawls and scarves, put the overcoat folded up into a roll for a pillow, and all this he did in silence with a look of devout reverence, as though he were not handling a woman's rags, but the fragments of holy vessels. There was something apologetic, embarrassed about his whole figure, as though in the presence of a weak creature he felt ashamed of his height and strength. . . .

When Mlle. Ilovaisky had lain down, he put out the candle and sat down on a stool by the stove.

"So, Madam," he whispered, lighting a fat cigarette and puffing the smoke into the stove. "Nature has put into the Russian an extraordinary faculty for belief, a searching intelligence, and the gift of speculation, but all that is reduced to ashes by irresponsibility, laziness, and dreamy frivolity. . . . Yes. . . ."

She gazed wonderingly into the darkness, and saw only a spot of red on the ikon and the flicker of the light of the stove on Liharev's face. The darkness, the chime of the bells, the roar of the storm, the lame boy, Sasha with her fretfulness, unhappy Liharev and his sayings - all this was mingled together, and seemed to grow into one huge impression, and God's world seemed to her fantastic, full of marvels and magical forces. All that she had heard was ringing in her ears, and human life presented itself to her as a beautiful poetic fairy-tale without an end.

The immense impression grew and grew, clouded consciousness, and turned into a sweet dream. She was asleep, though she saw the little ikon lamp and a big nose with the light playing on it.

She heard the sound of weeping.

"Daddy, darling," a child's voice was tenderly entreating, "let's go back to uncle! There is a Christmas-tree there! Styopa and Kolya are there!"

"My darling, what can I do?" a man's bass persuaded softly. "Understand me! Come, understand!"

And the man's weeping blended with the child's. This voice of human sorrow, in the midst of the howling of the storm, touched the girl's ear with such sweet human music that she could not bear the delight of it, and wept too. She was conscious afterwards of a big, black shadow coming softly up to her, picking up a shawl that had dropped on to the floor and carefully wrapping it round her feet.

Mlle. Ilovaisky was awakened by a strange uproar. She jumped up and looked about her in astonishment. The deep blue dawn was looking in at the window half-covered with snow. In the room there was a grey twilight, through which the stove and the sleeping child and Nasir-ed-Din stood out distinctly. The stove and the lamp were both out. Through the wide-open door she could see the big tavern room with a counter and chairs. A man, with a stupid, gipsy face and astonished eyes, was standing in the middle of the room in a puddle of melting snow, holding a big red star on a stick. He was surrounded by a group of boys, motionless as statues, and plastered over with snow. The light shone through the red paper of the star, throwing a glow of red on their wet faces. The crowd was shouting in disorder, and from its uproar Mlle. Ilovaisky could make out only one couplet:

"Hi, you Little Russian lad,
Bring your sharp knife,
We will kill the Jew, we will kill him,
The son of tribulation. . ."

Liharev was standing near the counter, looking feelingly at the singers and tapping his feet in time. Seeing Mlle. Ilovaisky, he smiled all over his face and came up to her. She smiled too.

"A happy Christmas!" he said. "I saw you slept well."

She looked at him, said nothing, and went on smiling.

After the conversation in the night he seemed to her not tall and broad shouldered, but little, just as the biggest steamer seems to us a little thing when we hear that it has crossed the ocean.

"Well, it is time for me to set off," she said. "I must put on my things. Tell me where you are going now?"

"I? To the station of Klinushki, from there to Sergievo, and from Sergievo, with horses, thirty miles to the coal mines that belong to a horrid man, a general called Shashkovsky. My brothers have got me the post of superintendent there. . . . I am going to be a coal miner."

"Stay, I know those mines. Shashkovsky is my uncle, you know. But . . . what are you going there for?" asked Mlle. Ilovaisky, looking at Liharev in surprise.

"As superintendent. To superintend the coal mines."

"I don't understand!" she shrugged her shoulders. "You are going to the mines. But you know, it's the bare steppe, a desert, so dreary that you couldn't exist a day there! It's horrible coal, no one will buy it, and my uncle's a maniac, a despot, a bankrupt. . . . You won't get your salary!"

"No matter," said Liharev, unconcernedly, "I am thankful even for coal mines."

She shrugged her shoulders, and walked about the room in agitation.

"I don't understand, I don't understand," she said, moving her fingers before her face. "It's impossible, and . . . and irrational! You must understand that it's . . . it's worse than exile. It is a living tomb! O Heavens!" she said hotly, going up to Liharev and moving her fingers before his smiling face; her upper lip was quivering, and her sharp face turned pale, "Come, picture it, the bare steppe, solitude. There is no one to say a word to there, and you . . . are enthusiastic over women! Coal mines . . . and women!"

Mlle. Ilovaisky was suddenly ashamed of her heat and, turning away from Liharev, walked to the window.

"No, no, you can't go there," she said, moving her fingers rapidly over the pane.

Not only in her heart, but even in her spine she felt that behind her stood an infinitely unhappy man, lost and outcast, while he, as though he were unaware of his unhappiness, as though he had not shed tears in the night, was looking at her with a kindly smile. Better he should go on weeping! She walked up and down the room several times in agitation, then stopped short in a corner and sank into thought. Liharev was saying something, but she did not hear him. Turning her back on him she took out of her purse a money note, stood for a long time crumpling it in her hand, and looking round at Liharev, blushed and put it in her pocket.

The coachman's voice was heard through the door. With a stern, concentrated face she began putting on her things in silence. Liharev wrapped her up, chatting gaily, but every word he said lay on her heart like a weight. It is not cheering to hear the unhappy or the dying jest.

When the transformation of a live person into a shapeless bundle had been completed, Mlle. Ilovaisky looked for the last time round the "travellers' room," stood a moment in silence, and slowly walked out. Liharev went to see her off. . . .

Outside, God alone knows why, the winter was raging still. Whole clouds of big soft snowflakes were whirling restlessly over the earth, unable to find a resting-place. The horses, the sledge, the trees, a bull tied to a post, all were white and seemed soft and fluffy.

"Well, God help you," muttered Liharev, tucking her into the sledge. "Don't remember evil against me . . . ."

She was silent. When the sledge started, and had to go round a huge snowdrift, she looked back at Liharev with an expression as though she wanted to say something to him. He ran up to her, but she did not say a word to him, she only looked at him through her long eyelashes with little specks of snow on them.

Whether his finely intuitive soul were really able to read that look, or whether his imagination deceived him, it suddenly began to seem to him that with another touch or two that girl would have forgiven him his failures, his age, his desolate position, and would have followed him without question or reasonings. He stood a long while as though rooted to the spot, gazing at the tracks left by the sledge runners. The snowflakes greedily settled on his hair, his beard, his shoulders. . . . Soon the track of the runners had vanished, and he himself covered with snow, began to look like a white rock, but still his eyes kept seeking something in the clouds of snow.

Printed in Great Britain
by Amazon.co.uk, Ltd.,
Marston Gate.